PRAISE FOR CATH

WIFE BY WED...

"A fun and sizzling romance, great characters that trade verbal spars like fist punches, and the dream of your own royal wedding!"
—Sizzling Hot Book Reviews (5 stars)

"A good holiday, fireside or bedtime story."
—Manic Reviews (4½ stars)

"A great story that I hope is the start of a new series."
—The Romance Studio (4½ hearts)

MARRIED BY MONDAY

"If I hadn't already added Ms. Catherine Bybee to my list of favorite authors, after reading this book I would have been compelled to. This is a book *nobody* should miss, because the magic it contains is awesome."
—Booked Up Reviews (5 stars)

"Ms. Bybee writes authentic situations and expresses the good and the bad in such an equal way . . . Keeps the reader on the edge of her seat."
—Reading Between the Wines (5 stars)

"*Married by Monday* was a refreshing read and one I couldn't possibly put down."
—The Romance Studio (4½ hearts)

FIANCÉ BY FRIDAY

"Bybee knows exactly how to keep readers happy . . . A thrilling pursuit and enough passion to stuff in your back pocket to last for the next few lifetimes . . . The hero and heroine come to life with each flip of the page and will linger long after readers cross the finish line."

—*RT Book Reviews* (4½ stars, top pick [hot])

"A tale full of danger and sexual tension . . . the intriguing characters add emotional depth, ensuring readers will race to the perfectly fitting finish."

—*Publishers Weekly*

"Suspense, survival, and chemistry mix in this scintillating read."

—*Booklist*

"Hot romance, a mystery assassin, British royalty, and an alpha Marine . . . this story has it all!"

—*Harlequin Junkie*

SINGLE BY SATURDAY

"Captures readers' hearts and keeps them glued to the pages until the fascinating finish . . . romance lovers will feel the sparks fly . . . almost instantaneously."

—*RT Book Reviews* (4½ stars, top pick)

"[A] wonderfully exciting plot, lots of desire, and some sassy attitude thrown in for good measure!"

—*Harlequin Junkie*

Taken by Tuesday

"[Bybee] knows exactly how to get bookworms sucked into the perfect storyline; then she casts her spell upon them so they don't escape until they reach the 'Holy Cow!' ending."

—*RT Book Reviews* (4½ stars, top pick)

Seduced by Sunday

"You simply can't miss [this novel]. It contains everything a romance reader loves—clever dialogue, three-dimensional characters, and just the right amount of steam to go with that heartwarming love story."

—Brenda Novak, *New York Times* bestselling author

"Bybee hits the mark . . . providing readers with a smart, sophisticated romance between a spirited heroine and a prim hero . . . Passionate and intelligent characters [are] at the heart of this entertaining read."

—*Publishers Weekly*

Treasured by Thursday

"The Weekday Brides never disappoint and this final installment is by far Bybee's best work to date."

—*RT Book Reviews* (4½ stars, top pick)

"An exquisitely written and complex story brimming with pride, passion, and pulse-pounding danger . . . Readers will gladly make time to savor this winning finale to a wonderful series."

—*Publishers Weekly* (starred review)

"Bybee concludes her popular Weekday Brides series in a gratifying way with a passionate, troubled couple who may find a happy future if they can just survive and then learn to trust each other. A compelling and entertaining mix of sexy, complicated romance and menacing suspense."

—*Kirkus Reviews*

NOT QUITE DATING

"It's refreshing to read about a man who isn't afraid to fall in love . . . [Jack and Jessie] fit together as a couple and as a family."

—*RT Book Reviews* (3 stars [hot])

"*Not Quite Dating* offers a sweet and satisfying Cinderella fantasy that will keep you smiling long after you've finished reading."

—Kathy Altman, *USA Today*, *Happy Ever After* blog

"The perfect rags to riches romance . . . The dialogue is inventive and witty, the characters are well drawn out. The storyline is superb and really shines . . . I highly recommend this standout romance! Catherine Bybee is an automatic buy for me."

—*Harlequin Junkie* (4½ hearts)

NOT QUITE ENOUGH

"Bybee's gift for creating unforgettable romances cannot be ignored. The third book in the Not Quite series will sweep readers away to a paradise, and they will be intrigued by the thrilling story that accompanies their literary vacation."

—*RT Book Reviews* (4½ stars, top pick)

NOT QUITE FOREVER

"Full of classic Bybee humor, steamy romance, and enough plot twists and turns to keep readers entertained all the way to the very last page."
—Tracy Brogan, bestselling author of the Bell Harbor series

"Magnetic . . . The love scenes are sizzling and the multi-dimensional characters make this a page-turner. Readers will look for earlier installments and eagerly anticipate new ones."
—*Publishers Weekly*

NOT QUITE PERFECT

"This novel flows extremely well and readers will find themselves consuming the witty dialogue and strong imagery in one sitting."
—*RT Book Reviews*

"Don't let the title fool you. *Not Quite Perfect* [is] actually the perfect story to sweep you away and take you on a pleasant adventure. So sit back, relax, maybe pour a glass of wine, and let Catherine Bybee entertain you with Glen and Mary's playful East Coast–West Coast romance. You won't regret it for a moment."
—*Harlequin Junkie* (4½ stars)

NOT QUITE CRAZY

"This fast-paced story features credible characters whose appealing relationship is built upon friendship, mutual respect, and sizzling chemistry."
—*Publishers Weekly*

"The plot is filled with twists and turns, but instead of feeling like a never-ending roller coaster, the story maintains a quiet flow. The slow buildup of a romance allows readers to get to know the main characters as individuals and makes the romantic element more organic."

—*RT Book Reviews*

DOING IT OVER

"The romance between fiercely independent Melanie and charming Wyatt heats up even as outsiders threaten to derail their newfound happiness. This novel will hook readers with its warm, inviting characters and the promise for similar future installments."

—*Publishers Weekly*

"This brand-new trilogy, Most Likely To, based on yearbook superlatives, kicks off with a novel that will encourage you to root for the incredibly likable Melanie. Her friends are hilarious and readers will swoon over Wyatt, who is charming and strong. Even Melanie's daughter, Hope, is a hoot! This romance is jam-packed with animated characters, and Bybee displays her creative writing talent wonderfully."

—*RT Book Reviews* (4 stars)

"With a dialogue full of energy and depth, and a twisting storyline that captured my attention, I would say that *Doing It Over* was a great way to start off a new series. (And look at that gorgeous book cover!) I can't wait to visit River Bend again and see who else gets to find their HEA."

—*Harlequin Junkie* (4½ stars)

STAYING FOR GOOD

"Bybee's skillfully crafted second Most Likely To contemporary (after *Doing It Over*) brings together former sweethearts who have not forgotten each other in the eleven years since high school. A cast of multidimensional characters brings the story to life and promises enticing future installments."

—*Publishers Weekly*

"Romance fans will be sure to cheer on former high school sweethearts Zoe and Luke right away in *Staying For Good*. Just wait until you see what passion, laughter, reconciliations, and mischief (can you say Vegas?) awaits readers this time around. Highly recommended."

—*Harlequin Junkie* (4½ stars)

MAKING IT RIGHT

"Intense suspense heightens the scorching romance at the heart of Bybee's outstanding third Most Likely To contemporary (after *Staying For Good*). Sizzling sensual scenes are coupled with scary suspense in this winning novel."

—*Publishers Weekly* (starred review)

FOOL ME ONCE

"A marvelous portrait of friendship among women who have been bonded by fire."

—*Library Journal* (best of the year 2017)

"Bybee still delivers a story that her die-hard readers will enjoy."

—*Publishers Weekly*

HALF EMPTY

"Wade and Trina here in *Half Empty* just might be one of my favorite couples Catherine Bybee has gifted us fans with so far. Captivating, engaging, lively and dreamy, I simply could not get enough of this book."
—*Harlequin Junkie* (5 stars)

"Part rock star romance, part romantic thriller, I really enjoyed this book."
—*Romance Reader*

FAKING FOREVER

"A charming contemporary with surprising depth . . . Bybee perfectly portrays a woman trying to hold out for Mr. Right despite the pressures of time. A pitch-perfect plot and a cast of sympathetic and lovable supporting characters make this book one to add to the keeper shelf."
—*Publishers Weekly*

"Catherine Bybee can do no wrong as far as I'm concerned . . . Passionate, sultry, and filled with genuine emotions that ran the gamut, *Faking Forever* was a journey of self-discovery and of a love that was truly meant to be. Highly recommended."
—*Harlequin Junkie*

SAY IT AGAIN

"Steamy, fast-paced, and consistently surprising, with a large cast of feisty supporting characters, this suspenseful roller-coaster ride will keep both series fans and new readers on the edge of their seats."
—*Publishers Weekly*

MY WAY TO YOU

"A fascinating novel that aptly balances disastrous circumstances."
—*Kirkus Reviews*

"*My Way to You* is an unforgettable book fueled by Catherine Bybee's own life, along with the dynamic cast she created that will capture your heart."
—*Harlequin Junkie*

HOME TO ME

"Bybee skillfully avoids both melodrama and melancholy by grounding her characters in genuine emotion . . . This is Bybee in top form."
—*Publishers Weekly* (starred review)

EVERYTHING CHANGES

"This sweet, sexy book is just the escapism many people are looking for right now."
—*Kirkus Reviews*

Beginning
of
Forever

OTHER TITLES BY CATHERINE BYBEE

Contemporary Romance

Weekday Brides Series

Wife by Wednesday
Married by Monday
Fiancé by Friday
Single by Saturday
Taken by Tuesday
Seduced by Sunday
Treasured by Thursday

Not Quite Series

Not Quite Dating
Not Quite Mine
Not Quite Enough
Not Quite Forever
Not Quite Perfect
Not Quite Crazy

Most Likely To Series

Doing It Over
Staying For Good
Making It Right

First Wives Series

Fool Me Once
Half Empty
Chasing Shadows
Faking Forever
Say It Again

Creek Canyon Series

My Way to You
Home to Me
Everything Changes

Richter Series

Changing the Rules
A Thin Disguise
An Unexpected Distraction

The D'Angelos Series

When It Falls Apart
Be Your Everything

Paranormal Romance

MacCoinnich Time Travels

Binding Vows
Silent Vows

Redeeming Vows
Highland Shifter
Highland Protector

The Ritter Werewolves Series

Before the Moon Rises
Embracing the Wolf

Novellas

Soul Mate
Possessive

Erotica

Kilt Worthy
Kilt-A-Licious

Beginning
of
Forever

CATHERINE
BYBEE

 Montlake

This is a work of fiction. Names, characters, organizations, places, events, and incidents are either products of the author's imagination or are used fictitiously. Otherwise, any resemblance to actual persons, living or dead, is purely coincidental.

Text copyright © 2023 by Catherine Bybee

All rights reserved.

No part of this book may be reproduced, or stored in a retrieval system, or transmitted in any form or by any means, electronic, mechanical, photocopying, recording, or otherwise, without express written permission of the publisher.

Published by Montlake, Seattle

www.apub.com

Amazon, the Amazon logo, and Montlake are trademarks of Amazon.com, Inc., or its affiliates.

ISBN-13: 9781542038553 (paperback)
ISBN-13: 9781542038546 (digital)

Cover design by Caroline Teagle Johnson
Cover image: © RomoloTavani /Getty; © zhengshun tang / Getty; © Barbara Prasnowska / ArcAngel; © Böhm Monika / Plainpicture

Printed in the United States of America

This one is for Dr. Carrie.
I could not have survived
the last few years without you.

CHAPTER ONE

"Happy birthday to you . . ."

Giovanni sat at the head of the table on the rooftop terrace of their family home. The seat was normally reserved for his mother, but Mari happily gave up her seat for the occasion.

The D'Angelos loved a good party, but birthdays were for family. And Gio couldn't have asked for more as his sang him "Happy Birthday."

His niece, Franny, sat on his lap, something he ate up, knowing she was growing out of the lap-sitting age. Soon there would be another baby in their family. His older brother, Luca, and his wife, Brooke, were several weeks away from welcoming the newest D'Angelo into the world. And even though his sister, Chloe, and her husband, Dante, weren't quite at the baby making stage, Giovanni knew it was only a matter of time.

In addition to his immediate family, Dante's mother, Rosa, was there, as well as a close friend of the family, Salena.

The San Diego spring air had a snap of cold that lofted away with the heat lamps on the terrace. The noise from the busy streets of Little Italy rose four stories to where they celebrated. On the ground floor, the family restaurant ran like the well-oiled machine that it was.

"You're getting old, m'friend." Dante patted Giovanni on the back once Franny jumped off his lap to help his mother cut the cake.

"Wait for it . . . ," Salena called from the other end of the table.

"You need to pick a wife!"

All eyes turned to the oldest D'Angelo, who didn't even bother to look up from the task of cake cutting as she gave her orders.

Salena, who seemed to be holding her breath, now sighed with a smile. "There it is." She winked at Gio. "How dare you be thirty and unmarried."

"Shouldn't that be 'find a wife'?" Gio asked his mother.

"Find one, pick one." Mari waved a hand in the air. "Call it whatever you want."

Gio laughed, his head more than a little fuzzy from the wine they'd been drinking throughout dinner.

Salena laughed louder than all of them. "We can start setting Gio up on blind dates, Mrs. D'Angelo."

"There isn't anyone in Little Italy that Gio hasn't dated," Chloe pointed out.

"That's not true," Gio defended himself.

"You exaggerate, Chloe. The high school senior class is completely untouched," Dante teased.

Gio motioned to Luca. "Help me out here."

"There will be a whole mess of freshmen coming into the city by midsummer." Luca leaned back, placed his hand over Brooke's as everyone at the table took a jab at the birthday boy.

There was no point in taking offense to his family's well-natured ribbing. He was the last of them to remain single, and now that Chloe and Dante's formal wedding had passed, the focus fell on Gio.

"Whatever happened to all that talk about settling down and having a dozen kids?" Brooke asked, reminding him of a conversation he had with her when they first met.

"I've been busy playing best man to all of you."

Luca and Dante exchanged glances with a shrug. "True."

Mari sat to his side once the cake was served and patted his hand. "You're a good son and generous brother."

"Thanks, Mama."

Luca grabbed an envelope that had been sitting in the center of the table throughout the meal and handed it to him. "This is from all of us."

"Is it a mail-order bride?" he asked as he accepted the large envelope.

"No," Chloe said. "But we do realize that you've put a lot of your plans on hold while we've been busy with weddings and baby showers."

"Not to mention flying all the way to Positano to beat me up," Dante added.

For a brief time, it wasn't clear that Dante was the right person for Chloe, and since Gio didn't approve of the match early on, he absolutely wanted to kick Dante's ass for messing with his little sister. Hence the last-minute trip overseas for said ass-kicking.

"The pandemic put my life on hold," Gio reminded them.

There was a collective groan at the table, followed by Luca saying, "And we kept it going."

"This is our way of telling you to take some time for yourself." Chloe smiled.

"And if you find a wife along the way . . . ," Mari said with a hum.

Gio opened the envelope and pulled out the papers folded inside.

Tour of Tuscany was written in fancy lettering with the image of a vineyard and a bus.

"What is this?"

Luca started to explain. "A three-week tour through Tuscany. Family-owned wineries of all shapes and sizes. This looked like a great way to kick-start what we all know is the life you want here."

Gio had been studying the art of wine making almost as much as he'd studied to earn his level one sommelier. He'd even considered increasing his certificate to the next level but wasn't sure that would get him any closer to his ultimate goal of growing his own grapes.

"The tour starts in Florence and ends there. You can visit Nonno before the tour leaves and stay later if you want. The return ticket is flexible."

Gio flipped through the pages of the itinerary, saw the tickets for the flight. "This is a week away."

Dante patted him on the back. "Better get packing."

The smile on Gio's face started to spread as excitement warmed up his spine. He hadn't visited Florence in years. "I don't know what to say?"

"*Grazie mille,*" Franny told him.

Everyone laughed as Gio stood and hugged his family, one member at a time.

~

The click of Emma's high heels echoed in the rotunda of the Napa offices of R&R Wineries as she walked through. Awards filled the display cases that splashed against the walls of the room, offering an exclamation point to her family's success.

There was a time she meandered through this building with an absolute sense of belonging. A sense of hope that one day she'd sit right beside her father and help make all the important decisions about their wine.

And even though she'd been asked to join the executive board meeting on this day, she held little hope that the time had come for her to move from Temecula to Napa.

Still, Emma kept her shoulders back and her chin high . . . while her cell phone was pressed to her ear.

"I'll be back in time for dinner."

Nicole, her best friend and dinner date for the evening, complained on the other end of the line. "It's your birthday. You shouldn't have to work on your birthday."

"It's a meeting."

"So . . . Zoom in like the rest of the world."

"My father doesn't ask for my presence very often. I'm not about to say no."

"Does he even realize it's your birthday?"

That . . . was a very good question. "Fifty-fifty chance."

Nicole moaned.

"Our reservation is at seven. My flight gets in at three thirty. I have plenty of time." Emma explained her plan.

"Call me if there's a delay and I'll meet you in San Diego and we can have dinner there."

"It won't be necessary. Trust me, I've done this trip a zillion times." Emma started up the stairs and ended the conversation. "I'll call you when I land."

"Please do."

Emma slid her phone into her purse and pasted on a smile as she walked through the open double doors of the main offices. Unlike the Temecula arm, Napa had full-time, everyday employees filling the space.

Her father, Robert Rutledge, and Emma's older brother, Richard, were the top two executives, with a dozen other employees that kept the office running. There were remote arms of R&R, the second to Napa was in Temecula, where Emma lived. Her parents had homes in both places, both sat on the edge of the vineyards that produced the grapes. Both had large operations on-site to produce and bottle the wine. This expanded the employee count a few times over. But the foremen and people that worked the land almost never stepped foot in the Napa office. And then there was Emma's position. Retail. Which arguably a trained monkey could probably pull off. Her dual degree in business and agriculture hadn't been exercised since the ink dried on the paperwork.

Emma helped find homes for their label. She headed up a small staff of sellers around the Southwest region of the United States. A position once held by her ex-husband . . . Kyle.

The fact that Kyle still worked for her father rubbed her all kinds of wrong ways and said a lot about her father's loyalty to her.

"Hello, Ms. Rutledge."

Emma was greeted by the office's main secretary.

"Good morning, Georgia." Emma looked around the relatively quiet office space. "Where is everybody?"

"They're already gathered in the conference room."

Emma looked at her watch. "I was told nine o'clock." It was eight fifteen.

"Mr. Rutledge wanted to start early."

Emma's heart skipped. "Great."

Georgia offered a smile. "I'm sure you can just sneak in."

The urge to roll her eyes was a physical pain to hold back. Why mandate she show for a meeting and then give her the wrong time?

Forty-five minutes early was plenty of time for coffee and gossip to try and arm herself for what the topic of discussion was going to be.

Emma headed toward the conference room, dropped her purse on one of the desks outside the door, and let herself in.

Only "sneaking" wasn't something she was going to do.

She opened the door wide and walked in.

Her father stopped midsentence from the head of the table while the rest of the testosterone took in her presence.

"Good morning," she offered.

"Emma." Saying her name was her dad's greeting.

Richard sat on her father's right, and gave her a smile.

Immediately next to her brother was Kyle.

He was the only one at the table who avoided looking her way.

"Good thing I arrived early, or I might have missed this meeting altogether," she said as she walked farther into the room. The chairs surrounding the conference table were completely filled. Chairs pushed to the side were sprinkled with her father's personal secretary and a couple of faces she didn't know.

Her father didn't offer an apology or an explanation. He simply tilted his head to the side and returned his attention to the men at the table. "As I was saying . . ."

Emma gave him half an ear as she moved toward the coffee station and poured herself a cup of *wake the hell up* juice.

"Lionel's resignation was a surprise to us all, but it's presented an opportunity to restructure a few things."

Lionel had been with R&R since before Emma had graduated from college. Even though the man could run circles around Richard, he wasn't the favorite son and had been passed over as the second in command when Richard took priority. To the man's credit, he stayed on for several years with no possible room for promotion. While the official word was he'd taken a job in a Washington State winery and there weren't any bridges burned, there was watercooler talk of raised voices and slammed doors right before everyone had been informed of Lionel's resignation.

Emma moved to the far end of the table, placed her cup of coffee down, and deliberately pulled a chair that sat against the wall to the table's edge. The men she squeezed between gave her room and a smile.

"We've hired a dedicated accountant for the sole purpose of bringing Richard up to speed on the chief financial officer duties."

Emma saw through Richard's forced smile.

Her brother might be good at numbers, but Emma knew he didn't like working with them. Besides, he was already president of operations.

"While he has committed to learning this, I am appointing a vice president of operations to share the workload, which will likely be a permanent position, considering our growth."

Emma opened the window of hope with the possibility of a promotion. After all, she could easily do Richard's job if only given the chance.

"Kyle." That dream was blown up with one word.

All eyes turned to her ex.

His gaze met hers, briefly, a slight glint in his eye.

Emma kept her hands on her coffee and acted unaffected.

Inside, her stomach twisted.

"And who will be replacing Kyle?" Emma asked, surprised her voice didn't waver.

"We're interviewing now," Kyle told her.

"You knew about this?"

"Of course."

Emma wanted to smack the smugness off Kyle's face but knew a catfight was all her father would need to throw at her and give him a reason to keep her at the bottom of the ladder.

"I'm sure there won't be any problem with you and your team reporting to Kyle while Richard is brought up to speed," Robert said directly to Emma.

Since she'd reported to Lionel, and on rare occasion Kyle, when she first took her position, this wasn't a complete shock.

But that didn't make it acceptable.

Emma channeled her father's behavior and said nothing as he continued.

Thirty painstaking minutes passed while her father went on about the boom of their sales and how their name opened more doors than they could solicit, the underlying message suggesting that Emma's role in the company was devalued as a result.

She half expected the meeting to end with a pink slip in her hand.

By the time her stomach had settled enough to pick up her cup of coffee, the brew had turned cold and the meeting came to an end.

Ten minutes from the time it was supposed to start.

The team dispersed, each of them laying congratulations out at Kyle's feet as if they were an offering, complete with flowers and incense.

"Perfect man for the job."

"I look forward to working with you."

"Well done."

Emma wanted to vomit.

Two sets of eyes skirted past her before heading out of the room.

She followed her father and raised a hand at her brother in a silent request that he not join her.

Robert looked over his shoulder, said nothing, and escaped behind the mahogany doors of his office.

Emma closed the door to prevent anyone from hearing what she had to say. "Why did you ask me to be here?" she asked before her dad could take a seat behind his desk.

"I didn't want you to hear about Kyle's promotion through an email." He lifted a paper from the stack on his desk, not sparing a look in her direction.

"And yet you started the meeting before I was scheduled to arrive."

"Best of intentions," he said without apology. "But now you know."

"You've made my ex-husband my boss."

That brought Robert's eyes to hers. He pointed using the paper in his hand. "You decided to divorce him. A mistake as far as I'm concerned."

"Years ago."

"No less true today. Kyle is the right man for the job."

Emma dropped her purse on an empty chair. "What about the right *woman* for the job? Did it ever occur to you to consider me?"

He laughed. A huffed drop of air that said, *Don't be ridiculous.* As if she was suggesting a hostile takeover was in order. "You haven't proven you're capable."

"You haven't given me the opportunity. My only responsibility with R&R is finding buyers and keeping tabs on a few employees in the southern region, which you just told everyone is a financial waste of time."

"Be happy you're employed."

The hair on her neck stood on end as she kept the words she wanted to say inside. "For how long? Until Kyle decides I'm no longer needed?"

"That won't happen."

Emma wasn't convinced. "Give me Kyle's job, then. The one you're taking résumés for."

"That would require you relocating up here. And before you tell me you will, let me add that walking through the tension of this office when both you and Kyle are here is not something I'm willing to endure."

She turned to face the window looking out over Napa Valley. "There it is. The bottom line to why I'll never be more for R&R."

"You have a trust fund. Working here is an option."

"Did it ever occur to you that I want to earn my keep?"

"Not at the expense of the peace in this office. Be content with the place you have in Temecula."

Be happy with a go-nowhere job with absolutely no room for advancement.

This wasn't going to change. Her marriage to Kyle had been the only time her father had given her any room at R&R. He would have gifted her a portion of one of the vineyards complete with a house . . . his direct words when she told him of her impending divorce.

Instead, she made the paycheck from R&R work with a rented condo in Temecula without touching her trust fund. Wasn't that secretly done to prove herself to her father? The transient living arrangement put in place in the hope that one day Daddy would ask her to relocate to Napa.

"I'm never going to be able to prove myself to you," she said under her breath.

Her father was already shuffling papers on his desk. Oblivious to her words.

"Maybe I need to do this on my own," she said a little louder.

"Excuse me?"

She turned. "On my own. Maybe I use that trust fund to find my own chunk of earth . . . here in Napa, Temecula."

"That's absurd."

"Not to me," she said with absolute certainty. "Unless you plan on holding the purse strings to my trust fund to only be used for 'father approved' purchases. Maybe I'm tired of living in a condo. Maybe Napa is ready for a second Rutledge label?"

Her father didn't rattle, but Emma could tell her words were weighing on him.

"I bet I can find a dozen wineries for sale right now in this valley," she said.

"Your trust fund won't support that kind of money."

"Loans, then?"

His eyes narrowed. "You'll end up blowing every dime I've given you."

"In light of the fact that I haven't touched one of them, I doubt that. But that would take care of everything for you . . . wouldn't it? No worries about Kyle and I having words in the office. I won't be in here asking you for any position that's available that you have no intention of considering me for. You won't have to fire me because the job you have me in isn't cost-effective. Just think, Dad. You can tell all your friends that I'm off trying to make a name for myself even though you warned me. Blame it on my willfulness . . . or even the red hair," she said, touching the end of said hair in her hand. "That would be a lot more pleasant of a conversation for you than the truth. 'Emma quit because I made her ex-husband her boss.' That can't be easy for people to swallow."

"I don't care what anyone thinks."

She laughed. Appearances were at the top of Robert Rutledge's list. Her father's list was suddenly placed on the bottom of hers.

She reached for her purse. "I haven't taken a vacation in three years. I'm sure the golden boy won't mind taking over my meaningless job for the next six weeks while I consider my options."

"Emma—"

"Or fire me. You have options, too . . . Dad." With that, Emma turned on her heel and opened the door, her entire body shaking. "Oh . . ." She turned a half circle. "Thanks for the birthday wishes." She placed a hand on her chest. "They were so heartfelt."

CHAPTER TWO

"Surprise!"

Emma's pulse jumped nearly as much as her legs did when a room full of screaming adults wished her a happy birthday.

Her handbag slid down her arm and she had to scramble to keep it from crashing to the floor.

She forced a smile and leaned in close to Nicole. "I'm going to kill you."

"Oh, stop. You love it."

No, actually. Considering how the day had started, the last thing she wanted was to be the center of attention in a group of people, many of which she spent very little time with.

Left with no choice, Emma swallowed it down and moved forward through the crowd of familiar faces, accepting birthday wishes and hugs. Gone were the thoughts of looking up properties and weighing her options over drinks with her bestie.

Someone turned on a speaker and Nicole's condo filled with music as Emma passed between people.

"Thirty is just a number."

"Welcome to the club."

"You don't look a day over twenty-five."

That one came from an old college roommate's husband. Of course she didn't look over twenty-five, she turned thirty, not fifty.

Nicole took Emma's purse and at the same time pressed a glass of champagne into her hand.

Emma met Nicole in the lobby of her building with the intention of calling an Uber so they could both drink. "You'll never believe what happened."

"*Hold that thought.*" *Nicole had started the tap dance with her hands on her pockets and then started rummaging through her purse with the guise of having left her phone at her place.* "*I don't like this coat anyway. Come up with me and help me pick a better one.*"

Emma should have seen it coming.

"Were you surprised, honey?" Emma's mother walked over and circled her small arms around her.

"I had no idea."

"Nicole's been planning this for months."

"No wonder she was stressed about my trip today."

"Hey, beautiful. Let me take your coat." Ryan, her brother, tugged her jacket off her shoulders.

Emma volleyed the champagne glass from one hand to the other to keep it from spilling.

Nicole quickly swept her jacket away and Ryan pushed in with his charismatic smile. "You look stunning, little sister."

"I thought we were going to a steakhouse bar." Hence the spaghetti-string little black dress and high heels. Most of the people in the condo were dressed for a house party. Slacks, dressy jeans, and nice shirts. A couple of them were even in shorts.

It was Temecula, and the spring temperatures had been north of eighty degrees for the past week.

"It isn't going anywhere," her mother said.

Emma sipped her champagne and looked around the room. "I can't imagine Dad is here."

"Oh, honey, no. He and Richard had to be in Napa this weekend."

No shit.

Emma's eyes slid to Ryan's. "He'd only be a drag anyway," Ryan said with a wink.

Nicole moved closer to Beth's side and tugged on her arm. "Can you help me in the kitchen, Mrs. Rutledge?"

Beth set down her glass and turned away.

"Dad had a different surprise for me," she said once her mother was out of earshot.

"Do I want to know?" Ryan asked.

Emma looked into her glass. At least the wine was helpful. "He promoted Kyle, which means he's now my boss."

Ryan's jaw dropped. "What the actual fuck."

"I literally just flew home from Napa a couple hours ago. I don't think Dad even remembered it was my birthday."

Her brother shook his head. "Best decision I ever made was getting far, far away from anything wine."

Ryan had zero tolerance for their father's ways and was always quick to make it known when they were in the same space.

"I'm starting to understand your wisdom."

Ryan looped his free arm through Emma's. "I'm sure Mom has a fat check with both of their names on it for you."

Fat enough to buy a winery? Probably not.

Before they could discuss it more, they were surrounded, and the subject was changed.

Emma clouded her disappointment by downing her glass of champagne.

~

Gio stood over the sink in his small kitchen and made quick work of cleaning up the dishes that lived in his section of their family home.

Chloe and Dante had already made their way home, and Brooke was putting Franny to bed.

Salena lingered at Gio's side, helping with the cleanup. "Are you sure you're okay with picking up some shifts while I'm away?" he asked her.

"It won't be the first or last time I help." Salena waited tables at a restaurant one block over and one block up.

Gio smiled. "You'll probably make better tips here."

"I make better tips not because of the location, but because of the looks." She batted her eyelashes and puffed her ample chest out.

"No doubt about that."

Salena was a very beautiful woman. And she knew it.

"Who is on the menu this week?" he asked, knowing the question wasn't offensive, not when the answer changed from week to week, or month to month. Salena was very much a catch-and-release woman. Gio liked to think it was because her standards were super high . . . or maybe she liked the chase more than the long-term reality. Either way, the two of them were similar in that way . . . at least until recently.

"I'm in a slump since my wingman got married."

Gio handed her a plate to dry. "Chloe will still go out with you."

"Yeah, but we had a routine. Now it's like she doesn't even notice the hotness surrounding us at the clubs."

"That's what marriage is supposed to do."

Salena put the dry plate on the open shelf. "Whatever. Summer will be here before you know it."

He handed her another plate. "Just be careful."

"They're the ones that need to worry. Not me."

"Yeah, yeah. Call anytime if your mouth is bigger than your biceps."

Salena nudged her shoulder against his as they finished the work.

~

"I didn't think they'd ever leave," Emma's mother said from across the room.

Ryan had stuck close until the last possible minute before following a group to a dance club.

They'd invited Emma to join them, but she wanted nothing more to do with crowds.

She reached for the half-empty glasses on a table to help clean up the mess left behind by the guests.

"Put that down," Nicole ordered. "It's your birthday."

Checking her watch, Emma shrugged. "For another hour."

Nicole pointed a finger her way. "It's against the rules to clean up after your own party."

"Says who?"

"Stop." Nicole was getting irritated.

Beth tapped the seat beside her. "Sit next to me. I have something for you."

No sooner had Emma's bottom found the couch than Beth stood and moved to the table filled with birthday gifts.

Nicole placed the handful of glasses on the kitchen counter. "Yeah . . . present time."

"I don't have the bandwidth for all of that." Emma waved a hand at the pile of gift bags, boxes, and cards.

Her mother sat back down with a brightly covered package in her hand. "You have time for this." Beth pushed the present onto Emma's lap.

Emma looked at the package, saw an envelope inside.

It was always the same. A check, a card . . . an *I love you* from both her parents written in her mother's handwriting.

"I'd really rather look at this tomorrow, Mom."

Beth sighed and patted Emma's knee. "I heard about Kyle's promotion."

"Kyle got a promotion?" Nicole asked, taking the seat on Emma's side.

The two of them hadn't gotten time to chat at all during the party. And truthfully, Emma didn't want to put a downer on the evening, although that felt like an impossible task now.

Emma nodded. "Yeah. He's my boss now."

"That's not how your father sees it," Beth said.

"Dad isn't great about telling you the truth of things when it comes to R&R."

Beth frowned. "I told him it was a mistake."

Her marriage to Kyle had lasted sixteen months, and that included the time it took for the divorce to become final.

When they met, he was in charge of sales along the West Coast. Older by eight years, Kyle was told to mentor the youngest Rutledge, aka Emma. It was during that mentoring an attraction developed.

Her father approved.

As a wedding present, Kyle was promoted to regional sales manager and reported directly to her father.

And Emma unwrapped toasters and air fryers.

When they divorced, a move her father didn't approve of, Kyle stayed in Napa, and Emma was cemented into the Temecula arm of R&R Wineries.

Kyle won.

"And I told Dad I was taking six weeks off to weigh my options."

Beth and Nicole exchanged glances.

"You're kidding," Nicole finally said.

"Nope."

"What options?" her mom asked.

"All of them." Emma stopped looking at her hands and sighed.

"We need more wine for this." Nicole stood and moved to the table full of gifts and picked up a random bag and removed the wine. She turned the bottle so the label aimed Emma's way.

Cabernet sauvignon, not a particularly bad vintage, but not particularly good either. It didn't matter, her taste buds weren't looking for something spectacular. She just wanted to get a little bit drunk. Or maybe a lot drunk.

"Dad is never going to take my position at R&R seriously. Promoting Kyle is a clear slap in my face."

"What I don't understand is why your father spent all that money on a good college if he was never going to use your talents," Nicole said.

"I can't be an *uneducated* trophy. That would be an embarrassment."

"Honey—"

"A trophy that lost her sparkle when she divorced. You know I'm not wrong, Mom." No taller than five three, with dark brown hair that only recently started to sparkle if she didn't get to the hairdresser within six weeks, Beth Rutledge had been the perfect wife, perfect mother. After all, she had no other jobs to occupy her. Emma wasn't even sure her mom had a hobby. What she did do was stand by her husband's side when asked, and sometimes point a finger at him when they were alone.

Nicole found three clean glasses and brought them to the living room.

"I'll talk to him."

"Don't," Emma told her. "Nothing you can say will make a difference. I told Dad that I was going to look into buying my own vineyard and starting my own label. Hell, I've seen him buy up property, demolish the house, and call the land a write-off for years before turning a profit. How hard can it be to buy something, move in, and make it work?"

Nicole handed her a glass and then poured one for Beth, who waved it off. "You're serious."

"Dad reminds me of my trust fund every time I ask for a promotion. 'Working here is an option.'" She lowered her voice to match her father's tone. "The kicker is he told me when Kyle and I divorced that he was in the process of buying us our own place. But I ruined it by divorcing the asshole. Our conversation today reminded me of that. I was good enough for that when I was married, divorced . . . not so much."

"The McGregor place," Beth said under her breath.

Emma looked past her nose. "You knew the property?"

"I helped pick it out. The house had good bones. Open floor plan. The kitchen needed a remodel, but it was perfect."

"Did Robert just let it fall through?" Nicole asked.

Beth shook her head. "No. He bought it and rented the house back to the owners. I'm pretty sure they moved out last year and it's sitting vacant."

"Ready for Dad to tear down," Emma said.

Beth shrugged. "I don't know, honey. You know your dad . . . he wants a bigger cut of land every year."

"Is this place in Napa?" Nicole asked.

"No. It's ten minutes from our property here."

Her parents had homes in both Napa and Temecula. The larger of the two in Napa. And if Emma had to guess, that design was to keep his marriage intact. If Beth and Robert had to comingle each and every day, her mom would have likely walked by now.

Emma took a drink of her wine. "Let me know if I can get a family discount on the place," she joked. "Or maybe he intends to give it to his third son."

"Not if I have anything to say about it," her mom chided.

"No offense, Mom . . . but Dad doesn't listen to you very often."

"A woman always has her ways," she said, smiling.

Her mom stood and picked up her purse. She pointed toward the gift bag at Emma's side. "I want you to make me a promise with that check."

Emma glanced up. "What?"

"That the two of you use it on the most lavish vacation you can dream of. Go to France . . . or Italy. Drink all the wine . . . and pick up the phone when I call."

The stubborn set in her mother's jaw was something Emma saw often in the mirror looking back at her.

"I all but quit my job today, Mom. I probably need this for my rent."

Beth leaned over, kissed her on the cheek. "Don't be ridiculous. You're a Rutledge. And it's high time you move out of that tiny condo and start living like one."

Emma didn't argue, she simply smiled. "I love you, Mom."

Nicole jumped to her feet and walked Beth to the door.

"I mean it. A long vacation. Both of you."

"You don't have to ask me twice," Nicole said with a laugh.

Nicole leaned against the door once Beth walked out. "How big is that check?"

Emma dug into the bag and ripped open the envelope. She grinned. "How does a few weeks in Italy sound?"

Nicole smiled from ear to ear. "Are you serious?"

"Can you get the time off?"

"For a few weeks all expenses paid in Italy? I'll fake a disease if I have to."

For the first time all day Emma put aside everything R&R . . . all of her disappointments, and felt the joy of her birthday.

Only looking at the clock, the hour had passed. "Go get your laptop and let's plan something epic."

CHAPTER THREE

The pasty aftertaste of a late night with a bottle of wine met Emma when she woke in the morning.

Birdsong was her alarm.

Not actual birds, but the kind an iPhone made when your alarm went off.

She'd forgotten to turn off the alarm when she fell into bed the night before.

Nicole's guest room and Nicole's pajamas met her eyes when she opened them.

Emma rolled over and turned off the birds and noticed two text messages from her mother.

The first read: Are you awake?

The second . . . Call me when you're up.

She stumbled out of bed and padded barefoot through the room and opened the blinds.

The sun was already high, the temperature past seventy-five degrees. Summer was going to roll in hot. A conversation she would be having with the foreman at her father's Temecula vineyards if she saw him.

Only she wouldn't be seeing him. Would she?

Well, she'd see him. Her family didn't stop being her family even if she no longer worked for them.

Emma dialed her mother's number and waited while it rang.

"You slept in," her mother said accusingly.

"We got to bed late."

"Did you stay at Nicole's?"

"I did."

"Did you pick a vacation destination?"

Emma smiled, despite the pain in her head. "Three weeks in Tuscany. Small group tour with all the stops and all the wineries."

"Sounds perfect."

Emma ran a hand over her face. "I'll either be ready to start my own place or switch careers altogether."

Her mom laughed. "About that . . . Can you meet me later today?"

"I'm practically unemployed and our trip doesn't start for a week. So yes, I'm free."

"Great. I'll text you an address. Let's say . . . two hours?"

Emma hesitated. "What's this about, Mom?"

"Two hours. I'll see you there." And her mother hung up.

After making a pot of coffee, and Nicole still not emerging from her bedroom, Emma slipped out of her best friend's apartment and made her way home.

An hour and thirty minutes later, Emma drove her SUV past her parent's estate and up the road indicated on the GPS.

Eventually the route indicated for her to veer off the main road and around the back side of the highly visible vineyards most of the natives of Temecula were familiar with.

After winding through open vineyards, she finally found the pillars that held the address to a house.

She slowed her car and inched along the drive after passing an open gate.

Vines stretched out in both directions.

A large parking area in front of the house held a single car . . .

Her mother's.

"What are you up to, Mom?" Emma whispered to herself.

She stepped out of her car and looked around.

It was quiet . . . as large properties surrounded by vineyards often were.

Peaceful.

The outside of the house bore a striking resemblance to her parent's home. Only smaller.

The landscape had been neglected but the house itself didn't look in that bad of shape.

Emma's mother walked out from the front door of the house, wearing large-rim sunglasses that hid her eyes.

The wind caught Emma's red curls, the ones she hadn't bothered straightening before she left the house, and blocked her view.

"You found it," Beth said.

"GPS is an amazing thing. What exactly did I find?"

Beth walked down the few steps to the drive. "This is the home I told you about last night."

Emma turned a full circle.

The house that would have been hers had she stayed married.

"Being Kyle's wife was too big a price," Emma said with a tiny laugh.

Beth ushered her over with a wave of her hand. "Come take a look."

"Why?"

"Humor me, Emma."

"Fine." Not really . . . but what was she going to say? "No, Mom, I'd rather not see the dangling carrot and skip right over to the second-place prize."

Beth had obviously shown up a bit earlier and had taken the time to open the blinds and windows, allowing the sunlight to spill in from outside.

The dust and musty scent of a home being closed up couldn't be missed, but the gentle breeze coming from the back of the house was helping move the stagnant air along.

The house had high ceilings and large windows that let in a ton of natural light. A California rambler fashioned after a Mediterranean villa is what popped into Emma's head as they walked around.

"I think this wall should come down and a huge island take its place," Beth said.

"That would open it up."

"I'm not sure of the color of these floors," Beth mentioned.

"Nothing a new stain wouldn't fix."

Her mother smiled and moved through the house.

There was a laundry room and a loggia that spanned half the size of the house in the backyard. There was a pool with a built-in spa, a staple in this part of California. And vineyards outlining the whole place. All four bedrooms had their own bathrooms.

It was beautiful.

And a lot like her mother's house. Which wasn't surprising since she was the one who picked it out.

Her mother had checked off all the boxes of a home, from the garage to the fenced-in portion of a yard with a pool.

They stepped back outside in front of the house.

"This driveway . . . it's so . . . plain."

Emma smirked. "It's a driveway, Mom."

"It's cement."

"What are you suggesting . . . cobblestone?"

Beth looked at her like she hadn't thought of it. "Now that would be lovely."

Emma turned to face her mother and sighed. "What is this all about?"

"Do you like it?"

"Who wouldn't like it?"

Beth smiled, as if that was all she needed to hear. "Good."

"Mom!"

"I'm going to have a little chat with your father."

Emma couldn't help it . . . she laughed. "A chat where he'll hand me the keys and walk away? I think you're delusional."

"The very thing he was going to do when you and Kyle were married."

24

"Yet somehow I'm unworthy as a divorcée. Besides, Dad may have purchased this property and given us the keys, but it would have always been his. Part of R&R. Something he could take away just as quickly. And honestly, Mom . . . as beautiful as this place is, I'm over being pulled around by my father's purse strings. You sent me to college to become something. And that is never going to happen with my *daddy* looking over me. He proved that yesterday. I'm the daughter of a millionaire wine tycoon who is capable of being more than a hood ornament on his dynasty."

"There are twenty acres of vines," Beth said as if she hadn't heard Emma's diatribe. "I learned that your father kept the original foreman from the previous owners and that they ship the grapes to us for production."

"Mom! Did you hear what I said?"

"I heard you, Emma. Now what you need to do is listen to me. The daughter of Robert Rutledge is not going to start out on some five-acre parcel of land with a single-wide and a lean-to to bottle her first harvest. And if your father isn't going to see fit that you find a proper place within R&R, he damn well is going to give you a leg up to do it on your own. If that means you take this property over and turn it into something instead of letting the house fall to ruin and the buildings blow over during the next storm, then that's what you do."

"Not if R&R holds the title. If I do this, I do it for myself. I control everything. I will not build something so that Dad can appoint Kyle to come in and take control."

Beth lifted her chin. "That is perfectly understandable."

Emma felt like she'd taken one step forward. "And I don't want this given to me. Take it out of my trust fund." Arguably, that was still a gift, but the money in those accounts was set up at her birth and had grown exponentially over time.

Her mother pointed to the larger buildings, which Emma assumed were for production and warehousing . . . and likely a cellar. "You're going to need money to get this place self-sufficient."

Emma pointed to her own chest. "Business degree, Mom."

"I know. I paid the bill."

Emma finally took her eyes off her mother and looked around. "Can you give me a minute?"

"Take all the time you need."

She placed her sunglasses over her eyes and headed toward the largest of the two outbuildings.

Emma pulled her hair around one shoulder and attempted to keep it from blowing in her face.

It took both hands and serious effort to push open the massive doors that led into the warehouse. It was a mess. Not only was there old, outdated equipment . . . or what was left of it, but there were dusty boxes and the remnants of someone's life. Broken furniture, rusty bikes . . . the space had obviously not been used to produce wine in some time. She meandered through the open building into a corridor that led to the second structure. Steps took her down to a cooler space. There were two remaining stainless-steel vats. One knock on them said they were empty. Old oak barrels only good as yard decorations at this point. Not much could be salvaged. But the space was solid. The walls sturdy.

"Hello?"

Emma turned to the male voice.

A man stood there. He looked to be in his fifties and wore a button-up shirt, jeans, and a pair of work boots that were well worn.

"Can I help you?" he asked.

Emma smiled and walked toward him. "You must be the foreman."

He shook her hand when she presented it. "I am. Raul."

"Emma Rutledge."

His eyes lit up and he started to shuffle his feet.

"Relax, please."

"No one said anyone was coming today."

"Likely because they don't know I'm here. My mother is at the house. She was showing me around."

His gaze skirted around her. "Is there a problem?"

"No. I'm . . ." What was she doing? "Can I ask you a few things?"

Raul shifted from one foot to the other. "Sure."

Emma tapped her sunglasses against her palm. "How long have you worked here?"

"Twenty years."

"You have a family?"

He nodded. "Four boys, two girls." He was smiling. "My oldest is about to finish high school. My wife stays home with them."

"You stayed on after my father bought the place . . . why?"

Raul blinked a few times. "I know the grapes. Jobs like this aren't available every day."

Of course. "Forgive me, but I'm not familiar with this property. What can you tell me about the vines?"

"What do you want to know?"

"Let's start with variety."

"We grow zinfandel, Sangiovese, a few acres dedicated to pinot grigio, and the rest are cabernet sauvignon."

That would explain the different vats in the cellar.

"And R&R comes in and harvests?"

Raul shook his head. "I bring in people and we take the grapes wherever we're told to."

"Not always R&R's production center?"

"The last couple of years . . . yes."

Maybe it took that long for the harvest to meet R&R standards. "Have there been any problems with disease or insects?"

Raul stood back. "None at all."

"Why did the previous owners sell? Do you know?"

Raul ran his fingers through his hair. "They were struggling. Production became an expense they couldn't justify. They cut back the watering. Sold off equipment and eventually put the place on the market."

"Why were they struggling?"

Catherine Bybee

Raul shuffled his feet. "Their son was sick."

"Oh . . ." She wasn't about to ask for more on that subject. Emma turned around and took in the space once more.

"Miss Rutledge?"

"Yes?"

"Do I need to worry about my job?"

Emma blew out a breath. "No. Not that I know of." What could she tell him . . . that if her mother could convince her father to sell her the place, then Emma was going to be Raul's new boss? And what would happen if Raul said that to whoever he communicated with at R&R? "I'm simply curious about the property."

"Okay." He didn't sound convinced.

Emma reached her hand out again, giving him no choice but to shake it. "Thank you, Raul. I hope to see you again."

"Have a nice day."

Emma left the cellar and went back into the Temecula sun.

She could do this . . . all she needed was her father to get on board.

CHAPTER FOUR

Florence, Italy

Where the Renaissance began and still lived and breathed.

It had been too long.

Gio had spent what he called *a summer in the city* here when he was thirteen. It wasn't the entire summer, and it wasn't exactly in the city. But his parents had shipped him off to visit his grandfather for six weeks.

At thirteen, Gio wanted nothing to do with leaving his friends in San Diego and going somewhere where he didn't know anyone his age.

Yet somehow, after less than two days, Giovanni D'Angelo found himself beside first cousins, second cousins . . . their friends, neighbors. The Italian he spoke at home sounded a bit clunky when he arrived, and smooth when he left.

The home his grandfather Lorenzo lived in sat just above the Piazzale Michelangelo that overlooked the city. The home had come from Gio's great-grandparents, and his great-great-grandparents. And while it was family homes and villas that dotted the landscape right next to the city, if you traveled only a few miles away, the hillsides were layered in vineyards.

It was Tuscany. And if there was a word that described the region better than any other, it was *wine*.

Thirteen-year-old Giovanni had sampled wine on more than one occasion. He was Italian, after all. But it wasn't the taste of wine at the time that made him fall in love with the long rows of grapes growing in the fields. No. It was the quiet of the fields. The peace of the home on the edge of a vineyard that came to life with the family inside. The way that family came together for a meal that included the fruit of their land.

Gio grew up in a four-story home that housed the family restaurant on the ground floor. As a child, he and his siblings and parents lived on the second floor. The third was guest quarters for family when they visited. And the fourth was a small space used mainly for storage.

When his older brother married, the third floor became his, and the guests were moved to the top floor.

And now . . . Gio lived on that top story with a terrace that overlooked San Diego. Not a bad deal, if he was honest. But not what he wanted.

Tuscany, and the impression of that one summer he spent with his *nonno*, lived inside his soul.

Yes, Gio worked in the family restaurant, but he didn't cook. Well, not like his brother and mama. He did, however, know wine. He studied wine. Became a sommelier, which admittedly did very little for the family business. But Gio loved everything about what created the bottled and fermented fruit on the table.

The smile on his face as the taxi drove up to his grandfather's home was felt deep in his core.

Lorenzo opened the door the moment the cab pulled up to the house. "Giovanni!"

Lorenzo walked over, kissed one cheek, then the next, and rocked back on his heels. "So good to see you here again."

They'd just seen each other for Luca's wedding.

Unfortunately, Lorenzo wasn't well enough to travel for Chloe's, which quickly followed. Gio wasn't surprised to see the added fatigue on his *nonno*'s face, or the slowing of his step that he'd noticed the last time he'd visited San Diego.

"It's good to be back," Gio said.

The taxi driver pulled Gio's duffel bag from the back of the car and set it to the side.

Gio thanked him in Italian.

When his grandfather reached for Gio's bag, Gio beat him to it. "I've got it."

With a wink, the older man stood tall and walked toward the front door of his home.

"How is your mother?"

"She's well. Said to give you a hug."

Lorenzo smiled as they made it into the house. "I'm so proud of her."

Gio smiled. "She knows it."

A simple nod finished that conversation. "So . . . you're here for a tour of Tuscany."

"I am."

Vaulted ceilings, which somehow looked smaller than the last time Gio had been there, spanned the living room of the home. "And you still want to own a winery."

"My goals haven't changed."

Gio dropped his bag in the living room and followed Lorenzo through the house onto the terrace that overlooked Florence.

The Arno River sat below, and the horizon of the city, complete with the Duomo, the Palazzo Vecchio, and the bell towers of the many churches, filled the view. The image had been etched in Giovanni's mind since the tender age of thirteen.

He drew in a deep breath and blew it out . . . slowly.

"It's something . . . isn't it?"

"I understand why you're here," Gio said.

"It wasn't easy leaving your mother."

"I know." Gio waved a hand in the air as if dismissing the conversation.

The story was simple. His grandparents had left the States when Gio's great-grandparents weren't well. After they passed, Gio's grandmother wasn't in the best of health. And so it went.

There was family here . . . extended to Gio, but family.

Y

Lorenzo turned back toward the house. "I made a little something for dinner. I hope you're hungry."

Gio turned to his grandfather with a smile. "I'll open the wine."

~

The conveyer belt where luggage circled the airport baggage claim had one bright orange suitcase going round and round . . . unclaimed.

Everyone from the flight had happily grabbed their bags.

All but Emma.

"This is a bad sign," Nicole said as she looked around at the people from their flight, who were all walking away.

"Damn it." Emma sighed and hiked her backpack higher on her shoulder and looked around them in search of someone from the airline to help with a lost bag.

Thirty minutes later . . . "It ended up in Seattle."

Emma looked between Nicole and the woman at the baggage claim counter. "What? How did that happen?"

"I really don't know. This is highly unusual."

"Is it still in Seattle?" Emma asked.

Instead of answering, the woman clicked a few keys on her computer with a shrug. "Might be."

"What do you mean, 'might be'?"

She glanced at her watch. "The tags are scanned going into the plane and leaving the plane. My computer says it's in Seattle, but there is a chance that your bag is waiting for the next plane out this way and not sitting in a holding room. As soon as it's scanned, we'll know where it is going."

"So, when will I get it?"

"We have to find it first. Couple days at most."

"A couple of days?"

Nicole leaned forward. "What is she supposed to do for a couple of days?"

"We're leaving on a tour the day after tomorrow."

The employee held up both her hands. "I will make some calls and see if we can get it here sooner." She handed Emma a form. "Fill this out. Describe the bag and any contents that might stick out. In case the luggage tag was lost."

Emma placed both hands on her face. "Does that happen?"

Again, the woman shrugged.

"And if that happened?" Nicole asked.

"Did you buy travel insurance? They pay for lost luggage."

Emma squeezed her eyes shut, turned around. "This isn't happening."

"You're in Florence. Go shopping. Chances are your bag will get here tomorrow."

Emma took the form the woman offered and filled out all the blanks. Where she was staying, the name of the tour company. Phone numbers. Passport information.

"Can you call me with an update before you're off today?" Emma asked.

"Absolutely."

A couple with a toddler walked up behind them. "Our bag didn't come down the chute."

The employee looked beyond Emma and Nicole and smiled.

With nothing more to do, Emma turned to the family behind them. "Good luck." And walked away.

"This is awful," Nicole said.

"My makeup. All my clothes."

"At least your computer was in your backpack."

"Yeah, but I packed my charger in my suitcase by accident."

Nicole rolled her suitcase beside them. "Then we have a lot of shopping to do."

"Just a couple of things to get through the night and tomorrow. It has to be on its way."

They walked out of the Peretola airport and around the building to find a taxi.

The driver spoke very little English but understood the address they gave him.

"We'll get to the hotel, take a quick shower, and hit a store," Nicole suggested.

Right . . . it would be fine.

Emma looked out the window as Italy sped by. "We had a connection in Dallas and London, how did they get Seattle in that mix?"

"No idea. It was so much easier when there were more direct flights getting out of the States."

"I'll be fine. I'll be fine," she said out loud. *What a freaking mess.*

~

"We found your luggage."

Relief flooded Emma's body. "Oh, thank God."

"It's on its way to Singapore."

The air dropped from her lungs.

"Unless there are delays it should be here in thirty-six hours. We'll have a driver bring it to your hotel in Florence."

"I won't be in Florence in thirty-six hours. I'm leaving on a bus tomorrow morning." Emma hadn't consumed enough coffee to be dealing with this.

"There's no way to get it to you any faster. We can send a driver to wherever you're staying."

"Hold on." Emma lowered the phone enough to talk directly to Nicole. "Do you have a copy of our itinerary?"

Nicole moved to her suitcase and dug for the information.

Once Emma had the papers, she spoke into the phone. Emma told the woman the name of the estate they were staying at when the suitcase was supposed to land. ". . . but we're only there for one night, so if it's late, you might have to take it to our next stop."

"And where is that?"

Emma told her.

"Oh."

"What, *oh*?"

"It's a bit far for a driver."

Emma was losing her patience. "That sounds like a you problem. I didn't check my bag into Seattle or Singapore."

"I'm sure we can figure something out. We can always reroute your luggage to an airport closer if—"

"Oh, no. Don't, please. You have my phone number. Call me when it gets here, and I can tell you exactly where I am at that time."

"We can do that. We are sorry for this inconvenience."

"Thank you for your help," Emma said before disconnecting the call.

"A day and a half?" Nicole asked.

"So much for seeing Florence before we leave for the tour. I need to buy more clothes."

"And nothing from your mom yet?" Nicole asked.

Emma shook her head. Apparently, her father was contemplating her proposal with the property.

The fact that he hadn't flat out said no was a shock.

Although that may have had something to do with the listing of Napa properties that Emma had provided . . . along with others in Temecula that could be used as a market-value point. Getting the property appraised would be simple . . . but hinting that she was willing to move to Napa was likely why her father hadn't refused Beth's request from word one. Robert's crowd lived in Napa. And the man made it clear he didn't want Emma in the mix.

Nicole nudged Emma's arm. "We promised your mother we wouldn't spend all our time worrying about the property."

Emma tossed her hands in the air. "I'm not going to worry about a house. I don't have any clothes."

Nicole hiked her purse higher on her shoulder. "Come on, *bella* . . . let's spend some of your money."

CHAPTER FIVE

The tour bus was parked just outside of Florence's main train station.

Gio dropped his duffel bag alongside the man in the bright orange shirt that had the tour logo imprinted on the back.

"Ciao," Gio said.

"*Buongiorno,*" the man replied.

"The paper said to find the man in the orange shirt."

"That's me. I'm Claudio." He extended a hand.

Gio shook it. "A pleasure. I'm Giovanni D'Angelo."

"You're Italian?" Claudio asked in Italian.

"I am. My grandfather lives here. I'm just visiting." Gio spoke to him in Italian, which brought a smile to the man's face. Claudio had to be in his fifties if not a bit older. A few worn lines making their way on his face, a little gray at his temples.

As Claudio looked at his list of names, he asked, "Where do you live?"

"Southern California."

"More Californians." He pointed to three men standing beside a bus. "They're from San Francisco. We tend to get a lot of guests from the States. Ah, here you are. Giovanni D'Angelo."

"Gio, please. My mother calls me Giovanni when she's angry."

Claudio laughed and switched to English. "We have you down as just one with a queen bed when we stop."

"That's right."

A couple walked up to stand behind him.

"We have at least two hours before our first stop. You might want to wait to get on the bus. Our driver, Alessandro, will take your bag."

"Thank you."

Gio picked up his duffel and let Claudio check in the next couple, then walked up to the three men talking with each other to introduce himself.

"Hey," he said when one of them made eye contact.

"You on the tour?"

"I am." He dropped his bag, reached out a hand. "My name is Gio."

"I'm Rob." Rob was clean-shaven, close to Gio's age.

"Pierre." Skinny guy, tiny mustache, with a French accent.

"I'm Chris." Chris spent some time in the gym. A lot of time in the gym.

Pierre looked beyond Gio. "You're traveling alone?"

"I am."

"I am, too," Chris said.

"Oh, you don't all know each other?" Gio pointed between the three of them.

Pierre lifted both hands in the air. "We do, but this is Rob's and my honeymoon. Delayed. We were married during the pandemic, couldn't travel, then life got crazy. Chris was supposed to be here with his partner, but . . ."

Chris rolled his eyes. "It didn't work out."

"We insisted he come," Rob added.

"I refuse to be a third wheel."

Four women wearing purple wide-brim hats who looked eligible for a senior living home walked up to Claudio.

"I don't think you're going to have to worry about that with this group," Gio pointed out.

One of the Golden Girls looked over her shoulder and winked.

Rob laughed. "This is going to be great."

"There should be welcome wine," Chris said.

"It's nine in the morning," Rob said, nudging him.

"It's Italy."

A man stepped from the bus and took the luggage from the couple that had registered behind Gio and rounded to the back of the small bus.

"You must be Alessandro." Gio walked toward the man and the other three followed.

"I am. Welcome."

As soon as the doors in the back of the bus were opened, Alessandro started to pack it with all of their luggage.

Gio shoved his bag on the side and stood back.

The Golden Girls walked over, each one with a bag half the size of them.

Gio reached for the first one that rolled up.

Alessandro reached for the second.

"Oh, thank you," the woman said.

"No problem."

"Are you Alessandro?" she asked.

"No, ma'am." He pointed over his shoulder. "He is."

The lady's bag had to be seventy pounds.

No sooner had he wrangled her bag into the back of the bus than a third Golden Girl slid him another. Just as big. Just as heavy. "You ladies don't pack light," he said.

"Half of it is medication," the woman with a feathered purple hat said with a laugh.

Gio turned his attention back to the four of them with a smile.

Alessandro patted him on the back and walked to the front of their bus.

Feathered Hat Lady placed a hand on her chest. "I'm Diane. This here is Barbara, Carol, and Jean."

Gio introduced himself.

Barbara nodded toward the bus. "C'mon, ladies, I want a seat in the front."

Claudio now stood at the door of the bus, looking at his watch. So far Gio counted the Golden Girls, the couple that looked nearly identical to Barbie and Ken dolls, and the three gay men from San Francisco.

He rubbed his hands together. *This should be fun.* "Do you want me to close this?" Gio pointed to the back of the bus.

Claudio shrugged. "We have two more."

No sooner had the words left his mouth than two women, one rolling a suitcase, the other holding a large bag that looked like it came from a department store, came running up.

The one with the bag brushed her long red hair away from her face when she came to an abrupt halt in front of the tour guide. "We're here."

"Emma and Nicole?" Claudio asked.

"Sorry we're late."

Claudio smiled. "It's okay."

When Alessandro didn't make an appearance, Gio reached for the rolling bag. "Let me get this for you."

The brunette smiled. "Oh . . . thank you."

That's when Gio met the green eyes of the redhead. No makeup, skin the color of cream, with a spattering of freckles that touched the tip of her nose and fanned out on her cheeks. She wore a shirt that had obviously come off a street vendor in town. *I love Florence* was written on it, with a heart where the word *love* should be. She was stunning. A bit less put together than the others getting on the bus, but gorgeous nonetheless. "Do you have a suitcase?"

She looked at her hand that carried the department store bag. "Pretty obvious I don't," she snapped.

"Ignore her," the friend said. "The airline lost her luggage. We stayed at the hotel till the last second, hoping they'd get it to us."

That explained the shirt and the bag.

"That bites."

"Tell me about it," Red said as she jockeyed her backpack off her shoulders.

The three of them walked around the bus, and Gio made himself useful by getting the suitcase, and paper bag, tucked away.

Alessandro made an appearance and closed the doors. "Thank you for your help."

Catherine Bybee

"I don't idle well," Gio told him.

He was the last one on the bus, with an empty seat in front of Chris. Rob and Pierre were across the aisle.

The redhead and her friend, Emma and Nicole . . . whose name belonged to whom he had yet to figure out, were in front of him. Barbie and Ken were across the aisle and huddled together in quiet conversation. The Golden Girls were spread across the two available front rows. One seat behind the driver was where Claudio now stood.

As Alessandro turned over the engine and closed the door, Claudio tapped his finger on a small microphone.

"Welcome to the best time in your life," he began.

The muttering on the bus simmered as they all gave Claudio some attention.

"As I've already told you, my name is Claudio. Alessandro is the safest driver in all of Italy."

That made a few of them laugh.

"I've been a part of this tour for five years, Alessandro just learned to drive the bus yesterday."

Gio chuckled.

"No, no. Ten years now, right, Alessandro?" Claudio asked.

"Sì."

Red leaned close to her friend, said something that made them both chuckle.

"We are going to be on this bus a lot. On our drive days, we will stop every hour and a half to two hours. If anyone needs a toilet, we will make an extra stop. But if you could all make use of the stops, that would be best . . . right?"

A chorus of yeses.

"You heard that, right, Jean?"

Jean nudged Diane.

"Because we're in this for some time, I always like to call out the names on my list and if you could tell everyone where you're from. My way of breaking the ice."

"Like the first day in high school after summer," Chris said behind Gio.

Claudio cleared his throat. "Kimmy and Weston."

Barbie and Ken raised their hands. "Hi," Kimmy said.

"We're from Denmark." Weston's accent was thick, but his English was good.

"And you both speak English, right?" Claudio asked.

They both nodded.

Next, Claudio named off Rob, Pierre, and Chris, all from San Francisco.

Gio came up next, which had the two women in front of him turning to look his way. "San Diego."

That had the redhead staring a little longer.

"Emma?"

Red raised her hand. "That's me. I live in Temecula."

"You're kidding," Gio said.

"No."

"Is that close to San Diego?" Claudio asked.

"Thirty miles," Gio told him.

"So, neighbors?"

"Kinda."

"Nicole?"

Emma's friend raised her hand. "Also from Temecula."

That left the Golden Girls. All of whom lived in The Villages, Florida, wherever that was.

"Who is ready for some wine?" Claudio asked.

The older women cheered.

"This ought to be fun," Gio muttered under his breath.

CHAPTER SIX

"He's looking at you again," Nicole whispered in Emma's ear once they climbed out of the bus.

"Stop it." The last thing Emma wanted was a distraction this early in the trip. It was bad enough that her mother had left a message saying her father was talking with his lawyers. Emma couldn't help but get her hopes up that the house in Temecula just might happen. As much as she wanted to relax and enjoy Italy completely, there was this crazy notion that her entire life was about to change the moment she returned to San Diego.

"He lives in San Diego."

"Yeah, I heard that." Emma pushed past her friend and toward the steps leading to the wine tasting room.

"You can't tell me you're uninterested."

Emma twisted on her foot, looked her friend in the eye. "Even if I was, it's a little early in the trip to be thinking about an Italian fling. We have three weeks on this bus with this guy." An Italian guy that lived in California. What were the odds?

"Sounds like a hellova fling."

"Sounds like a nightmare if it all blows up in a few days." That comment made Nicole step back.

"I didn't think of it that way."

Emma rolled her eyes, turned on her heel. "Now that we have that out of our system . . . let's taste some wine."

A few yards away, Gio stood holding the door open for them. "Ladies . . ."

"You're Mr. Helpful, aren't you?" Nicole asked.

"Blame my mother."

While Nicole gave him a hard time, Emma walked inside and thanked him.

"You're very welcome," he said almost under his breath.

Nicole giggled and planted herself at a table with four empty chairs. "So, Gio . . . what do you do in San Diego?"

Gio took a seat with them. "My family owns a restaurant."

"You run it? Or are you a chef?" Nicole asked.

"We all manage it. Or part of it. My brother is the chef. Sometimes my mother, but not as much lately."

Emma narrowed her eyes.

"I'm also a sommelier, but I'd be lying if I said ours is a restaurant that brings in the customers that are terribly picky about wine. We have some, of course, but most people only want a decent table wine."

"Cheap," Emma said.

"Exactly. I help some of our friends in the neighborhood with their wine selections. Otherwise, I'll jump behind the bar if it's needed, wait tables, schedules . . . some of the hiring and firing."

"A little bit of everything," Nicole said. "Where in San Diego?"

"Little Italy."

"We love Little Italy." Nicole glanced at Emma. "Right?"

"Yeah." There were a few restaurants there that stocked R&R's label. "What's the name of your restaurant?"

"D'Angelo's."

"Your family name?" Emma asked.

"Of course. Why make up a name? D'Angelo is Italian, we serve Italian food. It works." Gio looked between them. "What about you ladies? What do you do?"

"I work in estate planning," Nicole said.

"Sales." Emma had no desire to elaborate.

And when Claudio demanded everyone's attention, the opportunity for Gio to question further had passed.

"Since today is a drive day, we like to break it up with a stop. And if you haven't already looked at the complete itinerary, I'm here to tell you that you'll be getting more than just Tuscany while you're with us."

"I doubt anyone here doesn't know where they're going," Emma whispered.

"I told you that, Barbara."

Nicole hid her laugh behind a hand.

"I stand corrected," Emma admitted.

"I have to warn you, if you're thinking of filling up a suitcase with wine for your return to the States, they will only allow two bottles. So, if you want to buy anything here to drink along the way . . . buy what you want to drink here. Or, you have the option to ship wine home. You can see that the bus itself will have some limitations, so please keep that in mind as we move along." He turned to the woman at his side. "I leave you to Alice."

Emma listened as Alice introduced herself and talked about the winery, how long they'd been there, the grapes they grew. As she did, Emma slid a glance toward Gio. He really was something to look at. Strong jaw and a dimple to the side of his cheek when he smiled. He was so obviously Italian, something she may have guessed in the States but could tell undoubtedly after walking around Italy.

". . . there are very strict rules for a Chianti to be considered *classico,* classic. You'll hear this a lot. Eighty percent or more of the grapes used in this bottle have to be Sangiovese."

As Alice spoke, Gio mouthed the word *Sangiovese* at the same time she said it.

He turned his face toward her, and Emma snapped her gaze back toward Alice.

"But before we start with red, let me pour for you our rosé."

Alice stopped her monologue and walked around the tables, pouring the wine, and everyone in the room started quietly chatting.

Nicole turned to Emma. "Isn't that one of yours?"

Emma hushed her and glanced toward Gio.

"On your table there is a simple bread with the truffle olive oil we make here. It pairs very nicely with this wine." Alice stopped at their table, put a small amount of wine into each of their glasses.

When she was done, Gio lifted his. *"Salute."*

Emma put the wine to her nose, swirled the wine in the glass, looked at the color. She knew before she even tasted it the wine would likely be good, but not great. A taste later, and that was confirmed. She could certainly drink it but wouldn't buy it to take with them.

"Oh, I like it," Nicole said.

Emma laughed. "You like anything in a wineglass."

"Guilty."

Nicole sipped again and Emma pushed her glass away.

"You don't care for it?" Gio asked.

"It's not bad." She reached for the bread and took a bite.

Alice placed a piece of paper in front of all of them with the list of wines they were going to try.

"How long have you two known each other?" Gio asked.

Emma shrugged. "I don't know, seven, eight years."

"We met at that purple gym, remember?"

"That place was awful."

"Is it even there anymore?" Nicole asked.

"Purple gym?" Gio asked.

Emma nodded. "It was this circuit thing. The entire place was purple. The equipment, the paint on the walls. Even the carpet had these purple stripes."

"Trust me, it was bad," Nicole said.

Alice circulated around with another bottle of wine and demanded everyone's attention as she talked about the process they went through to make it.

Less than an hour later they were walking out of the tasting room, with only the Purple Hat Ladies hanging back to buy something.

"What did you think?" Chris asked as he walked up behind the three of them.

"I liked the Super Tuscan over the other two," Gio said.

"I agree," Emma chimed in.

Outside, the vibrant sun was tossing some warm temperatures down on them.

Claudio walked past. "About twenty minutes and we're on the bus," he told them.

"Something tells me the Golden Girls are going to take longer than that," Gio commented.

Chris laughed. "We've been calling them the Social Security Sisters, but I like Golden Girls better."

Emma looked over her shoulder at the two of them. "You guys are bad."

"C'mon, you don't have a nickname in your head?" Chris asked.

"Sure we do," Nicole said.

"Let's hear it."

Emma laughed. "The Purple Hat Ladies. Life goals if you ask me."

"What better way to enjoy old age than bus trips through Europe, drinking wine with your besties?" Nicole nudged Emma. Nicole had finished all her wine and was on her way to a buzz.

If there was one thing Emma had learned over the years it was to pace herself.

"From here we get lunch, right?" Gio asked.

"Yeah, the itinerary said small Tuscan town for lunch, then on to our first overnight," Nicole told him.

"God, I hope my luggage gets here."

They'd stopped under the shade of an oak tree to catch the breeze.

"The airline lost your luggage?" Chris asked.

"More like gave it a world tour. It ended up in Singapore."

"What? How did that happen?" Gio asked.

"That's exactly what I asked. So far, I've had the same corporate answer. 'We're really not sure but we're looking into it.'"

Chris looked at her T-shirt. "Well, that explains your fashion statement."

"You don't like my shirt?" Emma was laughing.

Chris narrowed his eyes. "You don't strike me as a five-dollar, street-vendor shopper."

"Oh? And what do I strike you as?"

"That luscious red hair and your curves . . . you belong in Chanel."

Emma felt Gio's gaze travel down those curves as Chris talked about them. It was brief, but she noticed.

Nicole chuckled. "He has you, Emma."

"And you." Chris pointed at Nicole. "Long legs, petite frame . . . Versace. Big, bold colors and sky-high shoes."

"I like it. Out of my budget, sadly."

Gio looked between all of them. "You know, if I'd said that, it would have come off as inappropriate."

Chris shook his head. "You have to be gay to be nonthreatening."

Nicole pointed at Chris. "Nailed it."

Gio placed both hands on his chest. "I'm not a threatening guy."

"No, but you're not gay." Emma's gaze challenged him. Their eyes locked.

"I could be."

Chris laughed so hard he started coughing. "Oh . . . no. Please, I mean, cute as you are, you're as straight as they come."

They were all laughing.

"I was just called cute by a gay man who has known me for less than three hours. I don't know if I should be flattered or offended."

"Why offended?" Emma asked.

He stared her in the eye. "I'd prefer sexy over cute."

Nicole tossed her hands in the air with a clap as she giggled. "And on that note, I'm going to find the bathroom."

"Good idea," Emma agreed.

As they walked away, Emma felt eyes on her back.

Chris's laughter followed behind them. "You're *so* not gay."

CHAPTER SEVEN

"How is it?"

Gio was on the phone with Dante while sitting next to the fountain in the small city's piazza.

"So far, so good. There are four women from a retirement community in Florida that were completely smashed before we settled for the night. A couple that are celebrating their anniversary, but they haven't said much to anyone. Three guys from San Francisco who are hysterical. And two women from Temecula."

"Temecula? Really?"

"Small world. We're in a hotel tonight, but tomorrow we'll be off to a villa. Wine tours during the day, big dinners at night. It's starting to get hot here but most of the accommodations have a pool, so that will help." Gio rubbed his chin at the thought of Emma in a swimsuit.

"Are you learning anything about wine making you didn't know?"

Gio shrugged. "Today was just tastings. Our longer stays give us the opportunity to really roam the vineyards and spend time talking to the winemakers. I think most of this crowd is more about drinking than learning."

"More one-on-one time for you, then."

"I agree. How's everything there?" Gio asked.

"I'm convinced your sister has an Amazon addiction. There's a new box at the door every day."

Gio laughed. "You married her." He still wasn't used to saying or picturing that. Dante had been his best friend forever. Between the two of them they must have dated half the appropriate-aged women in Little Italy.

"Best decision ever."

Gio glanced up to see Emma stopped in the middle of the piazza, yelling into her phone. He was too far away to hear the conversation.

"Hey, sorry to cut this short, but I see one of the women from the tour."

"Is she cute?"

Gio stood. "Cute is not how I would describe her."

"Is that a good thing?"

"I'll tell you about her later."

They said their goodbyes before Gio reached Emma's side.

". . . no, that's not what I said." She ran a hand through her hair, caught him out of the corner of her eye, and then pivoted full face. "Hold on."

"Are you okay?"

"No. My luggage made it to Florence."

"That's good."

She shook her head.

"That's not good?" Gio was confused.

"I told them about the early-morning checkout and told them to send it directly here if it arrived today and to our next location if it came late."

"I'm guessing they didn't do that."

"No. They sent it to the Florence hotel and now I'm trying to get the airline to go back to the hotel, pick up my bag, and get it to me here. And the guy I'm talking to is only catching every other word. He's trying but his English isn't great."

Gio saw the problem and held out his hand and placed the phone to his ear. *"Buonasera."*

The man on the line immediately started talking in Italian. "We delivered the luggage to the hotel."

"The wrong one. You need to go back, pick up the bag, and get it to us here." Gio gave the address for where they were staying.

"I have one runner and he is out until the morning."

"Tomorrow, then. But we will need you to take it to a different location." All this Gio said to the man in Italian. He paused for a moment and glanced at Emma. "Do you know the address where we're staying tomorrow?"

"Yes." She dug in her purse and unearthed a piece of paper that had scratch marks all over it. Emma pointed out the address, and Gio gave it to the man on the phone.

"Ohhh."

"What?"

"That's far."

Gio smiled at Emma, whose eager gaze prompted him to say, "We're getting somewhere."

"Thank God."

The man on the phone's voice lowered. "I don't know if that is possible tomorrow. We have one runner and more bags to get out. And I don't know if we take them that distance."

"You don't know?"

"I don't normally work in lost luggage. I'll have to ask a supervisor."

"Then ask."

"They're not here."

Gio lost his smile and swiped a hand over his face. The frustration in Emma's stance was rubbing off on him. "There has to be something you can do."

"Call back in the morning when a supervisor is on. I can't authorize . . ."

Gio pulled the phone away and told Emma what was going on.

"C'mon. This is ridiculous."

He didn't disagree.

"What is the name of the supervisor to ask for, and what time do they get in?" Gio directed his question to the man on the phone.

"They come in at eight, but I don't know who will be on."

"We'll call in the morning," Gio said before disconnecting the call and handing back Emma's phone.

"Did you get anywhere?"

He explained the situation and watched as Emma's frustration mounted.

Emma rubbed her temples. "This is a nightmare."

"We'll call them in the morning."

"I will call, you've done enough. Thank you."

"And if the supervisor's English is just as bad?"

She sucked in a breath, held it . . . and exhaled. "You're right. You sure it's not any trouble?"

"It's self-preservation."

"How so?"

He looked her up and down quickly. "If you're wearing the same clothes every day, everyone on the bus is going to be affected sooner or later."

For the first time since they met, Emma's smile met her striking green eyes.

"The good news is your luggage is in Italy."

"Until it's in my hands, it's like having sex without an orgasm. Worthless."

Gio tossed his head back and laughed. "I wouldn't know."

She placed a hand over her grin. "That probably wasn't appropriate."

"Funny, though."

Emma lowered her hand, looked around. "Damn."

"How about a gelato?" he asked.

"I could go for that."

They turned toward the gelateria and made their way to the line that formed outside.

"Is it really worthless?" Gio asked.

"What?"

"Sex without an orgasm?"

That sparkle was back in her eyes. "Maybe not completely. Depends on the guy, I suppose."

"Your connection," he said as if that was the answer.

"No," she huffed. "Okay, maybe . . . but if he has skills."

"How can you talk about skills if he doesn't finish the job."

She was getting flustered and Gio liked watching her squirm.

"There's more to it than just . . . you know."

"Than the finish line."

Emma narrowed her eyes. "Are we actually talking about this?"

"You were the one that started it."

"Ah, yeah . . ."

"Besides, if I were Chris, Rob, or Pierre, would you talk about it?"

"Probably, I don't know." She shifted her purse to her other shoulder.

"Listen, let me be honest. I didn't come on this trip to find a *finish line* with anyone." He kept the metaphor going.

Disbelief sat squarely between her eyes.

"I mean it. I just turned thirty. My older brother got married in December . . ." His voice drifted as he tried to make sense of what he wanted to say. "Actually, my baby sister got married the week before, but since it was Vegas, she and her husband remarried in the church for our mother last month."

"That sounds excessive."

"You haven't met my mother. Anyway, my point . . . it's my turn," Gio said.

"To get married?"

"Yeah." They inched forward in line.

"You have a girlfriend?"

He shook his head. "No."

"I'm confused."

He looked around them, kept his voice low. "I'm not looking for just a . . . *finish line*. I've kinda sworn that off." The words hurt to say. Especially with the way that Emma looked him up one side and down the other.

"You've sworn off sex?"

Gio looked behind them, smiled at the couple standing there.

"Uhm, y-yes." He tore the word out of his lungs.

Emma rolled her eyes and took a big step forward.

"I have. I mean until I find someone I think could be the one."

"The one."

"You repeat my words a lot."

"That's because they're bullshit," she said, deadpan.

"I swear." He placed a hand over his heart. "I want the house and the big family. And if I keep chasing *finish lines* I'm never going to get there." Even when those lines looked like Emma.

"You're admitting to being a player?"

He put both hands in the air. "Player is such a harsh way of looking at it."

They cleared the door of the gelateria, and Emma started scanning the glass case.

Gio greeted the man behind the counter and ordered in Italian. The worker asked if they were together and Gio said yes.

Emma ordered in English, which the man understood, and Gio reached for his wallet.

"I got this," he said.

"I can pay for my own ice cream."

He shrugged. "Fine, you get the next one. It's a long trip."

Emma relented and accepted him paying for her frozen treat.

Gelato in hand, they walked back out into the piazza and meandered slowly back toward their hotel.

Why did simple sweet cream with bits of chocolate taste better in Italy?

"This is so good," Emma said.

"I was thinking the same thing."

The sight of her tongue licking the side of the tiny spoon shot a nerve down Gio's spine.

"You're really looking for a wife."

"I am. I think it was turning thirty that really did it."

Another spoonful went between her lips. They were full, someone might call them pouty.

"Your biological clock is ticking?"

"Do men have those?"

She shrugged. "Why not?"

"I guess. I want to date with purpose."

"How very admirable of you."

He wasn't sure if she was teasing or serious.

Gio scooped another mouthful of gelato into his mouth, swallowed, and said, "Now that you know that, feel free to talk to me like you would our friends from San Francisco."

"That's a leap."

He tapped his chest. "I'm safe. My family would vouch for me if they were here."

"What about your best friend?" Emma gave him the side-eye.

Gio thought of Dante . . . all the trouble they used to get into. "Technically, my best friend is now family . . ."

"Yeah, but you hesitated."

"Dante would still vouch for me."

Emma sighed. "I don't get a creep vibe off of you."

He paused his steps, looked at her. "Thank you . . . I think."

She kept walking. "But I still call bullshit on forced celibacy while you're finding a fiancée."

"You have a right to your own opinion."

"When was the last time you had sex?"

Gio was pretty sure no woman had ever asked him that before.

"It's been a-a while."

"What is that? Two weeks? A month?"

He closed his eyes, shook his head. "Somewhere in there." Right before his birthday, but he didn't have to tell Emma that.

They made it to the hotel.

Emma tossed her empty cup into a trash can. "Well, Gio, you have three weeks on this tour. Let's see how you hold up." She patted him on the back and opened the door. "See you at breakfast."

He let her walk away, a bit dumbfounded that the most intriguing and beautiful woman he'd met in a long time had somehow challenged him to stay celibate on his Italian vacation.

Gio lowered his hand holding the cup. "What the hell did I just do?"

CHAPTER EIGHT

"Why is this so hard?" Emma looked like she wanted to throw her phone across the room once she stopped talking to the supervisor.

Nicole and Gio were staring at her.

The supervisor did speak English, they simply didn't say what Emma wanted to hear.

"That bad?" Nicole asked.

"They are going to try and get the bag here . . . but aren't sure if that will be tonight or tomorrow. They will call me when the driver is on his way."

"We leave in two hours," Gio stated the obvious.

"They won't bring it all the way to you?"

Emma presented a comical wrinkle to her nose, something Gio thought reminded him an awful lot of his nine-year-old niece.

"No. It's *too far!*"

"I can either stay here and wait for it, even though we don't know when it will actually arrive. Or I can send it home. Not an option." She pulled at the T-shirt bought from the last winery they'd visited. "Or, or I can keep going on the tour and when they call, rent a car, drive back, and pick it up."

"Or we can get a rental car right now and go back to Florence and pick it up," Gio suggested.

"Except it's being picked up from our last hotel and will be on the van all day as the guy doing the deliveries gets everybody else's crap to them." Emma sucked in a breath and let out a low growl.

Gio checked himself to keep from smiling.

The growl was stupid adorable.

"Damn!" Emma's face was turning as red as her hair.

Gio glanced at Nicole, who kept her lips shut.

"We have a what, four-hour drive today?" Gio asked for clarification.

"Probably five with the state of Jean's bladder," Nicole said.

The oldest of the Golden Girls did have the driver stopping more often than they expected to.

"And lunch," Emma added.

"Right, but Claudio said it would be about four hours on the bus total." Gio lifted his hand, showing four fingers.

Emma blew out a long-suffering breath. "Yeah."

"It's a complete pain in the ass, but it could be done. You'd miss all of tomorrow's wine tasting in order to have your own clothes."

"We'll rent a car. It will be an adventure." Nicole's voice had Emma trying to smile.

"You're right."

They'd been standing in the lobby of the small hotel and Gio motioned toward the door. "Let's grab some breakfast."

"I don't think I can eat anything," Emma said.

"Have a cappuccino and a *dolce*. It's Italy, not Texas," he reminded her.

"Fine." Emma moved faster than they did and reached the door first.

"She's not fine," Nicole whispered.

"I can tell."

~

"Could this be more beautiful?" Nicole asked Emma.

The lacy green vines early in their growth didn't end. Emma couldn't see the next property from the back porch of their room. Up on the hillside there was a structure, but it looked more like a castle than a home. "I don't think so."

"You know what would make it better?"

"What?" Emma glanced at her friend, saw mischief in her eyes, and knew what she was going to say before she said it.

"Wine." She walked over to where a complimentary bottle made at the villa sat.

"I won't say no."

The stop for lunch was not at a winery, but in a small town. The house wine there was drinkable, and Lord knew Emma was in the headspace to indulge.

While Nicole poured, Emma hung a few items of hand-washed clothing on the backs of the unused chairs on their tiny patio to dry. The villa was a sprawling home that had a hacienda feel, with spidery halls that had at least nine guest rooms. There was an upstairs on the main structure, but they were told it was for the family that owned the place. They weren't in attendance, which was unfortunate. Emma would have liked to speak with them.

Nicole handed Emma a glass. Both of them stared at the patio furniture.

"You know, this daily Laundromat look is growing on me," Nicole teased.

"At least we have an outside breeze to dry them faster."

"It's very Italian."

Emma tilted her glass toward Nicole's. "Cheers."

A sniff and taste later, Emma said, "Not bad."

"I love it!" Nicole took another drink.

Emma giggled and grabbed her phone to plug it into a charger.

"Any more messages from your mom?"

"No." Early in the morning, which would have been late at night back home, Beth had messaged to say her father had agreed that Emma should move into the property.

There were zero details and no guarantee that her dad had agreed to her terms.

"Do you want to try your dad again?"

Emma shook her head. "I left a message with his secretary." Not that she thought her dad would call her back.

"Do you really think he's going to hand you the property and walk away?"

"No."

They walked outside and sat at a small table opposite their "Italian Laundromat."

"Your mom seems to think he will."

Emma sipped from her glass. "If my dad wants me to be in that house, it's likely because he doesn't want me in Napa making good on my threat of buying something up there. He likes being able to avoid me. Keeping me in Temecula has given him some control. My dad likes control . . . over everything. So no . . . he won't just hand over the property. I don't care what my mother thinks."

"Why not just walk away, then, do what you say and do it all by yourself?"

Emma looked out over the vineyard they were surrounded by and sighed. She'd asked herself that question many times since she'd started this ball rolling. "I spent my twenties bending over backwards, doing everything short of circus tricks to get my father to see how capable I am. I even married Kyle."

"You don't think Kyle was ever in love?"

"He was into my father's money. Still is. I was the quickest way to it. I was young and stupid." Biggest regret of her life. "I think the fact that my father bought that property for his married daughter and holds it away from his single daughter makes me want it even more."

"Revenge?"

Emma shrugged. "Maybe. Regardless of the house, I am done working alongside or beneath my ex. And I won't have to talk to Kyle anymore."

Nicole lifted her glass. "Cheers to that."

Emma sipped with a smile.

They sat for a moment, staring out at the view, and her thoughts drifted to an entirely different subject. "What do you think about Gio?"

"I think right now he's trying to figure out how to get out of his celibacy oath." Nicole laughed.

Emma had shared the conversation with Nicole when she'd come back to the room the night before. "He cornered himself with that one. *I'm looking for the one.*' Sounds like a dating app line that always ends in a hookup."

"It does, but . . ."

They glanced at each other. "I know. He doesn't really fit the asshole type that would say that kind of stuff."

Nicole put her feet up on the chair across from her. "What do *you* think of him?"

"He's, ah . . . interesting."

"Is that a metaphor for hot?"

Emma laughed. "He is that, too. He definitely knows his wine."

"Something you two have in common."

She knew where her friend was going. "I'm not looking to be anyone's wife again. And a house full of kids? If that's what he wants, there is no use wasting his time."

"I'm sure you wouldn't mind wasting *some* of his time," Nicole said.

"Maybe." More like *absolutely.* Even though she thought the celibacy crap was just that, if he was actually looking for the real thing, she wasn't about to pretend she could be in the running.

Emma shook her head. *Why am I even thinking this way?*

"I say we take a walk around." Nicole lifted her glass. "With our wine."

"We should enjoy the place now since we're going to miss a day retrieving my luggage."

With that settled, they picked themselves up from the patio and walked out of their room.

The second they were out the door they saw Gio leaving his room.

His eyes found Emma's and the corners of his mouth lifted.

Her breath hitched.

"Hi," he said.

"Hey," she replied.

Nicole chuckled.

Gio looked at the glass in her hand. "I was about to go to the tasting room. Wanna join me?"

Emma shook her head. "This is more of a drinking day and less of a tasting day."

The man had such a striking smile. "I like how you ladies think. Let me grab a glass and I'll tag along. I mean, if you don't mind."

"The more the merrier."

He opened his door and disappeared inside.

Emma found herself looking at his butt as he did.

"He has a nice—" Nicole started.

"He sure does."

Ten minutes later, the three of them found half of their group by the pool.

Apparently drinking, and not tasting, was on the agenda for everyone.

"Come forward, future Betty Ford Clinic attendees, have a seat." Chris was already glassy-eyed and loud.

"Yeah!" Nicole sang and did a little dance.

"No swimsuits?" Pierre asked, his legs dangling in the pool.

"No luggage," Emma reminded him.

"Maybe tomorrow," Nicole said. "Wait, no . . . we're driving all day tomorrow."

"Only if we get a call." Emma updated the guys on the baggage fiasco. "It sucks."

"Good reason to get drunk tonight," Chris said.

Emma found a place under an umbrella and Nicole kicked off her sandals and sat on the edge of the pool next to Pierre.

"Wouldn't it be nice to have something like this back home?" Rob said.

"Little cold in San Francisco," Gio pointed out.

"This would cost a fortune in California."

Emma and Nicole exchanged glances but stayed silent.

"Are you guys close to the vineyards in Temecula?" Gio asked.

"I'm not," Nicole immediately responded. "Emma is."

"Hard not to be out there," she said, purposely vague. Although technically she still lived in a condo. "Do you guys get out to Napa much?"

"I don't," Chris said.

"What about you?" she asked Gio.

"Not as much as I should. When I was studying for my sommelier certificate, I did."

Chris patted him on the back. "Oh, that's right. I keep forgetting that you're our resident expert."

"I wouldn't say that." Gio's eyes caught Emma's. "I think Emma might give me a run for my money."

All eyes moved to her.

She shook her head. "Not sure why you say that."

"Because you taste the subtle differences and can narrow down the price point on the bottle."

"I'm sure everyone here can do that." Her eyes skimmed over the others in the group.

"Not me. I mean, this isn't cheap, but it could be twenty euros or a hundred," Chris said.

"If it was a hundred, it wouldn't be the complimentary bottle in our room," Pierre corrected.

Emma pointed her glass at Pierre. "See . . . it's all about deduction. Besides, every place we've been so far has started out with the cheapest wine first and then moved to the more expensive." She paused. "Which isn't what I would do. I'd start with the most expensive when your palate hasn't been saturated. But then white and rosé really do need to be tested before the reds."

She looked around. Everyone was watching her.

"Like I said, a run for my money," Gio said.

Nicole scrambled to her feet. "I have the perfect idea." She slipped on her sandals.

"What?"

She pointed to the villa. "I'm going to go find a bottle of everything they sell here, bag 'em up, and you two are going to have a taste-off."

"Nicole!" Emma scolded.

"Oh, this will be fun," Rob replied.

"C'mon. I wouldn't want to embarrass her," Gio said.

Emma's head snapped up. "Excuse me?"

"Ohhh . . ." Chris nudged Gio. "That look could kill ya."

Gio's eyes challenged her. "It's okay. You don't have to—"

Without looking Nicole's way, Emma said, "Put the wine on our room. And if *Giovanni* here wins, we pay for the wine. If he doesn't, he pays."

Gio gave a single nod. "I can do that. What are the rules?"

"Type of grapes, notes, age of the bottle, and price point," Emma said. "The one who tastes the most, gets the age of the wine and price point closest to the nearest dollar, wins that round."

"Why do I get the feeling that I'm being hustled?" Gio asked.

"This wasn't my idea." But she was going to win.

CHAPTER NINE

He'd yet to see Emma look this alive. Her green eyes sparkled when she was up to something, he decided. Like when she conned him into being celibate. It had been less than twenty-four hours and he quite literally thought about sex now as much as he did when he was eighteen.

All thanks to her.

Yet sitting across the table from him with her shoulders back, her chin high, she was confident she was going to win.

Word had gotten out that there was a competition going down by the pool.

Before Nicole could come back with the wine, staff from the villa arrived with wineglasses, a spittoon, and pads of paper.

On their heels, two of the Golden Girls showed up, as well as Kimmy and Weston.

Gio stopped the staff before they walked away and spoke to them in Italian. "Can you bring out glasses for everyone and an appetizer assortment?"

"Charge it to your room?"

"*Sì.*"

"Are you cheating?" Emma asked.

"No," the waiter answered for him. "He asked for more glasses and a bit of food."

Gio snickered. "Unless you want to drink *all* the wine. Then that's an entirely different contest."

"Not all of it," she told him.

"While we're on the subject. How many glasses of wine have you had already?"

"One."

"We're even, then."

She rolled her eyes. "You weigh more than me and you're a man."

Glad you noticed.

"Okay, the first two pours I drink it all."

"And from then?"

Gio looked up at the rapt attention of their audience.

"Ladies' choice."

She smiled, licked her lips. "I like to swallow."

Ahh, fuck!

"Girrrl!" Chris cried out.

Every drop of blood in Gio's body shot south. All while the crowd surrounding them erupted in laughter.

Emma kept her composure.

Beth Dutton would be proud.

"Your pours have to be bigger than mine," she told him.

He reached across the table, palm out.

The second their hands touched, all the southern heat lit on fire.

He was in big trouble.

They'd barely let go of each other's hands when Nicole returned. Jean and Barbara were at her side. Between the three of them they held seven bottles of wine.

Each was wrapped in paper so no one could see the labels.

Nicole instructed her helpers to set the covered bottles on the table to the side. "Have you figured out the rules?"

Gio and Emma exchanged glances. "I believe we have," Gio said.

"Okay, then." Nicole picked up the first bottle and uncorked it.

She poured into Emma's glass first and did an identical pour into Gio's.

"Ehh!" Emma scoffed at the small amount in his glass.

Gio made a waving motion with his hand that had Nicole giving him a bit more wine.

He looked Emma in the eye as they both reached for a glass.

He tilted his and measured the lighter rim around the darkest color of the wine. Young, he decided.

He swirled the contents in the glass before bringing it to his nose. Oak, but not overpowering. Roses. Funny, he hadn't noticed roses next to the vines. Floral. He couldn't tell what else was in there, but he knew it was floral. He expected a richer grape but thought for sure this was a pinot noir . . . He wrote everything down on the paper, gave it a price, and guessed a year. When he was done, he folded the paper in half and handed it to Nicole.

Emma did the same and they both sat back.

"How long have you been drinking wine?" Gio asked her.

"Eighth grade," she answered.

"Late bloomer," he boasted, but in reality, his mother had watered down the wine in a tiny glass for him as a child, and only on a holiday. Back when he was a kid, he didn't like it.

Emma tipped the glass back, finished it.

Gio followed her lead.

"Emma." Nicole cleared her throat and started to read. "Pinot noir aged in oak. Notes of roses and hibiscus. Two years old. Price point, twenty-two euros."

"You got all of that off of a sip of wine?" Carol asked.

"Gio." Nicole waved his paper in her hand. "Pinot noir in oak. Roses and another floral. Two to three years old, likely closer to two. Price, fifteen euros."

He smiled at Emma. "I didn't catch the hibiscus."

Nicole reached for the bottle and removed it from its cover and read the label. "It is in fact a pinot noir. Grown in the vast Tuscan valley with hints of roses and hibiscus. This was bottled two years ago, and the price is . . ."

Everyone hung on her last words.

"Eighteen euros."

"Slim margin but I think this round goes to Emma. She picked up on the hibiscus and was zeroed in on the age of the bottle, whereas Gio was closer to the price point."

Gio agreed and mentally rolled up his sleeves.

"All right. Round two." Nicole handed the bottle over to Chris, who poured a splash in his glass before sending it on to the person on his right.

This round, Gio took more time. A much more complex blend. And it was a blend.

Just as intent, Emma sipped twice, crossed out a note, and wrote something else.

Gio had always had a soft spot in his heart for competitive women.

Not that he was going to let her win.

Not on purpose, anyway.

They both wrote down the required information on their notepads.

He glanced at her for a nanosecond.

"Do I have to cover my answers?"

He liked her feisty side.

"No, ma'am."

With their answers in Nicole's hand, she started to read. "Gio says this is a blend. Cabernet sauvignon and Sangiovese. At lease sixty percent cab. Not a Chianti. Smoky oak, roses, dark cherry. Four years old, thirty-five euros."

Emma put her nose back in the glass. "I didn't catch the cherry."

"Subtle," he said.

"Now Emma. Cabernet sauvignon and Sangiovese. More cab than Sangiovese. Oak, roses. Four years old. Forty euros."

Off to the side, Gio heard Pierre say to Rob, "This should be a game show."

Nicole pulled the wine out again and narrowed her eyes at the label. She turned it to Gio. "What does that say?"

"Dark blend," he translated.

She looked at the back of the bottle. "It's all written in Italian."

Gio took the bottle back.

"No cheating," Emma said.

He placed a hand on his chest. "I'm wounded."

She rolled her eyes.

"Cabernet seventy-five percent with Sangiovese. Barreled in oak cured after a fire, giving it a slight smoky texture. It is in fact four years old." He winked at Emma, then looked at Nicole. "How much?"

"Fifty. They said it was a limited edition."

"Probably because of the fire," Emma stated.

"A point for Gio," Nicole announced.

While the wine bottle made the rounds, he sat forward. "A full cab from this year would likely bring out the flavor. The Sangiovese balanced it."

She finished her taste and followed it with water. "I agree. It's good."

"I might have to send some home."

The next two rounds Gio lost because of price point. If he picked up on a flower, she picked up on an herb. He was feeling the wine, she was all smiles.

Food was brought out, and Gio was pretty sure there were side bets going as to who was going to win.

Pressure was on him to win the next round or admit defeat.

"We could call it now," Emma prodded.

"Never gonna happen."

He took his time, did everything he could not to look at her.

This was an expensive bottle. Aged to perfection. *How aged?* he asked himself.

The more age, the more it cost.

Their description of the wine was almost identical. Gio pegged the wine at thirty years old, Emma said thirty-five. Gio won on the price point. He said seventy-five euros and Emma said fifty-five. The cost was seventy.

"You're looking pretty confident over there," he teased.

"You're looking a little skittish."

"More like buzzed." His heavy pours were settling in.

Everyone around them was snacking, which he was tempted to do.

But as long as she wasn't eating, he wouldn't either. He did not need his taste buds polluted with flavors that weren't in the wine.

"You're actually better at this than I thought you'd be," Emma praised.

"Why, thank you. But I admitted to knowing wine . . . you, on the other hand, did not. You are more than just a casual observer."

Nicole offered a sinister laugh.

Emma won the next round by a landslide. She picked up on a pear flavor, nailed the year and the price.

Gio lifted his hands in the air in defeat. "You beat me four to two."

Emma reached across the table to shake his hand.

He couldn't help himself, he leaned over and kissed the back of her hand.

Her eyes lit up and she smiled.

Gio liked when she blushed.

Emma cleared her throat, took control of her hand.

"Did you save the best for last?" Gio turned his attention back to Nicole, who still had one unopened and covered bottle.

"I honestly don't know. I wrapped them up and didn't look."

"One more, winner takes all?" Gio asked.

"I don't want to humiliate you."

"Ohhh. Damn, girl," Chris said.

Her green eyes stared into his.

Feisty . . . a little drunk. Good God, he was in trouble.

Emma made a motion with her hand for Nicole to pour.

The bottle was opened, both glasses were filled.

She reached for hers and Gio followed.

One sniff and they both wrinkled their noses and set the glasses down without tasting.

Neither of them went any further.

"What's wrong?" Nicole asked.

In unison, Emma and Gio said, "It's corked."

"What does that mean?" Jean asked.

"It's bad, Jean . . . the wine has turned to vinegar," Carol explained.

Nicole reached for Emma's hand and lifted it in the air. "We have our winner!"

"We need a medal." Chris lifted his glass high. The man was beyond tipsy.

"We can come up with something," Jean said.

Emma's eyes skirted to Gio and held.

Their fellow bus mates started mingling with each other.

"I owe you dinner," Gio told her.

She shook her head. "No. You owe me for the wine. But I'll take you up on dinner."

Nicole sat down. "Good, 'cause I'm starving."

He was thinking more one-on-one, but in light of where they were, he'd take what he could get. "Let's find some food."

CHAPTER TEN

Emma's alarm went off way too damn early for her liking.

Her mouth was dry, and her head was on fire.

She rolled over with a moan and slapped at her phone to shut off the noise.

Nicole muttered something Emma didn't catch and curled deeper into the covers.

Flipping back the sheet, Emma moved from her bed to the bathroom. One look at her face and she saw the late-night drinking under her bloodshot eyes. "What the hell was I thinking?"

The memory of Giovanni laughing warmed her inside. Oh, yeah . . . one-upping a man drink for drink probably wasn't the wisest of choices. Especially with wine.

She knew better but that hadn't stopped her.

Her body reminded her of her bad decisions as she used the toilet.

All she wanted to do was sleep for another four hours and attempt to get up then.

But no, the airline had said they'd sent a man out with her suitcase and it would be at the previous hotel that morning.

Gio, being Mr. Helpful, had disappeared after she received confirmation that her luggage was on the move, to ask the concierge about rental cars.

There weren't any. As in none in town that they could rent.

But before Emma even knew there was a problem, mainly because she was a part of the conversation with the concierge, Gio procured a car that the owners apparently used when they were in town.

So long as he drove it. At least that's the story that he told Emma. All said and done, Gio was meeting her and Nicole at seven.

After a quick shower, Emma padded back into the room.

Nicole was still sound asleep.

"Hey?" Emma said quietly. "Nicole?"

Nothing.

"Nicole?" A little louder.

"No . . . ," she moaned.

Emma grinned. "Headache?"

She rolled over, nodded, then turned white as a sheet, jumped out of bed, and ran into the bathroom.

Emma winced. Yeah, Nicole was not feeling it.

A couple of minutes later she emerged and fell back into the mattress. "This sucks."

"That bad?"

Nicole looked at her, eyes narrowed.

Emma sighed, pushed off the edge of the bed she'd been sitting on. "Okay. I got this without you."

"You sure?"

"I'm a big girl. Besides, Gio is coming, so . . ."

"I'm sorry, Em."

"No worries. Text me when you're moving. I'll be back tonight."

Nicole turned her pillow over, punched it, and laid her head down. "Thanks."

After getting dressed and tiptoeing out of the room, Emma searched for Gio in the foyer of the villa.

His back was turned.

The man knew how to wear jeans.

"Good morning," she said to get his attention.

He turned, instant smile.

"Why do you look like last night's drinking took no toll on you?" she asked.

He walked closer and that's when she noticed two cups with lids in his hands. "About an hour ago you wouldn't have said that."

"It's going to take more than an hour for my headache to go away."

He handed her one of the cups.

"No coffee. Not yet." She waved her hands against what she thought was in the cup.

"It's not coffee," he said. "It is what will make you feel better."

She pulled the cup to her nose to smell what was inside.

"Don't. Just drink," he encouraged her.

He must have seen the suspicion on her brow.

"You have to trust me," Gio said.

While she contemplated the cup in her hand, he asked. "Where's Nicole?"

"Doing a morning prayer ritual to the toilet."

He laughed. "I take it she's not coming."

"No." Emma removed the lid of the drink, really didn't like the color of the contents.

"Down the hatch," Gio said.

She shrugged. "Here goes nothing." A deep breath and she lifted the drink to her lips. It was thick, a little carbonated, something spicy and a suspicion of wine. Like taking medicine when she was a child, she guzzled it as quick as she could and gasped when it was done. "That's awful."

Gio was laughing. "It is, but it works. I promise."

Gone was the minty toothpaste flavor in her mouth, and it was replaced with what she imagined the floor of a bar would taste like.

Gio found the person in charge behind an open office door beyond the reception counter. He spoke in Italian and left the second cup with the person in the room. When he turned his attention back to Emma, he smiled and rubbed his hands together. "Ready?"

"As long as you're willing to drive."

He motioned with his thumb outside.

It was still early enough that the dew in the air had yet to be burned off by the rising sun. A few high clouds gave a hint that they might have a spring shower at some point in the day.

Gio led them to a small car, the name of it she didn't recognize. "Does anyone here drive an SUV?"

He laughed. "Have you seen the cities?"

He had a point. Narrow streets, no parking. Still, out in the country she expected something bigger. "Probably a good idea Nicole wasn't up for this." One of them would have had a tight fit in the back seat.

"We can't complain. They aren't charging for the car. Just fill up the tank."

"A bargain."

Inside, Gio opened a map app on his phone and set their route. "Three hours and fifty minutes."

"I can't tell you how much of a nightmare this luggage fiasco has been."

He pulled away from the villa and started down the long drive. "It's almost over."

She leaned her head back, closed her eyes. "Sorry." She forced herself higher in her seat.

"I'm driving. Lean back, get some sleep. Let my hangover cure take hold."

She blinked her heavy eyelids. "That shit was awful."

"Tell me that in an hour."

Seemed like his permission to sleep was all she needed. Emma's eyes started to drift. "I promise I won't sleep the whole way."

"Get some rest, Emma."

"Thanks, Giovanni." With that, she leaned her head against the window and allowed her body to relax.

~

When was the last time he felt this full?

All she was doing was sleeping.

Lips slightly open . . . a little spot of moisture on the side of her mouth.

Outside of family, Gio couldn't remember a time when a woman slept beside him that he hadn't slept with.

He instantly thought of the many times someone fell asleep on the bus.

That didn't count.

It was only him, Emma, and a whole lot of open road in front of them.

Why? Why did this feel different?

For twenty miles he pondered that thought.

Thirty . . .

Somewhere around the fifty-mile mark he realized his attraction was different because of the woman herself.

Unapologetic. Beautiful . . . of course. He was attracted, so her beauty was a factor. But it was more than what a mirror told him. A little mysterious. Old enough to not play petty games. He thought that even when remembering the night before when they were matching shot for shot . . . of wine, in a competition of who knew more.

Every time he thought they were matched, she one-upped him. And instead of that aggravating him, he celebrated her.

There was definitely more to Emma . . . what was her last name? Had she told him a last name? Didn't matter.

There was more to Emma than met the eye.

Gio couldn't remember a time when he was this intrigued.

His eyes focused on the road ahead instead of how she curled her legs under her in the seat beside him.

How her lower lip quivered on every exhale.

Stop!

He'd only been driving for an hour . . . ish.

Gio considered turning on the radio.

He should have done that before now. Now the noise might wake her.

Shifting in his seat, he chastised his body for twitching.

Where did the red hair come from? Her mother or her father?

Did she have siblings? Were they close?

What about her parents? Were they a part of her life? Were they alive?

He had questions. So many questions.

There were lots of back roads he needed to traverse to get them onto a major highway.

As Italy woke and the roads filled with people going to and from work, his pace slowed.

One would like to think that traffic was exclusive to the highways in the States, but they'd be wrong. If there was one truth in the world, traffic was everywhere. Even in nowhere places with tiny towns.

It was at a roundabout where he needed to stop in order to merge into traffic that Emma started to wake.

A little moan, a stretch, and she sighed. "Are we there yet?"

"Not even close. You've been asleep for about an hour. We're about five miles from the highway."

She stifled a yawn, covered her open mouth with her hand. "I needed that extra hour of sleep."

"How is that headache?" Gio finally had room in the roundabout and pushed on.

Emma tilted her head from side to side. "Wow. It's, ah . . . wow, not there."

"And your stomach? Any queasy thoughts?"

She took a moment. "None at all. What was in that God-awful concoction?"

He shook his head. "Oh, no. My secret. Besides, if you knew, you'd never drink it again."

"That's probably true." Emma turned in her seat. "Did you bring water?"

He motioned with his thumb to the back seat. "There's a few bottles in the back."

She unbuckled her seat belt and reached behind them. "Want one?"

"Yeah. Probably a good idea."

Emma righted herself in her seat, handed him a water bottle. "Thanks."

"I really do appreciate you doing this."

"You've already said that," he reminded her.

"I know, but it bears repeating. This is your vacation and giving up an entire day for someone you hardly know is very selfless of you."

"I want to know you better. So maybe I have a hidden agenda."

She laughed. "Not so hidden if you tell me that."

Gio drove with his knee while unscrewing the cap on his water. He took a sip. "So, are you going to tell me the real reason you know so much about wine?"

She blinked a few times, then stared out the window. "I guess that's the least I can do, considering what you're doing for me."

He knew there was more to the story.

Gio waited for her to elaborate.

"My last name is Rutledge," she said as if she were confessing something important.

"Okay . . . is that supposed to—"

"As in my father is Robert Rutledge, otherwise known as the owner of R&R Wineries."

Oh, snap. Yeah, that was big. "Napa Valley R&R?"

"That's the one. We have . . . *he* has vines in Temecula as well."

That was an interesting correction in how she worded her father's land.

"You grew up with wine."

"That I did."

"What do you do for the company?" he asked.

A short laugh escaped her lips. "That's a complex answer."

"We have just under three more hours on the drive to get where we're going. Probably need to stop for food a couple of times, and four hours back. So, if you want to give me the long answer, we have time." Besides, the way she was squirming around his question piqued his curiosity about her even more.

She sat taller and put her seat belt back on, which she'd left off after getting the water. "I'm in retail. Primarily for the wine we . . . *he* produces in Temecula. Although to be fair, I've found buyers for all the labels."

Gio moved over to the fast lane. "That doesn't sound like a complicated answer."

"Two weeks ago, it wouldn't have been."

"What happened two weeks ago?" he asked.

"I quit."

Gio let his eyes leave the road. "You what?"

"Quit. Technically I didn't quit. I said I was taking the six weeks of vacation owed to me to contemplate if I'm going to go back."

"What prompted that?"

She sighed. "I'll give you the short version because the long one will piss me off and make me miserable."

He didn't want that. Gio waited for her to speak.

"My father is a misogynistic ass who has never taken my role at R&R seriously. He promoted someone into a position that should be mine . . . or at least he should've given me a shot at it." She took a breath. "I wouldn't be surprised if he did it so I'd quit. He knows me well enough to know I would. He'd rather see me married, running a household and hosting book clubs, with another baby on the way, than see me succeed in *his* winery."

"That does not sound like you."

"It isn't." She took a swig from her water. "I might have figured out how to best him, though."

He liked the smile on Emma's face. "This I want to hear."

She shifted in her seat. "There's this house on twenty acres with mature vines that R&R already owns. It's in Temecula. The house has been vacant for a couple of years, but the vines are still producing. Apparently, according to my mother . . . the house and vines were slated for me."

"As in a gift?"

"Yeah . . . but there was this thing that happened . . . Anyway, my mother just showed me the property." She smiled and stopped talking.

"That good?"

"Yeah. The production space hasn't been used the way it should for several years. The place needs a dumpster or two to get rid of the broken and old equipment. But the vines are solid, the house is beautiful. Swimming pool, all fenced and gated."

It sounded like Gio's dream property.

"I told my dad I was willing to go out and start up on my own, something I know he thinks I'll fail at. My mother is convinced that he'll hand me over this property."

"A gift?" Gio asked for a second time.

"My dad is worth a lot of money. But no. I can't imagine there won't be strings attached. Besides, I'd rather buy it off him."

"You have that kind of capital?"

She paused.

"Sorry. That's none of my business."

"Emma Rutledge has a trust fund. But even if he took that away, Emma Rutledge has a college degree and a decade of experience. Something my father underestimates."

Gio could see how that would be a mistake. The woman sitting next to him was as determined as any woman in his family. And that was saying something.

Emma glanced at him. "Being a part of the family business was what I always wanted. Now my goals have changed."

A couple of seconds went by before Gio said, "You're obviously competent."

"I can run circles around Richard, and everyone knows it."

"Who's Richard?"

"My older brother. He's my dad's right hand. Yes, he's the oldest . . . and it was assumed that he'd take up beside my father."

Gio gripped the wheel a little tighter. "Do you and your brother get along?"

She shrugged. "We don't fight over Thanksgiving dinner if that's what you mean."

"That's not what I mean. Do you spend any time together, outside work? Is he there for you when you need him?"

Emma started laughing, settled, and started laughing again. "No. That's funny. Richard is entirely too into his own life. Ryan, my other brother, makes a point of coming around. We'll go out for drinks and talk on the phone."

"What does Ryan do with the winery?"

"Nothing. Never had any desire to enter the offices of R&R. Our father pushed against his resistance for a while but gave up early on. When I graduated from college, Dad tucked me down in the Temecula arm, which I was okay with. My parents have homes both in Napa and Temecula. Most of the time when I wasn't in school, I'd go to wherever my mother was. In Temecula I found more autonomy. I wasn't dismissed like when I was in Napa, so I owned it."

She stopped talking and Gio looked over.

He could see the frustration in how she kept blinking. "You don't want to hear all this," she said.

"I'm fascinated. And pissed on your behalf."

"You haven't even heard the best part."

He paused. "There's more?"

"My ex-husband is the man who took the job that should have been mine."

Gio's eyes snapped to hers. "You were married?" He didn't see that coming.

"Don't get excited. It wasn't for that long. Kyle worked for my father. He was told to mentor me. I think he felt it was a babysitting position at first. There was an attraction, obviously. Kyle saw how my dad was pushing me aside, and I felt like I had an ally. When we made it known we were dating, my dad approved and at the same time said that he wasn't going to lose a valuable employee should things not work out."

"Ouch."

"And that's how it played out. Kyle was promoted after we were married. For a short time, I lived in Napa with him."

"How did it fall apart?"

"I feel stupid," Emma said.

"No judgment here. We all have a past."

"Six months in he was pressuring me to have a baby. I was barely twenty-four. I went off of birth control pills and had an IUD placed. I was *not* ready to be a mother and as far as I saw it, this wasn't something that was going to change in five years. All of which we'd talked about before the ceremony. He was not happy. And it was then that I opened my eyes. Kyle was moving up the ladder. Kyle was being groomed for the boardroom. Kyle was getting an audience with my father for the future of R&R Wineries. After all, he was part of the family now. Kyle never wanted me. He wanted my name."

That cut. Gio could see it in Emma's eyes, hear it in her voice. "You deserve better. I'm sorry."

"I filed for a divorce a week shy of our first anniversary. Dad was pissed. Kyle stayed in Napa, I went back to Temecula. I grew up a lot that year."

"I'm not sure what to say."

Her smile was halfway. "I don't throw my name around to open doors, or cry on someone else's shoulder for their sympathy. I'm well aware that I have first-world problems. Problems most people would cut off a limb for."

"That doesn't make them less."

Her voice softened. "Thank you. I need to hear that once in a while."

"I'll tell you every day."

Gio stayed quiet as her story sunk in.

Then he heard her stomach growl. "Ready for breakfast?"

They both started to laugh while Gio looked for an exit that promised food.

CHAPTER ELEVEN

They made their breakfast stop quick, intending on taking more time for lunch after they picked up her bag.

For every complaint Emma had about her family, Giovanni praised his.

They were a half an hour from their destination, and she had his phone in her hand, scrolling through the pictures.

Within five minutes she recognized his sister Chloe's face, along with her husband, Dante. Gio's older brother, Luca, and his wife, Brooke, and Gio's niece, Francesca. "Why the nickname Franny?" Emma asked.

"I don't remember how it got started. My mother, I think. Gianluca, Giovanni . . . Francesca. These are names you hear a lot in our community. Maybe it was easier for my mother to call us out. We certainly listen more when our full names are used."

Emma flipped to the next picture. This one was Chloe's formal wedding. His sister was stunning. Olive skin, long dark hair. Rail thin. "I like Giovanni."

"You can call me that, I just might think you're mad at me."

That made her laugh.

Another picture was of his mother standing with Chloe. "Why hasn't your mom remarried?"

"You have to date to find someone to marry."

"She doesn't date?"

"Ew!"

That had Emma laughing. "Moms can't have sex, is that it?"

"I don't even want to think of my mother having sex with my father back when he was alive."

"Boys and their mothers," she said. "I bet Chloe encourages her to get out."

Another picture, this one of Gio and his mother dancing.

"My parents had the kind of love that most people can only dream about. I wouldn't be surprised if my mother never puts herself out there again. Besides, she's spent all her time raising us, keeping the restaurant going, and meddling in our lives, trying to get everyone married."

A few more pictures in and Gio was standing beside one of the bridesmaids. Italian, from what Emma could tell. A little shorter than him, beautiful, young. She was laughing, with her hand on his chest.

"This looks cozy," Emma said. "Your mother's matchmaking attempt?" she asked as she turned the phone his way.

He glanced at the picture. "No, no. That's Salena. Chloe's best friend. Someone we've known forever."

"She's gorgeous." Emma couldn't help but wonder if she and Gio had ever dated.

"She knows it, too."

"Conceited?"

"I wouldn't say that. Very self-aware." He glanced at Emma. "No."

"No what?"

"We never dated."

"Did I ask?"

"You weren't curious?"

Emma tilted her head to the side, found another picture of the two of them. "Well . . ."

Gio laughed. "Once, in junior high, there was a party at a mutual friend's. Chloe wasn't there, I don't remember why . . . Anyway . . . someone brought out a bottle. There may have been some underaged drinking. Spin the bottle was introduced."

"Your suggestion?" Emma asked.

"I don't remember." His smirk said he was lying. "So yeah, we kissed. Once."

"And?"

"It was like kissing a sister. Not that I've ever—"

"I get it," Emma interrupted.

"We vowed never to do it again."

Why did that make Emma feel better?

Another picture of Franny. "Your niece is adorable."

"She knows it. Gets away with everything, that one. Hard to say no to her."

Emma saw the love in Gio's eyes for the little girl.

"Everyone looks genuinely happy." The pictures on Emma's phone of her people always looked staged.

"Family is everything. It boggles my mind when I hear of other families that don't look out for one another."

"My mother is always there," Emma said. "And Ryan would be if I needed him."

Gio turned off the highway. "I look forward to meeting them."

Emma lowered the phone. "Are you meeting my family?"

"It isn't like you live far away. I can't imagine we'd leave here after three weeks, fly into the same airport on our return trip, and never see each other again. Do you?"

When he put it like that . . . "No."

"Good."

His phone went to a black screen, and Emma put it back in the holder.

Gio put the map app back on and started to navigate the familiar streets to the hotel they'd been at the day before.

She pointed out a tiny space where they could park and they both exited the car. The cooler temperatures had Emma rubbing her bare shoulders. "I can't believe it's taken this long to get my luggage," she said as Gio opened the door to the hotel for her.

"I certainly hope the airline compensates you."

"That's a fight for when I get home," she said.

The woman at the reception desk remembered them. "Ah, you're here for the bag."

"I am."

"They brought it late last night. It's in the back. If you'll excuse me."

Emma rubbed her hands together and turned to Gio.

"You're cold."

"I have a sweater in my suitcase."

The woman reemerged, a rolling bag at her side. "Here you go."

Emma froze.

Black bag.

Midsize, hard case.

Slowly she started to laugh . . . because what else could she possibly do?

All this effort. All this time.

She laughed harder until her stomach started to cramp.

"What is it?" Gio's question made her laugh even more.

By now both Gio and the receptionist were chuckling as well, as contagious laughs often went.

Emma found that funny, too.

"Are you okay?" Gio asked.

She shook her head no, then yes.

Emma pointed toward the bag. "It's . . . not . . ." Her head tilted back as a tear fell down her cheek.

"Oh my God. It's not yours?" Gio asked.

She shook her head, unable to form words.

He laughed with her now. "Why . . . why is this funny?"

"I don't know. It just is."

"It has your name on the tag," the receptionist pointed out.

Emma slowed her laughter and looked at the airline tag. It did indeed have her name, and the tag indicated the bag had been in Singapore and routed through to Italy. But it wasn't her bag.

"Damn, Emma. What do you want to do?" Gio asked.

Her laughter started to dry up. "We take it with us. Get it back to the airport at the end of our trip. Maybe there's something inside with an address and a name."

"Did your bag have that?" he asked.

"It had a luggage tag on the outside." She reached for the suitcase. "Whatever. I'm done trying to find it."

"I can call the airport and have them retrieve this," the receptionist suggested.

"It was hard enough to get them to come out here the first time. Someone else is out there just as frustrated as I've been. Clearly someone was asleep in the airline baggage department."

Gio took the bag and rolled it out of the hotel and to the car.

"What now?" he asked.

Emma placed both hands on her hips and looked around. "I need to shop. Buy the things I need for the rest of this trip so my hotel rooms stop looking like Grandma's laundry room." Her eyes landed on the clothing strung up on the balcony of someone's home.

Gio closed the trunk of the car and leaned against it. He removed his cell from his back pocket and started typing on it.

"What are you doing?"

"Looking for women's clothing stores. There's a couple towns between here and where we're staying that might offer something, but this is likely the best option."

Emma moved beside him and looked at his screen.

"Looks like there are a few choices." Gio pointed to their left. "Three blocks that way."

They both pushed away from the car and started down the street. Gio volleyed to walk on her side, closer to the oncoming traffic. "I'll try and make it quick," she told him.

"Why?"

"Excuse me?"

"Why? You're in Italy. Arguably the mecca of fashion. Shop. Find some great stuff that you'll wear long after you're back home. Maybe it will ease the pain of waiting for your long-lost luggage."

He had a point. Up until then she'd been buying cheap stuff that could be worn only to work out in when she got home. "You're just tired of my dime-store graphic T-shirts."

Gio looked her up and down before his eyes rested on hers. "You'd look like a knockout in anything you wore, *bella*."

A fluttering deep in her chest rose in her throat. *Wow!* "Do you go shopping with your sister?"

"Not if I can help it."

"Why?"

"Because she parades out of a dressing room, asking me if her ass looks big in a dress. Then I look, only because she asked, and I want to throw up."

Emma laughed. "I like your little sister already."

They found the first store a few blocks away.

Gio opened the door and waited for Emma to pass.

Inside, she walked to the palette of colors she liked the most and pulled a shirt from the pile. Too baggy . . . the style more for someone twenty years her senior. Maybe thirty.

Gio hung out by the front door.

A lap around the store and Emma decided to skip what they sold. "Nothing?" Gio asked.

She shook her head as they went back outside.

Tourists and locals meandered the streets. Not nearly as crowded as Florence, but busy enough.

The next store was much more promising.

Not completely casual, but nothing gala-worthy either.

She found a pair of linen pants in her size. Beige . . . they had them in white, but that might be riskier. Thinking of the heat they'd encountered on most of their trip so far, Emma loaded her arms with breathable fabric. Button-up shirts that could be layered over camis and tank tops.

Gio looked through a rack of light cardigan sweaters.

He must have felt her watching because he glanced over at her and smiled. He lifted a sweater up for her to see.

She nodded.

"Small?" he asked.

"Medium," she answered.

One of the store employees approached her and started talking in Italian.

"I'm sorry, I don't speak Italian."

Gio walked over. "She wants to take your things to a dressing room," he told Emma.

"Oh. Yes. *Grazie*," Emma said as she handed over the stack of clothes in her hand.

"Don't we have one semiformal event?" Gio asked.

Emma nodded. "I'd packed a dress that I could spice up or down. And heels." Really expensive shoes. "If we find something, great. But I'm not going to worry about it. What I really need is a couple of pairs of shorts. And a bathing suit."

That put a smile on Gio's face. "Shopping for a bathing suit sounds right up my—"

"It's the worst," Emma cut him off.

"Maybe for you."

She rolled her eyes, grabbed a pair of cotton capris off the rack, and turned toward the dressing room.

Once closed behind a curtain, Emma braced herself on the wall with the mirror. Giovanni was inching under her skin at such a slow and steady pace that he felt like he belonged.

And his flirting . . . warm and easy.

She shook her head and pulled her T-shirt from her shoulders.

Outside the dressing room she heard Gio talking with the employee.

Emma peeled off her leggings and replaced them with the linen. Already she felt more like herself. She buttoned up a shirt that matched and stepped out from behind the curtain.

Gio was sitting in a chair opposite her and a three-way mirror.

He watched her every step.

And because flirting went both ways, she glanced over her shoulder. "Does my butt look fat in these?"

Her goal was to make him squirm.

But it was her shuffling from one foot to the next when Gio's eyes slid down her body and rested on her ass.

Emma felt her cheeks warm.

The attendant emerged from the back of the shop. In her hand were two bottles of sparkling water.

She handed both to Gio and turned her attention to Emma. The woman fussed with the shirt and started a rapid fire of Italian.

"What is she saying?" Emma asked Gio.

First Gio addressed the woman talking, then Emma. "She asked if you had a belt. I told her your luggage never made it from home and that you didn't have anything."

"*Sì.*" She walked away and came back with a matching belt and wrapped it around Emma's waist. It looked very chic. Very Italian.

Before Emma could say a thing, the woman and Gio chatted again. Out came a pair of simple yet stylish flat sneakers that worked well with the outfit.

"She's saying that in Italy, women wear tennis shoes with almost everything. Especially in the cities," Gio translated.

Emma nodded. "Size thirty-six?"

The number the woman understood, and she disappeared again.

"Do you like the belt?" Gio asked.

"I do."

"Do you have anything like it at home?"

"No."

He removed the top of his water and sat back.

Back inside the dressing room, Emma took a long look in the mirror. Yup . . . she was in. Into how Giovanni watched her. How he flirted with her. How he was genuinely helpful. How he opened doors and walked on the outside of the sidewalk . . . and damn it, she was a feminist. And wasn't it a contradiction to want what Gio was offering?

She put on another outfit and walked out.

The attendant shook her head, said something, and walked to the rack where Emma had found the shirt.

"The shirt is too big," Gio explained.

"She's right."

"You're in luck."

"For what?" Emma asked him.

"There is a store a few blocks away that sells swimsuits and undergarments."

"Really?" That sounded like heaven. The daily sink panty wash was getting old.

"Really." The slightly seductive tone in how Gio replied prickled the hair on the back of her neck.

"I won't be modeling for you there," she said.

"That's unfortunate." But he was smiling.

"You know, Gio. For a man who said he was on a sexual sabbatical while traveling Italy, you sure aren't talking like it." She disappeared behind the curtain, replaced the larger shirt with the smaller one.

"I haven't caved yet," he teased.

Yeah, this shirt did a much better job of showing off her waistline.

From the way Gio looked at her when she emerged, he noticed.

Emma laughed and disappeared into the dressing room.

CHAPTER TWELVE

It was getting hard to breathe around the woman.

Her relentless teasing mixed with the curves of her body. One Gio would kill to see . . . touch. Damn.

He left her in the lingerie store that also sold women's swimming suits, in pursuit of something just as practical.

Emma accepted him tracking her on his phone so they could meet up should she leave the one store in search of another.

Gio found what he was looking for a block away.

Medium size, hard case . . . snow white.

Black suitcases always looked like the other guys. He bought a colorful luggage tag and, at the last second, a four-pack assortment of Sharpie pens.

Yup.

This bag will be hard to lose.

Before leaving the store, he opened the pens and wrote Emma's name in big, bold letters on one side of the luggage.

It wasn't enough.

He fired off a text message to Emma.

What is your home address?

A few seconds went by.

In Temecula?

Yes.

. . .

Why? she asked.

Gio shook his head. The woman asked questions about everything.

Trust me.

. . .

Her address appeared on the screen and Gio wrote it on the bag as well.

Even if she never used the suitcase again, at least this time it would end up at home once she returned.

The store attendant laughed as Gio left.

He walked into the lingerie store where he'd left her, and where her phone said she still was.

Two young women looking at lacy black bras took him in as he walked by.

"*Buonasera,*" he said before turning his attention to the direction of the dressing rooms.

An older woman working in the store was standing outside of a closed door. "Is that better?" Her English was good, her accent thick.

"I think so," Emma's voice called from behind the door.

The door opened and Gio's smile fell.

"Holy Mary . . ." Bikini. Emma in less than a bra and panties. Yeah, it covered the important bits, but damn . . . Her skin was flawless, ivory. He bet she burned if she didn't soak in sunscreen. He would love to help her put on sunscreen.

I should look away.

Didn't happen.

Emma turned in a circle.

"This one fits better," the older woman said. "Your boyfriend will like."

Emma twisted around. "He's not my—"

Their eyes met.

Gio swallowed . . . hard, blinked twice, and found his voice. "Why do I feel like a thirteen-year-old that stumbled into the girls' gym?"

"She's beautiful, yes?" the older woman asked.

"A goddess among women," he said in Italian.

The lady placed a hand to her chest.

Emma's brow furrowed. "What did you just say?"

"I said yes."

"I have about six words under my Italian language belt that don't describe food, and *yes* is one of them." Her hands perched on her hips.

"I said the equivalent of yes," Gio defended himself.

Rolling her eyes, Emma closed the door.

When she emerged, she was fully dressed. A crying shame, that.

Her eyes went to the suitcase at his side. "What is that?"

"A necessary item if you want to use more than paper bags to get all your new clothes home." Gio then swiveled the white suitcase around so she could see her name and address covering one entire side. "Safety measures."

She laughed. "That's too funny. Sadly needed, but funny. Thank you."

"You're welcome."

Once they left the store, Gio placed the bags Emma was accumulating in the suitcase and moved on to the next store.

"This can't be fun for you," she said.

"On the contrary, I'm having a great time." *Bathing suits help.*

"Yeah, sure."

For the next hour they went to three more stores, two of which took some time. It was then that they decided to start working their way back to the villa.

They decided on having a midday meal instead of stopping for lunch and then again for dinner.

Two hours closer to the villa, they stopped, found a restaurant with outside dining, and took their time.

"Wine?" Gio asked as soon as they sat down.

"Not for me. You can, if you want, and I'll drive the rest of the way."

He put that idea aside. "After last night, I'll pass."

Emma disappeared behind her menu. "It was fun, though. I'm a bit competitive."

Gio scoffed. "I couldn't tell."

"Ha. You're exactly the same."

"I like to win, when I'm matched. Otherwise, it's unsportsmanlike."

The waiter came, took their order, and disappeared again.

"Tell me, Emma . . . what do you hope to gain by traversing Tuscany when you already have a vast knowledge of wine making?" A question Gio had been pondering ever since she told him who she was.

"Who says no to Italy?" she asked.

"You have a point."

She grinned. "My mother gave me a big check for my birthday . . . and after she learned what my father had done, she insisted that Nicole and I spend it on a lavish holiday. I didn't need to be told twice."

"That's crazy. We were both gifted this trip."

"Oh, that's right. You said something about just turning thirty."

He nodded. "On the twelfth."

"You're kidding."

Gio shook his head. "Why?"

"We have the same birthday."

"Get out."

Emma pulled her driver's license from her purse and handed it to him.

"What are the chances of that?" he asked.

"Three hundred and sixty-five to one."

He handed her back her license. "No. It's much greater than that. Two people from the same part of the world, meet in a different part of the world, who both had birthday gifts that put them in the same place at the same time. Some might call that a sign." He knew she was listening.

"What kind of sign?"

"That we were meant to meet." He leaned forward, stared into her eyes.

She paused. "You're suggesting romantically."

"I didn't say that . . . but now that you mention it." He liked that her mind went there right along with his.

"Did you forget about the part where you're looking for 'the one' and I'm not looking at all?"

Gio couldn't help it. He looked at her lips and wondered briefly how she would taste. "Minor crossroads, *bella*," he said.

She shook her head. "You're one hell of a flirt."

"Says the woman who asked me if her butt looked good in her pants."

She giggled. "Touché."

"It's okay. I'm a patient man." He wasn't, actually . . . but the white lie sounded good to his ears.

"Is that your way of saying you're going to wear down my defenses?" Emma asked.

"I'm sure as hell going to try."

Her cheeks lit up, her smile didn't falter. "Men never talk to me like you do."

"I'm not like other men."

"And if I tell you that you're wasting your time?" she asked.

"It's my time to waste."

She blinked several times. "It was the bathing suit, wasn't it?"

It was his turn to laugh. "A vision that will come up every time I close my eyes."

"I wasn't looking for a compliment."

"Yes, you were. But no, *cara*, the swimsuit, while a bonus, is not what is prompting me to try." She intrigued him on every level.

"Don't say I didn't warn you."

"Duly noted."

~

It was his time to waste.

Who said things like that?

And what was up with the *bella* and *cara*? What did *cara* mean, anyway? She'd look it up once she was alone.

They'd finished their meal and found two more women's clothing stores in the town where they'd stopped.

The clouds that had threatened most of the day opened up while she was picking out the last of what she thought she'd need for the trip. Her credit card bill would not be pretty when she returned home.

On the other hand, she had some nice things that would forever remind her of this trip.

With her purchases bundled into a bag and held close to her body, she and Gio looked out at the rain that was coming in sideways.

"I can find an umbrella," he suggested.

"I don't think it will make much of a difference."

People outside were scrambling for shelter.

"We can make a run for it."

"Or wait it out." As soon as the words were out of her mouth, a clap of thunder rumbled through the shop.

Emma opened the weather app on her phone and showed Gio. "Until two in the morning?"

"We came from that direction, right?" Gio pointed to the left.

"Yeah."

Gio reached for the door. "Ready?"

Emma pulled the sweater she'd purchased earlier in the day closer to her body. "Might as well."

Outside, the temperature had dropped a good ten degrees.

The rain hitting her face didn't help.

Gio grasped her elbow and they both half jogged down the narrow street to the intersection.

"I think we're that way," Gio said.

The problem with Italian streets was that they all looked the same. And since they were in an unfamiliar town, even if it was small in comparison to Florence or Rome, it was still a catacomb with winding streets with cars parked all along the sides.

They turned down the block, got to the next one, and both stopped.

"Did we go down the wrong one?" she asked.

"The restaurant was only a few blocks from the stores."

Emma turned a one-eighty. "I think we needed to go the other direction."

Gio agreed and they doubled back.

They found the restaurant where they'd eaten and darted down another wrong turn.

By now they were both drenched.

Emma crushed the bag of clothes close to her body to keep the paper from ripping.

"We should have taken a picture of the intersection," she said.

They slowed their pace, turned in circles.

The streets had emptied of pedestrians, but cars and scooters still sped by.

"We rounded the block twice, then drove over two before we found parking."

"One more block over, then?" Emma asked.

Gio stayed close to her side as they slowed down and looked for a familiar landmark.

Her hair was starting to drip by the time they saw the car a half a block away. "There."

They picked up their pace.

Gio stood in front of the passenger side door and stuck his hands into his jeans pocket for the keys. When he finally had them in his hand, they flipped out of his fingers and onto the ground.

Emma started to laugh.

They both reached for them at the same time, their heads collided.

Gio was laughing as they stood up, rubbing their heads.

Their eyes met as rain dripped off their faces.

Giovanni stood within two inches of her body, the car to her back. His grin fell and his gaze traveled to her lips.

Emma's heartbeat picked up in her chest, her breath caught.

His fingertips reached for her hair and pushed the wet mess aside. That simple touch sparked hot, even against the cold, wet rain. His palm cradled her cheek, and his thumb traced the outside of her lower lip.

What would it hurt to let him kiss her?

Emma swayed a little closer.

"Am I wearing you down already, *cara*?" His voice was a whisper.

She nodded, and then shook her head.

Their eyes locked.

His lips parted, he lifted an eyebrow . . . and pulled away.

Out of the trance he'd managed to put her in without any effort whatsoever, air rushed from her lungs.

Gio retrieved the car keys that were still on the sidewalk and placed a gentle hand on her hip and urged her to move to the side.

Get a grip, Emma.

He opened the door and she scrambled inside.

It was going to be a very long last two hours of their ride home.

～

Still damp from their run in the rain, Emma and Gio walked into the villa, both of them rolling a bag at their side. They didn't see anyone as they walked the path to their rooms.

For two hours they both ignored the almost kiss and the electric tension that didn't seem to ebb even one kilowatt. They talked about the higher-end wines they both liked and compared notes as to which was better.

Anytime the conversation dried up, Emma found herself looking at the man and asking herself, *What if?* and *Why not?* For something temporary, of course.

She liked her single life. Liked having her own say in every part of her day. And in fact, would be getting more of that once she was home and starting her own winery . . . if her father agreed to her terms.

Once out of the car and such close quarters with Giovanni, she felt like she could breathe a bit easier.

They stopped at her door and he pushed the black bag closer to her.

"Thank you again," she said. "For everything today." For a moment she felt like she was saying good night to a date after prom.

"I had a great time."

She rolled her eyes. "Shopping for women's underwear?"

"That was the best part." He winked at her.

"You're incorrigible."

He laughed. "Are you going to meet the others?" Dinner hour was wrapping up, but Emma didn't want anything to do with a party.

"All I want is a hot shower and bed."

"I'll leave you to it, then. Good night."

He turned to walk away, and she stopped him before he opened his bedroom door. "Giovanni?"

"Yes?"

"Why didn't you? Why did you stop?" She didn't have to elaborate her question. Their *almost kiss* hovered over them like thick perfume in a crowded bar.

He rubbed the side of his jaw, smiled. "You're not ready."

Then, without anything else, he walked into his room and left her standing there.

Holy shit.

CHAPTER THIRTEEN

He was avoiding her.

A night of tossing and turning and wishing he'd taken her up on the invitation of a kiss made it hard to look at her without complete longing.

"Did something happen between you and Emma yesterday?" Chris asked the next day when he found Gio wandering the vineyards while everyone else soaked up some sun in the pool.

"What do you mean?"

"I don't know. Just seems you wouldn't give up an opportunity to see her lying out by the pool. Just because I'm gay, doesn't mean I can't appreciate a bombshell when I see one."

Gio groaned and walked deeper into the vineyard. "If I saw her in the swimsuit, I'd have to offer my services as suntan-lotion boy. And I'm certain I'd violate something in the process."

"And the problem with that is?" Chris asked.

"Nothing. Ultimately."

"I don't get it."

"Have you ever found yourself so intrigued with someone that you really wanted to get to know them better before anything sexual happens?"

Chris nodded several times and then switched his answer. "No. But maybe that's just me."

"I've followed close to that way of life myself. The majority of the time the women I've spent time with were on the same page. When I knew they weren't, I ended things. Emma is different."

"You haven't even known her for a solid week."

"I realize that. Besides, we have a bet going. I said I wasn't going there while on this trip."

Chris laughed. "That was dumb."

"Trust me, I know. I'm certain she's making her own wager on getting me to cave."

"That might be a bet worth losing."

"I know that, too."

"You two . . . talk about competitive," Chris said.

"I like the chase, if I'm honest."

Chris patted him on the back. "We all do, Gio. We all do."

~

The last dinner at the villa was set under strings of soft lights outside under the oaks. A long table stretched out for all of them, several bottles of wine, bread, olive oil, with an array of meats and cheeses.

It was seven o'clock and the sun was dipping across the horizon.

Gio stood beside the Golden Girls, laughing along with them. "How many bottles did you buy here?" he asked.

"Not that many," Carol told him.

"I sent a case home," Diane said.

"One? I sent three," Jean told them.

"We'll be the hit of our book club."

"Wine must be your fountain of youth," Gio said.

Carol put her hand on his chest, tapped twice . . . and then hummed. "Don't waste all that charm on us." She looked over Gio's shoulder.

Emma and Nicole were walking toward them, both in sundresses.

The closer they came, the more details he soaked in.

Emma's hair was down and straightened. Not the curly locks he'd seen most of the day before, especially after getting caught in the rain.

He knew, before she turned, that the dress she wore was backless. He also noticed that her arms were nearly the color of her hair.

"There you are," Nicole said. "Where did you disappear to today?"

"I've been around. Slept in." His eyes found Emma's. "Spent the day by the pool, did you?"

"I burn easy."

"Young lady, you're going to end up with skin cancer if you're not careful," Jean chided.

"I'll use a higher-SPF sunscreen the next time."

Carol nudged Gio. "What you need is a big, strong man to rub it in."

"You're terrible, Carol. Leave those kids alone," Diane said.

Gio couldn't let Emma's gaze go.

"Happy to help," he said.

"I bet."

"Are Kimmy and Weston joining us tonight?" Rob asked the group. The anniversary couple spent half of their nights alone. But they always emerged looking *refreshed*.

"I overheard Weston asking for food to be delivered to their room," Carol told him.

Nicole pulled out her cell phone and started taking pictures. "Squish in, everyone."

"You two in the middle," Carol instructed Gio and Emma.

Gio placed his arm around Emma's waist and used the opportunity to whisper in her ear. "Your sunburned nose is adorable."

Her smile radiated.

"Ready?" Nicole asked.

The Golden Girls flanked them while Nicole took several pictures.

They dispersed and the older women moved toward the table. Gio walked with them and helped them with their chairs.

"Your mother sure did raise you right," Barbara told him.

"I'll be sure and tell her that when I'm home, Ms. Barbara."

Gio took a seat opposite Emma, which felt safer. Only every time he looked up, he caught her eyes.

Maybe the other end of the table would have been a better idea.

Wine was poured and the plates of food traveled around.

"Is it true that the farther north we get, the more chances we have of tasting white wines?" The question came from Jean.

Both Gio and Emma answered at the same time. "Yes."

"Oh, good. I do like whites better."

"That doesn't seem to be stopping you from drinking and buying," Rob said, laughing.

"I know, but my digestion—"

"Is not something anyone here wants to hear about," Barbara interrupted.

Jean pointed a finger around those at the table. "Just wait. You'll all get there."

"Ladies." Gio directed his attention to the four oldest women at the table. "Since you might be a few years older than some of us. Do you mind if I ask you a question?"

Diane spoke up. "As long as you leave out age, weight, and religion."

"I would never be so personal. No, I want to know what life advice you might care to share. That one thing you did, or maybe wish you had done, if you could roll back the clock thirty years."

"Oh, that's easy," Jean started. "I wouldn't have married my first husband. Too young. I would have spent that time sleeping around."

Carol huffed. "You made up for it in the last five years."

"Yeah, but they're all old. One round, if that."

Gio glanced at Emma and Nicole, both of which were holding back their laughter.

"What about you, Carol?" Gio asked.

Carol patted her stomach. "Keep your core, ladies. When getting out of bed in the morning requires a trapeze over your bed, you've lost it."

"That's not what Giovanni is asking about." Barbara took her glasses off and started to clean them with the edge of her shirt. "Don't work so hard that you miss out. I've had two husbands. Edward, the father of my children. God rest his soul. Worked himself to the bone. He was a great provider, don't get me wrong. Back then you could have one person making the money. He kept fighting for the next promotion, the next raise. We didn't need as much as he wanted. Had a heart attack at fifty-eight, recovered, went right back out. Died three years later. Our kids missed out on really knowing their father. He missed the school stuff, the first dates, driving lessons. All of it. My second husband was the same way. He retired at seventy but didn't know how to live without work. We divorced within two years. Work should be a part of your life, not your only life."

"That's deep," Chris said.

"What about you, Diane? What advice do you have?" Nicole asked.

"Surround yourself with people you love and care about, who feel the same way about you. Sometimes they're family. Sometimes they're not. Don't get hung up on people you think you *should* love. If you have to *think*, then you don't." She paused, picked up her wineglass. "And take care of your teeth."

Several people chuckled at that last bit.

"I'm serious. Dentures are why old people eat too much sugar and salt all their food. Nothing tastes the same."

"I never considered that," Emma said.

Diane pointed to her mouth. "It's a big chunk of plastic. I should have gotten implants. Too late now."

Gio lifted his glass for a toast. "To new friends, and sound advice."

A chorus of cheers went up.

His glass touched Emma's, their gazes met. *"Salute."*

~

Emma lay on her bed, staring up at the ceiling. "What do you think about what Diane said tonight?"

"She's right about the teeth."

"Not that part, the being hung up on people you think you should love."

Wearing a T-shirt and ready for bed, Nicole talked from the bathroom, where she was removing her makeup.

"I don't think she's wrong. I've fought to have a relationship with my sister for years. Do I love her, yeah. But I wouldn't want to hang out with her. It's too much work to have a simple conversation."

Emma nodded, thought of her father, her older brother. "It's easy with Ryan and my mom. But Richard and my father? I always feel like I'm interrupting their life, their space."

Nicole finished in the bathroom and walked over to her bed, sat on the side of it. "Now that you no longer work for him, you won't have to interrupt their space."

"They're still family."

Nicole sighed. "Emma, don't take this the wrong way . . ."

She looked her friend in the eye. "What?"

"I can see why you're focused on all things R&R. Why it would bother you so much to be pushed aside. But I can't help but hear the things Barbara said tonight. Like working so hard that you forget about what you're working for. For as long as I've known you, you've pushed against the machine. That being your dad, or Kyle . . . what people think you *should* do versus what you *want* to do."

"I wanted to be a bigger part of R&R."

"And no matter how hard you've pushed, no matter how educated you are, or how much you can bring to the table, they're not letting you in."

Emma sat up in bed and rested her hands in her lap. "I'm not asking for that anymore."

"I can still see the disappointment in your eyes. I'm afraid that the need to 'get back' and 'show them' is driving you most. Pretend for a moment that this winery didn't happen. Hear what Diane was throwing down and surround yourself with people who support you and what you want to do with your life. Heed what Barbara said and find some balance. Don't become your father, who is obsessed with acquiring more instead of enjoying what he has."

"I only want my piece of the pie. I don't have to own it all."

Nicole tucked her legs under her. "We've been here for almost a week. I think you've been having a good time. But the other night, when you and Gio were going at it, wine for wine . . . you were on fire. Sassy, competitive without being a bitch. Laughing . . . flirting. I haven't seen that in forever. And last night, when you got in, you were practically glowing and yet you had every reason to be pissed. Luggage is all screwed up, completely rained out . . . you've spent a crap-ton of money on clothes you weren't expecting to buy. Long road trip, on a hangover, no less. But did you complain about any of that? No. You were all smiles and 'Gio said this, and Giovanni said that . . . and did you see the suitcase?' Compare that to every time we've stopped at a winery and you've compared it to R&R. You bring up the scale of the winery and family history. Which always makes you frown."

Nicole wasn't wrong. "I haven't meant to be a downer."

"You're not. I get it. Your dad did a douche thing and it's had a tidal wave of emotions and what-ifs. Let that go. Put your dad and every-thing R&R behind you. Surround yourself with people that make you smile and laugh. That support you emotionally."

Emma smiled. "Like you."

"Duh . . . and people like Gio."

"The man is looking for a wife."

"I didn't tell you to marry him. I suggested you spend time with him. When was the last time you even went on a date?"

Emma rolled her eyes. Had no intention of answering that question.

"Exactly," Nicole said. "Gio is fun. Carefree."

"And not nearly high enough on the social level that my father would approve."

Nicole tossed her hands in the air. "Who cares? Fuck him. He approved of Kyle and look how that worked out. Besides, your dad never has to meet Gio, or anyone you want in your life." Nicole moved to the side of Emma's bed. "You don't have to impress your dad or answer to him. I've heard you these past weeks. Going over all the 'what-ifs' of how your dad is going to swing this. Will he sell it to you? Will you accept a 'partner' deal? You can bust your ass to make something out of bare bones for who, you? Your dad? Will he show you more respect then?" Nicole held up her hand. "And before you answer that, let me . . . yes! You would do exactly that. And ten years from now, or five, you'll still be unsatisfied with how Daddy treats you. Not to mention you'd still be working for him. You could walk away now. You could say 'no thanks' and continue your day job. Or, even better, quit working for Dad and find another organization that would value your worth. Because, Emma . . . your dad doesn't value your worth and I know you know that."

Emma was breathing heavy with Nicole's monologue. Her words sunk in like a slow drip from a stalactite to a stalagmite. Each drop important for growth. Much as Emma hated to admit it, she had wondered how she would react to a "negotiation" her father would ultimately throw at her. Her last message to her mother, since contacting her father, was not getting her anywhere, so Emma had thrown out numbers of what the property was worth to try and negotiate a price.

That met with crickets.

Emma wanted to pay for it.

Her mother wanted it to be given as a gift.

And good ole Daddy hadn't responded.

"You're right." Emma kicked the covers off her bed and reached for her phone, which was plugged in and sitting on the nightstand.

"Who are you calling?"

"My mother."

CHAPTER FOURTEEN

Five fifteen the next evening, just minutes before the entire group loaded onto the bus from a pit stop to drive to their next destination, Emma's phone rang.

It was her father's secretary.

"It's my dad," Emma said to Nicole.

"Oh, snap."

Emma walked a few steps away from the group to talk without interruption.

"This is Emma," she answered the phone.

"Hello, Ms. Rutledge, it's Kerry." *Ms.* . . . the only people that referred to her as *Ms.* were at the office. Emma hadn't taken Kyle's last name, never had a desire to.

"Hello, Kerry."

"Your father is on the line. Please hold."

Not "Is this a good time? Your father would like to speak with you" . . . just *"Please hold."*

A full minute went by before he picked up the call. "Emma?"

"Hello, Father."

"I understand you're trying to get ahold of me."

Emma swallowed. "I don't think Mom needs to be the only one talking to you about this house."

"I'm sure she told you that I agreed with you moving in."

"She did." Emma's heartbeat picked up its pace. "But . . . I need to know what your intentions are. I'm not looking for a roof over my head, I want to turn this property around to become self-sustainable. And I'm willing to pay you for it."

Her father released a short laugh. One that said he didn't like what he heard. "You made that known. The lawyers are working on the best way to go about this. You should know that isn't something I'd do personally."

"You *would* direct your lawyers on what to do."

"Sometimes what I want to do and what can be done are two different things. Something you should know before you jump into a game you hardly understand."

She really didn't want to get into a pissing match with her dad over the phone. "I think we can both agree that the time for an internship at your side has passed us by. I've learned a lot about this business simply by having your name and growing up the way I did. I'm willing to learn the rest . . . on my own if need be."

Robert was silent. "Like I said. My lawyers are working out the details."

As frustrating as his answer was, at least there was no doubt of her intentions. "Once they have something figured out, have them send me the details. I'd like to know if I'm packing the moment I'm home, or if I'm hiring realtors in Napa or Temecula."

"That won't be necessary, Emma. Your mother has already hired a contractor who is busting out a wall in the house this week."

Emma tried not to let a smile cross her face . . . she failed.

More of their group crowded around the bus, catching her attention. "Have you already replaced me in my position?"

Another long moment stretched between them.

Emma waited for him to reply.

"You don't expect to be able to do both."

"My expectations and yours might be different. But since I wasn't given a pink slip—"

"You came short of quitting."

Emma glanced at the sky. *True.* "I should have handled that better." Actually, it was one of her finest moments. Somehow she didn't think her dad would agree.

"Yes. You should have. You weren't fired," he said.

"No. I certainly wasn't. I do want to meet your expectations. To do that, I need to know what they are about my position."

Her father sighed. "My understanding is Kyle is interviewing for your replacement. When you're back in the States, I expect you to help whoever fills the job if you're needed."

Kyle . . . of course.

Emma wanted to throw something. "That sounds reasonable."

By now everyone was on the bus and waiting on her.

"Thank you."

"You're welcome. If there's nothing else, I have to get back to work."

"I think that's all before I return."

"Enjoy your trip."

That almost sounded pleasant.

Emma disconnected the call and stared at her phone for several seconds. It sounded like this was going to happen. Details aside, she couldn't help but have a spring in her step as she climbed the steps onto the bus.

"Sorry, everyone. It was a . . . ah, important call."

"All good," someone said.

"I'm just happy it wasn't me this time," Jean announced.

Emma walked toward the back, saw Nicole sitting next to Chris. The seat next to Gio was empty.

Nicole offered a big grin.

Emma took a seat.

"Is everything okay?" Gio asked. "Nicole said that was your dad."

"It was. I had some questions about . . . things." Emma looked around, leaned closer, and lowered her voice. "I don't want everyone to know who my dad is."

"I get it."

She leaned back as the bus took off. "He's a hard man to get ahold of."

"You said as much before. I would think at this point his *operation* runs itself."

"He has narcissistic qualities. He doesn't think anyone can do it as good as him."

"Not even your brother?" Gio asked.

"Richard? Maybe a little, but not all." She paused. "Don't even get me started on Kyle."

"I won't," Gio said with a smile.

"It does look like things are moving forward."

Gio nudged her shoulder. "That's good news."

"It is."

"Then why the frown?"

"My mother suggested that everything was going like I wanted it to, but I doubt she knows what my father has set in place."

"You think there's something he's hiding?" Gio asked.

"I think my father does everything for a reason. And since my mother doesn't spend all that much time with the man, she's clueless about his motives." Emma tucked her purse under the seat in front of her and extended her legs.

"Your parents don't sound like they're a married couple. More like roommates."

"Roommates that live in separate houses." Emma paused. "I've always wondered if my parents are happy. If their mutual misery is why he works late, leaves early. Why my father uses every excuse to not be in the same home as my mother."

"What does she say about that?"

Emma looked at him. "I don't ask her. She keeps busy with clubs and her friends. Charity work. Typical socialite. Shows up when my dad needs her to."

"Married but separate?"

"Yeah."

"Yuck," he said. "Not for me."

She shrugged. "Works for them."

"I don't see the point. Why get married?"

"Kids? Although they were married for quite a while before Richard. Whatever. There's no reason for me to spend time thinking about it."

"I don't know about that. A parental relationship shapes us. You look at the relationships around you and figure out what you want and what you don't."

Emma knew he was right. Wasn't that in part why she married Kyle? It was expected. It was time. Only she wasn't cut out to live her mother's life. Not then . . . not now.

Gio's soft smile and genuine interest in the people that shaped her were unfamiliar territory coming from a man. She and her girlfriends, mainly Nicole, would dissect just about all the couples they saw.

"They are the real deal."

"They won't make it to five years."

"How the hell did she pick him?"

Emma's parents were not off the gossip meter.

Emma relaxed beside Gio. "How is it we're talking about relationships . . . again?"

Instead of answering, Gio slowly lowered his gaze from her eyes to her lips and then back up. He lifted an eyebrow and then turned to look out the window.

Emma squirmed in her seat, suddenly warm.

"What are you two whispering about up there?" Nicole asked from behind Emma's seat.

Emma glanced over her shoulder, narrowed her eyes, and turned back around without saying a word.

Gio silently chuckled.

~

Gio did what he could to not be completely alone with Emma for the next several days.

The tour skirted them around some of the bigger cities, likely by design from the organizers to bring tourism to the smaller towns. If they had a long drive day, they'd stay in one place for two nights. If it was a short drive, they left the next day.

The back of the bus was filling up with wine.

Not that there was any lack of drinking it.

The Golden Girls often initiated a party once they stopped, and the guys from San Francisco were always up for that.

"How are their liver lights not blinking yet?" Nicole asked Gio one evening as they gathered outside, waiting for Emma to join them.

Jean and Diane were already loud as ever, and whatever Chris was saying had all of them laughing.

"My body is craving exercise and water," Gio confided in her.

"Emma and I were just saying that. We're going to take a hike tomorrow. Wanna come?"

They were staying in what was best described as a castle. One now used for tourists, but it sat on a hill, surrounded by vineyards . . . of course. With a river nearby. Their host said there were trails to hike by the river when they'd arrived earlier that day.

"That would be great." Gio looked behind Nicole. "Emma still hasn't heard from her dad's lawyers, has she?"

"No. Her dad's an ass. I wouldn't be surprised if he waited two days before even requesting his lawyer send the information on. And we all know lawyers don't hustle for anyone."

"It's weighing on her. She's constantly checking her phone."

"I keep telling her to let it go but Emma doesn't roll like that."

He noticed. "If there is anything I can do, let me know."

Nicole laughed. "Oh, there's something you can do."

Gio tilted his head to the side. "Which is?"

Nicole covered her face with one hand, laughed harder. "Never mind. Forget I said that."

He was missing the joke.

"Nicole—"

"All I'm going to say is this, and don't you dare repeat it. I haven't seen Emma this relaxed around a man she was interested in since I've known her."

Gio knew Emma was on the same page, but to hear Nicole voice it stroked his ego a whole lot more than he expected.

Nicole continued, "My God, she hasn't been on a date in forever."

"She's a beautiful woman. I find that hard to believe."

"You've met her. She has a linear focus. One thing at a time. And work has kept her channeling the corporate world for too long. She needs someone to shake that up." Nicole pressed a finger to Gio's chest. "And you might be the right guy for the job."

He liked the thought of rattling Emma's world.

In fact, he'd thought of nothing else since setting eyes on her.

Before he could comment, Gio's phone buzzed in his back pocket. He looked at the screen, saw his mother's face. "I need to take this."

He answered her video call. "Ciao, pronto, Mama."

"Did I call at a bad time?"

"Not at all. How is everyone? How are you?"

"We're well. Sunday dinner isn't the same without you. You're still coming home to us, right?"

Nicole must have heard part of the conversation because she smiled at him and took a few steps away.

"It's a vacation, Mama."

"Good, good. Listen, Sergio has been sick."

Sergio was the head bartender and had been with them for as long as Gio could remember.

"Nothing serious, I hope."

"He's on the mend, just can't work. You know."

"Send my love."

"I will. Have you found any wine you love there? Something for our top customers."

By *top*, he knew that meant a midrange wine to his mother. They had to make a profit, and while their restaurant did very well, they didn't cater to the crowd that spent two hundred dollars on a bottle of wine.

"I didn't know I was looking."

"Well, look. We want something special when you come home. Giovanni's favorites from Tuscany. Brooke has a whole campaign figured out."

Brooke was a marketing expert. As Gio thought about it, the hook sounded good to his ears. "I like it. I've already purchased a couple of cases, but they're for my own collection. I doubt anything will arrive before I'm home, but if it does, wait for me."

His mother smiled.

From outside of the frame, Gio heard his sister's voice. "Is that Gio?"

"All the way in Italy."

Chloe popped in front of the camera. "How is my favorite pain in the ass?"

He laughed. "Isn't that my line?"

"Not after last year. You look good. Isn't it happy hour there? Shouldn't you be drinking?"

"I'm a little burnt out, to tell the truth." It was good to see his family. Even through a screen.

Chloe's smile fell into a fake frown. "Are you feeling okay? Giovanni D'Angelo, burnt out on wine? Say it isn't so."

"Every day . . . all day." Gio felt the weight of someone looking his way and he realized he was blocking Emma's path as she was attempting to skirt by without interrupting him. He started to move and then changed his mind.

"Emma?" He waved her over.

She hesitated.

"C'mere."

"Emma? Who is Emma?" Chloe's sultry voice dropped an octave.

"Be nice."

Emma moved to his side. "I don't want to interrupt."

"Not at all." He turned the phone enough to get Emma in the frame. "Emma, this is my sister, Chloe."

"Oh . . . oh!" Emma sounded surprised. "Hi, Chloe."

"Hello. Can I assume you're on the tour, too?"

"I am. We're all having a wonderful time." Emma slid a glance Gio's way.

"Emma lives in Temecula," he said.

"That's crazy. What are the odds?"

"Who are you talking to?" Gio's mother asked.

Chloe angled the phone to show his mother again. "Gio was introducing me to a friend of his. Emma, was it?"

"Yes. Yes." Emma squirmed.

"Mama, this is Emma. Emma, my mother, Mari."

"Aren't you simply beautiful."

The nervous laugh that escaped Emma, coupled with the rush of color to her cheeks, made everything about the call worthwhile.

"Did I hear Giovanni say you're from Temecula?"

"Yes, ma'am."

Chloe pushed into the frame. "You'll have to come to Little Italy."

"I-I'd like that." Emma nudged Gio's side.

"We should probably—" As he tried to end the call, Franny ran into the room.

"Zio Gio, Zio Gio!"

He glanced at Emma. "*Zio* means uncle."

"Good Lord," Emma whispered under her breath.

"Hi, Franny."

Franny's huge smile pushed in front of his mother and sister. "When are you coming home?" she asked, immediately followed by "Who are you?"

"I'll be back before you know it. And this is Emma."

Franny paused, narrowed her eyes. "Are you Gio's girlfriend?"

Emma busted out a laugh.

Chloe chided Franny. "You'll have to forgive my niece. She's the youngest and gets away with everything."

"We should let you get on with your day," Mari said for all of them on the California side of the line.

"Love you all. Ciao, ciao." Gio blew them a kiss.

"Lovely meeting you, Emma. We hope to see you in person when you're back," Chloe said.

Franny waved.

"Safe travels, *ragazzi*," his mother added. "Ciao."

Another chorus of *ciao*s and Gio disconnected the call.

Emma turned to face him, hands crossed over her chest. "Girlfriend?"

"She's a kid. Jumps to conclusions."

"Mighty big leap."

He shrugged, put his phone in his back pocket. "Now you have faces to put with the names."

"I already saw their pictures."

"Voices, then. As my mother always warns, my family is loud. Loveable, but loud."

Emma lost some of her defensiveness. "They seem very nice."

"Wait until you meet them in person." As he spoke, Gio put a hand on Emma's back and directed her toward the Golden Girls party.

"Who said that was going to happen?" Emma asked as her gaze slid to his arm.

"It will, *bella*. It will."

CHAPTER FIFTEEN

"So much for a quiet hike to the river," Emma said close to Nicole's ear.

Rob, Pierre, and Chris gathered next to Gio. The four of them divided up waters and snacks into two backpacks. Pierre and Gio took first shift carrying the provisions.

Even though Emma and Nicole volunteered to wear the packs, they were given a pass based on being the owner of a uterus.

Which in this case, Emma was willing to let slide. She was capable and she offered. What more was there to do?

"If you wanted to sneak off with Gio, I can make that happen," Nicole teased.

"Stop."

Only Nicole wasn't about to stop. Not if the last few days were any indication.

From moving seats on the bus to force Emma to sit next to Gio to the constant evening commentary of every time Nicole spotted Gio checking Emma out. Then the night-before meeting of the family . . . even on a phone call, Nicole was gunning for the position of matchmaker.

And Emma wasn't complaining all that hard. The more time she spent with Giovanni, the more she wanted to spend with the man.

"You ladies ready?" Rob called out.

"Waiting on you," Emma said.

The six of them started down the driveway, somewhat grouped together. Each had a bottle of water in their hands, with more in the packs should they need them.

Emma had pulled her hair back into a thick ponytail. She wore one of her now-famous street vendor T-shirts and a pair of shorts. The sneakers she had weren't ideal for hiking, but they'd have to do.

"Did anyone ask which direction we should go?" Nicole asked.

"Rob and I spoke with the owners before you guys came down," Gio told her. "Take the driveway to the main road, then a left, and almost immediately there's a cut in the clearing that the locals use to get down to the river."

"They said some of the walk is steep, so getting back up will take longer," Rob added.

Emma reached her hands over her head. "It just feels good to get outside and stretch."

"Do you hike a lot at home?" Gio asked her.

"Not as much as I'd like. But I have a feeling that's going to change." Living in a home on property instead of a condo was bound to give her more opportunities for outside exercise.

"What's driving the change?" Rob asked.

"I'm, ah . . . moving into a house. I've been living in a condominium since I left home for college. There's plenty of open space to stretch my legs where I'm going," Emma said.

"Sounds amazing. Rob and I have talked about moving out of the city at some point," Pierre told them.

"Not me," Chris said. "I love city life. I don't mind getting out with nature, but if we come across a snake or anything that has more than two legs and is bigger than my fist, I'll be the first one back to the castle."

"What about you, Gio? Does San Diego offer long hikes?" Nicole asked.

"Not especially. You have to get out of the city. Balboa Park has plenty of space, but I'd be lying if I said I spent a lot of time there. I get down to the water a bit. My brother-in-law has a boat. But it's more for business than pleasure, but we go out on it." Gio glanced at Emma. "Hiking vineyards is more my speed."

"I don't know if flat fields are considered hiking," she said.

"More than cement sidewalks and asphalt roads."

He had a point.

"I'm all about the treadmill," Nicole announced.

"You don't even like that," Emma reminded her.

"I said I was *about* it. I never said I *enjoyed* it."

They made it to the end of the long drive and took a left.

"Is that it?" Rob asked, pointing to a small clearing on the opposite side of the road.

"I think so," Gio said.

Chris held back by Emma and Nicole. "You guys go ahead and hit the cobwebs first."

The narrow trail allowed a single-file line.

Rob and Pierre went first, then Nicole and Chris . . . and Gio took up the place right behind Emma.

The dense brush offered slightly cooler temperatures than the main road. Even though it was still morning, Italy was showing off a heat index that would rival Temecula's. The difference, however, was in the foliage. Tuscany was not a desert that, when you added water, produced farmland. The average rainfall was greater than anything in inland California.

Their line spread out as they all carefully walked along the trail, mindful of where they put their feet.

"Are there snakes here?" Chris asked.

"I'm sure there are," Nicole said with a laugh. "But since you're in the middle of the line, we'll all step on them first."

"Ewww."

Emma found herself laughing. "Don't worry, Chris. Nicole will protect you."

Nicole lifted a hand in the air. "I got ya."

Up ahead, Rob and Pierre were hiking with speed. Out of earshot, but not out of sight.

The trail started a slow descent, and with that, zigzagged around trees.

"How long did they say it was to get to the river?" Emma asked Gio, who was a few feet behind her.

"Less than an hour."

"Hey, Gio . . . do you have a first-aid kit in that backpack?" Chris asked.

"Have a blister already?" Nicole teased.

"No. Just in case."

"Only food and water," Gio told him.

Emma slowed her pace to let Chris and Nicole get ahead. The trail opened up slightly, giving Emma and Gio the opportunity to walk side by side.

"I'm guessing Chris isn't all that outdoorsy," Emma said.

"It's not supposed to be a strenuous hike. He'll be fine."

"Unless our hosts hike Fiji for fun and they told you that based on their own experience."

"Good point." Gio looked down at their feet. "Are you slipping around in those shoes?"

"So far, so good."

"I never asked, but did you find anything in the suitcase that said who the owner is?" Gio asked.

"I found a card, but it wasn't in English."

"If it's Italian, I—"

"Nope. Not Italian. Nicole thought it was Thai, but I think it might be Indonesian. Either way, the suitcase belongs to a short, likely Asian, woman. We're guessing middle-aged."

"And you could tell that . . . how?"

"Wraps, cover-ups. Flat shoes and nothing flashy. Granny panties and bras that look like they should have been thrown away years ago."

"Are you saying younger women don't have old bras and underwear that are more than dental floss?"

She laughed. "Yeah . . . we have 'em, but we don't take them on vacation."

"I never thought of that."

Emma could see on his face that women in granny panties was a foreign concept. Yeah, chances were he'd heard of them but likely never seen them. "It's a guess. Not that I'll ever know for sure. I'll give the bag to the airport and hope they find the owner."

Up ahead, Chris and Nicole were talking to each other, and Rob and Pierre were nearly out of sight.

Gio's words repeated . . . rather slowly, in her head. "Dental floss?"

He laughed. "Thong panties."

"Yeah, I understood what you meant . . . but dental floss?"

He shrugged. "I don't get it. Underwear with a string up the ass? I'm not sure what a thong is supposed to accomplish. At least as underwear."

The first time she'd ever put them on she thought the same thing. Then society told her panty lines were not something men wanted to see . . . and gee . . . her friends all wore thongs. "I think it was designed for men to admire more than function."

"I'd be lying if I didn't say they were admirable but . . . they can't be comfortable."

They're not. "Most women's clothing isn't comfortable," she said. "Bras, for example. Yeah, we wear them all the time but it's the first thing to come off after we get home from work."

"High heels?" Gio asked.

"Exactly. Those come off in the car as we're leaving work. I always have a pair of flip-flops in the trunk of my car. Men have it made. The most they have to do is wear a tie once in a while. Wearing suits is limited to the corporate world."

"I own two and I can't tell you the last time I put one on. I rented a tux for my brother's and sister's weddings."

Emma thought about her wardrobe and realized she wouldn't have to dress nearly as well as she worked to get her winery up and running.

"Men definitely have it easier."

"I won't argue that," Gio said.

They walked for a few minutes in relative silence.

Emma couldn't help but wonder where Giovanni's concern for a woman's comfort came from.

Was it the fact that he had a sister? Had there been an ex-girlfriend he'd had who enlightened him on the plight of women?

The thought prompted her next question. "Why are you single?"

"W-what?"

"Single. Unattached. Not divorced, not married. Why?"

Gio looked at her, and then did a good job of investigating the terrain surrounding them.

She chuckled. "I can assume you're a player."

"That's a bit harsh," he replied.

"Is it? You're a good-looking man. I see the women looking at you."

"Men look at you, too."

"We're not talking about me. Have you ever been engaged?"

"No," he was quick to answer.

"Close?"

Gio shook his head.

Emma lifted her hand in the air. "Ah! Which means you're a player."

"I am not!" He paused, looked around. "The women in my life have wanted to be there."

Yeah . . . but that wasn't the whole story. "Name three."

"What?"

"Three. Give me three names of the women you've had relationships with that stand out."

Gio lifted both hands to his face, swiped them down. "Shelly."

"Who was Shelly?"

"High school. Senior year. I thought she was the one . . . she wasn't."

High school . . . young love. Emma pushed. "Why? You . . . or her?"

"Her," he replied. His eyes closed tight, then opened again. "Me. Both of us. We were kids."

Emma shrugged. "Fine, that's a pass. Give me another name."

He blew out a breath. "Ah . . . Erika. She worked at the restaurant."

"Ohh . . . employee relationship. That couldn't have ended well."

He winced. "It didn't. She claimed she was fired unjustly. Fact was she didn't show up for her shifts when we broke up. Instead of quitting, she waited to get fired to collect unemployment. Then threatened to take us to court. It didn't happen, but I never dated an employee again."

"You probably knew that going in," Emma said.

"I did but she was . . ."

"Yes?"

"Attractive, and I was stupid."

"Points to you for your honesty. But Erika stood out because of the mess left behind, not because there were deep feelings." Emma had slowed her pace and kept her head tilted to the side to catch everything Gio was saying.

"I didn't fall for her, if that's what you're asking."

"That's exactly what I'm asking. Is there a third name? Someone who meant something more than their attractiveness?"

Gio shook his head. "No, no . . . what about you? I know the name Kyle. Obviously, the fact that you're divorced suggests that was significant. What happened before him? What made you think Kyle was forever?"

Emma held on to a trunk of a tree to help her descent on the trail. "That's easy. Kyle was what was expected. He knew wine . . . he worked for my father and was therefore preapproved."

"That's all well and good, but what made *you* think he was worthy?"

Emma sucked in a long, agonizing breath. "He told me he was."

Gio laughed. "You don't strike me as someone who has to be told anything."

"I'm not." She walked a few more yards before adding, "I used to be."

She heard Gio sigh. He was right behind her now that the path had narrowed. "That's hard to envision."

"I . . . I wanted my father's approval, acceptance, so much so that I let myself believe that Kyle was a perfect fit. Between him and my father . . . I'm not proud, Gio. But I'm also no longer that young girl who lets someone think for her." As Emma explained herself, she felt the power of her words. Kyle had been a mistake. One she freely made with her father's approval. Her ending of that relationship was her first rebellion.

Her only rebellion.

For the past several years she'd been trying to rebuild the bridge between her and her father that she'd severed with her divorce. Yet that bridge was still failing.

"Kyle was a mistake. We've all made them. But was there someone before him? After him?" Gio asked.

"I had high school boyfriends."

"Plural."

Emma stopped walking, shot a look over her shoulder. "You're judging?"

"No! No . . . I would never."

She resumed walking. "High school . . . college. All hormones. I thought I fell in love every other month. Fell out just as fast."

Gio groaned. "Some would call that lust."

"Maybe it's a double standard. What men call lust, women justify as love when they're young. I convinced myself that I loved them all and trusted none of them. They all knew my father. Or at least his influence."

"How can you love someone without trust?"

Emma walked a few more feet, pondering his question. "You can't. Love is what young women convince themselves they're in so that they take the next step. That could be a first kiss, second base . . ." She smiled over her shoulder. "A home run. In the end, that's not the case. To be honest, I'm not convinced that love is real."

"How can you say that?"

"I'm serious. Is love my parents? God, I hope not. That's depressing as all hell. They married, had kids . . . and live completely separate lives. Kyle and I getting married appeared to be love. We looked the part in the beginning, but at the end of the day we couldn't find a TV show we both liked. A simple explanation of our differences, I know, but detailed enough for those that have been there to understand."

"Isn't love a feeling?" Gio asked.

"Yes but—"

"No. Everything you just described was a situation. An excuse to have sex . . . to get married . . . to stay married. You didn't dive into a feeling other than giving it a label of *love*. Love has to start somewhere."

"I suppose," Emma said.

"Everything starts as an attraction. Could be physical . . . intellectual or both. Like you and I."

Emma stubbed her foot on a rock, found herself off-balance. After a two-step dance, she found her footing. "Excuse me?"

"Our attraction," Gio said without apology.

Her throat felt dry. "Who said I'm attracted?"

One minute she was in front of Gio, the next he'd doubled his step and stood in front of her, stopping her in her steps. The backpack he'd had dangling from one shoulder fell to the ground.

Emma sucked in a breath.

His eyes found hers, his lips fell into a thin line.

She took a step back and then stopped herself.

Gio lifted his hand and placed it on a tree that stood directly behind her. "Are you suggesting that I'm completely wrong about the chemistry between the two of us?"

She looked at his lips, his eyes. "Physical."

"I'm not convinced that's all it is."

Emma lifted her chin.

"The risk is in the exploration." He leaned closer.

Somewhere on the trail in front of them their party was disappearing from sight. Not that Emma felt threatened by Gio's sudden move to keep her from walking away. Quite the opposite. His eyes drew her in, put heat deep in the pit of her stomach that started to spread.

"Isn't . . . isn't that what we're doing?" she asked. "Exploring through conversation?"

He leaned a little closer. "Yeah. We're doing that. You're smart as all hell. Feisty . . ." He reached for a strand of her hair that had fallen out of her ponytail and brushed it aside. The slight brush of the back of his fingers against her skin sent shock waves up her spine. "Unapologetic."

Emma swallowed . . . hard.

His lips were so very close to hers.

She felt certain he was inching in to kiss her. Unable to stop herself, she licked her bottom lip.

Gio noticed the move, his eyes dilated.

He moved closer still . . . his voice a whisper in her ear. "Your skin looks soft enough to taste, *cara*. Your lips . . . even when you're angry, I want to feel them against mine." Gio brushed his lips against the lobe of her ear, his breath warm against her skin.

Emma leaned into him slightly . . . her eyes fluttered shut.

Gio trailed his fingers down the side of her neck, and she tilted her head as if he were a vampire and she wanted him to taste her.

Was that him chuckling?

Emma wasn't sure and wasn't about to ask.

He pressed his lips to the side of her neck, and she felt her knees wanting to buckle from under her.

He was good.

Holy hell, when was the last time anyone turned on the fire in her body the way Giovanni did before a first kiss?

"Do you want to explore, *bella*?" His teeth grazed the side of her ear.

She opened her eyes, found Gio staring at her.

Emma offered a single nod.

"Me too."

His words were out, and his lips pressed against hers.

Emma's heart leapt in her chest with the contact.

Gio's open-mouth kiss made her want to drink him in. He kissed her hard, tilted his head where she had to follow . . . wanted to follow. His tongue was not timid, but smooth and so incredibly delicious.

Emma felt the tree at her back as Gio leaned in, their bodies touched from knees to tongues. The pressure of his body against hers would stay in her dreams long after this kiss was over, she knew that . . . felt it deep in her core.

So many sensations swept over her.

The fresh air and smell of something fragrant blooming nearby. The touch of Gio's hands as they ran up the sides of her body, stroking and bringing continuous waves of shivering sensations. Butterflies, if you could call the wings fluttering in her belly that, pulsed with every brush of his tongue against hers.

This was worth exploring.

So worth the risk.

Emma's breath felt raspy, her chest rising and falling against his.

While she wanted to touch more, explore deeper . . . they were standing on a trail with their friends up ahead by a few yards . . . or maybe a quarter mile by now.

Gio brought both his hands to her face and slowly eased back.

They stared at each other, breath mingling. "That was worth the wait," he whispered.

She leaned forward, caught his lower lip between her teeth, briefly.

Gio moaned, his eyes rolled back. "Damn, Emma."

She liked seeing him lose his shit, she decided.

He always appeared in control, but biting lips dissolved that in a second.

His eyes opened, lingered on her lips. "One more."

This time there was more fire. Emma let her hands wrap around him and fall past his waistline and over his ass.

There was no mistaking his arousal as his frame molded into hers, their bodies touching as much as they could and still be clothed.

Only when she tilted her hips did Gio pull back a second time. "The things I want to do to you right now."

She smiled. "Not the best place."

"You deserve cool sheets and champagne."

Emma looked over his shoulder. "Do you think they'll miss us?"

Gio smiled, leaned his forehead against hers. "Yes."

"Damn."

He untangled his body from hers but kept a hand on her hip. "We should catch up with them before they come looking."

"Probably a good idea."

Gio reached up, plucked a leaf from her hair. "Wow."

"Yeah. I agree."

He took her hand in his, grabbed the backpack, and turned toward the trail. "We're doing that again."

"That's the best idea I've heard from you since we met."

Gio squeezed her palm and didn't let go.

CHAPTER SIXTEEN

He was trembling.

There were kisses . . . and then there was that.

Emma was pure fire and response. He'd kept his distance until now. And Gio knew, as he kept her hand in his, even when the others came into view, that he wasn't letting go. This stumble into passion should have been a crash. But that cat-and-mouse game was over.

"There you two are," Nicole called from the edge of the river. "We were about to head back to find you."

Emma stood close to his side. "We were, ah . . ."

Chris looked between them. "Ah-huh . . . sure you were."

Pierre laughed. "Leave them alone."

Nicole walked over to Emma, made a motion to her own lip. "You have a little . . ."

Emma swiped at her lips. "What?"

Nicole chuckled. "Nothing." Her eyes met Gio's. "About time."

"We weren't gone that long," Gio teased.

Chris hummed and looked away.

"There's a clearing on the other side of the river," Rob said, pointing across the water.

"And how do you suggest we get over there?" Gio asked. The flow wasn't all that fast, nor was the river very deep, but there wasn't a bridge.

"I say we walk downstream and see if there is a way to cross."

Gio shifted the backpack higher on his shoulder. "I'm game."

Emma smiled. "Let's go."

Gio took up his position behind Emma, reluctantly letting her hand go as they took a single-file line along the riverbank. He found himself staring at her ass and forced his eyes away.

"Are there any waterways near your new place?" he asked.

"I honestly don't know. I didn't get a good look at the place before this trip."

"Are you excited to get back?"

"I am, but . . . it's going to be a lot of work. Not that I'm afraid of hard work. It just isn't something I thought I'd be doing this year."

He stepped over a log, stayed close. "I have faith in you."

"You hardly know me."

"I'm doing everything I can to fix that."

She glanced over her shoulder, looked him up and down.

"C'mon, you two. Don't fall behind again," Nicole yelled.

They didn't find a shallow enough spot on the river to cross without going for a swim. If anything, the current was getting faster, the water deeper. Instead, they made do with an open patch close to some fallen trees that gave them all a place to sit.

Gio and Rob broke out the food and the six of them talked about their travels.

"Big cities," Chris told them. "Manhattan, Chicago, Miami. All up and down the West Coast."

"Is this your first trip to Europe?" Nicole asked.

"Yes. But not my last, this has been one of the best experiences of my life."

"I was worried the bus rides would be awful," Rob admitted.

"They haven't been that bad," Emma said. "I think stopping for alcohol every few hours helps."

"And the bathroom breaks. Don't forget Jean's bladder," Gio reminded them.

"Are they not the biggest kick in the pants?" Chris asked. "I hope I'm that active when I'm old."

"I've heard stories about The Villages in Florida," Rob said.

"What's to tell? It's just a retirement community with golf courses, right?" Emma asked.

"All that, yes. But there is a serious swinger community and more STDs being passed around than you see at band camp."

Gio frowned. "It can't be that bad."

Chris put his hand in the air. "I asked Jean about it. She said something about the loofahs hanging from the mirrors on the golf carts. Apparently, that's how the swingers identify other swingers. Complete with a color code so you know just how into the swinger scene they are."

"Go, Granny!" Nicole said, laughing.

Gio leaned closer to Emma. "Remind me never to let my mother move to Florida."

Emma shrugged. "I think my mother should."

Nicole laughed. "I think so, too. Are there vineyards in Florida? Maybe your dad can buy some vines down there."

"There are wineries everywhere. Even in Florida," Gio told her.

"Wait, your dad owns a vineyard?" Rob asked.

Oh shit . . . that's right, Emma hadn't told the others about R&R.

She looked between Nicole and Rob, then the others. "Yeah," she said on a sigh. "My father is Robert Rutledge. R&R Wineries."

"Oh, man! That's crazy," Chris said.

Rob looked at Pierre. "I'm pretty sure we have a bottle of their cabernet in our wine fridge at home."

"That's huge. Why didn't you say anything?" Chris asked.

Emma shrugged, looked at Gio.

Nicole answered the question faster than Emma could form the words.

"Because people treat Emma differently when they hear she comes from money."

"Is that true, *cara*?" Gio asked.

"I told you about Kyle."

Gio reached over and took her hand in his.

"People suck," Nicole exclaimed.

"Don't worry, Emma, we'll keep making you load up the bus even if we know who you are," Chris said.

"That's Gio's job," Emma said.

"Oh, that's right." They all laughed.

"Wait, that means you were hustled, Gio." Rob tossed a fallen twig from the ground in Gio's direction.

"Hustled?"

"Yeah. Clearly Emma knew more about wine than she let on before your wine taste-off last week."

Gio smiled as he drew back and looked Emma's way. "It's okay. I liked the game."

"You're too easy, D'Angelo," she said.

He winked.

~

"What happened?"

Nicole was on Emma the second they closed the door to their room.

The walk up from the river was much more exhausting than the walk down. The whole way Emma envisioned Gio, as he walked behind, asking himself if she wore a thong.

A glance over her shoulder and she noticed the man blush, his eyes darting away from her ass.

For hours Emma hadn't thought about the missing email from her father . . . or his lawyers. She hadn't wondered how she was going to show her father up with the plot of land, or even if the whole thing was going to fall through.

No. All Emma had thought of was how soon she could find herself alone with Giovanni without worry of interruption.

They'd parted in the hall with the promise to meet by the villa's pool.

"Well?" Nicole stood impatiently, staring Emma down.

"He finally made a move."

"Hahaha . . . how big of a move?"

Emma flopped her butt on her bed. "I can honestly say I've never been kissed quite like that."

Nicole squealed.

"Nicole, he is . . . I don't know—"

"Don't know what? He's hot. He's Italian. He's single. And he's here and into you! What don't you know?" Nicole took up a space across from her on the bed.

"I know that part. Giovanni kisses in a way I forget my name."

Nicole commenced squealing once again.

Emma tossed a pillow at her friend. "Stop. He asks me about my life . . . my family, what made Kyle and I get married. Do you know the last time that happened?"

Nicole shrugged.

"Never. What if Gio knows this, somehow, and he's using this to fake this attraction?" Emma asked.

"I feel the need to point out two things here. First . . . no one . . . and I do mean no one, on this trip has suggested that Gio isn't exactly what he professes to be. He is into you, and I think we can both agree he could have had you several days ago but for some crazy-ass reason, the man backed off. Yes?"

Emma nodded.

"The second point I need to state in case your insecurities are tuned in more than my best-friend intention. *So what? So what* if his intention is to enjoy your company on this trip without seeing you when we're home? And for the record, I don't think I'm seeing that . . . but *so what?* Are you enjoying this . . . him?"

"I am."

"Then stop getting in your head." Nicole leaned forward and tapped Emma's forehead with a finger. "You don't have to be in a zillion percent control here. You enjoy Gio . . . he enjoys you. Re-fucking-lax, my friend. With all the mental fuckery that your father has put on you, you deserve this. Take a shower, get in your bikini that you know is going to make Giovanni sweat, and enjoy the attention."

"You're right." Emma pushed herself off the bed. "You're right. Why am I in my head?"

"Atta girl."

For a brief moment, the time it took for her to walk from the room to the shower and close the door, Emma felt like a football player leaving the locker room after a pep talk. Only now, alone with her thoughts, she stared at herself in the mirror and owned her truth.

She was in her head because she really liked Giovanni D'Angelo. And even though common sense suggested she keep herself guarded, her heart was singing its own tune. The man listened when she spoke. He genuinely cared about her story . . . or so it seemed.

Hadn't Kyle done the same thing?

Too many years had passed for her to remember every detail. But when she'd spoken to him about her dealings with her father, all of his suggestions involved the two of them getting married and proving the man wrong.

Gio had said very little about her family or her father. He'd voiced his concerns but not once suggested a single detail on how to deal with the man or the situation her father had put her in.

Emma shook off her thoughts and turned on the water to the shower.

Comparing Giovanni to Kyle was apples to oranges. The men were different in every way. And she'd married Kyle.

Giovanni could be a holiday fling with no tomorrow whatsoever.

And even though the thought of that made bile rise in her throat, she'd take that over nothing.

Get out of your head.

Emma leaned into the memory of Gio's kiss and stepped under the hot spray of water.

Get out of your head.

CHAPTER SEVENTEEN

Somehow Gio was expected to lie by the pool, watch Emma remove her cover-up, and not have a full-on erection for everyone else to see.

He'd seen her in the bikini before, in the store. But out here with the sun shining down and her legs spread out in front of her . . . wow.

Barbara and Carol were sitting on the steps of the pool, huge-brimmed hats covering their faces.

The other hikers were still missing, although they did say they'd be out soon.

Nicole took up the space beside Emma, her lounge chair in the full sun.

Emma spread a pool towel out on her chair before sitting. Her smile, although innocent enough, had a hint of daring behind her eyes.

"Can you bring the umbrella closer?" she asked Gio. "I burn really easy."

"Of course." Only now he had to stand up, semierect.

He cleared his throat and stood while adjusting his swim trunks in hopes of not being too obvious.

Nicole chuckled. "I'm going to grab a drink. Anyone want something?"

"Water is fine with me," Emma told her.

"Same," Gio added as he pulled the heavily weighted umbrella stand close.

"Don't forget the suntan lotion," Nicole said.

"Yes, Mom!" Emma teased.

"I wasn't talking to you."

Gio looked up.

"She burns and can't reach her back, lover boy." Nicole bounced away from where they parked themselves in search of drinks.

"Ignore her," Emma said once Nicole was gone.

"Lover boy?"

"She comes up with this stuff on her own."

Gio pushed his chair a little closer to Emma's to catch some of her shade. "I have a sister. I know all too well how much she and her girlfriends talk."

She looked his way, pushed her sunglasses a little lower on the bridge of her nose so he could see her eyes. "In that case . . ." Emma reached for the sunscreen and handed it to him.

He did not have to be asked twice. He made a twisting motion with his index finger for her to turn around.

Instead of just presenting him with her back, she removed the glasses and lowered the lounge chair so she could lie flat on her stomach.

Gio's eyes traced the path his hands would soon follow. Her delicate neck and slender back only covered by the thin strips of material that made up her bikini top. The way her ass tilted up and gave a ski-slope appearance before her bikini bottom covered her creamy skin.

He blew out a breath and moved to her side.

With a nudge of his hand, he encouraged her to shift over a little so he could sit on her chair with her.

"You do realize this is going to be torture," he said softly as he filled his palm with lotion.

"Where is the fun if it wasn't?"

He liked the playful side, even if it was at his expense.

Rubbing the lotion between his hands, he placed them on her back.

Emma reached for her hair and pulled it away from her shoulders.

She was soft, and still cool to the touch.

And damn, his hands were dark against her skin.

Gio rubbed in the lotion with light massaging strokes. Over her shoulders and up around her neck. The delicate spot where the back of her arms and shoulders met. He pushed around the bikini and trailed his fingers along her rib cage, teasing the edges of her breasts that pushed away from the material of her swimsuit.

The only indication that Gio received that she noticed where his hands were came in the way she shifted her hips, just a tinge.

With his thumbs he massaged the small of her back, added a little more lotion, and rounded her hips. "Mind if I pull this down a little? You wouldn't want a red line right here."

"Ahh hum," she murmured.

The woman liked to be touched.

And he was happy to oblige.

His fingertips met the cool edge of her ass.

She squirmed again.

He looked at her face, her chin resting on the lounge chair, her eyes closed. Rose-colored lips were slightly parted and he could see how her breathing had picked up the pace.

Instead of stopping at her lower back, he picked up the lotion and drizzled it on the back of her thighs.

She buckled. "That's cold."

He leaned forward, his voice a whisper. "I'll warm it up."

Gio scooted down the lounge chair, placed both hands on her legs, and with long, even strokes, kneaded the lotion into her skin. His thumbs traced the inside of her bikini.

Damn if she didn't rear up ever so slightly.

He was rock hard now. As long as he didn't have to stand up, he'd be fine.

Gio took a quick glance over his shoulder to see if they were being watched.

The Golden Girls were at the far side of the pool, chatting it up.

Nicole wasn't in sight, and no one else had come out.

He twisted enough to get the lotion down the back of her knees, her calves . . . and slowly moved back up. The softest skin sat on the inside of her thighs.

She was breathing hard now.

Unable to stop himself, Gio ran his index finger on the outside of her bikini dangerously close to where he wanted nothing more than to bury his tongue.

Emma's fingers fisted and she let out a tiny moan.

Gio closed his eyes and gave her bottom a little squeeze before removing his hands altogether.

"That should do it."

Her eyelids fluttered open, heat blared from her gaze. "That was almost indecent."

Gio's eyes drifted to his lap. "Which is why I'm going to sit right here for a few minutes."

She twisted in the seat and pulled the back of the chair into a sitting position.

Emma reached across his body for the lotion, when she did, one of her hands rested high on his thigh.

Their eyes locked, her smile wicked.

Before she could move away, he grasped her hand and inched it just high enough so he could feel the heat of her hand against his cock.

"If you want that to simmer down, you should probably give my hand back," she whispered.

A growl, low and deep, escaped his throat and he let her go.

The minx let it linger before pulling away.

"Where is Nicole with that ice water?" he asked.

~

The single most erotic experience in her life, and it happened in broad daylight, beside a pool filled with old women.

Giovanni moved back to his own chair as she finished covering her skin with lotion.

"Do you want me to do your back?" she asked.

"More than you know, *cara*. When we're alone."

And why weren't they alone right now?

Nicole walked up from behind them, three plastic cups pushed together in her hands. "Here you go."

Emma reached quickly to help her and then handed one of the ice waters to Gio.

He immediately rested it in his lap.

She tried not to laugh and bit her lip.

"You're not helping," Gio said in a hoarse whisper.

She giggled.

"Did I miss something?" Nicole asked.

Gio said yes and Emma said no.

"When you two figure it out, you let me know."

"Hey! Hey!" Chris waved a hand in the air. "The party can start."

The Golden Girls heard his call and cheered.

Rob and Pierre followed behind. They had a bucket of beers.

"We wanted to switch it up," Pierre said.

The three of them pulled lounge chairs closer.

Chris handed Gio a beverage.

"Emma?" he asked, a beer in his hand.

She shrugged. "Sure."

"Nicole?"

"I'll stick with my sangria."

Rob twisted around a couple of times. "We need music." He ran off to find some.

"Has anyone seen Kimmy and Weston?" Nicole asked.

"I heard they took a hike on their own."

Electric dance music filled the speakers surrounding the pool.

Emma reached for the bottle opener that was being passed around.

"We have wine over here if anyone wants some," Carol called from where the older women were perched.

"We're going with hops and barley, Ms. Carol."

"If you change your mind . . ."

"Do they ever sober up?" Nicole asked.

"Don't judge . . . that's you in fifty years," Emma told her.

"I should start collecting hats now."

Emma felt heat on the side of her face and turned to find the cause. Giovanni stared, a smile on his face.

"I'm thinking it's time for a swim." He nodded toward the pool, lifted an eyebrow.

She set her beer down. "Sure."

Leaving her sunglasses behind, Emma walked with him to the edge of the pool.

They both stared into the deep end.

"Do you jump in or ease in?" she asked.

"Today?" Gio looked down at himself, didn't answer the question, and jumped.

She laughed, despite the fact that his splash drenched half of her body.

He came up for air, shaking his head as he treaded water.

Emma sat on the edge of the pool and put her feet in the water. "Feel better?" she asked.

"Working on it." He swam over and placed a hand on the side of the pool next to her. "Are you getting in or do I have to make you wet from here?" he asked as he lightly splashed water onto her legs.

Unable to help herself, she said, "You already made me wet before getting near the water."

Gio's eyes instantly moved to her waist and then rapidly shut. "You're killing me, *bella*."

She scooted forward and reached for his hand.

The water instantly cooled her heated skin as she submerged into the pool up to her neck.

"That's better."

Gio released her hand and placed his on her waist.

They both kicked their feet just enough to stay afloat, neither of them speaking.

"I want to say something witty or ask more questions about your life . . ." Gio's eyes stayed on her lips.

"Right?" Except the get-to-know-you part of what they were doing here was dialed into the physical. She felt it.

Gio expressed it. "How soon can I get you out of this swimming pool and into my room?"

She placed a hand on his chest. "I'm not sure why we even came out here."

He looked over her shoulder to their group. "They're going to notice."

"I don't care."

His hand squeezed before letting go. "Give me a few minutes' head start."

Emma stretched out an arm and pushed away from the side of the pool, swimming to the other side.

Gio dunked his head one more time and swam to the side steps in the deep end and pulled himself out.

A few strides and he grabbed his towel on his chair and rubbed it over his face. If he said something to Nicole or the others, Emma couldn't tell. He walked away and toward the villa.

She waited until he was out of sight and followed his actions.

Nicole eyed her as she walked closer. "That was a quick swim."

"Sometimes that's all you need." Emma pulled her towel over her body, wrapped it around her waist.

"Where did Gio go?"

Emma looked over her shoulder, shrugged. "I don't know. I'll go check on him."

Nicole let out a laugh. "Real smooth, Em."

"Must have been something I said." Emma reached for her beer and then grabbed Gio's as well.

She knew the others watched as she left.

The air-conditioning inside the villa slapped her damp skin as she padded barefoot down the hall and toward Gio's room.

It had been a while since she'd been with anyone, and outside of college, she'd not been as bold as she was in pursuit of Giovanni.

It was liberating.

At Gio's door, she knocked using the tip of one of the beer bottles.

He opened the door, his smile ear to ear.

"You forgot your beer."

He pulled her arm until she was inside and let the door shut behind her.

Gio removed both beers from her hands, set them aside, and was back in front of her in three steps.

He'd changed into a dry pair of shorts, while she was still wet under the pool towel.

She hesitated, her breathing sped up, showing her nerves . . . or was that excitement?

They both moved at the same time, their lips crashed together, almost painfully.

Her lips were open, matching his. Indecent kisses that finally felt possible now that they were alone.

Her hands fell onto his chest, his wrapped around her and sucked her in.

Already her head buzzed and spun. The fire he'd sparked on the trail ignited like smoldering embers after a forest fire. Hot down in the core and ready for the right gust of oxygen to flame once again.

His lips left hers and found her ear. "I want to take you slowly," he whispered.

Emma wanted to cry with the pain in waiting. "Haven't we been dancing long enough?"

"*Bella.*"

She pulled the towel off her body and let it slide to the floor.

"Aw, fuck." Gio captured her lips again, one hand grasped the globe of her ass and fused their bodies.

He kissed her like his life depended on it. Head to the left, then right . . .

Emma snuck her hand into the back of his shorts, felt his cool, damp skin and gave it a squeeze.

Gio pulled at the fastening of her bikini behind her back. Once it was free, he tossed it to the floor and drew both of her breasts into his hands before dipping his lips to each nipple, one at a time.

Her head fell back. "Yes, please."

He said something in Italian. Something she didn't understand, but it sounded sexy and feral and made her body warm even more.

Standing was becoming increasingly harder to do. Emma backed up while Gio continued to pull her nipples between his teeth. Once at the bed, he let go long enough for them to fall together.

He kissed her again. "Are you still wet, *cara*?"

Wiggling her hips, she opened her legs slightly. "You tell me."

Their eyes met and held as Gio trailed a hand down her stomach, to the edge of her bathing suit, and beneath.

She lost her ability to smile when his fingers swiped past her clit and sunk into the damp folds of her sex. Her back arched and pelvis tilted as he stroked the most intimate part of her body.

Too stunned to do anything but feel, she gripped the bed covering with one hand, and Gio's hip with the other.

"Yes," she managed when he played her body like a bass player in a band.

"So responsive," he said over her lips.

She nodded yes, then no, then yes. She wanted him to continue what he was doing but wanted all of him inside of her more.

Emma lifted her knee enough to feel his erection against her thigh. "All of you, Giovanni. I want all of you."

"Whatever you want, my darling."

One more swipe of his fingers, and Gio lifted his body from hers and reached for the bedside table.

As he opened the condom, Emma lifted her hips and removed her bikini bottoms.

He kicked his shorts free and quickly covered himself.

Emma opened in invitation and reached for him.

"I'm going to make love to you slowly the next time . . . and the time after that."

She nodded. "Okay. But not this time." Emma took his cock in her hand, smiled at the thickness of him.

His eyes rolled back.

"Not this time," he repeated.

He plunged in and she couldn't breathe.

So much, so good.

He held still until she opened her eyes.

Then Gio kissed her and started to move. Together, hips matching the other's pace.

Emma wrapped her legs around his waist until she felt him hitting the perfect spots. "Just like . . . yes, there."

"Yes, *bella* . . . tell me exactly what you need." He shifted a little to the left.

"No. Other side . . ."

He moved to the right.

"There." Heat built in waves. She grabbed his ass, pulled him in faster.

Almost there . . .

Each rise and fall brought her closer, so much closer . . . until every internal muscle in her body contracted and she reached the red-hot tip of the fire's edge and exploded into a million pieces.

She rode the feeling, body pulsing.

Emma dared a look.

Gio smiled down at her, his eyes looked pained. "Better, Emma?"

She gasped and nodded.

He thrust in hard. "Good."

So deliciously good, she thought as Gio took over.

One minute she was on her back, the next he rolled her over until she was straddling him.

The man wanted his release, she could see that on his face.

But this new angle had some serious possibilities.

Emma sat tall and took even more of Gio inside of her. Yes, yes . . . this was very nice.

He reached for her breasts, squeezed them hard, and ran his hands to her hips, where he guided her.

She kept a tight grip on him from the inside, adding to her pleasure and, from the way he moaned . . . his.

Emma felt a little like a thief as a second wave started to crest.

Gio dove harder, deeper, and by the time her body stopped the spasms, he was calling out her name.

CHAPTER EIGHTEEN

"I don't know what I was expecting . . . but it wasn't that."

Gio dared a look to Emma's side of the bed, their legs still tangled together, their breathing slowing to a normal pace. "I'll need you to clarify that as soon as the brain cells return to my head."

She rolled onto her side and rested her hand on his chest.

Gio pressed his fingers against her hand and held it close.

"Why did we wait?" she asked.

"I can't remember."

"Oh, that's right, you swore off sex."

He gave her what he thought of as a "snake eye." "You're the one that came up with that doomed idea. Not me."

"I did. With good reason."

"Which is?"

She raked a fingertip along his chest. "If this had ended up being awful, I'd have to sit on the bus next to you for three weeks, trying to avoid eye contact."

His smile fell. "I never thought of it that way."

"Instead, I wasted nearly two weeks of my life in complete sexual frustration."

"And now, *tesoro*?"

She placed a kiss on his chest. "Do you think Nicole will be offended if I sneak to your room for the rest of this trip?"

He liked the sound of that.

Gio brushed her hair aside. "I'll buy her *all* the wine."

They stared at each other. "I didn't expect you, Giovanni."

"I came here for a wine vacation." And ended up with so much more.

Her smile fell, briefly, and her eyes flickered. "I, ah . . ."

"What, *cara*?"

"I'm usually good about setting boundaries before I ever sleep with someone. So that no one gets hurt."

Gio ignored the tightness in his chest.

"What boundary do you need?"

She eased back slightly. "I'm a strong woman. That puts men off."

"Because they're weak."

There it was . . . the smile he liked so much. "I don't like games. If you're out, you say it. Ghosting is for college kids."

Okay . . . he liked these boundaries.

"I remember what you said about 'the one,' and I'm not her."

Gio felt her stiffen beside him.

She looked away. "I don't want you believing this is the beginning of forever."

When her eyes looked back to him, they'd hardened ever so slightly. Like she was building back up the walls she'd lost as they had made love.

"What is this the start of, then?" he challenged.

She swallowed. "I don't know. I do know that the thought of getting married again makes me physically ill. I don't see that changing."

Gio dissected her words, her body language . . . and the meaning behind both. The fact that she remembered their conversation about his desire to find his future sat squarely in the middle of his head . . . and if he were honest, his heart. Did she want this encounter to stay in Italy? He didn't sense that.

"I still want you to meet my family."

"If meeting your family means you're thinking of the next step—"

He shook his head. "I'm Italian. My family has met many of the women I've dated. If they were more than one night. I don't want my mother's opinion of me to sour."

"Oh." She looked away. "I suppose that's okay, then."

"Good." He didn't have to tell her that their opinion of her . . . and maybe more importantly, him around her, was a barometer of them together. "I have a boundary."

Her eyes widened in surprise. "Okay."

"If you want to be with someone else, you tell me before it happens."

"You mean sleep with."

"Yes. Or feel an emotional attraction to." A foreign feeling inside of him boiled. It had been a long time since he'd asked this of anyone.

"You want us to be exclusive?"

He wanted her and didn't desire the picture of her with someone else slithering around in his head. "I do. I'll extend the same courtesy. If I meet someone and . . ." Even saying the words felt like a betrayal. "When I get home, I'll see my doctor . . . do all the things. I don't need to be out at the clubs looking for tonight. But if you want that for yourself, tell me now."

Emma smiled and nodded ever so slightly. "I'll see my doctor. I have an IUD, so . . ."

"No surprises."

She shook her head. "So, what do we do here? Shake on it?"

He reached for her, pressed her back to the mattress, and leaned over her. "I have a much better way to seal this deal."

～

They'd made love again before jumping into the shower. And while Emma knew they'd both be hearing it from everyone on that bus, she wasn't ready to share Gio quite yet.

She left the shower wearing only a towel while Gio finished washing off. "The key to my room is with Nicole and I don't have any clothes," she said from the space where the sink lived.

"Grab one of my shirts."

She giggled and faked a southern accent. "Why, Gio . . . people will know where I've been if I put on one of your shirts." Emma lifted the edge of his suitcase and found a T-shirt. She gave it a sniff before pulling it over her head.

"People are going to know, *bella*. Regardless of the clothes you wear." She knew that, too.

He turned the water off right as someone knocked on his door.

"Emma?"

It was Nicole.

"I hate to interrupt."

Emma opened it a crack and smiled. "We're between rounds," she teased.

Only Nicole wasn't smiling. "There's a situation."

"What is it?"

"Kimmy and Weston are missing."

"You're kidding."

"Not missing but—"

Giovanni called from the bathroom. "What's going on?" He emerged with a towel wrapped around his waist.

Emma opened the door wider, and Nicole continued. "Claudio had a partial message on his phone. Kimmy was crying, said something about Weston being hurt and they were along the river. He tried calling back, but the phone doesn't ring. It goes straight to voice mail."

Gio placed a hand on Emma's shoulder. "They can't be far. They went for a hike like we did."

Nicole waved a hand in the air. "We're putting together a search party. We have three hours before sunset."

"I'll get dressed," Emma said to Gio.

He gave her a swift kiss before she walked away. "I'll meet you in the foyer."

Emma followed Nicole to their room, hardly aware of the fact that she wore only a T-shirt. "Has anyone called the police to help?"

"No idea. We're not going to wait for anyone to get here to start looking."

In their room, Emma slipped on the clothes she'd worn while hiking earlier and wrapped her hair into a knot on top of her head. She grabbed her cell phone, which had been on the charger, and shoved it in her back pocket. In less than five minutes they were in the foyer with the rest of their party, including the Golden Girls.

Gio was at the manager of the villa's side, speaking in rapid Italian.

"What's the plan?" Emma asked when she reached his side.

"We go in pairs of two. Rob and Pierre, Chris and Nicole, you and I. Claudio and Alessandro will spread out with four of the employees," Gio told her. "They're already down on the main road."

"What about us?" Carol asked.

"We will split you up and have you stay on the road with the small carts." The manager handed them a walkie-talkie. "It's on channel two. If anyone reports in, you'll drive to them and report to the others. We only have three more radios. Remember, the cell reception is spotty by the river."

"We figured that out earlier today," Pierre said.

"Are there authorities coming?"

"Yes but . . . they are slow. I will get word to our neighbors and gather more people." The manager, who'd always had a smile on his face, didn't have an ounce of humor now.

"Do we know how badly Weston is hurt?" Emma asked.

"No. The message was brief. Kimmy was upset, from the sound of her voice."

Gio clapped his hands together. "Daylight is wasting."

With that, they all moved toward the front door.

"We need to share our location on our phones so we know where everyone is," Nicole suggested.

"Great idea," Chris said.

"If the phones won't work, what's the point?" Jean asked.

"Ms. Jean, the phones may not call out, but they can at least find the last location you were at before reception was lost," Rob told her.

"Oh . . ."

Outside, the small carts that looked like oversize golf carts sat waiting for all of them.

The older women climbed into the seats while the rest of them climbed up in the back.

Someone had placed flashlights, water, and blankets inside the carts.

Emma pointed to the flashlights. "They're expecting this to take some time."

Gio placed a hand on her leg as the cart moved them down the long drive. He elevated his voice to speak over the sound of gravel crunching under the tires. "It took us forty-five minutes to get down to the river on a trail."

"We would have seen them if they'd taken the same route down," Emma said.

"When Rob and I asked about the trails, we were told there were several, but some of them were overgrown since the teenagers in the area grew up and were no longer partying by the river. He said they were false starts that dead-ended."

"So maybe Weston and Kimmy took a dead end."

Nicole leaned forward. "Claudio said in Kimmy's message he heard the river."

Emma shivered. "But where? We looked for places to cross. Maybe they did the same . . ."

"Or went for a swim or fell in and were swept downstream." Nicole's words put ice down Emma's spine.

"Let's not think like that," Gio said. "We'll go down there, find them, and be back for a late dinner."

Emma appreciated his optimism . . . but she wasn't convinced it was going to be that easy.

They met Claudio and Alessandro, along with the staff members, on the edge of the main road. The other staffers that had driven the carts handed over the keys to the Golden Girls and everyone else stood by for instructions.

Claudio took charge. "We spread out, but not so far that we have more lost guests. Every thirty minutes, check in on the group chat messages."

The sharing of phone numbers and location settings then took place so they could find each other.

Emma looked over at Nicole and Chris. "Be careful."

They spread out in the space of a football field and moved into the dense brush and trees.

Emma followed Gio into what looked like a trail. "How long did we walk before it got steep?"

"Twenty minutes maybe? I was too busy looking at the view to pay much attention to the time that passed." He was making light of the situation, but Emma heard concern in his tone.

"At least it's a little cooler now."

"That helps."

"Do you know any first aid?" she asked.

"No. Do you?"

Emma kept looking at the ground, searching for evidence that someone had recently walked through this area. "No. Let's hope all that time watching medical TV shows kicks in."

She heard someone calling Kimmy's name in the distance and followed suit. "Kimmy! Weston!"

No reply.

"Does this look like the trail?" Gio stopped, looked left, then right.

Emma pointed to the right. "That way."

Gio dug his heel into the dirt, making an arrow. "I forgot to bring bread crumbs."

"We should have thought of that."

"I have a pretty good sense of direction," he told her.

Emma glanced above her head at the angle of the sun. "I do, too . . . in the mall."

Gio laughed.

"Kimmy . . . Weston?"

They kept the same cadence until the ground started its descent. The trail had somewhat fizzled out, but the terrain around them was much more open than on the trail they'd taken earlier in the day.

Gio picked the path with the easiest footing. Because they were walking much faster, they started to hear the water right as their first thirty-minute check-in needed to take place.

They could hear the others calling out Kimmy's and Weston's names, which gave Emma a sense of relief.

"Did the text go through?" Gio asked.

"Yes." Good thing, since they didn't have one of the radios to communicate with. "I don't think this was on the tour packet," she said.

"Ha. The stories we'll tell our families when we're home."

Emma slapped at a mosquito that was having dinner on her arm.

They met the edge of the river with no sign of anyone.

"Do you think they went for a swim?"

Gio shook his head. "They don't seem that adventurous."

Emma looked each way. "Do we go upstream or downstream?"

"I say down. They could have slipped in, and even though the current doesn't look that strong, that can be deceiving," Gio said.

"Solid plan." Emma typed their intention into the group text before putting her phone in her pocket.

"Weston . . . Kimmy?"

An hour flew by. According to the group chat, two of the search parties were moving upriver instead of down. Pierre and Rob had to double back when the terrain became impossible and had yet to meet the river's edge. The authorities were on the scene and had added to the search party.

"An hour and forty-five minutes till sunset," Emma announced. "Kimmy must be freaking out."

"We'll find them." Gio placed a hand on Emma's arm.

Noise from downstream caught their attention at the same time.

"Kimmy?"

They both started running toward the sound.

"Weston?" Gio yelled.

"It's us. Nicole and Chris."

Emma's heart fell in her chest.

"We see something," Chris called out.

Gio and Emma picked up their pace.

Both of them ignored the branches that rushed past their bodies, scraping their skin as they ran by.

The bright orange shirt that Nicole was wearing stuck out in the green brush.

They came to a stop by Chris's side. He pointed to the riverbank that was now a few feet below them.

A chunk of earth looked like it had recently fallen away. A long-scored section of earth looked like it could have been the heel of a shoe sliding along the ground.

"Does that look right to you?" Chris asked.

"No," Gio said.

The current of the river had picked up in this section, with larger rocks breaking the water's path.

Gio looked at Chris's radio. "We should call this in and then walk downstream."

Chris lifted the radio to his ear. "We think we found something."

They all started walking, swiftly, as Chris informed the others of what they saw. "Kimmy?" Emma yelled.

The terrain they could walk on rose in elevation before it started to dip back down.

All four of them called Kimmy's and Weston's names over and over and scrambled alongside the river's edge, looking for any sign of their friends.

Sunset felt like it was working double time as the light of day was becoming a memory. And the bugs were starting to feast.

They must have walked a quarter of a mile before Emma heard a noise. "Everyone stop."

"Please help me." A female voice.

Hope flared. "Kimmy?"

"Here."

The four of them turned in circles. "Downstream?"

"I think so," Gio said.

They half jogged.

Chris was on the radio. "We hear Kimmy."

There were cheers over the radio.

"Kimmy, keep yelling," Nicole called out.

"Here!" Her voice was closer.

They marched up what felt like another hill before coming down the other side. That's when they saw them.

Weston was lying on the ground, his back propped up against a tree, and Kimmy was on her feet, waving her hands in the air. "Over here."

An outcropping from where the river had eaten into the earth and carved it away and then receded at some point was where Kimmy and Weston had found refuge.

From the appearance of their clothing, they'd both been in the river, their clothes molded to their bodies, Kimmy's hair fell in damp strands down her back.

Gio took the lead and found a way around the steep terrain, but there was still a good four-foot drop.

"Chris, stay behind so you can help us back up."

"You got it."

The static from the radio countered the river's current as Chris gave the others an update.

Gio reached for Emma's hand to help her down. Once there, Gio reached for Nicole, and Emma rushed to Kimmy's side.

The woman threw her arms around her. "I was so scared."

She was shivering from head to toe.

"You're safe now." Emma released Kimmy and dropped to a knee. "What happened?"

"We fell and the river took us here."

Dried blood streaked down Weston's face and neck.

Gio knelt on Weston's other side.

"I hit my head hard. Every time I stand, I get so dizzy I can't walk." Weston's words were slow, his eyes blinked repeatedly.

"I can't carry him," Kimmy said.

Gio used the flashlight to look at Weston's head. "That's a pretty good gash."

"How is he?" Chris called from above them.

"I'm not a doctor, but he is going to need stitches at the very least. Maybe a concussion," Gio said.

Emma nodded. "That would be my guess."

"Do you think you can manage with one of us on each side of you?"

Weston nodded. "We can't stay here."

Gio slid under one arm and Emma did the same on the other. Nicole walked with Kimmy to where Chris waited.

One at a time, Chris helped Nicole and Kimmy to his level.

When it came time for Weston, Chris pulled and Gio gave the man a foothold and a push. Weston fell to his butt the moment he was over the edge.

Gio gave the same foothold for Emma before taking Chris's hand.

Between Chris and Giovanni, Weston managed to stay on his feet.

By now their flashlights were on as they carefully picked their way through the brush. With no path to call a trail, Emma felt like her body was becoming a human magnet to every biting insect and every thorn. All of them would likely need a tetanus shot before the end of the evening.

Finally, they saw the lights of other flashlights coming their way. "Over here," Emma yelled, waving her light in the air.

Men she didn't recognize found them.

Two of them appeared to be medics of some sort. They had Gio and Chris stop and sit Weston down.

After a few minutes of asking questions, the medics took over for Gio and Chris.

Kimmy kept pace with her husband, and Nicole, Chris, Gio, and Emma walked behind. "What a crazy night."

"I need a shower," Nicole said.

"I need a tetanus shot," Emma said, voicing what she'd been thinking for the last hour.

Chris rubbed his hands over his bare arms. "Me too. Remind me to never again go into the woods."

Giovanni took Emma's hand in his and squeezed.

The damage of their rescue mission became evident in the lights of the villa.

The mosquitos had dined on all of them.

While Giovanni hadn't gone untouched, it was nothing compared to the welts that were growing on Emma's skin.

An ambulance had taken off with Weston and Kimmy while the rest of their tattered crew gathered. Even the Golden Girls were covering their yawns.

"*Cara . . .*"

Emma turned, knowing Gio's endearment was meant for her.

He reached out and lifted her arm. On the back of it was a large scrape that bled in a few places.

"It's just a scratch," she told him.

"I'll get a first-aid kit and bring it to your room," he said before turning away.

"And Benadryl, if they have it."

"A cream?"

"Yes, but the pill, too. These bites are starting to itch."

He winked and left her sight.

"C'mon," she said to Nicole. "Let's get cleaned up."

CHAPTER NINETEEN

The search party sat around the communal dinner table in exhausted silence. Everyone ate together, even the staff.

The Golden Girls hadn't even bothered. All of them chose to stay in their rooms.

Gio sat beside Emma, who looked like she was sleeping with her eyes open.

Claudio stood and lifted his glass. "Why so somber?" he asked. "We should be celebrating. Thanks to everyone's efforts, we found our friends and they're safe."

"We're just tired," Nicole said.

Emma scratched a welt on her arm. "And missing a few pints of blood."

That brought a laugh from everyone there.

Claudio lifted his glass higher. "A toast, as you say . . . to Kimmy and Weston."

Half of the party lifted a glass of water, the others lifted their wine.

Before they placed their glasses back down, Chris spoke. "And to us. We've made some great memories, but tonight's actions remind me of the humanity in people."

"*Salute,*" Gio offered.

Emma looked into his eyes as they drank.

She sighed and rested her head on his shoulder as others picked up plates of food and started passing them around.

"Food and then bed, I think," he whispered and then kissed the top of her head.

"You'll have to wait for me to sneak to your room," she told him.

"Of course, *cara*." But he liked that she remembered what she'd said earlier that day.

"Did Kimmy say how they fell into the river?" Rob asked.

"She didn't, but we found a fresh patch of the hillside that looked as if it gave way, and then we turned our search downstream," Gio told him.

"Smart thinking," Claudio said.

"It really could have been so much worse." Emma dug into her pasta, held her fork to her mouth. "Weston could have been knocked out altogether and . . ."

Gio caught the eyes of several of them. All thinking the same thing.

"A good thing we'd taken that hike earlier ourselves. We were a little more familiar with the landscape," Chris added.

"And I didn't hear you squeal once," Nicole teased. "Even when we were covered in cobwebs."

Chris closed his eyes. "I'll have nightmares for years. Probably have to seek therapy."

"Overcome your fears by diving into them." The words came from Alessandro.

Gio held his breath. "I like that one."

Chris shook his head. "I'm comfortable on this side of the spider hole, thank you very much."

Everyone picked on Chris for a few minutes, which he took in good humor.

Gio noticed Emma's head snap forward and back up. Literally as she tried to fall asleep at the table.

He wiped his face and placed his napkin to the side of his plate before scooting back his chair. "C'mon, *tesoro*. Before you nose-dive into your dinner."

Emma nodded. "I'm sorry, guys. I can't keep my eyes open."

Gio pulled her chair back as everyone said good night.

He placed an arm around her waist as they left the dining room.

"I can get back on my own."

"Yes, but then who will kiss you good night?"

Her eyelids were heavy. "It's the Benadryl. Makes me sleepy."

"And here I thought it was because of our earlier activities."

She lifted an index finger in the air. "You have a point."

At her door, she removed her key from her back pocket and turned to face him.

Emma smiled and lifted her chin. "I'll see you in the morning."

He dropped his lips to hers, slowly . . . savoring her tired kiss. "Sleep well, *cara*."

She stepped inside and closed the door with a smile.

By the time he arrived back in the dining room, everyone was talking about the two of them.

Nicole waved a hand in Rob's face. "You owe me."

"I told you," Pierre said. "When women are that tired, nookie is not going to happen."

Gio narrowed his eyes as he grasped the back of his chair. "Are you guys betting on us?"

Chris shook his head no and said, "Yeah."

Rob pulled out his wallet and handed Nicole twenty euros. "We're even."

Gio sat. "Even from when?"

"This afternoon," Nicole said, making the money disappear in a pocket. "I thought you two would be back by the pool within the hour. Rob bet you'd be out for the night."

The expressions on Rob's, Pierre's, and Chris's faces were in tune with *What? Doesn't everyone make financial wagers on someone else's sexual encounters?*

"You guys are seriously flawed." But Gio was smiling . . . because deep down, he liked that he and Emma were that obvious to everyone around them.

~

They were back on the road in two days.

Weston had an overnight stay in the hospital and a dozen stitches. He and Kimmy were en route back to Florence, where they were going to stay for a few days before flying home.

Kimmy had returned to the villa to thank everyone, gather addresses, and collect their things.

While it was sad to see them go, not one of them thought they'd continue the trip.

Emma switched between sitting beside Nicole and Gio while they moved from one part of Tuscany to the next.

The final week of their tour had only two day stops.

They stopped at the coast in Cinque Terre, where Emma and Gio snuck away for a private dinner on a private boat during sunset.

"How did you come up with this idea?" Emma asked as the captain of the boat helped her on board.

"I had help. My friend Dante suggested it."

"The friend that married your sister?"

"Right. Brother-in-law. It's hard to say that."

"Because of your sister, or because of him?"

"Chloe, of course. I know Dante's secrets. All of them. The thought of him dating my sister made me ill."

"Does it still?"

The captain led them to the back of the boat, where a half-round couch looked over the water. On the table by the couch sat a bucket with chilling champagne.

"No. He makes my sister happy, and he knows if he messes up, my brother and I will . . ." He let his words trail off.

The captain said something in Italian to Gio.

"*Sì, sì.*"

The captain picked up the bottle of bubbly and started to open it.

"You don't seem like the violent type," Emma said, getting back to what Gio had implied.

"I'm not. But I am willing to protect the people I love."

The captain handed them glasses of champagne. *"Salute!"* he said.

"Grazie," Emma and Gio said together.

While Emma and Gio sipped, the captain left their side to pilot the boat.

"This is delicious," Emma said as she picked up the bottle and looked at the label. She'd never heard of the winery. Like so many of the places they'd been.

The boat started to move, and they made use of the couch and the view.

"So, the boat idea came from Dante," she said, getting back to what they were talking about.

"Yup. He has a boat in San Diego and is starting a business taking small groups on tours and catering private dinners."

"Just like this?"

"Yup."

Gio placed an arm over Emma's shoulders. She was wearing linen pants that flowed in the breeze and a simple loose-fitting shirt that fluttered open enough for him to get a glimpse of the tops of her breasts. The Italian sun had kissed her skin, and the bugbites from their unexpected rescue mission had freckled her body with bumps for days. She didn't bother with makeup . . . she didn't need it.

Emma narrowed her gaze. "Do you have Italian citizenship?"

"Ah-huh. My parents were born here. We took advantage of the link. And why not?"

"I would, too. Have you considered moving here?"

He hesitated. "Seriously? No. I couldn't leave my family. Although it would be less expensive for me to open my own winery here, I'd spend the difference traveling back and forth to the States."

The boat picked up speed once they puttered away from the dock and reached the open sea.

"That leaves Temecula," Emma said.

"Yes. This trip has opened my eyes to what I want to make happen."

Emma twisted a little to watch him more closely. "And what is that?"

"It starts with vines, my own property, and home. But there was an experience we've had here in Tuscany that I don't think the Southern California wineries have completely tapped into. Anyone can put a tasting room on-site. But what about intimate dinners cooked by the family or host staff? What about co-oping with other vineyards the way Claudio's company does? A bus that takes you into San Diego." Gio spread his arm to the ocean. "That works with a local ship's captain to entertain this small party . . . a local restaurant with an Italian chef that teaches the guests how to make fresh pasta? And in all these places the wine is there. Celebrated, drunk."

"There are plenty of wineries with restaurants all over Temecula," she pointed out.

"But do any of them have the heart of the home that we've experienced in the smaller villas that we stayed in?"

She considered his question. "I'm not really sure. But running a winery and opening up a hotel are different. Besides, there are larger places in Temecula that have that."

"Large venues. True." Gio lifted his hand and put an inch of air between his index finger and his thumb. "Not on a smaller scale. I wouldn't start with overnight accommodations. But while you're waiting for your first harvest, or first bottle that can sell, there might be a way to pull in some return on your investment."

Emma thought about what he was suggesting. "You'd need an extensive investigation into the viability of that idea . . . but I like how you're thinking."

He grinned. "Are you going to steal my idea?"

She placed a hand on her chest. "I'm not the one with a family with a restaurant or leisure ships at their disposal."

"Your father doesn't have restaurants at his wineries?"

"No. Wine tasting, special events for wine tasting . . . gift shops on-site in the Napa tasting room, but Temecula only has a tasting room."

"A wasted opportunity. Your name has a great reputation."

"My father was never interested. And in all fairness, I've never thought about it either." She turned to stare out at the ocean as the wind did a great job of tossing her hair all around.

"Maybe you should. Thinking costs nothing."

"Researching does. At least if you hire to get it done."

Gio laughed. "My time is free. I'm talking small scale all the way around. I don't have to build what I create to such a level that my secretary has to speak with my children."

Emma blinked without saying a word.

Gio sighed, lowered his voice. "*Bella*, that was insensitive of me. I'm sorry."

"Don't be, it's true." Even if it hurt to hear.

"No. That was inexcusable."

"And something you've thought about but haven't said. You're right. R&R consumes my father and brother. I don't think my twenty acres are going to be as intensive. For the first two weeks of this trip, I walked into each villa and compared and contrasted. I've seen the smaller scale and fight to see myself in that." She pictured the land waiting for her when she returned home. "But I'll never create what my father has."

"Will it bring you happiness?" Gio asked.

She honestly didn't know. "I guess I'm going to find out."

Gio captured her hand. "Have you heard from your father's lawyer about the details?"

Emma offered a coy smile. "I haven't looked. Not since you and I . . ."

He lifted her fingertips to his lips, kissed them. "I'm distracting you."

She shook her head. "You reminded me that this was supposed to be a vacation. Checking my email every day is counterintuitive to relaxing and finding a reset button."

"A good distraction, then."

"Fishing for a compliment, Giovanni?"

He leaned forward, kissed her briefly. "If I wanted a compliment, I'd ask if my butt looked good in my jeans."

They were both laughing when the captain cut the engine, dropped the anchor, and moved to the kitchen to prepare their meal.

CHAPTER TWENTY

"I expect an invitation to the opening day of *Casa de Emma*." Rob pulled Emma into his arms in a hug that felt like it came from family.

Not necessarily her family, but a chosen one.

"I absolutely will."

The trip was over. Three weeks of their lives that formed friendships Emma knew she'd keep for years.

Nicole was making the rounds, hugging and saying goodbye to the ladies from Florida. The four of them were staying two more days in Florence before making their way home.

Giovanni was helping Claudio and Alessandro unpack the bus for the last time.

"For what it's worth, I think you and Gio make a cute couple," Pierre said when she hugged him goodbye.

"I'll play with him for a while," she said with a wink.

"Ha. You don't strike me as a player."

"You guys have a safe flight." She moved to hug Rob.

Gio walked over, dragging two suitcases in each hand. His and the extra lost luggage bag, and Emma's and Nicole's. "Well, guys . . . I guess this is it." He offered a handshake that turned into a hug from the men in the group. "Remember, if you're ever in San Diego . . ."

"We might be down for Pride next year," Chris told him.

"I have friends in Hillcrest that will clue you in on all the things," Gio said.

Pierre waved his phone in his hand and pointed toward the road. "That's our driver."

"Ciao, ciao."

Finding her inner Italian, Emma waved her hands in the air as she wished them goodbye.

"Our ride is five minutes away," Nicole said.

"Did you ask for a bigger car?" Emma looked at all their luggage. The white suitcase with her address written on it with a Sharpie made her laugh every time.

"I did."

"You sure you want to come to the airport early?" Emma asked Gio. His flight was leaving nearly an hour after theirs.

"An hour isn't early, it's on time. Besides . . . you'll be there."

Nicole made a choking noise. "Sappy much?"

"Don't be jealous. I have friends I could . . ." His voice trailed off, his eyes closed, and then he shook his head. "Never mind. I know why they're single."

Emma considered his words. "And what would those friends say about you, I wonder."

"That I'm the best catch in town."

She rolled her eyes.

Nicole snorted. "Men who say that seldom are."

"My mother is never wrong."

The car they were waiting for pulled up and Gio opened the door for them.

Apparently, the same mother who thought her son was the number-one bachelor in town worth finding also taught her son the gestures of being a gentleman.

The driver traversed the streets of Florence as they wove their way to the airport. "I can't believe it's over," Emma said as she watched the ancient city fall into the background.

"I'm ready to go home," Nicole said.

"I have to pack, hire movers." Her mother had sent her pictures of the finished work at the new house, all of which Emma was getting more excited about than she'd been before she'd left.

"I thought your mom was going to hire them while you were gone," Nicole said.

"I told her to wait. I want to read over the transaction paperwork and maybe even ask a lawyer to take a look before I actually move." The email had come through three days before, but Emma hadn't opened the attachment. She was waiting until she was on the plane. That way, if there was anything in the paperwork that looked fishy, she could digest the information and decide what she wanted to do before landing. That would avoid any instant outburst or otherwise rash actions on her part.

And if there was something Emma knew about her redheaded disposition, it was that she could come off with fireworks when she was upset.

"Your mother wouldn't tell you one thing and it be another," Nicole insisted.

"My mother wouldn't know."

Gio and Emma had talked about this subject more than once.

As he sat beside her in silence, his hand held hers and squeezed.

"I'm sure it's fine."

Emma hoped her best friend was right.

"How much stuff do you have to move?" Gio asked.

"I'm in a one-bedroom condo. Not a lot. The house is going to look empty."

Nicole clapped her hands together. "Shopping!"

Gio shook his head. "As soon as you know you're good to move, let me know. I'll be there."

Emma shook her head. "It's grunt work, Gio."

He pointed to his chest. "I'm cheap labor. And I'm not the guy that only shows up for dinner and a movie."

"Careful, I may take you up on that."

"I insist you do."

Nicole chuckled. "You're bossy."

The driver pulled up to the curb at the airport and jumped out of the car. A few minutes later Emma and Nicole were in line to check their bags, Gio in another since they were on two different airlines.

It took ten minutes and a supervisor for Emma to explain the extra-bag situation.

As for her lost bag, she would jump through all the hoops needed with the airline once she was home and no longer jet-lagged. She then presented her new bag, address written all over it and everything, and said, "Try not to lose this one." It was a bitchy statement, but something none of them could argue with.

They met up with Gio before going through security and then found a place to sit with a cup of coffee since they had some time before their flight.

"Saturday . . . ," Gio started. "What time can you be ready?"

Emma glanced at Nicole, then Gio. "Saturday? Did I miss something?"

"Unless you need me to help with the move before then. In which case I'll be there."

Emma paused.

"He wants to take you out on a date, Em. I know it's been a while, but this is how it's done. Guys don't *ask* if you want to go out, they assume the answer is yes and ask what time," Nicole told her.

Emma blamed the lack of sleep from the night before. The one where Gio made good on his slow and very thorough lovemaking and kept her up half the night. Not that she was complaining, even in her own head.

She offered a sideways glance. "Are we assuming things?"

He leaned over; his lips hovered above hers. "Can I do that, *cara*? Can I assume when it comes to Saturday nights with you?"

The man put warmth in her belly like no one had before. "We can give it a trial run," she teased.

"Trial . . . do I get a six-month lease? A year?"

That sounded long term to her ears. "How about month to month." Even that sounded like commitment.

Gio kissed her briefly and pulled away. "We'll renegotiate in thirty days."

Her heart was pounding, this time it wasn't in excitement, but nerves.

"I'll make dinner reservations for seven. But come early to help you pack. Or help you move, and we can order food in. Whatever you need," he said.

"What about what you need?" The man was always trying to do something for her.

"All I need is to see you again . . . soon."

"Oh my God. Can you two keep the pillow talk to the bedroom?" Nicole's tone was pure teasing annoyance.

An hour later, boarding for their flight opened and Emma said her goodbyes.

Giovanni kissed her in a way that should have been indecent . . . and would have been if they were anywhere but in an airport, but no one seemed the wiser. "Text me when you land in London and when you get to San Diego," he said.

It was nice that someone cared. In all the times she'd flown in the past, no one asked for a safety update.

"I will."

She and Nicole inched through the line, and as she started down the jet bridge, she looked over her shoulder to find Giovanni watching her.

He smiled and waved.

And an unfamiliar wave of emotion bubbled up inside her.

"Holy crap . . . are you crying?" Nicole asked.

Emma blinked several times. "No. Don't be ridiculous."

~

"We waited a whole day. But now, you tell us everything."

Gio had to give his mother credit. When he'd arrived home the day before, and all but fell into bed from the lack of sleep from the long flight, Mari hadn't done more than greet him, give him food, and say good night.

Even though it wasn't a Sunday, the entire family gathered on the rooftop terrace of their home, the table was set . . . and the wine was poured.

A home-cooked meal sounded divine . . . although if Gio was being honest with himself, what he really craved was a burger. Italian family meant Italian food . . . and even he was a bit burnt out on pasta and wine.

There was no way out of forced family time. Which he wouldn't change for the world.

What did Emma go home to?

An empty condo with boxes ready to pack.

Her text message was on his phone when he'd landed the day before. I'm home and exhausted.

Since his flight came in after Emma's by a few hours, he didn't comment or text a reply until morning, afraid he would wake her with the pinging on her phone.

Here he was, late afternoon the next day, and all he'd managed with Emma was a couple of pleasant text messages, with a promise to talk later in the evening.

"It was truly one of the best experiences of my life. I can't thank you all enough."

The whole family sat around the table. He and his mother took up each end while Chloe and Dante sat on one side and Luca, Brooke, and Franny evened it out on the other.

"Details, Gio . . . Mama is asking for details," Chloe teased.

"I lost count of the places we stopped. All of them had a certain amount of charm and none of the wine was awful. We've all had bad wine, so that is hard to do." Gio talked about Claudio and Alessandro and how they basically worked for three weeks straight. "When we stopped for longer stays, they would rotate who was around . . . taking a day off, but someone was always there."

The family sat in rapt attention.

"There were four women from Florida . . ." The antics of the Golden Girls and the sheer amount of wine they drank and purchased was talked and laughed about. Rob, Pierre, and Chris . . . their laughter and willingness to participate in anything and everything. He told them about Weston and Kimmy and the search-party experience.

And when Gio paused long enough to shove some food into his mouth, his mother offered a sweet smile and tapped her fingers on the table.

"You've said nothing about Emma."

Gio chewed slowly and looked around the table.

Everyone was quietly watching him.

He slowly swallowed with a grin and followed it with a drink of water. "What do you want to know?"

Mari lost her smile. Slapped a hand on the table. "What do I want to know?" She rolled her eyes, lifted a hand in the air, and switched to Italian. "For an hour you've talked about everyone but the woman you introduced us to."

"C'mon, Gio . . . give it up," Chloe said, kicking him under the table.

"Hey."

"Is she your girlfriend?" Franny asked without hesitation.

Gio winked at his niece. "Emma is someone I hope you will all meet very soon."

"Bene, bene . . ." His mother was smiling again.

"I won't say she's a girlfriend, but we are more than friends."

Mari's smile fell to a flat line. "Why not a girlfriend?"

"Mama, we've only known each other a few weeks."

"This means nothing to me. When you know, you know." Mari swirled spaghetti with her fork. "Your father and I—"

"Yes, Mama, we know. Instant love, marriage, and babies. It isn't like that nowadays."

Brooke cleared her throat and placed a hand on her protruding baby bump. "I disagree."

Dante laughed. "It took Chloe and I more time."

Mari tossed around gestures with her free hand. "You were childhood friends. That's different. And since you eloped without a whisper to the family, something must have been instant. Not that I want you to share."

Dante stood down.

Smart man.

"This Emma is beautiful, and the way you smiled at her . . ."

"It was sappy adorable, Gio," Chloe said in agreement with their mother.

He was infatuated with the woman, there was no pretending otherwise. "Her guard is up a bit. She's been married before."

"Children?" Mari asked.

"No, Mama. But when someone is divorced it takes a little longer to trust."

All eyes turned to Luca. The only person at the table who had any personal authority on the subject.

Gio waited for his brother to agree.

Instead, Luca placed a hand over Brooke's at the table and shook his head. "Not when you find the right person."

Gio rolled his eyes. "It still takes time."

"Wasting time, you mean," his mother said.

Gio spread his hands to each side of the table, indicating his sister and brother. "Mama, two weddings in one year . . . isn't that enough?"

"No," she said flat out. "My youngest son still isn't married. There is still room at this table. So, no. It's not enough. When you're married, it will be enough."

"It's a trap, Gio," Dante said.

Chloe hit his arm.

"Not marriage . . . the *enough* part. Soon as you're married the question switches to babies."

The two things Emma said she didn't want.

"Oh," Chloe sighed. "That's true."

"None of this when you meet Emma. We don't talk about my lack of being a husband or anyone's biological clock. I don't want anyone scaring her off."

"What's a biological clock?" Franny asked.

Dante started laughing.

"I mean it!" Gio pointed his fork at his sister and mother.

"She means something to you," Luca said quietly.

Gio paused, thought of her smile, her laugh. The freckles on her face and how crazy her hair turned in the humidity. "Yeah. She does."

"Then we will do our best to keep our opinions about weddings and babies to ourselves. Don't you think, Mama?" Luca asked.

Mari released a deep sigh. "Fine. I can do that."

Gio felt the tension in his shoulders ease.

Franny leaned over, tapped his arm. "What's a biological clock?"

CHAPTER TWENTY-ONE

Emma had crashed into her pillow and didn't come up for eight hours. Unfortunately, that woke her in the middle of the night.

She could tell that Gio had read her message, but he hadn't left one.

While it would have been nice to hear from him, chances were he didn't want to wake her with a call.

For two hours she lay in bed, willing herself to go back to sleep . . . but it didn't come.

Giving up, she brewed a pot of coffee and opened her laptop.

She again combed through the paperwork her father's lawyer had sent.

The first thing it said was that Emma could occupy the residence effective immediately. That was very clear.

It went on to say that Emma would be responsible for the property and harvest. Which seemed straightforward enough. Only responsible and owning were different things.

The lawyer went on to say that they were working on putting the property into her trust. Not using her trust to pay for the property, but making it a part of her inheritance.

Her father didn't do anything without strings. At least in her experience.

Did this mean Casa de Emma was R&R Wineries 2.0? Yes, she had a trust fund, one she was allowed to draw on, but once the property was there, did her father control it at all?

For hours on the flight, she'd vacillated on what to do, what to say . . . how to approach her father.

She needed a well-thought-out approach with actual solutions.

Did she want the home and the winery if in fact her father had any part of it?

After three weeks in Italy and seeing the smaller but more welcoming operations and the joy of the families involved in these estates . . . And yeah, maybe Giovanni had something to do with it. He and Emma showed great interest in the different locations and spoke with the operators and owners for hours. They loved what they did and wanted to share what they had.

They were happy.

When was the last time she saw her father with a smile on his face? A genuine *I love life* smile?

And why not? The man had everything he could want.

A beautiful, devoted wife.

Three healthy children.

A multimillion-dollar successful business that made people in the industry absolutely green with envy.

All for what?

To take those long family vacations where the five of them could sit around and play Yahtzee and have a campfire and reminisce on the time they did that one thing . . . or the time they went to that one place?

They did things as a family, but Emma had always felt that as children, they were interrupting their father's life with their needs.

Isn't that why she dove into the wine industry to learn everything she could? Went to college to become something her father would be proud of? To spend time with her father in the one place he couldn't avoid her?

That hadn't worked.

When she was married to Kyle, she'd managed a little more time with her dad, but staying married to a man who didn't love her . . . who she didn't love . . . wasn't worth it.

She needed to approach her father with a business plan to remove his name from his *gift*. And to do that she needed advice from someone who had been thinking along the lines of a small vineyard their entire life. *Giovanni.*

While Emma had experience in the business, she never thought she'd be in a position to start something up from scratch.

For the first time in weeks, Emma logged out of her personal email and into her business one.

There were twenty messages.

Fifteen were company spam, the things R&R sent to anyone on payroll.

One was from a customer in LA that needed information on the points of the previous year's harvest, and the other four were from people Emma spoke with on a weekly basis.

And two of those emails were from the same person. The only one that asked a personal question.

"I heard you're taking an unexpected vacation. You deserve it . . . you work too hard and make the rest of us look bad."

It was from Amy. She was a rep in Texas.

They'd met on Zoom meetings but never in person.

When Amy replied the second time, her email was even more personal.

And . . . informative.

"You're leaving? It's your family business . . . how do you leave that?"

Amy left her personal phone number and asked if Emma would call her once she was back Stateside.

There was nothing . . . absolutely nothing from anyone else she worked with inside R&R.

At ten in the morning, Texas time, Emma dialed Amy's number.

"You're alive!"

Amy's Texas drawl put a smile on Emma's face.

"Barely. Jet lag is kicking my butt."

"Sounds like a first-world problem."

Amy always kept things real.

"One I'm happy to experience," Emma said.

"I hope you had a good time. In the four years I've been working for this company, this is the first time you took more than a couple of days for yourself."

Was that true?

Emma thought of the last time she took any real time off. It had been on her honeymoon . . . the time when her husband worked hard to convince her that she didn't have to work at all. He would take care of everything.

Emma shook her head . . . and the memory from it. "Big birthdays deserve big celebrations."

Amy sighed. "Happy to hear it. What is this about you leaving? I wasn't expecting you to ever quit."

"Sometimes life offers you opportunities you don't want to pass up." The last thing Emma wanted to do was suggest anything was wrong in the life of R&R and have that get back to her father.

While Amy was expressing, and likely feeling, the weight of Emma's departure from her family business, there was no way to know for certain that Amy wouldn't talk directly to Kyle or even her father about the information Emma was providing.

"So, there is something you're leaving for? That's exciting. No one has said a word about what you're doing next," Amy said.

Emma paused. "I'm not ready to tell anyone quite yet."

Amy chuckled. "Well . . . it was a shock to hear you were leaving, but even more, who replaced you."

She'd already been replaced? That would explain the near-empty inbox.

"I'm sorry. I wasn't a part of that process." You would think her father would give her the courtesy of telling her who took her place.

"I always thought Davila was more of a beer drinker."

Amy's words had Emma's back up straight. "Davila?"

"Yeah . . . I thought you knew."

Emma blew out a breath. "I didn't."

Davila worked directly with Kyle. A cozy hire that screamed inter-office relationship.

"I'm surprised. She doesn't have a tenth of your knowledge and zero management skills . . ." Amy went on about a contract she'd been trying to land for four months that finally was inked while Emma was in Europe.

While Amy chatted away, Emma pulled up the portal with R&R to check her accounts.

Davila's name was changed on the point of contact. Two of Emma's accounts were crossed out as active and placed under pending.

When she tried to dig into why, Emma found herself blocked by a password that didn't belong to her.

Davila . . . and likely Kyle.

Why? What did it matter if Emma saw what had happened to pull two prominent restaurateurs that collectively owned several four- and five-star establishments?

Emma backed out of the system with her name and pushed back in with her brother's.

All while Amy chatted with very little encouragement from Emma.

In Richard's files, she found everyone in retail and then saw Davila's name. She clicked on the two accounts that said pending and looked at the notes.

Both said identical things.

Clients were unhappy with the service from their previous rep, and upon renewal, they were likely to cancel their contracts.

Previous rep? That was her.

Amy was well into her personal life when Emma interrupted her. "Really? That's crazy . . ." Emma had no idea if her response was appropriate but pushed forward anyway. "Listen, we're going to have to continue this conversation another time. I have a call beeping through from my father and I have to take it," she lied.

"Of course. Go. Don't be a stranger."

"I won't. Thank you."

She hung up to stare at her computer screen.

Unhappy with their rep.

Emma called bullshit. She pictured the two clients and the elaborate dinners she had with them. The personal attention and conversations with the head chefs.

She went on to look at the other accounts on her file . . . now Davila's file.

Phone calls were made informing the businesses that their representative was changing, as would be expected. There were two notes suggesting that Davila's communication had been the only one since the account had been secured. Which was utter bullshit.

Not only had Kyle's pet project taken over Emma's job, but she was attempting to slander Emma's name after taking over. Or at least make the books look like she was crappy at her job.

Why?

What possible reason would Davila have for doing this?

Emma was already out.

Unless Davila worried Emma would return and wanted to try and cement her name in the position.

Yeah, that made sense. Insecure people did stupid things.

Not knowing if her backdoor entry to the company files would last forever, Emma printed out the database of her previous clients, their numbers and contacts. And because she was feeling spiteful, she jumped onto Kyle's base, which was limited since he had the supervisor role, and printed his out as well.

With the sun high in the midmorning sky, Emma took a quick shower and got dressed.

A good-morning text had come in from Gio while she was drying her hair.

The simple greeting put the biggest smile all morning on her face.

Can you talk? he typed.

She needed to think more than talk. I have a busy morning. How about tonight?

I'll hold you to it.

Without makeup and her hair in a ponytail, she jumped into her car and headed to the new house.

She pressed in the gate code her mother had told her to use and pulled into the now-cobblestone driveway. "That was fast," she muttered to herself.

A brand-new fountain splashed water on the newly planted landscape. Her mother had run with Emma's vision. A vision brought on, in part, by her mother's sense of style. A proper villa needed a fountain and circular drive. How many had she seen like that in Tuscany? Too many to count.

It was beautiful.

There wasn't one construction truck in the drive. Her mother must have had a staff on standby with big bonuses to finish the construction in less than a month.

Emma cut the engine and stepped into the heat.

Spring had given way to summer while she'd been in Italy. And the Temecula heat took no prisoners in its assault.

Emma unlocked the front door.

Her mother had put the temperature on frigid.

Emma found the thermostat and bumped it up five degrees.

She set her purse on the island that now separated the kitchen from the great room.

It was pretty spectacular. Again, her mother's eye for details shined. Two iron chandeliers hovered over the kitchen island . . . a space that would sit five easily. A massive double wine fridge had replaced the single one Emma had noticed when she viewed the house that first day.

The floors had been refinished with a darker stain, and all the walls had a fresh coat of paint.

She slowly walked into the great room, looked at the fireplace. She envisioned a Christmas tree to one side and rows of deep green garland laced with tiny lights over the hearth.

Dark furniture would make the room feel cozy. Area rugs over the hardwood floors would warm up the space even more. The image of her and Gio warming their feet by a winter fire, toes bundled in fuzzy socks, made her smile even more.

Back in the primary bedroom she realized her queen-size bed would look like a child lived in the room. Brighter colors in here . . . she decided.

Outside, the pool also had new landscaping and potted plants filling corners and edges. Pots of citrus reminded her of the fields in Italy.

They, too, reminded her of Gio. *"I want lemon trees so I can make my own limoncello."*

"To sell?" she asked.

"No, bella, to drink."

Emma thought of everyone on the tour gathered around the patio and pool, music playing and wine and food flowing.

The vineyard beyond the pool kept the smile on her face.

She hadn't asked for this, but now that it was in front of her . . . Emma wanted it.

On her own.

And if that couldn't happen, then visions of Christmas trees would just have to wait.

CHAPTER TWENTY-TWO

"I miss you already."

Emma leaned into Giovanni's voice, hearing his slight Italian accent that seemed to have gotten thicker as the days went on while they were in Italy. She pictured his grin and the way his hair always seemed ruffled by this time of night.

"It's unsettling how often you popped into my head today," she told him.

"A compliment and an insult in the same sentence. This is a gift you have."

She supposed it was.

"Why unsettling?" he asked.

"Because before I left for Italy, I was steadfast in believing that I'd toss this house and property in my father's face if he was still in control of it."

"Oh, no . . ."

"The house is in the trust. *My* trust fund. I told my parents I wanted to pay for the property out of my trust, not put the property in the trust. And since I haven't touched any of that, I'm not really sure how it works. I do think, at the end of the day, my dad holds control over all of that."

"I know nothing about trust funds."

"You would think I would . . . but I don't. Then there is the verbiage about the vineyard. It reads like a political speech. On one hand, it says I'm in control, but it doesn't exactly say it's mine."

Gio sighed. "Do you need a lawyer, *bella*?"

"I'm looking for one now."

"We have one I can recommend. He works with a lot of businesses in San Diego. My mother has used him for years. Very up-front. If you need something he can't manage, he'll tell you."

Considering most of her contacts were also in contact with her father . . . "That might not be a bad idea."

"I'll send you his number."

"Thanks." It was only seven o'clock, but Emma had already put on her pajamas and was curled up on the couch while talking to Gio. She tucked her feet under her and stared at the wall. "I kept hearing your voice asking me what I wanted. Do I take the opportunity this house and vineyard offers? Even if that means working with R&R? Do I want to find a way to buy this property out from under my father and make it successful without his help?"

Gio hummed. "I put those thoughts in your head?"

"Yes. Before you, I would have either walked away or sat back and let my father pay for everything. Then worked my ass off to prove myself. Now I'm trying to dissect my father's lawyer's legal stuff and at the same time devise a business plan to pay for my own everything. How do I come up with money for employees over the next couple of years before the first bottle is even sold? Especially if I need to spend every dime in my trust fund to get started? Do I try and get a loan against the property . . . this one or another, for start-up costs? I don't have a job to pay for the loan and no collateral."

"Emma, darling . . . take a breath."

And just like that, she did. The tension that her monologue had built inside of her eased.

"Giovanni D'Angelo makes me question myself and *that* is unsettling," she finally admitted.

He chuckled. "Do you want my advice?"

"I have a feeling you'll give it to me anyway."

"No, actually. I won't. I'm surrounded by strong women, and every time I try and fix their problems, or offer unsolicited advice, my ass is usually handed to me. Only when I'm asked are my thoughts given consideration."

Emma wasn't sure she'd met a man who didn't think he knew more and told her so at every opportunity.

"Okay, Gio, what would you do?"

"No, no . . . what I would do and what I think you might want to consider are different."

"Why is that?" she asked.

"I've been preparing myself to take the step to own what is being half handed to you, on my own, since I was old enough to drink wine. You've only had these thoughts rattling around in your head for a month. You told me you envisioned your future within R&R, under the wings of your father, and that thought never wavered."

"That's true. I've been pushing for more at R&R for a while. I never thought I'd leave the company."

"So, taking on your own place is a complete plot twist in your life. Even with a hundred percent help from your father."

All true. "You think I should continue taking his money and work to show him I'm capable to run this place . . . for him?"

"No, *cara* . . . I don't suggest you do that. Not completely, anyway."

"What do you suggest?"

"Go slow. Continue to ask yourself what you really want. What your father wants and what is motivating him should be considered, but regardless of what the answers to those questions are, Emma needs to know what Emma wants. I don't know your father and would never profess to understand what is going on in his head . . . but I'm beginning to know you. I see a smart, kind, and capable woman and can't imagine those qualities are lost on your father. Not completely. And if he sees even half of what I see, I don't believe he would be setting you up for failure. From what you have told me, he doesn't sound like a cruel man."

"I wouldn't use the word *cruel*," she said.

"What word would you use?" Gio asked.

Emma looked at the ceiling as if the answer would be written there. "Disconnected. Emotionally unavailable."

Gio sighed. "That's what I hear from your stories. Let's assume, if we can, that your father wants physical distance from you being involved with R&R. Then this move and property does that. But he still wants to look like the hero here, so making you pay for it probably doesn't sit well with him. From what you've told me, image is important to him. Am I right?"

"Yes. He doesn't play outside of his social class. Hell, he didn't bother coming to my birthday party because my friends don't measure up."

"Is it safe to say that if you fail, it's a reflection on him?"

Gio hit the nail on the head. "Exactly. My divorce was somehow harder on him than me."

"Then that explains why your father isn't going to outright give you this house or this land. It's a placeholder. He can't have his daughter working for a competitor, and yet he couldn't keep you in the position you've been in forever. You're much too willful for that."

Emma let Giovanni's words settle in. So many of his conclusions rang true in her head. "I move slowly and figure out what I want . . . then what?"

Gio laughed.

"I don't know what's funny," she said.

"*Then what? Then what? Cara*, listen to yourself. Asking 'then what' contradicts 'slowly' and 'figuring it out.' The 'then what' is completely dependent on what you really want." Gio paused and started again. "See the lawyer, gather the facts. Know exactly what your father can and cannot do with how he has it set up. With that, ask yourself if you can work within those guidelines. Do you *want* to work within them? Do you want this? Do you want the house, the vines . . . *Casa de Emma* to be how you envision it? *Then*, you either draw up a contract with your father, on your terms, to accept his capital . . . or use his capital as a loan like any other bank. Owner financing, if you will. Or you try and get an SBA loan . . . or a private loan. See how none of that matters right now since you don't have all the facts and likely haven't answered the biggest question of all."

His logic sunk in. "What do I really want?"

"Exactly. You really need to want this, Emma. It's going to be a lot of hard work, long hours, and little reward in the beginning."

"I know that."

"I'm sure you do, *bella*. But I'm going to remind you of that. With your father's help it's going to be hard. Without it, even harder."

She rubbed the back of her neck. "But likely more fulfilling."

"No doubt in my mind about that."

Emma looked around her rented condo, so small in comparison. Not that she needed a bigger home. It was only her. She could have bought her own single-family home at one point, but stayed fluid in case her father wanted her in Napa.

She was thirty now . . . and that road map of her life had been detoured.

"Thank you," she said to Gio.

"Have I helped you focus?"

"You have. I've been jumping around in my head all day."

"If I was there, I'd massage your temples until you fell asleep."

Emma closed her eyes and drifted into that thought. "That sounds perfect." She pulled in a deep yawn.

"Saturday can't come quick enough," he told her. "You sound like you're getting tired."

She moaned. "Jet lag. I woke up in the middle of the night and couldn't get back to sleep."

"It's always tough . . . but completely worth it. Get some sleep, *cara*. We'll talk tomorrow."

She wished him a good night.

Once the call was disconnected, Emma looked at her phone with a smile.

Having a man in her life that constantly asked what she wanted was a first.

Emma was starting to get used to it.

~

Emma parked her car outside of the tasting rooms at the Temecula vineyards of R&R Wineries. She looked up at the bougainvillea-laden trellis that sparked bright red flowers and a welcome sign. There were only a couple of cars in the main lot, and from the looks of it, several more where the employees left their vehicles.

This location was as much a part of her childhood as a corner playground would be for kids in the city. The tasting room sat on the far edge of the family's Southern California property. The estate itself was nestled up against the hillside. The home where Emma's mother spent most of her time.

As grand as it was, it didn't hold a candle to the Napa vineyards.

Emma thought about the land that was now in her name. Or half of it, anyway. And the image of the three bears from a childhood book came to mind. The big one for Daddy, the smaller one for Mommy . . . and the tiny one for the baby. The image fit her situation perfectly.

She stepped from her car and adjusted her shirt.

Her heels made clicking noises as she crossed the parking lot and moved up the steps to the tasting room and offices.

The air-conditioned room was a welcome relief from the rising temperatures outside.

Two employees were behind the counter and three pairs of customers were tasting and laughing.

"Hello, Miss Rutledge," Dena, an employee that had worked the day shift in the tasting offices for five years, greeted her.

Emma had to smile. If there weren't customers in attendance, Dena called her Emma. When there were people standing by . . . it was always Miss Rutledge.

"Good afternoon, Dena," Emma said. It was only eleven in the morning, but pointing out morning drinking to paying customers was avoided. Wine tasting in the afternoon sounded less . . . *alcoholic*.

"Is she the owner?" the customer in front of Dena asked.

"Mr. Rutledge's daughter."

The couple turned to look at her and smiled.

Emma nodded slightly and continued her way to the back.

The skeleton staff consisted of a receptionist that took on the responsibilities of the office secretary. Meghan cared for everything and everyone and catered to Emma's father when he was in the office. Which didn't happen that often.

Richard, on the other hand . . . spent about a quarter of his time in Temecula. He almost never told anyone he was coming. Emma's theory was that Richard never knew when their father was going to send him south. And Richard, always striving to please their father, never argued.

"Hello, Emma. How was your birthday trip?" Meghan asked with a genuine smile.

"Out of this world. Have you been to Tuscany?"

Meghan laughed. "I wish. On my bucket list."

Emma could tell by the lack of stress on Meghan's face that her father wasn't there. Not that Emma expected him to be.

"How is everything here?"

"Never changes much. But I heard you're leaving us."

Emma kept a smile on her face and forced a laugh. "I'm not getting kicked out of the family."

Meghan rolled her eyes. "That's not what I meant. Is it true you're starting a new branch of R&R?"

Is that what people were being told?

She walked to the coffee pot and went through the act of helping herself to a cup of java.

"I mean . . . it's about time your father gave you a better position," Meghan said, her voice lowered slightly. "If you're asking me."

Emma didn't confirm or deny Meghan's words. Instead, she looked beyond the secretary to the closed door behind her. "Is my father here?"

Meghan shook her head. "No. Your brother showed up yesterday. Said he's going to be here for a couple of days."

"Oh, good . . ." Emma walked around the desk, her coffee in hand. "Just the person I wanted to see."

Without knocking, she opened the office door and walked inside. "Richard."

Richard's chin shot up. "Oh my God, Emma. What are you doing here?"

She set her cup down on the table right inside the door and her handbag beside it. "Good to see you, too."

Her older brother pushed back from the desk and got to his feet. He offered a hug and a kiss on her cheek. "You look tanned and rested."

"I am." He, on the other hand, looked stressed and overworked. "You should try a vacation. It does amazing things for your skin."

Richard's hand shot to his face.

When he realized she was teasing, his hand dropped.

"Happy birthday, by the way."

"My birthday month is almost over. But thank you. I'm sorry you and Kristen weren't at the party." She took a seat on the sofa inside the room.

"There was this thing . . . Father insisted."

"Yeah, I remember. The Kyle-becoming-my-boss thing."

"I don't know what to say about that." Her brother looked genuinely sorry.

"It's not your place." Emma switched the subject. "How is Kristen?" Richard's wife was a lot like their mother. Happy to stay at home and play hostess. From what Emma could tell, Richard and Kristen had a relationship similar to their parents'.

"She's good. She said to say hi if I saw you."

"Be sure and tell her I send my love."

With the pleasantries out of the way, Richard leaned against the desk and crossed his arms over his chest. "What really brings you in today?" he asked.

"Father asked that I guide my replacement, but it seems I've already been removed from my second-level security login."

Richard frowned. "That's odd."

He unfolded from his perch and sat behind his computer and started typing.

While he typed, Emma talked. "I'm sure you've heard about the property I'm taking over."

Richard's gaze was fixed on his screen. "I have. It makes sense."

"Makes sense how?"

He glanced at her briefly, expression neutral, then back to his computer. "You've wanted out of sales for a while."

"I'm wired for upper management. Not a rep under my ex-husband."

"Yeah . . . yeah . . . which makes the property make sense."

"How is that?"

He paused. "You want a job that isn't available. Father figured out a way to make you happy."

Was that how their father was selling this?

"You agree with him?"

Richard narrowed his gaze. "He's the boss, Em. We both know that."

And neither one of them had gone out of their way to force what they wanted. In Richard's case, he was thrown in as second in command and took all the stress that came with it.

"I hear the house is nice. Mom seems excited about it."

"It's beautiful. A little bit like yours and Kristen's." Their home had been built on one of the R&R properties close to the family home in Napa.

"We can't wait to see it." He clicked a few more keys. "This is odd. Why would anyone take you off the clearance list?"

"I'm not sure. Can you switch it back?"

He shook his head. "Not my area. I'll talk to Kyle."

Emma clenched her hands into fists at her sides. "Don't you find it odd that Kyle has more authority in this company than I ever had?"

Richard leaned back in his chair. "Kyle worked for Dad long before your marriage or divorce."

She sighed. "Wine is thicker than blood, right?"

Richard was quick to defend their father. "Dad put you in charge of the new winery. Not Kyle."

In charge of the winery and owning the winery were two different monsters.

The distinction needed to be made . . . and it needed to be made soon.

CHAPTER TWENTY-THREE

"I need to go to Napa," Emma told Gio on a video call while sitting in her car. "To confront my father."

Gio could see by her expression that she was spinning. The wheels in her head were turning a mile a minute.

"Has the lawyer gotten back to you?"

"Not yet. But I know what he's going to say. I saw my brother today and from what he told me and what I've learned is that the common understanding is that my father bought land for me to manage for him."

"I feel like you've already voiced this," he said.

"I have, but hearing my brother's take on things told me, even without a lawyer checking the legal crap, that my hunch is right. I knew my father loves his control more than anything."

"All right . . . so you go to Napa, confront your dad. What's the goal? To feel better?"

"I have to do something, Gio. I feel like a pawn on a chessboard. He's 'hinting' to me that this is mine, but telling everyone else something different."

"So instead of playing into his hand, have your pieces hovered and ready to win." Gio was starting to understand that Emma was a person of action and not talk. Even if that jumping might get her into trouble. He'd heard that personality trait about redheads but had yet to see it for himself.

Until now.

"Have you answered last night's question?"

She sighed. "Do I want the house?"

"Yeah."

"I know what I don't want. I don't want to work for my dad anymore. I don't want my ex-husband to have a position higher than me in my family business. I don't want to be pulled around like a puppet waiting for Daddy's approval. God, I've wasted the last decade doing that."

Gio wished he was at her side to soothe her nerves that were dangling everywhere. "I doubt that time was wasted."

"I want to yell at my father. To his face."

"Will he respond to that?" Because it didn't sound to Gio that her father cared.

"No. He hates temper tantrums," she growled. "I'm so frustrated."

"If you don't take the house and you no longer work for your father, what will you do?" Gio was trying to get her to see what power she did have. Right now, he didn't think Emma saw anything other than the wall in front of her.

"I could get a job in another winery in a heartbeat. And probably crawl up that ladder . . . unlike my own family winery."

"Do you want that?"

She shook her head. "No. Not really, but I will if I have to. Or I make good on my threat and find a property of my own instead of this one."

"I like the idea of you starting your own before you take a job with someone else," he offered.

She sighed. "I do, too. That's going to take time. All while this property just sits there."

"Emma, darling. Hold off on the tantrum. Call me. Yell at me. And when you can answer the first question . . . then a plan can be made."

She squeezed her eyes shut.

Gio knew she was frustrated, but damn, she was cute doing it.

"I hate this."

"You know what you need?" He lowered his voice, lifted one corner of his mouth.

Emma caught on and smiled. "The answer to everything isn't sex."

"Maybe not everything, but it will help you relax."

Her eyes started to shine as her thoughts shifted.

"I'll be there tomorrow, *bella*. Unless you want me there tonight." All she had to do was ask.

"Tomorrow is fine."

Damn. "Am I helping you pack?"

"I have boxes, but I haven't started. Not until I'm certain what I want to do."

"Smart."

"Will you meet me at the house?"

"Casa de Emma?"

She smiled. "I want you to see the scope. The work my mother has put into the house is fantastic. I hate to see that go to waste. Maybe you can help me make a decision."

"*Cara*, that isn't my decision to make."

"No, but you've talked me off the ledge two days in a row now. I do value your opinion."

Gio liked the sound of that. "I'll meet you there."

~

If you hit traffic at the right time, the drive to Temecula's wine country wasn't bad.

Gio pulled off the freeway a little over an hour from when he got on and started winding up the main road leading into the vineyards.

It really was beautiful. Maybe not Tuscany gorgeous, but lovely in its own way. He'd been drawn to the area as soon as he was old enough to drive.

His GPS pulled him off the main road a quarter mile before he saw the gated entrance to Emma's home.

Shivers went up his arms as he took in the view.

Finished driveway, fountain . . . mature trees and a sprawling home that said Mediterranean, but not perfectly Spanish or Italian. Perhaps a Californian Mediterranean style was the best description. Tile roof and stucco walls, with a stone facade and iron porch lights.

As he did his best to close the gap in his lips from the enormity of what Emma was talking about, she emerged from the front door.

She wore a sundress, her hair flying in the breeze.

His heart flipped.

He missed her. It had only been four days and he missed the hell out of this woman.

Gio stepped out of his car and shoved his keys in his front pocket.

"Bellissima." He jogged up the steps, wrapped her in his arms, and spun her around. Before she could say a word, his lips were on hers. She tasted like a light summer rain on a hot day.

Slowly, he felt the tension in her body ease and Emma opened like the flower she was. Only then did Gio pull back and watch her until she opened her eyes. "I missed you, too," he said softly.

"Putting words in my mouth?"

He grinned, pecked her lips again, and pulled away.

"You found the place okay?"

"Technology is a wonderful thing."

Emma slid a hand down his arm and tugged. "Let me show you."

"Guide the way, *cara*."

The expectations promised from the outside of the home absolutely delivered on the inside. While the home was completely empty, it managed to have a cozy feel. Warm tiles, stone, and hardwood floors.

"Wow."

"I know, right?" she asked.

Gio stepped into the great room and ran a hand over the heart of the fireplace. "I can picture a Christmas tree right here," he said, pointing to the corner of the room.

Emma started to laugh.

"And this kitchen . . . do you cook?" he asked.

"I manage, but . . ."

He shrugged. "My mother would make use of every cupboard, every space on the countertop."

Emma walked him around the rest of the home. All the bedrooms, the bathrooms . . . another great room that might serve as a man cave or place for children to claim as their own. The outside patio would host great parties and family gatherings. And the pool simply made sense in the heat that Temecula sported most of the year.

Then, of course, there were the vines, rich in their summer growth. He looked for the path leaving the fenced-in yard to reach what he saw as the main attraction.

Emma told him about the varieties that were grown there and how she'd been talking with the foreman and had already increased the watering schedule and was calculating the extent of renovations needed to the working part of the property.

"The previous owners hadn't produced wine on-site for years. They sold the grapes. My father has used them in our blends . . . his blends."

Which explained the state of the equipment in the distillery. "You'd need an equipment loan," he mused aloud. "There are auctions for used equipment, but there is likely a reason it's for sale."

"Buying old equipment is like buying an old used car. You're taking on someone else's headache most of the time."

Gio offered a smile and let her show him around the rest of the place. Another barn structure held an old truck that was likely used during harvest. Old oak barrels that were better off used as containers for plants at this point.

Still, the bones were good.

"What do you think?" she asked once they were back outside, staring over the vineyard.

Gio took that moment to look at Emma. Really look at her. She had a smile that reached her eyes and a bounce in her step as she gave him the tour. She interjected the ideas she had for where things would go, and a future tasting room . . . and wouldn't it be nice to have a path that would carry guests away from the driveway, directly into the vineyard, to a covered patio where a long table could be set up for meals. Just like the one they'd visited in Tuscany.

"I think you're in love."

She hesitated. "It's really nice."

"*Bella*, it's spectacular." Gio draped an arm over her shoulder and turned her to the south. "You could have a clearing, not a big one, for a vegetable garden. And along the back of the equipment barn, a small chicken coop for fresh eggs every morning. Remember the place outside of Pisa that had the hens flittering around? How amused we all were?"

She hummed. "Fascinating creatures."

"That give you breakfast every day."

"My parents never wanted animals."

"This won't be your parents' home," he reminded her.

"Technically—"

Gio waved off her technicality. "Do you want this, *cara*? The door is open and only you can make that choice."

She started nodding, slowly at first, and then her eyes met his. "I do. I really do." As the words left her lips, Gio saw the conviction in her eyes. "I need to find a way to do this on my own."

"Then that's what we do. We do our homework, map out a plan, and when you present it to your father, he has to go along with it." Gio was certain they would find a solution.

"And if he doesn't?"

"We're not going to think like that."

They walked back into the house and Gio took in all the features a second time. "In the beginning, one of the rooms can be used as an office."

"I thought that, too. Then I considered the bonus room."

"You can't close it off then. Which will make you feel like you need to continue to work long after you should call it a day."

"That's true. I've worked from my laptop so much in the past few years, every time I look at it and I'm not working, I feel guilty."

"Living above a restaurant my entire life has forced me to look beyond the work when I wanted a day off." They stopped in the kitchen and it was there that Gio poked around. "There's a ton of storage."

"I can fill maybe five of the cupboards."

Gio looked across the room. "Do you have any furniture that will work?"

"Not really. Even my bed is only a queen, and that primary bedroom . . ."

"It needs a Cal king."

"That's what I thought. My mother is pretty good at this kind of thing, but if I ask for her help, she'll want to pay for it. Like she did the remodel."

Gio shook his head. "And this is a problem?"

"If it was just my mother, no. But it's my father's money she'd be spending."

And Emma didn't want to be beholden to her father for any more than she already was.

"It's hard for me to wrap my mind around the division. What was my father's was my mother's, and vice versa. There was no *his* and *hers*. My brother and his wife . . . same thing. Chloe and Dante, it's all *ours* and *we*."

"My mother hasn't worked outside of the home in their marriage."

"Would your father have wanted her to work?" he asked.

Emma looked shocked. As if the thought disturbed her. "No."

"Then what's the difference?"

"I hear ya. My father doesn't restrict my mother's spending. Not that I know of, anyway."

Gio tilted his head. "It's you that doesn't want to take any more from him."

"I don't, Giovanni. Maybe that would be different if my dad was a loving, generous man who simply wanted me to be happy. Like how you describe your mom. Robert Rutledge is not that man. This is meant as a shiny new toy to distract me and keep me busy while removing me from his place of business. Richard confirmed that." She hopped up on the kitchen island, her legs dangling off the side. "I don't even know if he expects any great reward from these vines. He may be expecting a loss year after year to use as a tax write-off. Something he's done before with smaller acquisitions. Then he'd be able to tell anyone who asks that his daughter may have thought she knew what she was doing, but look . . . it fails. And he'll come out as the hero because he takes care of it."

Gio walked around in front of her, met her eye to eye. "That's nauseating."

"I know. If this is fruitful, he will take the credit. If it fails, he's the hero." She placed a hand on her neck and pretended to squeeze.

Gio framed her body with his arms and snuggled into the space between her legs. "The only hero I want in your life is me," he said, distracting her.

Emma placed her arms on his shoulders and leaned forward. "You've really kept me focused. Not an easy task."

He placed his hand on her bottom and scooted her closer. "Can I focus your attention somewhere else?"

"I don't know. What did you have in mind?" Her smile suggested she knew exactly where his thoughts were.

He slid his hands down her thighs and then back up under the dress.

"Oh . . . that's what you had in mind."

Her eyes widened when he found the edge of her panties and ran his thumbs down the warmest part of her body.

"I hope that's okay."

Emma leaned forward and placed her lips on his. Like every time they kissed, energy surged between them both, making his blood boil and his heartbeat surge.

Her arms pulled him close while Gio teased her center with his fingers.

She retracted sharply when he found her favorite spot and then she wiggled closer.

When Emma gasped, he released her lips and kissed the base of her throat that she offered so sweetly when her head fell back.

He liked this surrender. The way she unfurled under his touch.

Gio trailed kisses down the open V of her dress to the tops of her breasts. All while her body damped his fingers through her panties.

The image of her lying back, open for him to taste, on the kitchen counter was simply too delicious to pass up. What better way to break in her new home and cement her memory of him?

With his mind made up, he tugged at her panties. "Lift your hips, *cara*."

She obliged and he wiggled them down her legs and set them on the counter beside them.

He spread her legs farther, her hooded gaze took him in. "Relax."

"What are you . . . ?"

Gio dipped his head and took his first taste.

"Oh, hell . . ." She leaned back and Gio leaned in.

He loved how she moved against him, how she tasted on his lips.

Gio teased and played, nibbled and tugged until he found what worked for her. And even though her thighs shivered and then held him in, he didn't stop the pace. Kept it exactly where she needed it.

Then her breath held, and he felt her orgasm on his tongue, heard her cries echo in the empty room. When she pushed him away, he took one more drink before letting go.

Gio smiled over her body, his erection calling for attention.

Emma was laid out, exactly how he wanted to see her, an arm tossed over her eyes. "That was . . ." She didn't finish her sentence and just started laughing.

"A great way to test the quality of this countertop. It passed."

She laughed even harder and opened her eyes. "What about you?"

Gio shook his head. "You owe me one."

"I'll make good on that."

He had no doubt.

CHAPTER TWENTY-FOUR

Even though Gio had made dinner reservations, they decided to cancel them and eat in.

Emma changed into a pair of shorts and a T-shirt once they arrived at her condo and then got to work packing.

Gio called a local hardware store and reserved a truck for the following day. The goal was to get her bed in the new house before Gio left on Monday. By the following Friday he would return with a helper to move the bigger furniture.

"I can hire movers," she insisted.

"Is that how you want to spend your money, *bella*? I'm here and I'm free."

A budget. What a concept.

While the two of them filled the empty boxes that she had, they talked of ways to obtain a loan to have the ability to buy her father out of any controlling interest.

Gio had thought of this angle long and hard since he didn't have a parent able to sock millions of dollars into his winery ambition.

They woke early the next day and drove together to pick up the rental truck.

Gio had been intuitive enough to pack a small bag with clothes, something Emma hadn't suggested. It wasn't that San Diego was so far away that he couldn't go home and come back, but why?

They'd spent a lot of time on the phone since their return from Italy, it was like he was there anyway.

And he grounded her.

Emma had been told she was hot-tempered, "a feisty redhead." But exercising that fiery personality against her father hadn't happened since she was a teenager.

Yes, she wanted to scream at him, at the injustice of his actions and her placement within the company. But she never did. And now that she wanted to tell the man off more than ever before, there stood Giovanni, holding up the caution flag.

He was right.

Emma needed to approach everything with knowledge and power to get what she wanted.

Back at her condo they loaded the truck with her bed and then stuffed the rest with boxes and suitcases filled with summer clothes. She loaded her groceries into bags that she could transfer into the kitchen.

Next came utensils, a coffee maker, and a wine opener.

Back at Casa de Emma, the name that was used originally by their San Francisco friends in Italy, but that had grown on her since . . . she opened the electric gate with a remote as Gio followed behind in the truck.

She stepped from the car and welcomed the silence.

And she smiled.

This is really happening.

Gio hopped out of the truck and rounded in front. "There's the smile I love to see," he said.

"I'm feeling good about this decision."

He gave her butt a playful slap. "Open the door, *cara* . . . let's get this stuff inside."

"Hey!"

Gio winked and walked to the passenger side of her car to help unload.

Thirty minutes later, the boxes they'd managed to pack were scattered around the house and they were lugging the mattress inside.

Emma never considered herself all that athletic, but the two of them managed to get the bed from her condo to the truck, and now into the house. The bed frame had broken down into several pieces, which Gio insisted he deal with taking apart and putting back together on his own.

While he did the heavy lifting, Emma started putting the refrigerated groceries away.

She laughed at how ridiculously small her provisions were for the amount of room the kitchen had.

Gio walked by with her small toolbox that held only the bare minimum of tools. He stopped at her side, planted a kiss on her lips. "I'll be in the bedroom putting your bed back together."

She placed a hand on her rumbling stomach. "I'm going to run out and get us some lunch."

"Sounds good."

"Any preference?" she asked.

He nodded and started to walk away. "Not Italian."

She couldn't stop her laugh. "I ate all that last night."

Gio pivoted and pulled her close with his free hand. His kiss was instant, open-mouthed, and hot as hell. "I'll give you all the *Italian* you desire." He squeezed her butt and let her go.

She grabbed her purse and keys from the counter and walked out the door and paused. "I can get used to this."

~

Gio propped his phone against a wall and turned on some music while he worked.

Emma had given him a full debate the night before about moving her bed into her new room instead of setting it up in a guest room. She wanted a bigger bed, but did she want to spend the money on that right away? Her bed was perfectly fine. Even with the two of them snuggled against each other in it, it worked. Then she concluded that the need for living room furniture and a bigger dining room table and lighting and outdoor furniture outweighed the bed. Exhausted with her own conversation about all of it, she decided to move her queen bed into her king-size room.

All the while Gio simply listened.

Despite Emma's frugality of keeping her current sleeping accommodations, he concluded that she had no concept of a budget. And why would she? According to her, her father had each of his children on the payroll at an early age. A tax move people do to save money. That money went into an account and eventually paid for her first car and helped pay for college. When she finally moved out of her family home, she bought everything she needed for her small place with the money she made as a sales rep. Thankfully, she and Kyle never bought a home together or anything major, so her trust fund was completely intact.

She did what she wanted to do when she wanted to do it.

A life that Gio knew.

He'd never had to pay for many of life's big expenses. The family home was paid for. The restaurant afforded all of them a comfortable lifestyle. When their father had passed, a life insurance policy gave their mother a cushion and put money into accounts for all three of them. Their mother, being insightful, dropped that money into a market account that had tripled in nearly ten years.

Gio's pile of money might not have been as big as Emma's, but it was enough to get started.

All of this rolled around in his head as he manually screwed together her headboard.

When he came back the next weekend, he was bringing power tools.

Noise from the kitchen drew Gio's attention away from his task. Emma must have forgotten something.

He turned his music down to ask her just that when a female voice that wasn't Emma's called her name.

"Emma?"

Gio dropped the screwdriver on the floor and stood.

"Are you back there?"

Gio walked into the hall to find who was talking.

A woman who stood a little shorter than Emma and was at least twenty-five years older than her walked toward him and then stopped. "Oh." She was dressed in linen and fine jewelry, and Gio was fairly certain he was looking at Emma's mother.

"You just missed her. She went out to get us lunch."

The woman hesitated and then looked around. "Oh . . ."

Gio turned on his charm like a switch. "I didn't think Emma had an older sister."

The woman's smile was slow to travel but soon she huffed out a breath. "That's very sweet, but I'm Emma's mother."

"Beth, of course. You have the same nose." Gio continued in Italian and said they also shared the same beautiful smile. Switching languages was a surefire way to make a woman feel flattered, so long as the words were said with a smile and sincerity.

Beth Rutledge melted into a pile of putty. Her shoulders relaxed and her cheeks heated with the same flush he'd seen in Emma's. "You're Italian."

"Guilty," he said. "Emma speaks highly of you."

"That's wonderful to hear."

Gio could see by the expression on her face she'd heard nothing of him.

"I'm Giovanni. A friend of your daughter's."

"A *friend*?"

He winked. "I do spend a lot of time looking at your daughter's nose." That made Beth laugh.

"Should we move this conversation out of this hallway?" he suggested.

Beth shook her head and turned around. "I'm sorry to just drop in like this. Emma sent a message that she was home but hadn't started moving yet. I wanted to make sure the new plants were getting watered."

The excuse sounded legit on the surface, but Gio knew there was a foreman who made frequent rounds. Gio wasn't about to point out what he knew. Not to mention, Beth Rutledge wasn't dressed to be out watering plants.

"I think everything is taking root. We haven't noticed anything wilted."

"This heat will do it."

They stopped in the kitchen, where Beth looked around at the boxes. "I told Emma I could hire movers."

Ahh, that's where Emma picked up on hired help.

"There's something to be said for doing things yourself," he told her.

"A sore back?"

"Lack of need for a gym," he countered.

"Enjoy that while you're young."

"Oh, please, Mrs. Rutledge, you're much too young to be talking like that."

She narrowed her eyes. "I can't tell if you're really this charming or you're pulling my leg?"

Gio lifted his chin. "I've yet to meet a woman who doesn't like to be flattered. Besides, if I don't make a good first impression, how will I ever secure a family dinner invitation?"

Once again, Beth gave him a guarded look. One Gio was certain he'd seen on Emma's face a time or two.

"How long have you known my daughter?"

"We met in Italy."

"You're from Italy?"

"No. San Diego. But Emma and I met on the same tour *in* Italy."

Beth smiled. "Not long, then."

"Long enough to know your daughter is a thief."

Beth gasped. "Excuse me?"

Gio placed a hand to his chest. "She's stealing my heart."

Beth rolled her eyes. "Aren't you something."

In all the times he'd used that line, he'd never meant it. With Emma, on the other hand . . .

Gio pointed to Beth's face. "You both roll your eyes exactly the same way."

"She gets it from me. I've been rolling my eyes at her father for years."

Funny, Gio had pictured Beth as someone who was submissive to her husband. Maybe he was wrong.

He looked at Beth's light brown hair and brown eyes. "Which grandparent has the red hair?" he asked. Gio had looked up Robert Rutledge shortly after he learned who Emma was. The man, while turning gray now, had dark hair when he was younger, and so did his first son, Richard.

"Women do dye their hair."

He shook his head. Emma was red . . . everywhere. "Not your daughter."

"Oh . . . you have *that* relationship, do you?"

As if she couldn't tell. "I don't kiss and tell," he said.

"Mmm-hmm. Well, I'm told that my great-grandmother had red hair. You can say Emma got it from me."

"Her fiery spirit, too, I think."

Beth crossed her arms over her chest. "I like you, Giovanni. Even if you have more pickup lines than a sailor on shore leave."

He laughed. "And what would you know about sailors on shore leave, Mrs. Rutledge?"

She was having fun. Her smile worked from ear to ear. "I had a life before Mr. Rutledge."

I bet you did!

Before Gio could comment further, the front door opened, and Emma walked in.

"*Cara* . . . look who's here." He moved quickly to take the lunch bags from her hands and kissed her before turning back to Beth.

"I wasn't expecting you," Emma said.

"I was starting to worry. You've been home for days and hadn't moved in yet."

Emma looked between him and her mother.

"She was waiting for me to have time to help," Gio offered, a white lie to keep the truth out of the conversation.

Emma let the explanation stand and moved over to hug her mother.

"You look tired," her mother said.

Gio could tell that Emma took the comment as an insult.

"That's my fault, Mrs. Rutledge," he offered with a wink.

Emma gasped and Beth laughed. "My God, where did you find this man?"

"Am I wrong?" he asked.

"Gio. This is my mother!" Emma looked a little dazed.

"Who had a thing for sailors before your dad came around."

"W-what?" Emma's jaw dropped.

Beth waved a hand in the air. "Nothing." She pointed at Gio. "You need a warning label."

He nodded. "My mother would agree."

Beth was close enough to pat Gio's cheek. "You have the dinner invitation."

Gio moved in, kissed Beth's cheek, and called her adorable in Italian.

Beth grasped the handle of her purse and crossed her free arm over it, almost like the queen of England.

"Call me when you're settled. I've talked with Benson's about a few of their pieces I think you'll like."

"I told you I wanted to pick out my own furniture."

"I know, but for some reason there are backlogs on almost everything these days. The sooner you get on that, the better, or you'll be sitting on fold-up chairs come Christmas."

Emma relented. "I should have time midweek."

"Good." Beth glanced over her shoulder and tilted her head Gio's way. "And without this one. We need to talk about him," she said, smiling.

Emma shook her head as her mother left the house. "What in the heck was that all about?"

Gio placed a hand on his heart. "Your mother loves me."

~

Saying goodbye was harder than Emma expected.

The morning sun had tipped over the horizon and Gio was drying his hair with a towel after a shower.

Emma walked up behind him, in front of the mirror, and wrapped her arms around his waist. "Have I thanked you for all your help?"

"Oh, so many times."

She kissed his bare shoulder.

Gio smiled at her through their reflections.

He made a point of lifting the toothbrush he'd brought with him and setting it in a cup next to hers. "I'm leaving this here."

"Bold move, D'Angelo." She was joking.

"I'm not brushing my teeth in any other woman's bathroom," he said.

"I'm not brushing mine in any other woman's bathroom either."

Gio growled, twisted in her arms, and spun her around. Once she was pinned between him and the sink, he lifted her up to sit on the edge. "I'm going to miss you."

"You'll be back on Friday."

He kissed her nose. "I know. But that's four very long and lonely nights without you."

"It will give me a chance to stock up on condoms."

He wiggled his eyebrows. "That reminds me. I made an appointment with my doctor for next week."

"Your doctor? What's wrong?"

"Clean bill of health, *cara*. In case the condom fails."

She'd completely forgotten about that. "Right. I'll call my doctor today."

"Good." His hands traveled down her back. "Now, if you don't walk away, I'm going to be forced to make love to you again and sit in traffic for hours."

She draped her arms on his shoulders. "You're the one who tossed me up here."

He smiled, looked in the mirror, and started to frown. "Is that from Italy?"

Emma twisted and looked in the mirror.

Gio pointed to the scratch that had happened almost two weeks prior on their journey to find Kimmy and Weston. "Yeah. Crazy that I still have a bruise."

"Are you anemic?"

"Not that I know of. I do bruise easily."

"Maybe you should have that checked."

She shrugged, thinking nothing about it. "Look at you, Mr. Concerned."

His smile faltered. "Have the doctor look, *tesoro*, please."

"Okay." She kissed him briefly and he helped her off the counter.

She slipped her arms into a light bathrobe and followed Gio out of the house a short time later.

He kissed her again, whispered something in Italian she didn't understand, and turned away.

"Text me when you get home," she told him.

He blew her a kiss from his car before getting behind the wheel.

Alone for the first time in her new house, Emma wrapped her arms around herself and smiled. "I'm home."

CHAPTER TWENTY-FIVE

Emma insisted on picking her mother up for their midweek lunch and shopping trip. Emma knew that if she didn't placate her mother with a trip to the furniture store, mysterious gifts would start to appear on her doorstep.

Driving her mother also gave Emma an excuse to drive to the working side of the Temecula winery and have a discussion with Noland, the operational manager, or foreman, as Emma referred to him.

Dressed to shop and not traipse around wine cellars and factories, Emma walked carefully through the buildings, greeting the workers she knew by name. Most had been there for years.

She found Noland next to a barrel of cabernet that had been aging for three years.

"Good morning," she said, announcing herself.

His smile was instant. "Emma, what a surprise."

"It's been a minute."

"The days are long past that you were running around here getting into trouble."

She pictured those times he was referring to. "What self-respecting teenager being raised at a winery doesn't bring her friends in to test the stock?"

Noland's laugh was as warm as his personality. "Do I need to find you a glass, or is there another reason for your visit today?"

"I'm on my way to pick up my mother. We have a full day planned. But I was hoping to run into you and ask for a favor."

"Anything for you."

She knew that's how he would respond.

"Do you know about the property on Edgewood Street?"

"I do. I visited the site a couple of times."

Emma smiled. "I'm taking it over."

"Is that right?" he asked, smiling.

"It's a long and drawn-out explanation, but at the end of the day, my plan is to be able to harvest the grapes this season and process them on-site."

Noland narrowed his eyes. "If I remember right, there isn't a processing plant there."

"There isn't. The owners before my father hadn't produced wine on the land for some time. The equipment, what's left of it, doesn't seem up to par. I can't truly tell. It's been a while since I've been in the factories during harvest. I'm likely going to have to scrap everything that's old and start with new equipment."

"Old equipment, old problems."

Emma nodded. "My thoughts, too. Raul, the foreman there, isn't up on the changes that have happened in the past several years when it comes to production."

"You want me to help set things up?"

"I would love that . . . but I can't steal my father's employees. Helping me on that big of a scale is a job and not a favor. What I was hoping for is a little guidance. I'm going to create a list of all the things I think I need and if you can look it over and tell me what I'm missing, that would be great. And maybe when the time comes, perhaps give me a few hours with Raul and your honest opinion on his capabilities."

Noland kept smiling. "You don't even have to ask for that. I'm happy to help you out."

She sighed. "Good. Thank you."

"I'm confused, though."

"About?"

"Your father is likely to send a crew over and set everything up."

"That's not the plan. This is going to be completely separate from R&R."

His face lit up. "How exciting is that?"

"I'm getting there. I won't go into details about the finances, just know that this isn't all on my dad. I'm not going to rely on him or R&R."

"Your father won't let you fail."

She shook her head. "I'm not going to fail. I have what it takes to make this work. I may never produce the tens of thousands of bottles my father does, but I don't have to. I don't want my father's sweep of a pen on the bottom line doing this. I want to do it, from the ground up. This favor is for me . . . not paid for by my dad."

Admiration filled Noland's eyes. "I'm proud of you, Emma. You'll get a lot more out of this doing it yourself."

"That's my thought. So, you'll help?"

"Anytime. You know where to find me."

Emma extended a hand, which Noland shook with a chuckle.

"One more thing?"

"Shoot."

"Let's keep this between you and I. I don't want others speculating on what's going on."

"It's a small community, others will find out."

He was right. "They will, but I'd like to be the one to tell my father I don't want his help first."

She shocked him, Emma saw it on Noland's face. "You're serious."

"I am."

He blew out a breath. "I'll keep my lips shut. Considering I almost never see your father, that shouldn't be difficult."

"Or my brother."

Noland leaned against the barrel. "We communicate through email . . . if at all."

"Thanks, Noland. I'll be in touch."

Fifteen minutes later, Emma pulled into her mother's drive, rolled down the windows, and left her car.

Emma didn't bother knocking. "Mom?" she called from the foyer.

She heard soft music playing toward the back of the house and followed the sound.

Beth was in her primary closet, shuffling things from one purse to another.

"You ready?" Emma asked.

"Almost."

"Where is Christy?" Christy was the woman who helped keep the house clean and sometimes cooked meals.

"It's her day off."

"We all need those once in a while."

"I think she's seeing someone. Lately she's been asking for more days to herself."

A hardship for her mother. "You could probably do with her coming in only a few hours a few times a week."

Beth paused, then shook her head. "What about when your father is home? He can't put his clothes in the hamper to save his life."

Emma laughed. "So that's the real reason you two live in separate houses."

"It helps. And we don't live separately."

"Really? When was the last time you two were together?"

They walked out of the closet and the light automatically switched off.

"I was in Napa for nearly a week when you were in Italy."

Emma called bullshit. "While there was construction going on at my place?"

"Okay, maybe four days . . . but still. And I'll be back there in a couple of weeks for an event your father wants me to attend."

"What event?"

"One of those magazines that he loves to get his name in."

Emma could think of three off the top of her head. There were always photographers and women dressed in formal gowns and men in tuxes. Emma had only been to one of those events, right after she and Kyle were married. Never before had her father wanted her there, and not since.

"Have you picked out a gown?" Emma asked.

"Not yet. Heaven forbid I wear something I have in my closet."

They stepped outside the house and over to her car. "Have you ever considered renting a gown?"

Beth rolled her eyes. "Don't be ridiculous."

She wasn't.

As soon as they got in the car, Emma rolled up the windows and blasted the air. They made it to the main road before the questions started.

"Now that we've talked about my housekeeper and my clothes, I want to hear everything about Giovanni."

Emma laughed and looked at her watch. "You know what, Mom? I'm proud of you. That took over fifteen minutes."

"He *is* charming."

"You like anyone who can speak a different language."

Beth cleared her throat. "I'm sure you like that, too."

It didn't suck.

"What do you want to know?" Emma asked.

Beth didn't miss a beat. "Is it serious?"

"It's only been a little over four weeks."

"No, then?"

Emma shrugged. "I wouldn't say we're casual."

"Is there something between casual and serious?"

"Of course there is."

"What's that called?" her mother asked.

Emma blinked several times. "Whatever we're doing."

"Do you want it to be serious?"

"Oh my God, Mom." Emma gripped the steering wheel hard.

Catherine Bybee

Beth paused. "He makes you smile more than Kyle did."

Emma glanced at her mother. "You've met him once."

"And in one visit I saw you smiling more than your whole time with Kyle."

"There are thousands of dollars' worth of useless wedding pictures that would say differently."

"Only because a photographer told you to."

"Is smiling your barometer of happiness?" Emma asked.

"It certainly helps."

"I don't see you and Dad smiling very often."

Beth dismissed her. "Oh, honey. We've been married for so long that doesn't matter anymore."

Emma shook her head. "That's ridiculous."

"We smile. You just don't see it."

"I'm not buying it. I'm convinced that you and Dad have only had sex three times in the missionary position with a timer set. And neither of you were smiling." The thought made her skin crawl, but the image was in her mind, nonetheless.

Her mother laughed. "I assure you that wasn't the case."

Emma stopped for the red light. If her parents' marriage was the goal, Emma would happily stay single. A conclusion she made during her brief time with Kyle.

"How did we get onto your father's and my relationship?"

"You were telling me how I smile when Giovanni is around, and I was comparing you and Dad based on your assessment of my relationship with my boyfriend."

"Ha! He *is* your boyfriend."

"Mom!" Traffic started to move again.

"What does he do for a living?"

"His family owns a restaurant."

"Oh . . . a restaurateur." The singsong of her mother's voice said she was impressed.

216

"One family restaurant does not make him that. He is also a sommelier, hence both of us being on the tour in Italy."

"Something the two of you have in common."

Emma pulled into the parking lot of where they were going to have lunch. "Kyle and I had wine in common, too . . . so I won't hold that against Gio."

"Gio?"

"Yes. It's a nickname. He said there are a half a dozen Giovannis in his neighborhood and growing up, it was easier being called Gio."

Emma turned off the engine and Beth reached for the door. "He introduced himself to me as Giovanni, so that's the name I'll use."

Emma hesitated before getting out of the car.

This was going to be exhausting.

~

"Thanks for this," Gio said to his family. Their weekly dinner took place on Sunday without him since he was with Emma, but they went ahead and had a second one midweek to accommodate him.

"Eventually you'll bring your girlfriend here so we can meet her." Mari passed the plate of chicken as she spoke.

He didn't correct the *girlfriend* comment since that was how he viewed Emma, even if they hadn't gone so far as to give the other a title.

"I'll help her get settled into her new place and then bring her. She's pretty busy right now."

"I think it's sexist of you to only invite the men to help move her next weekend. I can help," Chloe offered.

Dante had already agreed.

Luca was tied up in the restaurant kitchen since one of their chefs was on vacation.

"I need brawn, not beauty," Gio told his sister with a smile.

"That's a backhanded compliment."

"I can help," Franny announced.

Gio pressed a finger to his niece's nose. "Soon, *bella*."

"When is all this wine that you bought in Italy going to arrive?" Mari asked.

"I wouldn't expect anything for another month. Customs is always slow," Gio told her. "Speaking of wine . . ."

Mari glanced at Luca, Luca looked at Chloe . . . then they all turned to Gio.

"Yes?" his mother asked.

"What was that?" he asked.

"We're all waiting, brother," Luca said.

"Waiting for what?"

"For you to start the conversation about your place in Temecula."

Chloe leaned forward. "None of us believed that you'd return from Italy and be happy here for long. You've been talking about a winery in Temecula since Papa was alive."

Gio released a breath. His family supported him in everything he did, but in this, it would take more than a few days, weeks, or dollars. "I'm going to need every dime from my accounts, and once things are in motion, I won't be here to help with the restaurant. I'll be in debt up to my eyeballs. Probably have stress streaming from my ears."

"Sounds like a party," Dante said.

"I'm serious. I'm going to help Emma find the loans and get on her feet. Get through the first harvest. If land is going to go on sale, it will be after the grapes are off the vines. I'm hoping this winter I can find something." If Gio could find half of her size of land, with a quarter of the house, he could make it work.

Chloe reached for her wine. "Count us in," she said.

"In for what?"

"Us, too," Luca added.

Gio shifted his gaze between his brother and sister. "I'm confused."

"Investors. Papa's insurance money might be growing, but it isn't making any of us happy."

Gio shook his head. "That money is your future. I can't risk that."

"But you can risk your own?" his mother asked, her voice stern. "We're a family. We do things together as a family." She pointed to Chloe and Dante. "Dante speaks of another boat by next year to double his business . . . we help. Not because we need the money but because his happiness is our happiness. And the same goes for you. Luca, Chloe, and I talked of this before we sent you on your birthday trip. We knew this was the push you needed to take the leap you've always dreamed about. I offered to take a loan out on the building—"

"No, Mama."

She stopped him with a wave of her hand. "I know, I know. Bad decision, but I'll help in every way short of that. And you'll accept that help. All of it."

The warmth in Gio's chest rushed to his head. Their investment would make every step of this that much easier.

"I'll write up contracts."

Mari cussed . . . in Italian. "The hell you will."

Gio slapped his lips shut.

She shook her hand in the air and raised her voice. "Family!" she said as if that was the answer to a question. "Contracts are for strangers."

Emotion welled inside of him. "Thank you. All of you."

"Now eat. The food is getting cold."

Luca lifted his glass. "To the future wine with the D'Angelo name on it."

"*Salute!*"

CHAPTER TWENTY-SIX

Emma had to stop herself from staring at Giovanni and Dante as they juggled her furniture into and out of the moving truck Gio had rented early Friday morning. The two of them working and laughing together, both of them winking at her with *bella* this and *bella* that . . . It was as if they were biological brothers and not just friends.

Dante had greeted her with a kiss to each cheek as if he knew her.

They were absolutely lovely to look at.

"I have a feeling you two got into a lot of trouble in high school," she told them after they'd moved her couch into the great room.

"What one person calls trouble, others call fun," Gio told her.

Dante was laughing. "We had a lot of fun."

Emma was in the kitchen, unpacking the rest of her boxes.

Her entire week had been spent packing and researching what she needed to make Casa de Emma work.

"Broken hearts everywhere," she said.

Gio walked up behind her, kissed the side of her neck. "I saved my heart for you, *cara*."

Her mother was right . . . Gio had all the lines.

Lines that didn't suck to hear.

They walked back out the front door to bring in something else. The truck Gio had rented this time was bigger, and they managed to pack her entire life into one load. Well, two, if she counted the one they'd done the week before.

The tissue paper she'd used to keep the glasses from breaking was piling up on the island, and every time a gust of wind drifted in from the open doors, paper flew in all directions.

The guys strained under the weight of her dresser. "Where do you want this?" Gio asked.

"Bedroom."

"Show us where."

Emma jogged in front of them as they maneuvered around a corner and eventually into her bedroom.

She pointed to an empty wall. "There."

They set the bulky furniture down and huffed out a breath.

Both of them stood there looking at her.

"That's good, I think." Emma glanced around. The primary bedroom was huge. Plenty of wall space for big items.

She found Gio staring.

"What are you waiting for?"

"For you to change your mind."

"No. This is good."

Gio and Dante shrugged and walked out.

Emma considered the traffic flow through the room to the massive doors leading out to the backyard.

When they returned, they both held two of the drawers that filled the empty slots in the dresser.

"You know . . . maybe this wall over here will be better."

Gio grinned. "You sure?"

"Yeah. That way I won't run into it on the way outside." She walked the desired path as if they needed a demonstration.

Gio and Dante both lifted an end of the chest and huffed it to the new location.

Yeah . . . that was better.

She sat on the edge of the bed, her eyes narrowed.

The guys walked out.

Now the room felt lopsided.

Back they came with more drawers. "Actually . . . this isn't working. Can you move it back?"

Dante laughed, pointed at Gio. "You owe me a beer."

"I'm sorry," she told them.

"Don't be."

"It doesn't really matter. In a few months all of this furniture will end up in one of the spare rooms."

Gio walked by, kissed her. "It matters for the next few months, then."

She walked out of the room before she could change her mind again. It was getting close to noon. Lucky for all of them, Gio's mother had sent him with trays of food that only needed to be heated up.

Emma pulled the lid off one of the catering trays and marveled at the amount of food. "I hope your mom doesn't expect us to eat all this," Emma told Gio as he walked by again.

"Speak for yourself. I'm starving," Dante said.

Following Mrs. D'Angelo's instructions, Emma put the tray of pasta into the oven and set it to the right temperature. There was a container filled with freshly grated parmesan. The caprese salad was enough to feed ten people. There was bread and a bottle of olive oil and balsamic vinegar. Another small tray had asparagus that looked like it had been seared and now rested in a garlic butter sauce.

Emma's mouth watered.

It was Italy all over again.

Food like this deserved wine, so she found a bottle she liked and removed it from her wine fridge to open and let breathe.

While Gio and Dante continued to lug in every last box of belongings she owned, Emma set her small round dining room table that filled a breakfast nook area of the kitchen. A bigger dining room table was on the list of things to buy, but for now, this would do.

She found everything she needed, including wineglasses, before the oven timer went off.

"Lunch is ready?"

"Yes!" Dante dropped the box in his hands in the middle of the living room and moved to the sink.

Emma laughed.

"Slacker," Gio called him out and walked down the hall with the box in his arms.

A few minutes later they were sitting around the table, filling their plates. "I appreciate you coming to help," she told Dante.

He winked and shoved a piece of bread dipped in oil into his mouth.

"Everyone wanted to come," Gio said.

"Like, the whole family." Dante talked around the food in his mouth.

"They can't wait to meet you. I thought we might hold off until you're unpacked. Or for a time you can come to us."

She felt nervous just thinking about it. "It will be a while before I'll be set up to entertain here."

Gio scoffed. "You don't need anything fancy to entertain my family."

"We'll find two sawhorses from a shed with a piece of plywood to make a table, and boom, done." Dante made it sound easy.

"Owning a restaurant that does the occasional catering means we come equipped with everything you need for a party." Gio winked her way.

Twenty minutes later Emma placed a hand over her stomach and called it. "I can't take another bite."

"I saw you put away more food than that in Italy," Gio teased.

"In Italy all we had to do was eat and drink. Any more and I'll need to crawl into bed for a nap."

Much as they all hated to get up from their break, Dante had a deadline to get back to San Diego.

It was just after three in the afternoon when Emma and Gio stood on the porch, waving goodbye to Dante.

He'd stayed long enough to move everything bulky and helped empty out a few boxes and then promised to return with a swimsuit and a cooler full of beer.

By seven in the evening every box had been unpacked and items distributed around the house. Gio had connected her television and moved her speakers around the room until it provided the sound he felt she needed.

Then, after several trips to the dumpster that sat on the far side of the house, close to the cellar, they both fell onto her sofa like deflated balloons after a party.

The house still felt empty, but they were done.

"I'm wrecked."

"You're a beautiful wreck," Gio said, grasping her hand and putting it in his lap.

"I couldn't have done it without you."

"Yeah, you could have. It just would have taken you longer." He kissed the back of her hand, put it back in his lap.

She stared at the blank walls and empty corners of the room. "I have so much to learn about being a homeowner."

"Like what?"

"Maintenance stuff. What does a water heater need? Do I have to have that kind of thing serviced every year?"

"No, but your air filters need to be changed annually."

She looked at him. "What are those?"

He smiled. "I'll help you."

"I should probably invest in some power tools. Things went faster today because you brought them. And a decent toolbox for the garage. I've never had my own garage."

"Your garage makes me drool," he admitted.

It was fit for three cars, with plenty of storage for all the things men put in garages.

"And what about the fountain outside? The sprinkler system? I was gone most of the day on Wednesday, and when I came home it looked like someone had been here to mow the lawn and clean up the leaves. Is my mother paying him? Does Raul see that things are picked up around the house? His job is the vines, not the house."

Gio twisted around to look at her. "You're doing it again."

"Doing what?"

"Jumping to the next thing and making it feel bigger than it is."

Yeah, it was a nasty habit of hers.

"Tomorrow we'll write a list, and when I'm not here, you'll keep adding to the list. And we'll prioritize that list. The only thing urgent about a sprinkler system is knowing where the shutoff valve is if it springs a leak. Same thing for the gas line—"

Her eyes lit up. "I didn't consider the gas line."

Gio tucked a strand of her hair off her face and behind an ear. "Not everything is an emergency. I'll show you what I know, and we'll find others to fix what is beyond my abilities. It's an adventure, not a chore."

"Good, damn it . . . why am I so uptight about this?" Emma had been twisting herself up into mini tornadoes almost daily since moving in.

"It's not your area of expertise."

She shook her head. "It's not. I'm much more versed in the production and selling of wine. Talking to others in the business, sales predictions." She thought about the event her parents were attending that her mother needed a dress for. "I'm always able to make people listen when I talk wine."

"I've seen *that* woman in action," Gio said.

Her mind drifted to her father and how he would spin her having this house, this land. What would he tell his friends in the business about it? "When I do confront my father, I want to be able to talk intelligently about every aspect of this property. Even the house."

"You will."

Emma looked at him with a soft smile.

"When I tell him I'm capable of doing this on my own, I need to know I'm telling the truth."

"You will," he repeated.

"I need him to take me seriously."

"I know."

"That I'm a partner in this, not an employee or just his daughter. That I belong at the table. And when I'm there he can't ignore me."

Gio tilted his head. "You spoke with Silas last week. He offered ideas on how to navigate a new contract with your dad, right?"

Silas was the lawyer Gio had connected her with. He confirmed that the paperwork in regard to the property did say she could occupy the house and manage the grapes. But that there was nowhere that stated she owned the grapes or had the right to produce her own label. Since the trust was part of their family trust and the property was part of R&R Wineries . . . yeah, it left a lot to interpretation on who was in charge of what.

There was plenty of room to negotiate a contract with her father. The cleanest thing would be for the property to come out of the trust and be put in her name solely.

Emma didn't see her father going for that. Not when he could use the land as the tax write-off it would be until it was operational. And who knows, maybe her father expected that she would never make a go of the place.

Emma saw that perfectly.

She could hear his argument the moment she suggested he take this path. He would flip the script and make her sound ungrateful for asking.

However, if Emma came to him with a plan to buy the equipment, care for the harvest, and start production . . . without a dime more from him, then maybe he would realize that his charity to her was nothing more than a father helping his daughter start her own business. She could use her trust fund to pay for the property itself . . . or acquire a small business loan . . . or maybe a large business loan from a bank, to pay her father back, and if that wasn't good enough, she'd find silent investors if her father balked at the idea.

And what better place to find silent investors than a gala event in Napa?

Emma examined her options while staring blankly across the room. "There's a wine event in Napa in two weeks. Black tie . . . a who's who in the industry. My mother was talking about it."

"Is it something you want to attend?" Gio asked.

She caught his eyes and slowly started to smile. "What better place to meet potential investors if my dad doesn't agree to my terms? And won't he be surprised to see me there."

"You wouldn't tell him you're going?"

"Hell no. Why tell him I can play this game, find my own investors, when I can show him?"

"As chess pieces on the board go, I think that's a great move. Any chance of that backfiring and your father telling you to move out?"

"He wouldn't risk his reputation. Besides, my dad doesn't hate me. He doesn't believe in me."

Gio squeezed her hand. "Now the real question is, do you want me to come with you? I mean, who else is capable of keeping you from spinning out of control?"

Emma considered his words. Honestly speaking, she had a hard time standing up to her father and she needed someone in her corner.

"I do want you there," she finally said.

"Then I'll be."

"Black tie," she reminded him.

"I know where to get a tux. And plane tickets."

"I bet you look great in a tux." She snuggled close.

"I look fantastic."

She laughed, lifted her lips toward his. "Such a humble guy."

Gio smiled as his mouth settled on hers.

CHAPTER TWENTY-SEVEN

"What brings you in today, Emma?"

Dr. Sandy, who preferred when you called her by her first name, had been Emma's concierge doctor since she turned eighteen. A perk of having parents who didn't want to deal with waiting rooms was spending extra money on a doctor that would see you within twenty-four hours for urgent needs and a few days for things that could wait.

With health care the way it was in the States, concierge medicine made sense.

Emma hoped she would always be able to afford the luxury.

"I am in a new relationship. We're both seeing our doctors for a clean bill of health."

"That's easy enough." Dr. Sandy typed a few things into her computer that sat on a rolling cart. "Are you sexually active with him now?"

"Yes. But we've been good about condoms."

"And you want to have intercourse without them?"

Emma smiled. "It would be a nice option."

"The perks of monogamy." She looked at her notes. "How is the IUD working out?"

"Fine. I think I spotted maybe twice this year. No hormonal headaches. I love it." Birth control and zero periods. It was a winning combination as far as she was concerned.

"You're due to have it switched out."

"I thought as much."

"And you know I don't do that here. You'll have to see the gynecologist."

Emma remembered. "I'll make an appointment." Her OB-GYN was not a concierge doctor, and that appointment would likely take a few months to get in.

"What about your last Pap smear?"

Emma wasn't exactly sure. "A year and a half ago, I think."

"Annual means annual, Emma," Dr. Sandy scolded with a smile. "We can do that today. Check for HPV, bloodwork for all the other offenders."

A nice way to say sexually transmitted diseases. Not that Emma was worried. Her sex life had been pretty bankrupt before Giovanni.

"You just turned thirty."

"Don't remind me."

Dr. Sandy shook her head. "No complaining until you hit menopause."

Which Emma assumed Dr. Sandy had personal knowledge of. Not that the woman showed it. Petite and well put together, Dr. Sandy felt more like a friend than a physician.

"I would like you to make an appointment on your way out for a complete physical. You haven't had one in a while."

"I can do that."

"Is there anything else while you're here you want me to look at?"

Emma started to shake her head, then stopped herself. "I've noticed myself bruising a lot." She lifted her arm. "I had one back here that took over two weeks to go away." Emma lifted her pant leg to show where she'd bumped into a lone box filled with books during the moving process. "That was from three days ago. Barely bumped into something."

Dr. Sandy gently squeezed around the bruise, ran a finger over it. "I'll do some bloodwork since we need to poke you today anyway. You've never been diagnosed with anemia, right?"

"No."

Dr. Sandy smiled. "We'll figure it out." She handed Emma an exam gown. "I'll be right back to do that pelvic exam."

~

Emma was on the way to San Diego a day before she and Gio were flying out to Napa, to meet the family.

While driving, she had Nicole on speakerphone.

"Are you nervous?"

"A little, I guess. I feel like I know them already. Dante was here when I moved in and I somewhat met his mother and sister over the phone when we were in Italy."

"Yeah, but this is in person. It's not the same as a phone call."

Emma kept her eyes on the road and hands on the wheel. "Are you trying to *make* me nervous?"

Nicole laughed. "I'm sorry I couldn't help you move." She'd been sick and neither of them wanted to risk spreading the joy.

"Moving is a pain in the ass. You didn't miss anything."

Nicole laughed. "How are things going with Gio?"

Emma found herself smiling. "The sex is out of this world."

"You're into him for more than sex."

"I am. He helped me move, lifted all the heavy stuff. His mother sends meals with him if she knows were going to be too busy to cook."

"All shallow stuff, Em."

He was much more than any of that. "He keeps me grounded, Nicole. I find myself wanting his opinion on all kinds of things. Together we've strategized how I can run Casa de Emma without a profit for two to five years without relying on my father."

"That sounds great."

Emma found her smile slipping. "It does . . ."

"I hear a 'but' coming."

She took a deep breath. "But . . . I'm moving that dependence from my father to Giovanni. And how smart is that? The last time I depended on a man was Kyle and look how that turned out."

"That's horseshit. You never depended on Kyle."

"He turned my head and made me think I needed him."

"Yeah, but you figured it out and got out. And does Gio do that? Is he taking control and leaving you behind?" Nicole asked.

"No. He's helping me figure things out. He asks me a lot of questions and only offers an opinion when I ask. At least when it comes to the winery and dealing with my dad."

"Sounds to me like Kyle and Gio couldn't be more different."

Emma could see what Nicole was saying, but her heart and body were reminding her of this familiar, heartbreaking ground. "Still scares me a little." Or a lot.

"Why, because he left a toothbrush at your place?" The two of them had talked about that right after it happened.

She shook her head. "Oh, he has left something at my place every time he comes." Which was every week, for a couple of days. He even made it midweek for a meeting with Noland to go over equipment options. But he'd gone home instead of staying the night. Emma had found a jacket he left behind that he felt he needed when leaving San Diego but most certainly didn't need in the heat of Temecula.

"He has a drawer already, eh?" Nicole was laughing.

"It's not funny. It's scary."

"Ah-huh . . . so you're bringing all of his stuff with you right now to give back to him."

"No."

"Then it's not scary. It's just stuff. And in light of the fact that the man doesn't live down the street, it's practical. In time you'll probably have stuff at his home. It's natural. The part that's eating at you is the desire to keep the men in your life from keeping you from your goals. And since Gio owns a penis, he gets lumped into the gender roles. But, Emma, not all men want to quietly control you. If he was, I'd be the first to say it. I honestly thought he might have been a holiday fling. What happens it Italy stays in Italy, you know?"

Emma dismissed the thought. "I never felt that way."

"Good. I'm happy for you. I think you might have found one of the rare, good ones. Find out if he has any single friends he can hook me up with."

That made Emma chuckle. "I will."

"Let me know how he is with his family. They say men can be judged by how they treat their mothers, children, and animals."

"I don't think they have any pets." And Emma already knew he had mad respect for his mom.

"Kyle was allergic to anything with fur."

Emma rolled her eyes. "He didn't even like pubic hair."

Nicole busted out in laughter. "Call me as soon as you're home from Napa. I want to hear all about that kickass move."

The system in her car told her another call was coming through, this one from Dr. Sandy.

"I gotta go. My doctor is calling me."

"Doctor?"

"It's nothing," Emma's finger hovered over the disconnect button. "Just lab work."

"Go, go. We'll talk later."

"M'kay."

Emma switched over the call. "Hello?"

"Hi, Emma, it's Dr. Sandy."

"Hey, Doc."

"So good news. Condoms are optional on your end. All your STD tests are negative."

One less thing to think about. Not that Emma was truly worried.

"There was a concerning result on your iron panel, but I don't want you to be alarmed."

"What kind of concern? Am I anemic?"

"No. Your iron is high, but your blood counts are normal."

"What does that mean?"

"I don't want to speculate right now. I want to repeat the blood-work and add a couple of things to it."

That felt odd to hear. "Okay."

"You said you were in Italy on a wine tour recently?"

"Yeah, for three weeks."

"And did you drink a lot?"

Emma laughed. "It was a wine tour through Tuscany. We did a fair amount of drinking. I wasn't hammered every night if that's what you're asking."

"Good, good."

"Could that be why my iron is high?"

"Your liver enzymes are a tiny bit elevated as well. My check-engine light would be blinking, too, after a month in Italy," she said with a slight laugh. "I don't want you to be worried about this. Everything else looks perfect. We'll repeat the bloodwork and go from there. Can you come by later today?"

"I'm on my way out of town." Emma glanced in her rearview mirror.

"Monday, then?"

"Sure."

"Great, hold the line and I'll have you talk with Sophie to schedule. I'll move some things around and we can get that physical out of the way since you'll be here."

"Thank you for calling."

"You have a great weekend."

Emma released the call, and her radio station took care of the silence in the car.

No matter how calm and collected her doctor's voice had been, the words *don't worry* and *Can you come by later today?* were a complete contradiction.

~

Gio tracked Emma's location from his phone.

It was a Friday in Little Italy, and it was hopping. The outside patios at the restaurant were completely filled and the inside was pushing the limits of their staff.

Luca had jumped into the kitchen to help and Mari was in her kitchen upstairs, preparing the "meeting Emma welcome meal" for the family.

It seemed like Sunday dinners now happened completely around Gio's schedule.

He knew that couldn't last forever. Sundays had been the tradition for a couple of reasons, mainly because staffing issues were easier on Sundays as opposed to Fridays and Saturdays. Chances were none of them would have to miss family time to cover a shift in the restaurant. And because Mari reminded them they were Catholic on Sundays and taking the one day out of the week to be a family is what kept them together.

The family had proved in the last month that dinners could move around. With all the changes in their family, it was probably a good thing to shake it up.

Gio stood outside, looking at both his phone and the street to see when Emma drove by. As soon as she exited the freeway, he called her.

"Are you stalking me?" she answered with a laugh.

"I am. I'm standing outside, but there isn't any parking. I moved my car so you can park behind."

"Ahh, that's so sweet. Can I sleep on your side of the bed, too?"

He chuckled. "You already do."

"I'm turning down your street," she told him.

Eyes searching, he saw her white SUV clear the corner. "I see you."

Gio stepped away from the curb and to the edge of traffic on the one-way street. Cars moved slowly on this main road, as pedestrians were constantly walking in front of the drivers. The light at the intersection had turned red, forcing Emma to stop.

Gio walked over to her car and pointed down the street.

"Go up one block, where you can turn right, then back down this intersection. Before the light there is a driveway on the left that says 'Private Parking,' turn in."

"You got it."

Gio stood back and watched her pull away.

God it was good to see her. In his town.

He couldn't wait to show her off.

Gio walked through the restaurant and out the back door that only their family and the employees used.

As he passed the kitchen, Luca called out. "Is she here?"

"Pulling in now."

Luca walked to a sink and started washing his hands.

In the parking lot, Gio watched Emma navigate the narrow space with ease. He was at her door and opening it for her before she lifted her purse from the passenger seat.

"You made it."

"Traffic was light."

Emma stepped out of the car and lifted her lips. "Hi."

He kissed her briefly. "Hi. You're about to be inundated by my family. I hope you're ready."

"It can't be that bad."

He closed the door. "Not bad, just overwhelming."

Emma walked to her trunk and opened it.

A small suitcase and a garment bag sat there. "Not the white one?"

"I'm not checking a bag to fly to Napa."

Gio removed both items from the trunk and closed it.

Emma took a deep breath and stared up at the back of their building. "So, this is the famous D'Angelo's?"

"It's better on the inside." The back alley that doubled as their parking space was utility in nature. Nothing beautiful about it.

Carrying her bag, he walked beside her to the door, leading them inside.

Luca was there with a warm smile. "The woman we've all been waiting to meet," he said.

"Emma, this is my brother, Luca."

"I've heard a lot about you," she said.

Luca winked and took her hand. "Ignore his lies. I'm the older, more charming brother."

Gio rolled his eyes. His brother's flirting was as natural as breathing. Something they both mastered before their teenage years.

"With a pregnant wife if I'm not mistaken," Emma called him out.

"The love of my life." Luca placed a hand to his heart. "But that doesn't stop me from being the older and more charming brother, no?"

Emma laughed.

Any tension Gio noticed in her shoulders slid off with the warm welcome Luca offered.

Luca stepped aside. "I'll be up in a half hour," he told them.

Gio guided Emma around the corridor to a family entrance to the stairway leading to their apartments. "I told you we didn't have an elevator, right?"

"You did."

"I'm all the way at the top."

They made it to the second floor, where his mother's apartment was. The door was wide open.

"Gio, is that you?"

"My mother," he whispered to Emma, who had stopped on the landing. "Yes, Mama. I'm going to get Emma settled before—"

Mari walked into view and interrupted Gio's words. Like Luca, she grasped Emma's hands almost before saying hello. "Look at you. *Bellissima*. Those green eyes. So stunning."

"Emma, my mother, Mari." Gio put the suitcase down and stood there holding the garment bag.

"We met on the phone," Emma reminded her.

"Yes, but I didn't notice the color of your eyes. We're so happy you're here."

"Thank you for having me."

Mari patted Emma's cheek. "Anytime." Mari turned to Gio. "Your sister and Dante are on their way. Rosa is bringing her *limoncello*."

"It's homemade," he told Emma.

"Who is Rosa?"

"Dante's mother."

"Oh."

Mari waved a hand in the air. "She's family. You get settled. I'll be up in a few."

"Onward," Gio said, picking up the suitcase and taking another flight of stairs.

Third floor . . . Luca and Brooke's apartment.

Fast footsteps meant only one member of the family.

Franny.

"Mama," she yelled. "Gio's girlfriend is here!"

His nine-year-old niece was on the landing and right in Emma's business without apology. "Hi."

"You must be Franny."

"And you're Emma. Is your hair real?"

Gio had to laugh.

Emma chuckled, too. "Yes. Is yours?"

Franny looked at her like she was crazy. "Yeah. My friend's mama dyes her hair pink. Is yours dyed?"

Brooke emerged from the apartment to stand behind Franny. Her baby bump getting bigger by the day. "Franny. It's not polite to ask if someone dyes their hair. Sorry," Brooke apologized.

"Don't be. Kids are honest. And no, Franny, my hair is naturally red."

Gio winked at his niece. "I think you should dye your hair blue," he told her.

"Don't give her any ideas," Brooke grumbled. "I'm Brooke."

"Nice to meet you."

Brooke pulled Franny back into the apartment. "We'll see you up there."

Emma started up the stairs again. "Anyone else I should know about?"

He laughed. "I warned you."

"Yes, yes you did."

CHAPTER TWENTY-EIGHT

Gio's one-bedroom apartment on the top floor of the building reminded Emma a lot of where she'd moved from. Only a little smaller.

He'd said that the place had been used as a guesthouse, of sorts, for out-of-town company. The kitchen was tiny, but any guest of the D'Angelos wasn't expected to cook, so the tininess of the space made sense. No one ever went hungry.

There was a small living space with light, welcoming colors. When she'd commented on them, he quickly gave credit to his mother. The only thing Gio was responsible for was his personal things.

But the best part of the space was the terrace. He had a large sliding glass door that opened out to a rooftop terrace. A massive table was centered under strings of lights and outdoor heaters for when the weather turned cold. Considering they were only a few blocks from the San Diego Bay, Emma assumed the nights would be slightly cooler and damp. When she'd left Temecula, it was in the nineties, and she'd guess the temperature in Little Italy wasn't over seventy-five. San Diego was known for its mild weather that was hard not to love.

A separate entrance from the stairwell to the terrace gave everyone access.

The view of the bay was fantastic.

Gio hung up her garment bag and rolled her suitcase into his bedroom before joining her on the terrace.

"What do you think?"

"I see why you love it here."

"My family makes it special."

"There is a lot of them."

Gio pulled her into his arms and kissed her. "You'll love them, too, before the night is over."

The door to the terrace opened wide and Gio's sister announced herself. "Finally. We meet the woman my brother can't stop talking about. I'm Chloe."

Chloe was the very vision of an olive-skinned Italian woman with long dark hair and deep brown eyes.

"Are you trying to embarrass me?" Gio asked.

"You hold the crown for that, Gio."

Chloe didn't bother with a handshake or simple gesture, she hugged Emma without hesitation. "So happy to meet you."

"You, too. Between Dante and Gio I feel like I know you."

Chloe looped her arm through Emma's and pulled her away from Gio's side. "Dante said your place is epic."

"I like it." Nerves inched up out of nowhere.

Dante walked their way with a woman at his side. "Hi, Emma."

The familiar face made her smile.

"Hey, Dante."

"My mother, Rosa."

Rosa looked around the same age as Gio's mother. "Look at you."

Emma wasn't sure about all the attention. She glanced over her shoulder to find Gio watching her. "Nice to meet you."

"It's about time Gio brought a woman around," Rosa announced.

"He told me he brings his dates around often." Emma stared at Gio.

"Yeah, but not in a long time," Chloe said.

"You're more than a date, *cara*," Gio said.

Chloe, who hadn't let go of Emma's arm, tugged her toward the stairs. "Let's help my mom bring the food up."

"Sure."

Chloe turned to Gio. "Mama wants the heaters on."

As soon as they were out of hearing range of those on the terrace, Chloe whispered, "Gio hasn't brought anyone around in two years. And none of us liked her."

Emma wasn't sure who *her* was, but Chloe's explanation told her why so much attention was given to her visit.

"None of you know me yet."

Chloe looked at her. "We know what we need to. You make my brother smile. He hasn't snapped at anyone since he left for Italy."

"Regular sex will do that," Emma blurted without thought.

Chloe's laugh said she wasn't offended. "Oh, we're going to get along just fine."

Two flights of stairs and they were in Mari's apartment, where plates of food were covered in foil and ready to transport.

"I brought help," Chloe announced when they entered the room.

Mari looked up, clicked her tongue. "Chloe, Emma's our guest."

"A guest today is a friend tomorrow. What can I do?" Emma asked.

"Ah, so sweet." Mari removed the apron from her waist and tossed it on the counter. "Grab a plate and head upstairs."

Following instructions, Emma felt the tension ease simply by doing a task. She grabbed a chilled platter and headed out the door.

Franny skipped down the stairs in a near run and almost bounced right into Emma.

"Francesca!" Mari yelled at her.

"Sorry, Nonna."

"Grab a plate and stop running."

"Yes, Nonna."

"Franny will keep you on your toes around here," Chloe said right behind Emma as they walked back to the terrace. "The waiters started to call her the D'Angelo Tornado."

"She's adorable."

"She knows it, too," Chloe said.

Back on the terrace, Gio was talking with Brooke.

Franny came from behind Emma with a dish and rushed it to the table. Then she ran to Gio to say something.

Right behind them Luca arrived, a massive plate in his hand. Mari carried a smaller one.

"Dante." Mari caught his attention. "There's one more plate."

Dante jumped to his feet.

"And Giovanni . . . where is the wine? We can't have dinner without wine." Mari barked orders and everyone snapped to.

"On it." He turned to Brooke. "What is the baby drinking tonight?"

"I'm fine with water."

Emma sat her dish down as Gio walked by.

He stopped, kissed her cheek without saying a thing, and continued out of sight.

Mari pulled out a chair. "Emma . . . please. You can sit next to me so I can soak you up."

"No pressure there, Mama," Chloe said, giving her mother a hard time.

"What? My baby brings home a beautiful woman for only one night, I have to make the most of it."

"Don't make the poor girl uncomfortable, Mari," Rosa said.

"I thought I was the baby," Franny announced.

Then, before Emma could say a single word in the mix, Luca said something to Franny in Italian. Chloe continued to defend Emma's need for some space, and Rosa argued in half English, half Italian.

It was a scene right out of a Big Fat Italian Sitcom.

Brooke walked quietly over to Emma. "It's a loud family. But they mean well . . . I promise."

"This is crazy."

"Are you an only child?" Brooke asked.

"No. Two brothers."

"Well, then . . . you know how it is."

Emma shook her head. "We have painfully civilized, boring holiday meals that we can't wait to escape."

Brooke frowned. "There is nothing boring about this family."

"I can see that."

"You should have been here when Chloe and Dante showed up as a couple for the first time."

"What happened?"

Brooke nodded toward Gio, who had returned with a carrier filled with wine bottles. "Gio wasn't happy that his best friend was sleeping with his sister."

"Did they fight?"

Dante walked over to Gio, the two of them laughed about something and glanced her and Brooke's way.

"I wouldn't say 'fight.' Gio punched Dante once and Mari broke it up."

Emma had a hard time envisioning Gio that angry. "I can't see Gio being violent."

Brooke moved to Emma's side and they both stared at the gaggle of D'Angelos. "None of them are . . . until you threaten their family. They'll go to the ends of the earth to protect that."

"What are you two whispering about over there?" Dante rose his voice to get over everyone else there.

"I was just telling her about the time that Gio welcomed you with a knuckle sandwich."

Gio looked directly at Emma. "He deserved it, *cara*. Trust me."

Mari pointed a finger at Gio. "Never again in my home."

"Yes, Mama."

"Come on, Emma. Let's eat." Mari once again indicated the seat next to her.

Emma took a fortifying breath and walked to the table.

As soon as she sat, Franny asked, "What's a knuckle sandwich?"

~

"My ears are still ringing." Emma sat curled in the nook of Gio's shoulder after they both climbed into bed.

"I warned you."

"Do they ever run out of energy?" Dinner had lasted nearly three hours. It rivaled anything Emma had experienced while they were in Italy.

"They were excited that you're here."

"They're not like this normally?"

"No. They're like that all the time, maybe a little more since they had someone new to share their stories with." Gio graced her arm with his fingertips in a lazy, loving way.

"Like you beating up Dante."

"I did not beat him up. I defended my sister's honor."

Emma had been waiting all night to hear his side of the story.

"Your sister can't have sex?"

"She can have sex, just not with my best friend. Dante broke the guy code. First page in the rule book."

Emma chuckled. "What changed?"

"He married her. Would slay dragons for her."

"Everyone likes a good dragon slaying."

"I'll dust off my sword."

"I'll give you a warm place to put it."

Gio placed a finger under her chin and tilted her face to his. "Is that an invitation?"

She reached between them, ran her hand over his hip, and snuggled closer. "I don't know. It's been a long day."

Gio rolled her onto her back and hovered. "I'll do all the work."

Emma stretched her arms out to the side. "Okay, you talked me into it."

"Oh, *cara*."

His lips descended and she stopped him. "I saw my doctor. I'm all good." Her thoughts flickered briefly to Dr. Sandy's conversation, but Emma pushed that away.

"That makes two of us, then."

Gio had seen his doctor that Monday.

"We should celebrate," she suggested.

He hesitated. "No condom?"

"No need for it."

"You sure?"

"Not unless you're sleeping with someone else."

He placed a hand to the side of her face. "I have room for one woman in my life and that is you."

His words felt like a declaration.

His kiss felt like a promise.

~

Gio watched the slow transformation of Emma from smiling and animated to stoic and guarded.

It began on the flight to Sacramento. Their playful recount of the night before shifted to the events that were about to unfold at the gala.

"My father is going to be shocked to see me."

The statement was repeated a few times.

"He won't let on unless he doesn't have an audience."

Right, right . . . Gio had heard this, too.

Once the plane landed, they rented a car and drove for well over an hour before reaching the hotel.

Gio offered what he thought she needed to do and hear. "Remember your goals."

"We're there to mingle. Meet people in the industry and put a face to the name so when and if I need to call, they remember me."

"And when you do face your father?" Gio asked.

"Act like anyone else in the room that owns a vineyard and believe I belong there." Her words were convincing even though her expression was not.

"I'll be right there to help keep you grounded."

Her smile was forced, but Gio would take it.

They arrived at the hotel in time to shower and get ready.

Emma showered first and then parked herself in front of a vanity mirror.

When Gio emerged, her hair was still in a towel and she was finishing with her makeup.

"Beautiful, darling."

She smiled at him through the mirror, and he walked away.

Gio pulled on a pair of briefs and hopped up on the bed. There was no reason to get into his tux until the last minute.

He flipped through his phone, checked a few emails . . . found his sister's Instagram page and saw a picture of him and Emma smiling at the camera. The comment section was filled with questions from mutual friends.

"Who is that?"

"Is Gio finally off the market? Now maybe I'll have a chance."

"She's too beautiful for him."

Gio had an account but didn't spend much time on it.

As much as he wanted to scream to the hills that he'd found the right woman, that woman wasn't ready to scream it back. He felt her getting closer, but he also saw how much she struggled with the need to be independent and the desire to depend on him.

Every time he tried to do something simple for her, she asked him to show her how so she could do it herself.

The hair dryer turned on and Gio glanced at the time. Ten minutes later he picked his lazy butt off the bed and unzipped his garment bag. As he pulled on the tux, he couldn't help but think about how unfair it was to women that they went through a complete ritual of makeup and hair . . . finding the right dress and shoes, the right underclothes to wear. "I'm glad I'm a guy," he said out loud when the hair dryer turned off.

"I am, too," Emma said from the other room. "But is there a particular reason as to why?"

"It only takes me fifteen minutes to get ready and that includes a shower and a shave."

"Lucky bastard."

He laughed.

"Okay, I need you to turn around and face the wall."

"Sounds kinky," he teased.

"No. I want to grab my dress and I don't want you to see me until I'm ready."

Gio turned toward the wall and buttoned up his shirt. "I already know you're beautiful."

"Why, thank you . . . but I want the wow effect."

"*Bella*, you've already given me that."

He heard her open the closet door and close it. "You can turn around again."

He did, but she was back in the bathroom.

Gio finished getting dressed and ran a comb through his hair, then teased the front of it. *Yup . . . men have it easy.*

He caught movement out of the corner of his eye and looked up.

"Whoa." He could not form words. And *wow* was not enough.

The green in Emma's eyes sparkled, and they were outlined with such precision he couldn't look away. Bold, red lipstick . . . her beautiful hair piled high on her head with tendrils falling all around, giving freedom to her natural curls.

And the dress . . . holy shit, the dress.

Off the shoulder, floor-length, with a slight sparkle from rhinestones built into the top layer. It hugged her luscious curves and made his mouth pop open like a drooling dog after a long run.

"Wow," he finally said.

Her smile was instant, her joy from his reaction evident in her eyes.

Emma twisted to the side, showed him the back. "Does my butt look big in this?"

"Are we going to this thing or am I throwing you on that bed?" he asked, avoiding her question.

"Bed throwing will have to wait." She looked him up and down, walked over, and adjusted his tie. "We clean up well. Maybe we should do these things more often."

He rested a hand on her hip, wanted nothing more than to smear her lipstick.

"I'm sure it can be arranged." He watched her lips. And an image of her wearing white, walking toward him, stole his breath.

"There." Her hands fell from his bow tie, her eyes flittered before looking into his.

"Don't you dare kiss me," she whispered.

Gio ran his fingertips down the side of her exposed neck. Sparkling earrings fell from the lobes of her ears. "What about here?" he asked.

Emma wavered his way, then pulled back. "You're evil."

He chuckled. "Let's do this . . . so we can come back here and do that."

CHAPTER TWENTY-NINE

A fire truck raced in her chest.

There weren't individual beats of her heart, but a siren screaming through the streets as Emma stepped out of the rental car with a valet attendant standing there.

Giovanni took her arm as they walked into the event.

"Breathe, Emma."

She did as he told her, as if he commanded it.

"Do it again."

She did.

"You've got this."

His encouragement pulled her shoulders back and tilted her chin high.

A short line kept them from the inside.

Emma couldn't help but look around to see if she recognized anyone.

Mainly her parents.

As dedicated as she was to making an impression at this entire event, she'd done her homework. The internet provided the faces behind the names of some of the most prestigious wines in the valley. Some she knew . . . most she didn't.

The organization that was putting on the event happily extended an invitation when they heard her name. She'd asked, as politely as she could, for the event coordinator to not tell her father. She wanted to surprise him after he gave her such a lavish gift of her own winery. A story the wine magazine wanted to know more about.

She promised an interview in the future.

Beside her, Gio looked like he belonged.

While she felt like an imposter.

How did he do that?

They stepped up to the attendant at the door checking their invitations.

Giovanni removed them from the inside pocket of his tux and handed them over.

Emma didn't realize she was holding her breath until they were inside, and she exhaled.

Groups of people fell together like the same colors on a puzzle board. They didn't necessarily fit, but they mingled in the same neighborhood.

Gio led them to a space against the wall of the massive room distant from the bigger crowd.

"How are you feeling?" he asked.

"Better, I think."

He stared her in the eye. "You look like a million dollars."

Damn, he knew exactly what to say.

Her shoulders eased.

He turned back to the room. "Okay . . . who do you recognize?"

Emma scanned the room. "Ten o'clock. Tall, gray hair. The woman beside him is wearing a drape over her dress. Caldwell. Mike and Nancy. My introduction to them was brief."

"Friends or enemies?" Gio asked.

"I don't believe there's a lot of love between my father and Caldwell. I couldn't tell you why." Emma kept looking. "Bernard Wilson. Overweight, mustache with the red tie, twelve o'clock."

"Who is he?"

Emma looked at Gio. "Wilson Winery? You're not familiar?"

The light turned on in Gio's head. "Oh, that Wilson."

"Yes . . . *that* Wilson. I'm not a fan."

"Of the wine or the man?" Gio asked.

Emma rolled her eyes. "You can't blame the grapes for the man. The only time I ever entered this kind of room was with Kyle. Bernie there was with a woman half his age. A woman who was not his wife. The ass-kissers in this room pretended not to notice. I was told to smile and pretend she was the niece he told everyone she was."

"Who told you to do that?"

"Kyle. He fit right in with this part of the game. Pretending to be something you're not to get what you need." Emma was a slow learner in that area.

Yet here she was doing just that.

Gio's hand sat comfortably on her waist and gave it a squeeze. "You belong here. We'll play this game for as long as it serves us and then leave."

For the next few minutes Emma pointed out the faces she knew, or those that she'd learned of in the past couple of weeks.

Then a face came into view that made her jump.

She stepped in front of Gio, her back to the room. "They're here."

Gio scanned the room.

"Don't look obvious."

He must have spotted them because he stopped turning his head. "Your father looks older in person."

"Internet pictures are from ten years ago when he still had hair."

"Ha . . . I shouldn't laugh, Lord knows where I'll be in ten years."

That eased Emma's nerves. She turned to the side and caught a glimpse of her father again. Behind him, Richard stood talking to someone who . . . "Damn it."

"What?"

Emma looked into Gio's eyes. "Kyle's here."

Gio snapped his neck to the side so fast the hair on Emma's arms stood up. "Where?"

"Behind my father. My brother is the one with dark brown hair . . . Kyle is blond."

Gio looked toward the room, then down at her and back. "You two were never meant to be."

"I figured that out." And the fact that her father continued to invite Kyle to these events and not her pissed her off.

Gio turned her around. "Okay, *amore.* Are we doing this? Or standing in the corner all night?"

She squared her shoulders. "We're doing this."

~

Anger motivated her.

That was Gio's conclusion as they stepped into the fray.

While Emma was laser focused on the task, Gio took his blinders off and read the room.

Emma made a stir just by being there. Arguably the most beautiful woman in the room, certainly one of the youngest.

And she was with him.

They approached Bernard Wilson first.

Before they made it to his side, Gio whispered, "Nothing makes people more at ease than laughter."

Emma nodded and painted on a smile.

Gio's spine grew stiff when Wilson saw their advance and eyed Emma up and down as if she were strutting down a runway wearing a bikini.

Gio despised him on sight.

"Bernie . . . so lovely to see you again," Emma said the moment they approached the group of five.

Clear confusion marred Wilson's face. "I'm sorry, I . . ."

"Don't be." Emma placed a hand on her chest. "Emma Rutledge."

Recognition flashed in his eyes. "Robert's daughter."

She nodded. "Right."

Wilson's gaze dipped a little too low on Emma's frame for Gio's liking.

"This is my companion, Giovanni D'Angelo."

Gio extended a hand, gripped Bernie's a little too hard. "A pleasure. I've enjoyed your wine many times."

Wilson took his hand back, regarded Gio with a less enthusiastic smile. "We love to hear that, don't we, gentlemen?"

The other men in the circle laughed.

One by one they introduced themselves, and when the handshaking was over Gio placed that hand on the small of Emma's back, making damn sure they all understood what the word *companion* meant.

Bernie shifted his gaze between the two of them. "I seem to recall the last time I saw you, you were newly married."

Gio felt that the comment was meant to pull Emma off her center.

For a brief moment, Emma hesitated, and Gio jumped in. "Worst sixteen months of your life, right, *amore?*"

The two of them locked eyes. "It could have been worse," she replied. "It could have been two years."

The men laughed.

Well . . . all but Wilson.

Emma found her voice. "Funny . . . I remember when we last met, that you were with a . . . niece was it? What was her name?"

Wilson's leering smile started to fall.

One of the men in the circle cleared his throat.

"Yes. My niece."

Emma looked around the room. "Is she here tonight or did you bring Mrs. Wilson?"

Gio wanted to hug and high-five Emma at the same time. Her sting was so on point the other men had to shift their faces away to hide the fact that they were trying not to smile.

"My wife wasn't feeling well. She stayed home."

"That's unfortunate. I was so looking forward to meeting her. Next time."

Gio didn't give the silence that followed room to grow. He nodded toward another group in the room and leaned close. "*Cara*, I do believe we're being waved over."

Emma went along with his cue. "Yes. Gentlemen, if you'll excuse us."

They offered nods as they walked away.

"I want to kiss you," Gio whispered in her ear.

"That guy's an asshole. I don't care what happens, I'd never try and go into business with him."

"He'd want to be paid back in sexual favors."

She shivered. "Don't make me throw up."

Gio looked over his shoulder. "If he ever looks at you like that again I'll have to introduce him to my fist."

Emma smiled up at him. "I thought you said you weren't violent."

"Only when provoked, *cara* . . . only when provoked."

They approached Caldwell. Emma's stride was much stronger than the first walk across the room. "I would do business with Caldwell. Not only does he produce great wine, but I'm told his employees love working for him."

"Is that his wife?" Gio asked.

"Yes. There's no way for me to know for sure, but I don't think he plays in the same arena as Bernie and his many nieces."

"This is the man your father doesn't like."

"From what I can tell."

"Then let's make sure your father sees you with him."

Emma moved in beside Mrs. Caldwell and placed a hand on the other woman's arm. "I have to tell you how much I'm admiring your dress."

Gio knew that the Caldwells were in their sixties, according to his research, but Nancy didn't look a day past fifty. Tall, lean . . . built a lot like Chloe. He would guess this woman spent a lot of time in a yoga studio.

Nancy was all smiles. "That is so kind of you to say. I noticed yours when you walked in."

Women bonding over clothes.

Again, Gio wanted to high-five Emma on her approach.

"You look familiar, have we met?" Nancy asked.

"We have, but I wouldn't expect you to remember. Emma Rutledge."

When she said her name, Mike Caldwell shifted his eyes off the couple they were standing beside to Emma.

"Beth and Robert's daughter. That's right."

"There aren't many of these events I've had an opportunity to attend. But that's all changing."

Mike turned to Emma. "Did I hear Rutledge?"

"Yes, Emma Rutledge."

Caldwell looked directly into Emma's eyes, no dipping of his gaze to look where a married man shouldn't.

Emma shook his hand and turned to Gio. "Let me introduce you to Giovanni D'Angelo. Mike and Nancy Caldwell. They produce some of the finest merlot that you'll ever taste."

Gio shook hands. "I'm sorry I haven't had the pleasure."

"We can fix that." Mike lifted his hand in the air and a waiter walked over with a tray.

"Are you sponsoring this event?" Emma asked.

"Almost always, Emma. Mike loves the attention," Nancy said.

"More like the write-off." The older man beside them introduced himself. Gerald and Elena, who were dear friends but didn't own a vineyard.

Gio and Emma both took a glass from the tray. *"Salute."*

"You're Italian."

"Guilty," Gio said as he tilted the glass to the side and looked inside. "Emma and I were just in Tuscany on a very intensive tour. Lots of wine, right, *amore?*"

Emma brought the wine to her nose, they both looked at each other and smiled.

Gio took the first sip.

Then Emma.

"Not the merlot," they both said at the same time.

"Cabernet," Emma said.

"Oak aged . . . five years?"

"Maybe seven."

Gio smelled the wine again. "Honey."

"No, that's hibiscus," Emma corrected him.

"You always taste the floral notes better than me."

Emma glowed when she talked wine.

"You two are simply adorable," Nancy said with a sigh. "That was very entertaining."

"You certainly know your wine," Mike pointed out.

"I hope so . . . all things considered," Emma said.

"You have cabernet grapes on your land, right, *cara*?"

"Not a lot, but yes."

"Your land?" Mike asked.

"My parents have helped me get started on my own vineyard. Completely private label," Emma told him.

"Is that right?"

Gio once again used his free hand to touch Emma's back. He liked where she was going with this.

"Yes. In Temecula. The vines are sturdy, but my production needs some TLC before harvest."

"Good for you," Nancy quickly said.

"Say that in a couple of years when I have entries in the black column."

"I've seen your plan, *amore*. It may not take two years," Gio told Emma.

"One could hope. Truth is that's part of why I'm here," Emma told her captive audience. "Networking is part of the job, right?"

Mike smiled. "When your father owns what he does, you probably don't need that."

"I don't plan on failing, and I'm not counting on bailouts." Emma lowered her voice and inched a little closer. "My father hasn't been too receptive of me taking responsibility within R&R. He reserves that for my brother."

"We've seen Richard quite a bit over the years," Nancy told her.

Emma's smile was starting to fade. "And now you'll see me."

Mike regarded them both and then waved at another waiter. "I promised you the merlot. Try this one."

Gio took Emma's still-full glass from her hand and moved them aside, then accepted the next vintage.

He turned to face her, saw she'd regained her smile. They went through the same routine of swirling and smelling. As they did, two more parties of people turned to watch them.

"Much richer," Gio started.

"The merlot for certain. Chocolate," Emma said.

"More hibiscus?" he asked, knowing that was exactly what he smelled.

"Absolutely."

They took a taste together and Emma hummed.

It was that good. "I'm going to say ten years aged in oak."

"I think you're right." Emma took another taste. "An expensive bottle to be serving at a function with this many people."

"When you're ready for more information on write-offs, Miss Rutledge, give my office a call," Mike told her.

"I may just do that."

Gio saw the invitation to keep in touch for the win it was.

"Well? Were we right about the wine?" Gio asked.

"One hundred percent."

Gerald lifted his glass. "I just know it tastes good and gets the job done."

They all laughed and lifted their glasses. "Cheers."

"Emma? Is that you?" Beth's voice was behind them.

Gio saw Emma suck in a breath before she turned around.

CHAPTER THIRTY

Emotion tore through Emma's soul . . . from the high of having Mike Caldwell give her an open invitation to call him for advice to the crushing low of turning around to see her father's stern expression and her ex-husband standing by his side as if he belonged.

"Mom."

Gio took the glass from her hand before Beth had a chance to move in for a hug.

"Did we know you were coming?"

"Last-minute decision," Emma lied. She pulled away and moved to her father.

"I'm surprised to see you here," he said. His lips smiled . . . his eyes didn't.

Emma kissed his cheek and did everything in her power to keep from shaking.

"Isn't this where owners of wineries go, Father?" she asked.

Kyle huffed a short laugh.

Emma didn't give him the courtesy of a glance. "Richard, you look good." Her brother offered an awkward hug. "Where is Kristen?"

"Headache."

I bet.

"Giovanni, it's so good to see you again." Beth hugged Gio.

"Mrs. Rutledge. You're absolutely stunning."

"Oh, please," Kyle uttered before taking a swig out of the wine in his hand.

Gio turned, his shoulders pushed back. "And you are?" Gio asked.

Kyle dared him with a look. "Emma's ex-husband. And you?"

Emma took a step closer to Gio.

"Her future," Gio said, deadpan.

Emma's heart beat so hard she was sure everyone heard it.

A split second of silence followed the exchange that no one missed.

Thankfully, Emma's mother cut the tension. "Giovanni, I don't believe you met Emma's father. Robert . . ."

Gio turned his attention away from Kyle and shook her father's hand.

"Beth had a lot to say about you. Restaurant business?" Robert said.

"Correct."

Emma watched as her father and Gio took each other in.

Gio didn't linger, he went right to Richard. "You're the oldest brother."

"Richard . . . yes. Good to meet you."

With the introductions out of the way, Emma took a step back and once again felt Gio's hand on her hip. Its presence was a constant reassurance.

"I didn't realize your daughter was so engaging, Robert," Mike pointed out.

"You've been keeping her from us," Nancy added. "We need more young people in this room. Keeps things interesting."

Emma felt the heat under her father's gaze. "Emma's been here before."

"Very true." Emma glanced at Kyle, paused. "One time." She looked away. "But now that I have my own label, I'm back."

Her dad blinked; fake smile plastered.

"We offered our daughter a piece of our land . . . she decided to be a veterinarian instead," Nancy said.

"It will all go to her eventually," Mike said. He looked at Emma. "She's an only child."

"Oh . . . well, hopefully she likes wine." Emma tried to keep the conversation going while her parents, Richard, and Kyle simply stood staring.

"Sometimes I wonder," Nancy said with a laugh.

Her dad lifted his chin. "How are your vines faring after the fire?" Robert asked Mike.

"Not bad. We were able to save around forty percent . . ."

In that moment, Emma felt the dismissal of her father.

Gio squeezed her waist.

She turned to him. "If you'll excuse me. I need the ladies' room."

Nancy set her glass down. "I could take a break, too."

Gio kissed her cheek. "You're doing great," he whispered.

"Don't start a fight," she whispered back.

He winked before she walked away, and then started a conversation with her mom.

Nancy led them both to the bathroom. Once behind the doors, Emma let out a sigh.

"Are you okay?" Nancy placed a hand on Emma's shoulder.

She swallowed. "Of course."

"Oh, don't start that. There's enough plastic and fakeness out there to keep cosmetic surgeons in business for years. You don't have to pretend with me."

Emma let her smile fall and decided to be honest. "It's a bit off-putting that my father brings my ex-husband to these things. It's as if he picked a side after our divorce and it wasn't mine."

Nancy invited Emma to sit in the lounge area of the ladies' room. "A lot of people bring the wrong plus-one to these events."

"Like Wilson?"

Nancy laughed. "Exactly. You held your ground with the entire interaction."

"Was it that obvious there is tension?" Emma asked.

"I wasn't kidding about the need for excitement at these things. Your friend certainly has your back."

Emma lowered her eyes to her lap. "Giovanni is more than a friend."

"That was obvious."

"Together we hope to make everything come together, with or without my father's continued help."

Nancy narrowed her eyes. "It does appear that your father doesn't want you here."

"No, he doesn't. Which is why I didn't tell him I was coming." Emma kept her voice low when she heard noise in the area of the stalls. "Sometimes, as a woman, if you aren't invited to the party, you simply need to crash it."

Nancy laughed. "In this male-dominated field, you're not wrong."

Emma closed her eyes and breathed. "Thank you for taking a moment to calm me down."

Nancy took her hand. "Anytime. Now, do you need to use the facilities before we head back to the fire?"

"No. This was an excuse to fortify my convictions."

"Let's get back out there before your boyfriend flattens your ex's ego."

~

Emma sat in the passenger seat on the way to the airport in Sacramento.

Despite her near panic attacks, Emma left the event feeling stronger than when she arrived.

Her father had no choice but to introduce her to several of his friends and colleagues. After about the third one, Kyle silently slipped away.

The awkward silence that ensued every time a random person put together that Kyle was her ex-husband . . . and the man still worked with her father . . . the ice between Emma and her dad became sharper.

Once Kyle left, that ice began to thaw.

And while everything was civilized, Emma knew she'd made all the impressions she needed to.

Gio had taken the time to talk with the actual coordinators of the event, making certain that their names were on the invite list for the future.

"Do you think Kyle will ever be on the guest list again?" Gio asked when they reached the freeway for the hour-long trek to the airport.

"Not if I'm there. You saw my father."

"He was everything you described."

"I can't tell if it's that he just straight doesn't like women, or if it's me."

"The majority of the people in attendance were chest-bumping men. All of them one-upping the next guy. I don't think it's you."

"Watching Kyle slither away was rewarding. Even if no one ever called out the fact he chose Kyle over me, it was apparent that people noticed."

"Nancy Caldwell tossed out a few comments."

Emma smiled at the friend she'd managed to make. "She's something."

"Your mother is much more reserved around your father."

"Peacekeeper . . . balance-maker. It's been her role for as long as I remember. Parents aren't supposed to pick a favorite kid, but Ryan and I knew from the beginning that we weren't the chosen."

"I'm sorry, *cara*. You deserve better."

"I do. And I'm finally able to say that out loud without feeling guilty. Watching everything unfold last night drove home what I already knew. Now when I go to my father and present him with options, he can either take me seriously—"

Emma's phone rang. "It's my mother."

"Do you want to deal with that right now?"

She smiled and answered the call on speaker. Emma placed a finger over her lips for Gio to stay quiet. "Hi, Mom."

"Good morning, Emma. I hope it's not too early."

"Not at all."

"Good. Your father and I wanted you to come by the house for breakfast this morning."

That was out of character.

"That's not possible. Gio and I are on our way to the airport right now. We have an early flight."

"Can't you delay it, honey? Your father would really like a chance to talk to you."

Emma rolled her eyes. *I bet,* she mouthed to Gio. "Not possible, Mom. I have a meeting first thing in the morning and Gio is needed at the restaurant." Emma was getting good at setting boundaries. "Besides, if Father wants to talk to me, tell him to advise his secretary to put me on the books. I've been trying to talk to him since I came home from Italy."

"Hold on," Beth said.

Emma could hear that her mother had pulled the phone away and was talking to someone. Likely her father.

Sure enough, when her mother got back on the line, she started with "Your father says he wants—"

"Mom. Just stop. Put Dad on the phone."

"Emma."

"I mean it. Is my dad so afraid to talk to me that he needs a go-between every time?"

Beth huffed. "You're right. This is ridiculous. Robert. Talk to your daughter."

Emma smiled at Gio, who was silently laughing.

After a few seconds, her father picked up the call. "Hello, Emma."

"Hello, Dad. What is it you wanted Mom to say for you?"

"What was last night about?"

"I'm sorry?"

"Last night. You flying all the way up here, without telling me, and coming to *my* event?"

"Your event?" Emma asked, avoiding his question. "I didn't realize you were one of the sponsors."

"R&R is always a sponsor."

"Now I know for the future."

"Oh, no. This is not a regular event for you."

She clenched a fist.

Gio reached over and wrapped a hand around it.

"Excuse me?"

"You heard me. R&R Wineries is represented by your brother and me."

"And Kyle," she reminded him.

Robert huffed. "We're not going over this again, young lady. You chose to divorce him. You understood the ramifications of that choice."

Gio shook his head.

"Regardless, Father. I wasn't at the event representing R&R. I was there representing myself. I haven't quite settled on a name for my label, but I like Casa de Emma."

"What are you talking about?"

"My winery. The place I just moved into. The one your lawyers gave me legal access to. Remember?"

"I remember—"

Emma interrupted him, her words perfectly picked to have this conversation. "I've been trying to get ahold of you for weeks to talk about the logistics. My lawyer found a few phrases that have us concerned."

"Your . . . your what?"

"My attorney."

"What do you need with an attorney?"

"Dad . . . you sent me to college. An expensive one. I graduated with honors. One of the first rules in business is to seek legal advice whenever in doubt. Especially with contracts."

"R&R has plenty of lawyers."

Emma smiled at Gio. For some strange reason she was getting a kick out of this entire exchange. "But Casa de Emma does not."

"What in the hell . . . there is no *Casa de Emma*. Your property is an arm of R&R."

Emma opened her mouth wide as if in shock and looked at Gio. *Surprise!*

But before she could say a thing, she heard her mother talking to her dad. "You told me Emma had control of that land."

"It's . . . she does," her father stuttered.

"As an arm of R&R?"

263

Her parents continued to argue while Gio and Emma heard every word.

"Go, Mom," Gio said quietly.

Emma raised her voice. "I wanted to believe that what my lawyer was concerned about was somehow lost in translation."

"You expect me to hand you a fifteen-million-dollar piece of property without holding any rights to the wine?"

And there it was.

"Actually, Father . . . I didn't *expect* that of you at all. I explained I wanted to start out on my own. I'm prepared to negotiate a sale from R&R to Casa de Emma."

"I can't believe you, Robert." Beth was mad.

Emma continued. "Since I've already moved in . . . and the legal paperwork you provided gives me possession of the home and control over the vineyard as part of my trust, I'm sure you'll be prepared for negotiations moving forward."

"Negotiations for what, young lady?"

Gio made a cutting motion against his neck and mouthed the words *Cut him off.*

"I don't have my computer in front of me since we're on the way to the airport. Maybe you can have your secretary call me and arrange a better time to talk. I think my schedule is open Tuesday afternoon."

Gio was holding back laughter.

"This is absurd," Robert said.

"Give me that phone." Beth took the call back. "I will take care of this."

"Mom. I appreciate your help, but I can handle it."

"For Christ's sake, your father gave Richard fifty acres and an executive salary."

Emma thought Richard only lived on those acres. He wouldn't bark at actual ownership. Their father had his balls in his pocket.

"This is not on you, Mom. I have this."

"I'll be back next week. Earlier if your father shoves his foot any farther up his own ass."

Emma's eyes opened wide. She'd bet money her father had left the room. "I love you."

"I love you, too, honey. Give Giovanni a kiss. Make sure he knows I like him a hell of a lot better than I ever liked Kyle."

Gio made a heart shape out of his fingertips.

"Bye, Mom."

They hung up.

"She loves me more than she did Kyle," Gio repeated.

"That entire conversation and that's what you pick up on."

"You don't need anything on the rest of it. You were a rock star. You stated the facts, gave your father an out and a place to lie if he needed to . . . and then backed him into a corner."

"And then shut him down so we can regroup."

"*I have room in my schedule on Tuesday.*' That was priceless." Gio raised a fist in the air, to which Emma bumped it with her own.

"We talked to enough people last night to let them know that my father's generosity is giving me a seat at the table. And hopefully that will be talked about. His ego is much too big to look like a two-faced liar. He'll have to negotiate with me."

Gio changed lanes to get around a semi. "People will be talking. I made sure of that."

"How so?" Emma asked.

"I spoke with the editor in chief of the magazine running the event. I reminded them of your conversation and then added a love story to spice it up."

Emma's jaw dropped. "You did not."

"I most certainly did. Wine and romance? What more could a magazine article want? Your father added the drama by inviting Kyle . . . and you know people will talk about that."

Emma stared out the windshield. "That's a spark of genius."

Gio patted his own back. "I know."

"Humble much?" Emma asked, joking.

"I am many things, *amore* . . . humble is not one of them."

~

Hours later, Emma lugged two giant bags of food that Gio's mother had prepared into the house.

She dumped the bags, her purse, and her keys on the counter and sighed.

Emma pulled out her phone and texted Gio. I'm home.

Good. You're safe.

I feel good about today.

There was a pause and then dots flashed on her screen. You were a force.

Emma glanced at the food on the counter. Thank your mother again for me.

We're Italian. Everything begins and ends with food.

And wine.

She glanced at her wine fridge, saw some of the bottles she'd purchased in Italy stacked and chilling.

If you start to doubt what happened today. Call me. Day or night.

Emma ran a hand down her face, her smile actually hurt. You know me too well.

Standing up to your father is huge. There is bound to be a recoil. Call me if that happens. Promise me, amore.

I will.

She sent a kissing emoji and he sent a heart.

Amore . . .

Didn't that mean "love"?

An endearment. An Italian endearment.

Emma shook it off and grabbed her keys to shove in her purse.

She hesitated . . . tossed them in the air . . . twice.

Then picked up her phone.

"Hey, sis! How the hell are you?"

Emma loved how down-to-earth Ryan was. He was a symbol that her family could be normal.

"I have food . . . I have wine . . . and I need you to help me change the code on my gate and give me the name of a locksmith."

CHAPTER THIRTY-ONE

Wearing a thin blue and white hospital gown, Emma sat in the exam room, waiting for Dr. Sandy to walk in.

She'd spent the previous night catching up with her brother, eating and laughing and dissing their father.

Ryan was understandably outraged and yet not surprised by Robert's actions.

It was when Kyle was brought up that Ryan wanted to take a stand.

"I don't care if Kyle walked the moon and the earth. He has no business keeping that man in his inner circle and you on the sideline."

Emma couldn't have agreed more.

"When can I meet this Giovanni guy? I need to approve before it gets any more serious."

Emma's heart melted.

Ryan didn't think Kyle had been the right guy either.

When she called Ryan out on not saying something at the time, he reminded her that she'd been focused on one thing. Pleasing their father.

Now . . . Emma sat in a doctor's office and realized she'd said nothing to anyone about this appointment.

So focused on her financial future, she didn't think this was worthy of talking about.

Yet now as she sat there . . . her hands shook.

Dr. Sandy walked in the room only minutes after Emma had changed and made herself comfortable on the exam table.

"Good morning."

"Hey."

"How was your weekend?" Sandy sat on a rolling stool and focused her attention on Emma.

"Good. Great, even."

"Glad to hear it. I'm going to run another blood panel."

"Yeah, you said that. What are the numbers?"

"You didn't log in to the portal to look?" she asked.

Was that a thing? "I didn't realize I could do that."

"Well . . ." For the next five minutes Dr. Sandy talked about iron saturation and how the number for Emma's body was unusually high. Then she talked about binding capacity . . . and then something called a ferritin level. Super high. Sandy paused. "My suspicion is that you have hemochromatosis."

"What is that?"

"It's a genetic disorder that makes it so that your body doesn't process iron like everyone else."

"So, my bones are stronger?" Emma knew almost nothing about blood iron.

"No. Your body can't burn off iron. But before we go there . . . let's run the tests and make sure."

"It could be a fluke?"

Dr. Sandy's smile didn't convince Emma.

"You mentioned liver enzymes . . . what does that have to do with this?"

Sandy took a deep breath. "If you do have hemochromatosis, the iron in your bloodstream has to plant itself somewhere in your body. One of the first places it goes is your liver."

Everything in Emma's body stilled. Her eyes widened. "What does that mean?"

"Your liver enzymes are only slightly elevated . . ."

"Which means you know the iron levels aren't a mistake."

"We need to double-check," Sandy said.

"But my liver is telling you you're right."

Emma met Sandy's eyes. "Most likely."

"And then what?"

"I don't want to 'then what' yet," she said.

Emma snapped her head up. Her hand shook. "'Then what' anyway. What am I looking at?"

"Before we go there . . . let me examine you. Ask a few questions."

"Okay."

Emma sat there, eyes wide. What did this mean? She had zero idea what Dr. Sandy was talking about.

"Lie back."

Emma tried to relax on the half table while the doctor poked around, asking if something hurt.

Nothing hurt.

Wasn't that an indication of a problem?

"How is your energy level?"

"I'm a little tired. But I've been running. Moving . . . traveling. Starting a business."

She poked at Emma's hands. "Any pain in your joints?"

Emma shook her head.

"What about your bowel movements? Constipation, loose . . . different color?"

She felt a glitch . . . a memory . . . "A few times it's been light."

"In color?"

"Yeah." In Italy.

"All the time?"

"I don't look all the time."

Dr. Sandy stopped examining her and stood back. "Any headaches?"

"A few."

"One a week? A month?"

"I take something over the counter a couple times a week. I've been a little stressed."

Dr. Sandy smiled.

But it didn't meet her eyes. "This is what we're going to do. I'm going to repeat the blood tests. That's where we start. I'm going to order an MRI of your liver, get that started, and hopefully your insurance will approve sooner."

"Then what?"

"If . . . if your bloodwork continues to point in this direction, I'm going to request a consult with a hematologist and a hepatologist . . ."

-Ologist this and *-ologist* that. Emma shut off.

Nothing else went in.

Nothing registered.

Sandy talked and Emma turned off.

The nurse walked in . . . drew her blood.

As Emma left the office, she had the information for the patient portal. Something she never thought she would need to look at. And a follow-up appointment.

A numbness fell over her like nothing she'd ever felt before.

She'd been told words she'd never heard. And considered everything she did know about liver disease.

None of it good.

Her phone rang as she drove home. It was her mother. There was no way Emma could talk to her . . . not with her head spinning on everything she'd just been told.

She let the call go to voice mail and finished the rest of the drive on autopilot.

At home, Emma dropped everything on the kitchen island, found her computer, and started typing in all the new words that had been added to her vocabulary by her doctor.

The printout of her previous bloodwork sat in front of her.

Within an hour she started to understand.

If your body couldn't process iron, that iron needed to stick some-where in the body. The liver . . . head, heart . . . joints.

Emma flexed her fingers.

No pain.

It was genetic. Not something brought on by diet or too much wine.

Nearly every article she'd found on the disorder had disturbing images of patients with diseased organs. Too much iron in your liver meant disease if untreated, and that seemed to be a resounding theme.

Emma found herself down the rabbit hole of liver disease. Alcoholic and nonalcoholic liver disease. The results were the same. None of them pretty.

It was when she looked up cure and treatment for hemochromatosis that Emma cringed.

"What the hell?"

~

"I hear you have a girlfriend."

Gio looked up from the office desk, where he was working on the inventory and employee scheduling.

Salena stood in the doorway, pointing her finger in his direction.

"Who told you that, Instagram or Facebook?"

"Both," she said without apology.

Gio dropped the pen he was holding. "Sometimes the internet doesn't lie."

Salena smiled and scrambled to sit across from him. "She's beautiful."

"I know. I'm a lucky man."

"You met her in Italy?"

Gio paused. "You've been talking to Chloe."

"Your sister is my best friend. That's a given."

"I did in fact meet her in Italy." He pictured her standing there with a bag in place of a suitcase. "She's special."

Salena's jaw slacked. "Oh my God . . . Chloe wasn't kidding."

"What?"

"You're all in."

He glitched. Like a computer not completely syncing with the internet connection.

"Holy crap . . ."

Salena started to laugh. "Yeah . . . holy crap. No one is going to believe it. Giovanni D'Angelo is off the market."

Gio pictured Emma with her hair piled high, standing in a room of people that didn't matter smiling at him. "I'm beyond off the market."

Salena sat back and a tear ran down her face. "I'm happy for you."

"Thank you."

"Looks like I'm the last of us to find the one."

Salena was beautiful, spicy . . . self-assured. "You will."

Silence followed. "Whatever."

Salena stood, opened her arms. "I look forward to meeting her."

Once Salena left, Gio picked up his phone and sent a text to Emma.

Good afternoon, cara.

When she didn't reply right away, he set his phone down and got back to work.

He smiled into the things Salena had said. "I'm off the market," he whispered to himself.

~

Tuesday morning arrived after a night of tossing and turning.

Emma's father's secretary called. Emma didn't pick up the phone.

By nine in the morning Dr. Sandy had confirmed what Emma knew in her heart was true. The lab work wasn't a fluke. "I'm sending you to the hematologist to manage this. They're going to want to do some genetic testing to confirm the cause. Which is likely genetic."

"Likely?"

"I won't say a hundred percent until they test. I'm ninety-nine percent sure that's the cause. The other causes of iron overload, hemochromatosis, don't apply to you. You're not being treated for cancer or are on any drugs that would cause this. I've already called Dr. Andrews and she will get you in this week."

"And my liver? According to what I read, the extra iron in my body is absorbed by my liver but doesn't leave and, if left untreated, could cause cirrhosis." Emma shivered when she said the word *cirrhosis*.

"Which is why we want the MRI and the liver doctor to see you."

"Jesus."

"I have no doubt we'll find some iron in your liver. Dr. Chow is excellent. I spoke with him yesterday and he'd like you to come in this week. We're going to get the ball rolling and start taking care of this."

Fear crept up Emma's spine. "And the treatment . . ."

"Phlebotomy. We need to take blood out of your body. Sounds archaic but it's—"

"Leeches. Didn't bleeding people to better health end in the Middle Ages?" Emma had been shocked when she'd read that online.

"I thought the same thing until I was in medical school. But no. The treatment is to remove blood from your system, half a liter at a time . . . consistently until your body is no longer overloaded with iron. Diabetics have insulin to control the sugar that their bodies can't process. You need to remove red blood cells that are saturated with iron so your body is forced to make new cells that have no iron in them. That blood circulates and pulls the iron into those new blood cells—almost like a sponge—and they are discarded again. Over time the excess is depleted from your system."

"How much time? How many trips to the vampires do I have to have?"

Dr. Sandy chuckled. "I don't have the answer to that. This is where Dr. Andrews comes in and monitors the progress. Once you're no longer overloaded the phlebotomies slow down."

"What are we talking about?" Emma found herself "then what-ing." A term Gio had coined when it came to everything wine and vineyards.

"Routine trips to the blood bank. I have other patients on maintenance with this, and they donate blood three or four times a year. But when they were first diagnosed, they went in every week, some twice a week or every other week. For months . . . or years, depending upon how it's spread out."

Emma's stomach twisted. "I've never donated blood in my life."

"That's about to change."

Emma paused. "Thank you for your honesty."

Dr. Sandy's voice softened. "Are you getting any sleep?"

Emma couldn't help it . . . she laughed. "No."

"I know this is hard, but try and stay off of Dr. Google, okay? I will be in constant contact with the doctors on your team and touch base with you every week until we have all our answers."

Tears formed. "I have a team."

"Yes. A good one. Make your appointments and then take a walk. Have your boyfriend give you a massage and try and get some sleep."

Her boyfriend . . .

Gio knew nothing about any of this.

"Thank you."

Emma hung up the phone and stared at it.

"I have a team."

CHAPTER THIRTY-TWO

Gio tried calling Emma Monday night. She didn't pick up.

Her text messages consisted of two or three words, none of which matched the energy she'd had coming out of the weekend.

By Tuesday afternoon, he was channeling every insecurity in his mind. They'd spoken almost every day since coming home from Italy. And their text messages were so often that Gio felt like he was always by her side.

All of that felt like it came to a crashing stop.

Gio sat on the terrace with his phone in hand. Emma hadn't called him back, and her last text message was the night before.

He'd sent three messages that day and zero replies.

"Screw it."

He dialed her number.

Every ring that didn't go answered dropped his heart further in his chest.

Right before the fifth ring, she picked up.

"Hey," she said.

Gio smiled. "I needed to hear your voice. I haven't heard from you and was starting to worry."

"Uhm . . ." Emma cleared her throat. "I'm sorry about that." Her voice wavered.

Gio lost his smile. "What's wrong?"

"Uhm . . ."

Was she crying?

"Is it your dad?"

"No. No . . . I haven't talked to him."

"That was today, right?"

"I, ah . . . didn't take the call." She sniffled.

"You're crying." He could hear it in her voice.

"Yeah . . . I'm having a bad day."

Gio ran a hand through his hair. "*Amore*, talk to me. What's going on?"

She hesitated. "Remember how I said I saw my doctor?"

Doctor? "Yeah. Clean bill of health." Gio stilled. Was that wrong?

"Sexual health . . . and that's still good. But she did some other bloodwork and that isn't good."

Five minutes into Emma's monologue about the "not good" bloodwork and the need for doctors and tests and MRIs, Gio walked into his room and started shoving clothes into a bag.

He scratched a note on a piece of paper, grabbed his keys, and jogged down the stairs.

"Hey?" Luca caught him.

Gio put a finger to his lips and handed his brother the note.

Emma needs me. I don't know when I'll be home. I'll call later.

Before Luca could ask anything, Gio was out the door and in his car.

". . . and what does that mean?" Gio asked.

"It means it's probably genetic . . . ," Emma continued.

His car picked up the call and put it on speaker as he pulled out of the drive.

As Emma talked, her tears dried up.

As the tears went away her voice grew stronger.

So many new words were thrown in Gio's direction so quickly he couldn't process them all. Liver doctors, blood doctors . . . "Emma, why didn't you tell me this was going on?"

"My doctor mentioned something on Friday on my way down to your place. I blew it off. We had other things going on."

"Nothing is more important than your health, *amore*."

"Yeah . . . I'm learning that. When I went to the doctor yesterday, I went numb. Today she confirmed what we suspected and all I can do is cry." And just like that the tears were back.

Gio glanced at his speedometer and then his rearview mirror.

"I'll be there in thirty minutes." They'd been on the phone for a half an hour already. And Gio wasn't exactly following the speed limit.

"You don't have to—"

"Don't finish that sentence," he told her. "Have you eaten?"

"What?"

"I'm Italian, have you eaten?"

"No," she finally said.

Of course not. "Listen to me. Go to your refrigerator and pull something out. Anything my mom sent home with you."

"I'm not—"

"Don't finish that sentence."

Emma sighed. "Fine."

Fine was never a good word coming from a woman. But he could hear her moving in the background. Then he heard the beeps coming from her microwave.

Gio smiled. "Have you told anyone about this yet?"

"Only you."

"And when is your appointment with the hema . . . blood-ologist?"

Emma chuckled. "Tomorrow."

What was the name for the liver guy? "And the liver-ologist?"

"Friday."

The microwave beeped.

"I'm going to eat now."

"Go ahead. I'll do the talking."

"You want to listen to me chew?" she questioned.

He smiled. "I have had a lot of meals with you. Listening to you chew is kind of adorable."

"Ew . . . nobody likes to hear someone chewing food."

She wasn't wrong, but Gio wasn't going to disconnect the call.

"What did you heat up?"

"It's ziti, I think."

Gio liked getting what he wanted. "Did she put sausage in it?"

"I think . . . yes. She did."

"It's the best."

Hearing her take a bite was music to his ears. "Oh, yeah . . . this is good."

"I keep saying it needs to be on the menu."

For the last half of the drive, Gio directed the conversation to food and some of his family history with the restaurant. He told her how Brooke and Luca met over Franny running through the restaurant and Brooke catching her before she collided with a waiter carrying hot plates. Gio did everything to keep the conversation going and give Emma time to eat.

Thirty minutes sped by.

He pressed the new code to her gate and let himself in. "I'm pulling up."

"Okay."

It was then that he ended the call.

Emma stood at the door wearing sweatpants, a T-shirt, and fatigue written all over her puffy face.

His heart broke at the sight of her.

He took the steps two at a time and crushed her into his arms.

She started to shake.

"I've got you. It's going to be okay."

A sob tore from her throat, and her knees gave way.

Gio picked her up and walked her inside.

~

Gio snuck out of the bedroom and quietly closed the door.

He'd held Emma as she cried, soothed the worries that he could, and lain with her until she fell asleep. It was just after seven in the evening, the sun was still shining, but Emma hadn't slept since Sunday night.

Gio took his phone with him as he stepped outside so he could call home.

There was one text message from his mother. **We're worried. Call as soon as you can.**

"Hi, Mama."

"Oh, thank God. Giovanni, this isn't like you. What is going on?"

He launched into an explanation without giving every detail. The whole time his mother cooed and gasped at all the right times.

Mari clicked her tongue. "She must be scared to death."

"And shocked," he said.

"Does she feel okay? She didn't look sick."

"That's just it, Mama, she's not ill. She feels fine outside of scared, shocked, and exhausted. And before you ask, yes, I'm making her eat."

"I'll make more and bring it."

Gio smiled. "We're fine for now."

"I want to do something."

"And I'll let you. Right now, Emma needs to rest and get ready for the week. If you come here, she'll feel the need to entertain."

Mari clicked her tongue. "Entertain. Please, I don't need entertainment."

"I will let you know when you can come."

"Your pain is our pain, you know that."

"I do."

"And Emma is a part of us all now."

"I know that, too, Mama." God, he loved his family. "I don't know when I'll be back."

"We have everything covered here. Don't spend another moment's thought on the restaurant."

Gio knew his absence in Little Italy was felt, but it wouldn't stop the family business from running. "I love you."

"Oh, my heart. Take care of Emma. Call if you need anything."

Once he ended the call, Gio opened the internet app on his phone and started searching Google.

~

Emma sat in a chair with Giovanni at her side, holding her hand, in Dr. Andrews's office.

"I want to start your treatments next week."

"How often will I have to go?"

"Once a week to start."

Giving blood every week sounded problematic to Emma's ears. Dr. Andrews made it sound routine. "Okay."

Gio squeezed her hand.

"How long will the weekly trips take to get Emma to normal?" Gio asked.

Emma smiled, thankful he asked.

"Three months . . . six months. Hard to say until you start treatment and we see how you're responding. If you're feeling too tired or need to go out of town or need to skip a session, that's perfectly fine."

The doctor paused. "Any other questions?"

Emma nodded. "Yeah. If it's genetic, then I've had this my whole life, right?"

"Correct."

"Then why am I just finding it now?"

Dr. Andrews looked at her computer. "Why were you seeing Dr. Sandy?"

"Routine. I told her I thought I was bruising too much, and she did the bloodwork."

"No joint pain?"

"Nothing like that," Emma told her.

"When was your last period?"

"I have an IUD. I haven't really had one for five . . . no, six years."

A light went off in Dr. Andrews's head . . . Emma could see that in the other woman's eyes.

"The average age that women find out they have this is often over fifty-five. After menopause. If you haven't had a period in six years, that iron had no way to leave your body."

Emma felt chills as it all started to make sense.

"You can always take the IUD out and it would likely speed this process up."

"Enough to where she won't need the phlebotomies?" Gio asked.

"No. Phlebotomies are going to be needed."

Emma felt a little more grounded with the information. "One more question."

"Go."

"Genetics . . . does this mean my brothers could have this, too?"

Dr. Andrews nodded. "Absolutely. But just because you have it doesn't mean your brothers will. There are a lot of factors. Your parents are likely carriers of the mutated gene, or could possibly be suffering with this without knowing."

"My parents are in their early sixties."

"Symptoms of this are often ignored until the organs the iron deposits in are affected."

"The liver," Gio said.

"Yes. Joints, liver, head, heart . . . This often goes undiagnosed until it's too late. Are your parents healthy?"

"Yes. So are my brothers."

"Everyone should be tested before major damage can set in."

"According to my bloodwork, my liver isn't a hundred percent happy."

"Not a hundred percent, but not awful either. Is your liver involved? Probably. Is it too late?" Dr. Andrews shook her head. "I don't think so. I don't want to give you false hope, but I don't want you working yourself up on something you couldn't have done anything about."

"I'll try."

"Good." She studied Emma's chart. "How much do you drink?" Dr. Andrews looked between the two of them.

The doctor spent some time talking about the dangers of excessive drinking and moderation . . . and abstaining until the liver doctor had all the test results he needed.

Emma pointed a finger at Gio. "He can taste the wine."

The doctor smiled, her shoulders relaxed. "You're an adult. As long as you're not playing drinking games, you should be fine. My patients with this who don't have liver disease drink in moderation."

"Okay." *I can do this,* Emma chanted in her head.

"Anything else?"

"No."

"Great. Stay here so we can get some more bloodwork." Dr. Andrews walked out of the room.

Giovanni turned to her the moment they were alone. "How are you feeling?"

"Better. Numb . . . It's a lot to take in."

"I like your doctor."

"I do, too."

Gio offered a smile. "No more wine tasting challenges."

That made her chuckle. "Those weren't really games."

"Ehh . . ."

"Okay, maybe they were."

Gio leaned over and kissed her briefly. "We've got this, *cara*."

CHAPTER THIRTY-THREE

The morning air stirred from the open window in the primary bedroom.

Gio pulled in a deep breath and reached a hand over to Emma's side of the bed.

He moved it a couple of times and opened his eyes.

She wasn't there.

The light from outside spread a soft glow into the room, telling him the sun was barely over the horizon. The clock on the side of the bed confirmed the early hour.

He kicked off the sheet covering his body and reached for a pair of lounge pants he had sitting on a chair in the room before searching for Emma.

"Emma?"

The kitchen and great room were empty.

A fresh pot of coffee and a clean cup sat beside it.

Gio smiled and helped himself.

With a cup in hand, he looked out the front door, found the porch empty. He then decided to look in the back by the pool.

Emma sat curled in a chair, her gaze off in the distance.

A light bathrobe covered one shoulder, the other draped to the side, displaying a tiny string that held on a nightgown Gio was getting used to seeing her in.

"There you are," he said softly to get her attention.

Emma slowly turned her head and smiled over her shoulder in his direction. "Did I wake you?"

He walked close, set his cup beside hers on a table, and kissed the top of her head. "No. Not at all. How long have you been out here?"

She looked into her cup.

It was empty. "Before the sun rose."

Gio took the chair beside her and brought the first sip of java to his lips. "Did you sleep better last night?"

"A little, I think. Better with you here."

What man didn't like hearing that?

"Bad dreams?"

She shook her head. "No. I wake up and for the first few seconds I feel normal. Like nothing is going on . . . then I remember. If I lie in bed even half-awake, my head starts spinning with all the possibilities and worry."

Gio hated the sadness on her face. "What can I do? We're not going to have any more answers for a while."

She tried to smile. "I think I need to keep busy. There's so much to do here. Maybe if I exhaust myself, I will sleep through the night."

Gio took a sip of his coffee, handed it to her since hers was empty. "Where do you want to start?"

"The cellar. There's years of crap built up in there." Emma sipped the coffee, handed it back.

"Okay, then. Let's make some breakfast and get to it." Gio stood.

"I'm not that hungry."

He reached for her hand. "It wasn't a suggestion," he teased.

Emma rolled her eyes, a tiny smile on her lips, and let him help her to her feet.

An hour, and one breakfast, later, they opened the doors to the cellar and production building wide.

Emma stood with her hair in a ponytail, wearing an old pair of jeans and one of the graphic T-shirts she'd picked up in Italy. One that said, *Wine a little, you'll feel better.*

They both put on work gloves and stared out over the mess.

"I say we get everything out of here. What is absolute trash has a date with the dumpster. Anything that can be recycled in a pile, and anything useful in another pile. But we empty it completely," Emma suggested.

Gio nodded. "Then we can see how sturdy everything is, get a reading on the internal temperature and see if we need to fix the climate controls."

They walked in and Emma kicked at something on the ground. "Not to mention rodents."

He looked at her feet and what was likely droppings from a mouse. "Should I expect you to scream if we find a mouse?"

Emma grinned, a genuine smile he hadn't seen all morning. "I grew up playing in vineyards, the only thing that makes me scream is a rattlesnake. Which reminds me, *city boy* . . . don't put your hands where you can't see. Those damn things love to hide around left-behind crap."

Gio draped an arm over her shoulders. "Noted. Now . . . are we going to look at this all day or get our asses moving?"

She playfully pushed him away.

Gio smacked her butt and they dug in.

Within an hour, Raul had shown up, and whatever he'd planned to do that day turned to helping them out.

Old barrels were taken out and lined up.

Parts of old equipment that amounted to nothing but scrap metal were put in a different pile.

The small dumpster was quickly filling up with garbage left behind by the previous owners.

"Why wouldn't your father send someone over to deal with this?" Gio asked as he lugged yet another crate of empty wine bottles outside.

"Who knows?"

"I asked many times what R&R wanted me to do with this space," Raul said. "I was told to leave it. Keep the grapes growing and the landscape around the house alive."

Emma passed Raul and picked up another handful of trash. "With the place vacant for nearly two years, I hope you brought your kids around to use the pool," she said.

Raul straightened, glanced at her. "Uhm."

"What a waste if you didn't," Gio said.

"Maybe a couple of times," he admitted.

"Good," Emma said.

Right before lunch they managed to find the bottom of the cellar floor. Cement, stained with all kinds of sin living in the corners.

"I have a friend who has a power washer," Raul told them as they all stood around looking at the mess.

"That would be great," Gio said.

"Is that something we need to buy?" Emma asked.

"No."

"If we need to pay him to use it . . ."

"He's a friend, Miss Emma. I let him borrow my things, I borrow his."

Gio patted Raul on the back. "We appreciate it."

They ate sitting on the front porch of the house, where the shade kept them a little cooler. For hours Gio hadn't heard Emma say a peep about all the things she was facing. They were dirty and hot . . . and working their way to exhaustion.

Just like she'd asked.

Emma pointed to the pile of scrap metal. "Should we take that to the dump?"

"Scrap metal is worth money," Gio told her.

"Enough to make a difference?" Emma asked.

He wasn't sure. Gio had never taken a load like this to a recycling plant.

"I have a friend," Raul said again between bites of his sandwich. "He has a truck. He takes a percentage of the load but takes care of it for you. Loads it. Unloads it."

Gio glanced at Emma, gave her a thumbs-up.

"Sold."

"He might have to come after his day job."

Emma laughed, finished what was left in her water bottle, and jumped to her feet. "Whenever."

"Shall we start on the winery?" Gio pointed to the production building.

Raul wadded up a napkin and stood. "Let's go."

"We really appreciate your help, Raul," Emma said as they walked across the driveway.

"It's my job, Miss Emma."

She shook her head. "Technically, you're my vigneron. Cleaning out old buildings does not fall into your job description."

Raul tilted his head back and laughed. "No one has called me that. Foreman is a good enough title for me."

Raul left briefly and returned with the power washer and said he didn't need it back until Monday.

The utility truck was pulled out of the equipment barn and a whole new mess was unearthed.

Gio didn't consider himself a mechanic. But he knew when an engine on a car didn't sound right.

"Hey, Raul . . ."

The man smiled. "I have a friend . . ."

Emma laughed. "You have a lot of friends."

"I'm a blessed man," Raul told them.

Later that night, with the winery and cellar looking slightly better, but the property surrounding the buildings looking like the backyard of a thrift shop . . . Emma and Gio said goodbye to Raul, called it quits, and dove into the pool.

Emma sat on the steps, submerged up to her waist and leaning on her elbows. "There were a few times today that I had an opportunity to forget about everything that is going on."

Gio swam over to her. "Me too. Hard work does that."

She looked at him with a sad smile. "I'm really glad you're here."

He framed her body with his hands. "There is nowhere else I want to be."

"Eventually you'll have to go home."

"That's debatable," he said.

She narrowed her eyes. "Hmm."

"Let me worry about that."

"Okay."

Gio knelt in front of her in the pool and ran his hands up the sides of her body. "I have a very serious question for you."

"You do?"

He found the string to her bikini top and played with it. "Why on earth are you wearing this in your private pool?"

Her smile told Gio he was asking the right questions.

"I'm not used to going skinny-dipping."

He pulled the string and the top fell open. "Oops."

~

They sat outside of the liver-ologist's office inside the air-conditioned car with the engine running.

"That felt like a formality." Gio said what he thought they were both thinking.

"He didn't tell us anything we haven't already heard."

"Except that your MRI was approved."

The reminder had Emma digging into her purse for her phone.

Gio put the car in gear and pulled out of the parking lot.

He listened to one side of the conversation as she booked the appointment. "Monday? Really? No . . . I thought I'd have to wait. Oh, okay. Yeah, no . . . that's fine. Ten? Yeah."

She disconnected the call. "That was easier than I thought."

"We'll have more answers on Monday."

"I won't hold my breath for the results on Monday. They said by Tuesday."

"Monday MRI. And a week from Thursday your first phlebotomy—"

"Vampire treatment." She was trying to find humor in what wasn't funny.

Gio went along with it. "Your first vampire. Should I be concerned? I hear vampires are something women crave."

"Considering the love bite on my right boob, I'd say you have nothing to worry about."

He tried not to smile. "I am sorry about that."

"No, you're not."

"No, I'm not." Gio pulled into the hardware store parking lot. "When do we tell your family?"

"I don't know. After the genetic test comes back, I guess. I'm not ready to deal with them."

Gio pulled the car into a parking space and cut the engine. "You're the boss."

She looked up at the sign on the home improvement building. "If I'm the boss, then what are we doing here?"

"My brother and mom do the fancy Italian dinners. I am the boss of a barbeque. And you don't have one."

Emma smiled. "I like barbeque."

~

Emma held the phone to her ear, keeping her tone low as she talked to Nicole. The conversation had started with Emma telling her best friend everything that was happening. There were questions and more tears and a whole lot of *"What can I do?"*

That's when Emma explained that Giovanni was doing everything and that more people calling and asking about her health . . . questions she couldn't answer . . . would make her anxiety and worry escalate.

"It wasn't anything like this with Kyle. Gio and I've been working with each other. Meals, cleaning up . . . laundry. I don't think I ever saw Kyle put a load of laundry into the washer. Ever."

"Kyle was convenient. Gio is the real deal. They are not even on the same planet," Nicole told her.

"He makes me laugh and holds me when I cry. *'Go rest, Emma. Save your energy, amore.'* He hasn't left since this started."

"Any man who truly cared about you wouldn't leave."

"We distract ourselves with cleaning the place up during the day and searching for the equipment we'll need to get the winery up and running before harvest. Even though we're both exhausted by bedtime, sleep isn't easy."

"This can't be easy. I'm shocked just hearing about it. You're living it."

Emma watched a hummingbird flip around the glass feeder Gio had hung up. "I go from disbelief . . . like this is a dream, to staring off, to having to move and get shit done. Working is helping me get out of my own pity party."

"You're allowed to feel sorry for yourself, Emma."

"Allowed, yeah. But I don't like where it takes me. Worry crawled up my back like a spider fighting against the water flowing down a drain. That's when I start spinning. What if the MRI is all bad news? What if my liver is so polluted that disease has set in? That's not reversible, Nicole."

"But you're not sick."

"I haven't exactly been feeling great either. The doctors start asking questions and I'm like . . . yeah, I've been tired. My bathroom habits are off. And when I look all this up online, the signs point to a real issue. Dying of a liver problem looks slow and painful."

"Stop talking like that. You're not dying," Nicole snapped.

"No, I'm *what-iffing.* That's what Gio calls it. And if I'm not *what-if-fing,* I'm *then what-ing* . . . If this comes back positive, then what? If that comes back wrong . . . then what?"

"I get it, Em. I mean . . . I don't get it. I'm not you, but when you find yourself down the rabbit hole of doom, try turning that around. It's one thing to have a plan on what you can do, it's another to rock in a corner in need of aerial spraying of Prozac. What if the MRI is fine? What if they caught this so early that there is nothing else wrong with you? As your friend, that's what I'm going to do. You are young, healthy—"

Emma snorted.

"Healthy!" Nicole practically yelled into the phone. "You're not an alcoholic. Hell, I'm the one that likes to drink more than you."

"That's because you work in finance."

Emma heard Nicole laugh a little.

"Maybe. You have a major support system. Gio isn't going anywhere. I felt that at the airport in Italy when we were leaving. And he's proven it by sticking at your side."

Emma glanced at her watch.

Gio was inside, getting ready to take her to her MRI appointment.

"I don't want him to leave. Even when he goes to the grocery store, I find myself looking for him. The thought of him going back to San Diego for several days makes me feel empty inside."

"I think that's great, Emma."

"I never thought I'd feel this way. I'm sure some of it has to do with what I'm going through."

"So what if it does? I doubt it will change when all of this is behind you," Nicole said.

Emma heard the door behind her open. "Ready, my darling?" Gio asked.

She smiled, pushed out of the chair. "I have to go. Wish me luck with the MRI."

"Call me as soon as you know anything. I can duck out of the office if you need me."

Emma smiled. "Love you."

"Love you, too, Em."

Gio closed the door behind her. "Who was that?"

"Nicole. I needed to tell her what was going on."

Gio smiled. "Good. You need your friends right now."

"And you," Emma admitted. "I need you."

He pulled her into his arms. "You couldn't get rid of me if you tried. You ready to put one more test behind you?"

She faked a smile. "I am."

~

The MRI took less than a half an hour from start to finish . . . but the waiting for the results carried through the weekend.

Gio was convinced that Emma had nerves of steel . . . that was until she started snapping at him.

"Damn it!"

He heard her cuss before he heard the sound of something hitting the floor.

"You okay in there?" he called from the great room, where he was hanging two iron candleholders on the wall surrounding the fireplace.

"Why did you put this here?"

Gio left his hammer on the mantel and walked back to the primary bedroom. "Put what where?"

He rounded the corner and Emma was shoving the dresser, trying to move it. "This? It's in the way. I just stubbed my toe on the damn thing."

There was no way he was going to remind her that the furniture was exactly where she'd told him and Dante to place it. Instead, he moved to her side and said, "Where do you want it?"

"Over there," she huffed and pointed her finger and limped as she moved away.

"I've got this."

"It's in the way."

Tread lightly, he cautioned himself.

One by one Gio removed the drawers to the dresser and placed them on the bed. All while Emma removed the socks she was wearing to examine the aforementioned toe that had been stubbed.

"Is it broken?"

"No," she snapped. "Hurts, though."

"Will ice help?" *Suggestions, not solutions,* he reminded himself. Emma needed control wherever she could find it.

"Maybe."

He wasn't about to tell her to get some . . . instead he went through the motion of taking everything off the dresser to lighten the load.

Eventually, Emma huffed out of the bedroom to what he assumed was the kitchen to retrieve ice she likely didn't need.

By the time she returned, holding a plastic bag filled with ice, he'd lugged the dresser to its new position.

She sat on the edge of the bed, glaring at the dresser. "That looks dumb there."

Gio swallowed his smile.

"I have a suggestion."

Her nose flared, her lips a flat line. "What?"

"C'mere." Gio motioned toward the walk-in closet and waited while she reluctantly followed.

"What?"

He stood in the middle of the room that would be considered an apartment in Manhattan and turned a full circle. There were single shelves with single rods filled with Emma's clothes. Shoeboxes were stacked on the floor, a hamper off to the side. "There is a ton of space in here."

"The dresser would look even more ridiculous in here."

He moved to her side and gently placed an arm over her shoulders. With his other hand, he made a sweeping motion. "Picture an island with drawers for all the things you have in the dresser that doesn't fit. And instead of one rod, you put two on each side, leaving some space for long dresses and coats. How about a shoe rack on the back wall . . . maybe a full-length mirror? Now the dresser that doesn't really fit in the bedroom can be moved to a spare room and you'll never need to stub your toe again."

Emma tucked hair behind her ears as if the very hair on her head was her enemy.

A shift of her body weight from one foot to the other was all Gio got as a reply to his question for several seconds.

And then he heard her sniffle.

He dared a look and saw a tear fall down her cheek. "I'm being such a bitch."

His arms circled around her and she buried her head into his shoulder and started to cry. "Shhh." There was a physical ache in Gio's chest, hearing her cry.

"Why can't the doctors look at the test results right away? They do in hospitals."

"I don't know, *cara*."

"Maybe the news is bad and they don't want to tell me."

"They wouldn't do that. They deal with this stuff every day."

She sucked in a breath. "I'm scared."

Gio stroked her hair. He was, too. "Shhh."

"Two weeks ago we were crashing parties in Napa and now I'm waiting to hear from my latest doctor about my latest problem. How did this happen?"

He held her tighter. "I don't know, *amore*. It doesn't feel real most of the time."

"I just want to wake up from this bad dream."

Gio pulled away so he could look at her.

He wiped the tears from her eyes with his thumbs and tried to smile. "In five years, we're going to look back on this time and kick ourselves for all the worry we're creating."

"Are you sure?"

No.

"Yes," he lied.

Emma lifted her chin and squared her shoulders as if his words impacted her in a way to move her forward. "I like your idea about the closet."

He couldn't help but chuckle. "Back to the home improvement store?"

Her smile was heaven in his heart. "You don't mind?"

"Are you kidding? I love that place."

CHAPTER THIRTY-FOUR

Tuesday morning, Emma's phone rang while they were having coffee.

Dr. Chow's, the liver-ologist's, name popped up on her screen.

She dropped the cup onto the counter, spilling coffee everywhere.

"Is that your doctor?" Gio asked.

"Yes."

When she didn't reach to answer it, Gio grabbed the phone. "Hello?"

"Can I speak to Emma Rutledge?"

The phone was on speaker.

"I'm here," Emma said.

Gio reached for her hand.

"This is Dr. Chow's office; can you hold for the doctor?"

"Of course."

When elevator music came across the line, Gio placed a hand on her cheek and made her look into his eyes. "We got this."

Did she?

She nodded, even if she didn't believe her own motions.

They'd spent the weekend doing so much yet absolutely nothing. The closet was half-built while Emma painted one of the guest rooms . . . twice because she hated the color after it had dried.

They ate and tossed and turned at night.

Even though she loved having Giovanni at her side, they hadn't made love all weekend.

He held her every night, and woke with her every morning.

Emma couldn't ask for more.

"Miss Rutledge?"

"Yes."

It was Dr. Chow. "I have the MRI results. As we expected, your liver is where the iron in your bloodstream decided to deposit itself."

Emma looked at Gio.

"How bad is it?"

"Uhm . . . it's pretty impressive. I'm surprised, given your ferritin levels and your lack of symptoms."

That didn't sound good.

"What does that mean, Doctor?" Gio asked.

"Do I have cirrhosis?" Emma blurted out.

Dr. Chow cleared his throat. "Iron in your liver was expected, or none of your doctors would have added me to your team. The MRI gives us a starting point to work off of while you're going through treatment to de-iron the excess in your body. Do you have cirrhosis?" He paused. "We won't know until we do a FibroScan."

Emma's shoulders slumped.

That wasn't a no.

"I thought cirrhosis was diagnosed with a biopsy." Emma had read that on the internet.

Dr. Chow sighed. "I believe a FibroScan will tell us if we need a biopsy. Biopsies are invasive, painful, and unnecessary at this stage. The FibroScan determines the degree of scarring of your liver and will tell us if we need to dig deeper."

Another test . . .

Another fucking test . . .

Gio squeezed her hand. "Any advice at this stage, Doctor?" he asked.

"My specialty is the liver. Avoid alcohol until we know exactly where we're at."

Emma ran her hands down her face and tried not to cry . . .
Again.

~

The morning of Emma's first date with the vampires, Dr. Andrews called with the genetic testing results.

She spat out some crazy series of letters and numbers and confirmed that, yes, this was a genetic marker for hereditary hemochromatosis.

"I'll write orders for your immediate family members to get tested whenever they're ready to come in."

"Thank you," Emma said.

"I'll see you in three months. Standing orders are written for your lab work and treatment. If you need anything, don't hesitate to call me."

"Thank you."

Emma pulled out the notebook and turned it to her "Then what?" page.

She put a checkbox next to the words *Genetic test* and then underlined where she'd written *Tell family.*

That was not going to be fun.

Her father's secretary had called again.

Her mother . . . three times.

And again, Emma ignored all the messages. Maybe once everyone heard the reason why, they'd understand.

The two of them stepped out of the house and started toward the car.

Raul slowed his truck and rolled down the window. "Good morning," he said.

Emma waved.

Gio opened her door for her. "Good morning. We'll be back in a few hours. If you need anything, call."

"I'm checking water lines today. Unless you think there is a greater need somewhere else," he said.

"Sounds good to me." Gio turned to her. "Emma?"

She smiled at the man who was keeping things going with all the appointments she and Gio were juggling. "Thank you for all you're doing."

"My pleasure, Miss Emma. You have a nice day."

Not likely, but she appreciated his words.

En route to the infusion center, Emma told Gio her plans regarding her family. "I'm going to ask that my father and Richard fly down for a family meeting this weekend."

"Will he do that?" Gio asked. "He doesn't seem like the kind of man who takes orders."

"I've never asked. I'll tell them I've been seeing a doctor and it's important. How do you say no to that?"

"You don't if you're talking to someone you love," Gio told her.

Emma wasn't sure what to expect when she walked into the infusion center. Thankfully, no one she knew had cancer and she'd never had to congregate with people who did.

Until now.

They walked in holding hands, which, she had to admit, even to herself, was exactly what she needed. All around were patients of all ages, races, and colors. People in wheelchairs and others using walkers. Some with bandanas on their heads to hide their baldness . . . and every one of them wearing a mask. This was not optional in a place where nearly everyone had a compromised immune system.

A strange wave of guilt washed over her as she waited for her name to be called. She was there to have someone take blood out of her. The others in the lobby were there to have toxic medicine infused into them. They were bound to be sick for hours or days after their treatments . . . Emma was likely to be tired and fatigued but bounce back in a day or two at most. And that was where the guilt came in.

Emma couldn't help but wonder if this seemingly simple visit was the beginning of something worse. A dark cloud of worry never felt far away.

"You're only here for the vampires, *amore*."

Either Gio was reading her mind, or he was thinking the same thing.

The two of them sat in the waiting room, quietly chatting.

Finally, her name was called, and they both stood up.

The man taking them back introduced himself as her nurse and asked her to confirm why she was there.

"And this is your first treatment?"

"Yes."

"Have you ever given blood before?"

"No."

They were led to an open room where curtains offered privacy to patients sitting in large reclining chairs who had IVs and medicine flowing into their veins.

Emma felt a little dizzy before sitting down.

"Your blood pressure is a little high."

"I'm nervous."

The nurse pulled up a rolling chair and opened a cart and started removing several things.

Emma looked around and saw a dozen employees scurrying about.

"How are you two today?" As the nurse asked the question, he tied a tourniquet around Emma's arm to start her IV.

Her poor, tattered veins looked like she had a drug habit. "We'd be better if I didn't need to come here," she answered honestly.

"What was your name again?" Gio asked.

He turned his badge around.

"Robert . . . but call me Bob."

Emma started laughing and looked at Gio.

"We won't hold that against him," Gio said.

"Do you have a bad Bob in your life?" Bob asked.

"Kinda."

"You're going to feel a stick."

Emma held still. "I'm getting used to it."

"Doesn't make it fun."

Emma stiffened as her skin was poked.

"Sorry. We have to use a bigger needle since we're taking blood. We don't want it clotting."

Bob tapped the cannula in place and hooked up an empty IV bag with a long tube to Emma's arm and replaced the tourniquet he'd taken off briefly. "Too tight?"

"It's okay." It hurt, but she wasn't going to complain. Not when all the people behind the different curtains were in much worse shape.

He placed a ball in her hand and told her to squeeze.

Slowly . . . like a snail moving down a path, her blood started to fill the tube.

Bob moved her arm, pulled at the IV a little.

"Yeah, it's how I thought." He sighed.

"What?"

"Normally your blood will just flow into the bag. But your blood is too viscous and won't." He removed a large syringe from his cart and attached it to a valve in the tube and started to pull. "I need to draw it out."

Emma could see the muscle in Bob's arm twitch with effort as he worked to draw the blood out of her veins. And when he did, she felt a fluttering in her vein. *Thick blood, fluttering.* Emma closed her eyes, leaned her head back, and felt her stomach turn. "I think I'm going to faint."

"Emma?"

"It's okay. I'm going to lay you back."

Her ears started to ring, and voices faded. She felt the chair reclining, and her head sunk to the side.

"Emma?" Gio called at her side.

The blood pressure cuff on her arm started to squeeze.

Beeping next to her ear went off, but the fear of throwing up was too great for Emma to see what was making the noise.

"Someone go get Dr. Salazar," Bob called out.

"What happened?" Gio asked.

Emma heard everything but felt as if she was in a cloud. Someone pulled off her cotton mask and placed an oxygen one over her face.

"What's going on?" a new voice asked.

"This is her first treatment. I had to start pulling, got the first fifty cc's out and she said she was going to pass out. Blood pressure sixty over thirty."

"Stop the phlebotomy and give her a half liter of normal saline. Miss Rutledge? I'm Dr. Salazar. Are you coming back to us?"

Emma opened her eyes . . . slowly and nodded. But damn, she felt like crap.

"You're okay. You had a vagal reaction. Very common. Your blood pressure is already coming back up. Do you have any pain?"

"No. I-I just thought I was going to pass out and throw up."

"Are you still nauseated?"

"It's better now."

"Did you eat today?"

"Yes, she did," Gio answered.

"We'll give you some fluids, let this pass, and if you're up for it, start again." The doctor patted Emma's arm, turned to the nurse.

Gio, who had backed away, moved to her side and grabbed her hand.

"Take some deep breaths," Bob told her.

The wave of crazy started to pass.

Emma smiled at Gio.

"Better, *amore*?"

She swallowed. "I feel stupid. It's just blood."

"Shh, enough of that." He brushed her hair back.

Emma turned her head to the nurse.

"That was a pretty good impression of Casper the ghost," Bob told her.

Emma looked at Gio. "Did I turn white?"

"As a sheet."

The blood pressure bag inflated again.

"Much better. I think we can take this off now." Bob removed the oxygen.

While fluid went in instead of out, Gio talked to her softly.

Twenty minutes later, Bob started pulling blood again.

This time Emma stayed lying down.

When Bob was done, he said, "I'm going to give you another half a liter of fluids and then you can go. You have an appointment for next week on Thursday."

"Yes. I'll try not to faint next time."

"I'm going to make you lie down and give you some orange juice before we start next time."

Emma agreed with that suggestion.

Thirty minutes later, they were ready to walk out the door.

"Lots of fluids, no alcohol, and rest. I'll see you next week," Bob told her.

"What about gelato?" Gio asked.

"Only if you bring back some for me."

~

Gio applauded himself on keeping his shit together.

But damn, when Emma went down, he'd almost lost it.

They'd come home and Emma had threatened to go back out to the winery and continue the work they'd started over the weekend.

Gio put his foot down. *The hell you will.*

He made her take up residency on the couch and brought her lunch and a bowl of ice cream. Was that absolutely necessary? No. Was that exactly what Gio needed her to do to feel like he had some control over what was going on? Yes.

They both concluded that the stress of everything just hit her at the same moment and her body needed a reset.

The doctor and the nurse assured them that everything was fine, which Gio knew on an intellectual level was true, but emotionally . . . he was a wreck.

Emma didn't fight him all that hard when he turned the TV on and found something for her to binge-watch. She turned her phone off and gave in to his pressure of taking the day off.

Dante called an hour into the show, and Gio excused himself to answer it.

Gio explained what happened and ended it with ". . . I lost five years off my life watching her pass out."

"She's okay now, though, right?"

"She is."

"How are *you* doing? I know you're taking care of her, but are you getting any rest?"

"You sound like my mother."

Dante laughed. "She put me up to the questions. You're with the woman you love when she needs you. Chloe ran off to fucking Bali and wouldn't return my calls. No sympathy for you, my friend."

"God love my sister."

"I'll keep her anyway."

"Damn well better."

They laughed.

"Seriously, though . . . you know everyone is dying to get over there and help."

Gio scratched the stubble on his face. He hadn't shaved and it was starting to itch. "How about Sunday? Emma has a big test on Monday, and she could use a positive distraction."

"You sure?"

"Yeah."

"Okay. I'll let the others know," Dante said.

"We don't have sawhorses or plywood in the sheds."

"We'll come prepared."

CHAPTER THIRTY-FIVE

"Are you ready for this?" Gio asked right before they turned up the drive to Emma's parents' Temecula home.

"No. But we're doing it anyway."

Emma told Gio the gate code when they approached.

"Looks a lot like your place," Gio observed out loud.

"Only bigger."

"Exactly my thought." Gio turned to her once they parked the car. "Do you think he's really in there?"

"My mother said he was coming."

"*Your father won't likely come,*" Beth said.

"*You're very persuasive, Mom. Make him.*"

"*What's going on?*" she asked.

"*It's something that affects everyone in our family. I'm sorry for sounding cryptic without explanation, but I only have the stamina to tell all of this once. I refuse to have this conversation four times.*"

"*Stamina? Are you okay?*"

"*I've had better months.*"

"*I'm worried.*"

"*I'll see you on Saturday.*"

Shortly after the conversation with her mother, a text message came through confirming the time.

Ryan was easy . . . His worry was evident, but he didn't press.

"My mother has a live-in housekeeper. Her name is Christy," Emma informed Gio when they got out of the car.

"A servant?"

"Superrich people don't like to do their own laundry."

"I'm not a fan of laundry either," he teased.

She chuckled and Gio grasped her hand.

It was twilight, and a dinner invitation had been given. Emma wasn't sure how that was going to go. The intention was to get the news out of the way as quickly as possible so it didn't weigh on her during a polite meal.

Gio knocked on the door.

Emma sucked in a deep, fortifying breath.

Beth answered. "Since when do you knock?"

She put her arms around Emma and hugged her.

"When Dad is here, I knock."

Beth turned to Gio, hugged him, too. "Thank you for having us," Gio said.

"Come in, come in."

Emma placed her purse on the table in the foyer and walked beside Gio through the hall and to the great room of her parents' home.

She heard the voices of her brothers and father.

The smells coming from the kitchen said roast with onions and garlic.

Ryan jumped to his feet the second she rounded the corner. "Emma." He hugged her hard, put his lips to her ear, and whispered, "He's in rare form tonight."

Great!

Ryan pulled back, extended a hand to Gio. "You must be Gio. I've heard a lot about you."

"All good, I hope."

Ryan laughed. "If it wasn't, we'd be having a less polite conversation."

Emma's jaw dropped.

Gio shook Ryan's hand with renewed enthusiasm. "I like that attitude."

"Testosterone much?" Emma asked.

"Setting boundaries and expectations early is important," Ryan said.

"Duly noted," Gio replied.

Emma smiled. If there was one family member she wanted Gio to get along with, it was Ryan. Her brother took little shit, was honest to the point of rudeness, and had more integrity than a monk.

Gio pushed forward and extended a hand to Robert. "Mr. Rutledge, nice to see you again."

"Surprised to see you. I thought this was a *family* meeting."

"I'm here for Emma."

Richard shook Gio's hand, and then Gio returned to Emma's side.

"What can I get you to drink?" Beth asked. "Emma, chardonnay before dinner?"

Emma smiled. "I'm fine."

Beth raised an eyebrow.

"Giovanni?"

"I'm good as well."

Robert narrowed his gaze. "That's unlike you, Emma. Seems you always have wine when there's a family meal."

"It helps with the tension," Ryan called out.

Every one of them had a drink in their hand. Her father held a short highball glass, likely filled with scotch. Richard had a glass of wine, and Ryan curled his fingers around a beer bottle.

"You're pregnant," Robert said flat out, eyes accusing. "Is that what this is about?"

Beth gasped.

Anger rose in Emma's chest. She looked at Gio. "That would be easy. Wouldn't it?"

Gio sighed. "Much easier."

"No, Father. I am not pregnant. I wouldn't call a family meeting if the condom broke."

Beth blew out a breath. "Can we please sit?"

Emma and Gio sat on one end of the sofa.

Ryan sat poised on the edge of the fireplace hearth.

Richard and Beth took up wing chairs, and her father stood leaning against the fireplace as if he were lording over all of them.

"You've ignored my secretary's calls," Robert said accusingly.

"I have."

"You show up in Napa. Talk to nearly everyone in the room, spreading an interesting version of what the land you're living on is for . . . then tell me when you're available to talk and proceed to ignore my calls."

It was no shock to Emma that her father instantly tried to dominate the conversation and make this all about him.

She squeezed Gio's hand and closed her eyes.

"If you would give Emma a chance to talk, Mr. Rutledge, you'll understand why."

"And who are you?" Robert tossed his anger at Gio. "Beth said a restaurateur, but I looked up your name. A family trust, two-bit nothing in San Diego does not make you—"

"Robert! Enough. Can't you see what you're doing?" Beth yelled.

"Smooth, Dad."

Emma felt the tension in Gio's arms beside hers.

"The only reason I'm not up in your face right now, Mr. Rutledge, is because I can see through your insecurities and need to show dominance when you're not in control," Gio said, his jaw tight.

"Excuse me?"

"However, if you use the words *two-bit* and *my family* in a sentence again, I'll happily give you an education on what it means to stand by the people you love."

Robert put his glass down. "You will not—"

"Shut up, Dad." Emma came out of her fog.

The room instantly got quiet.

"Shut up and listen." Emma pinned him with a stare.

He turned and started walking out.

"I'm not drinking tonight because three of my doctors have advised me not to."

Robert stopped mid-room.

"And no, none of those doctors are in obstetrics." Emma's voice didn't sound like her own. Not when talking to her dad, in any event.

"Honey, what's going on?" her mom asked.

"I had some routine bloodwork right before Giovanni and I flew to Napa. They discovered that I have a genetic, hereditary disorder that affects my blood." Emma stopped looking at her father and turned to her brothers. "And since I have this genetic mutation, you two might have it as well. *That* is why I asked for a *family* meeting."

Richard put his wine down. "What is it?"

"Are you okay?" Ryan asked.

Gio patted her hand. "It has a fancy name, but the bottom line is, I can't process iron in my bloodstream. Iron has been building up inside my body for years." Emma looked at her mother. "In order for me to actually have this issue either you or Dad has it as well, which you'd probably already know because of your age . . . or the more likely scenario is you both carry the gene, but don't have the disorder. It's complicated. I can show you a chart, but the bottom line is, Richard and Ryan have the same chance of having this genetic mutation as I do. And if left untreated, it can be life-threatening."

"What do you mean, 'life-threatening'?" Ryan asked.

"If iron can't leave your body, it builds up in places like your liver and heart, causing other disease." Emma felt her throat constrict.

"Like nonalcoholic cirrhosis," Gio added.

"Jesus, Emma . . . is that you? Do you have—"

Emma cut Ryan off. "We don't know yet."

"Oh my God." Beth got up from her chair and moved to sit beside Emma.

"I've been in more doctors' offices and been poked so many times I've lost count." Emma lifted both of her arms and looked at the bruising everyone could see. "My liver MRI impressed my hepatologist. I have a more accurate test on Monday to determine if we need to worry about cirrhosis." Emma looked up and found that her father was looking at the wall across the room. "So yes, Dad. I blew off your secretary's calls. I had more important things that needed my attention."

Why she cared that her father wouldn't look her way was beyond her.

Her dad said nothing, just drank from his glass.

"Everyone needs to be tested. Especially you two," Emma said to her brothers. "My doctor has orders when you're ready to go in."

"I'm not sick," Robert said without preamble.

They all turned to him, somewhat shocked.

"What the fuck, Dad. Emma just told you she has a blood disorder and is facing her liver being fucked up and you come up with *I'm not sick*?" Ryan stood. "What are you going to say next . . . genetics have nothing to do with you? Hereditary, Dad. The word means it's passed on from our parents." Ryan was pissed.

"If Emma says we all need to be tested. We get tested," Richard spoke up.

Emma felt the support in the room shift.

Ryan glared at their father, lifted his beer to his lips, and stopped himself. "Fuck." He set it down.

Beth placed an arm over Emma's shoulders and looked at her husband. "Robert?"

Her parents stared at each other.

Her dad shook his head.

"Robert, we need to tell them."

Emma turned to her mom.

Her father's head snapped toward them. "Beth . . . don't."

"They're going to find out."

Robert emptied the contents of his glass in one swallow.

"Don't tell me you knew about this." Emma shrugged away from her mom.

"No, honey. I would never keep anything like this from you."

"Beth, I'm warning you." Robert pointed at her.

"You heard her, Robert. Genetics don't lie."

"What are you talking about?" Richard questioned.

Beth looked from Emma to her brothers, took a deep breath, and let it out. "Your father and I couldn't have children the normal way."

"God damn it, Beth."

Emma froze.

Beth scooted down the couch.

"What? We're adopted?" Ryan asked.

"I remember Mom when she was pregnant," Richard told Ryan.

"But I look like you," Emma said.

Beth tried to smile. "The problem wasn't with me."

The realization of what that meant sunk in. Her mom could have babies . . . did have them, only their father wasn't the sperm donor.

Everyone turned to Robert.

"I can't believe you're doing this." Robert moved to the decanter of liquor, poured himself another drink.

"You're not our biological father." The cloud lifted from Emma's head.

"Then who is?" Ryan asked.

Their mother's voice softened. "I don't know. We conceived with the help of a doctor. We looked at sperm donor profiles and—"

"Stop, Beth. They do not need to hear any of this."

In two steps, Ryan got in their father's face. "Why the secret, *Dad*? Aren't we old enough for the truth? And who the fuck cares?"

Gio clasped Emma's hand in both of his.

That's when things clicked in her head. "Because it somehow makes you less, is that it?" Emma asked. "Your fish don't swim and there is no way in hell you're going to let anyone know that. Did it make you less of a man?"

Robert looked at each of them, said nothing.

"That's it." Emma stood, released Gio's hand, and walked to the family picture above the fireplace taken right before Emma graduated from high school. Her finger shook as she pointed to the images.

"Richard and Ryan can easily pass as your sons. Maybe because they're men . . . maybe the sperm donors looked a lot like you." Her gaze fell to the red, curly locks of her hair and pale skin. "But I come out and hold no resemblance of you whatsoever." How had she not seen it before?

"That never mattered," Beth said.

"To you. But to Dad?" Emma looked at her parents. "You were afraid someone would figure this out, so what better way to avoid that than to keep me out of your hair. Tuck me down here in Temecula, keep me out of the office, stop anyone from asking if I look like the mailman."

"No one has ever asked," he replied.

"You and your brothers have similar features, honey. That's not a worry," Beth added.

Emma wasn't so sure. "Then your disdain for me being in the office is straight-up corporate misogyny. Not a woman's place."

Her father didn't deny her conclusion. "I have always taken care of you, young lady," Robert fired at her. "Stop being ungrateful."

"Ungrateful? Am I supposed to show gratitude for being born?"

"We wanted all of you," Beth cried.

Emma shook her head. "Dad wanted one. One to prove he was a man. I can see that so clearly now."

"I just gave you a home and this is how you talk to me?" Robert squared his body to hers, and Gio jumped up and in between them in a heartbeat.

Gio fisted his hand. "Don't give me a reason."

Emma's blood was pumping so hard she thought steam was boiling from her ears. "I'll start packing tomorrow. I don't want your damn charity."

Robert lifted his chin.

Beth pushed in between all of them, squared up to Robert. "Have you lost your mind? If our *daughter* moves out of that house, I will move out of yours. Our divorce will rip your reputation in half, and everyone will know why it's happening."

"Beth—"

"I'm serious, Robert. You are way out of line here."

Gio put an arm around Emma, looked her in the eye. "Let's go, *amore*."

Ryan grabbed his jacket off the back of a chair. "I'm out." He walked to Beth and kissed her cheek. "I have a couch." He turned to their father. "Fuck you."

Richard stood. "You're wrong on this one, Dad."

Emma, Gio, Richard, and Ryan all walked out of the house together. They stood at the bottom of the steps, staring out over the property.

"Holy shit." Ryan said what they were all thinking.

"I didn't see that coming," Richard added.

Somehow, Emma wasn't surprised. The disconnection from her father had been there for years. At least now she understood why.

Gio kissed the side of her head. "I thought my family was loud."

She laughed.

Richard offered a half-ass grin. "God, it sucks to be the chosen one right now."

Ryan patted his brother on the back. "You can always jump ship."

"All I know is wine."

"If Mom divorces him, she'll need help running half of Dad's business," Emma said.

"You think she will?" Richard asked.

"I don't think she's been happy for years. And after tonight, I wouldn't be shocked."

They all stood in silence as that thought sunk in.

"When is your test on Monday?" Ryan asked her.

She told him.

"Will you know right away?"

"My doctor said by the afternoon."

Ryan rocked back on his heels, looked at Gio. "I'm a phone call away."

Gio nodded.

Richard opened his arms and Emma slid in. "I love you, sis. I'm sorry this is happening."

Tears stung her eyes. "Thank you. I'll email you both everything I know about it and give you my doctor's number to schedule the blood tests. Although now you only have half a chance of having this condition."

Richard pulled away and kept shaking his head. "I can't believe he's not our biological dad. This is crazy."

"I'd be celebrating right now if it wasn't for what you're going through," Ryan told her.

Emma smiled.

Ryan hugged her next. "Don't keep anything a secret. The minute you know there's a problem, you or Gio need to call me."

Emma nodded against his shoulder. "I love you."

He kissed her cheek. "I love you, too."

Richard sighed. "I need to get drunk."

Ryan patted him on a back. "I have alcohol and a couch."

Richard looked behind them toward the house. "Good thing, because I sure as hell am not going back in there."

The men shook hands, both her brothers thanked Gio for being there.

In the silence of the car, Emma felt her body melt into the seat.

"How are you doing over there?" Gio asked.

"You know . . . I'm strangely relieved."

They paused, lost in their own thoughts.

"Are we packing when we get home?" he asked.

"Would it bother you if I said yes?"

Gio was quick to shake his head. "You tossed out that possibility faster than I could form the words. Whatever you want, my love."

"Let's see where the fallout settles. We can *then what* after Monday's tests."

"Let's go home."

CHAPTER THIRTY-SIX

Gio and Emma had a lazy morning after sleeping in.

Emma took the bombshell that was dropped the previous evening like a champ.

The light of the new day gave them both some clarity on her family situation. While Emma had yet to suggest they start looking for a new home, he could tell by the way she walked around and looked at Casa de Emma that she was picturing herself without it.

"None of it matters without your health," Gio told her.

"Boy, have I learned that lesson."

He came up behind, wrapped his arms around her as she stared out a side window at the vineyards. "Home is where the people you love are."

She leaned her head back and sighed. "Maybe that's why I like it here so much."

Gio's heart warmed. "Are you telling me you love me, *amore?*"

Emma twisted in his arms, placed hers around his waist. "Love is scary."

"Not when two people love with the same amount of their hearts."

Tears filled her eyes.

"Don't cry."

"I love you even if it is scary."

Gio grasped both sides of her face and lowered his lips to hers, he poured his soul into their kiss. When he drew away, his lips moved to her ear. "I love you, Emma. You never have to be frightened with me."

They held each other tight.

"I don't want you to leave. The thought of you not being close by actually hurts."

"Shhh, I'm not going anywhere."

"I want you to move in with me," Emma told him, her cheek resting on his chest.

"Haven't I already done that?" He laughed.

"I guess you have. What am I saying? I might be homeless in a few days."

Gio pulled back, kissed her again. "We'll figure it out."

The bell to the gate at the front of the property rang and they both looked at the intercom. "Your family is early."

Gio let her go and answered the gate. "Hello?"

"It's Beth, Giovanni."

"Come in." He pressed the button for the gate to open.

Gio held back when Emma opened the door for her mother.

Beth's eyes were visibly red and swollen. She attempted to hide the stress with makeup, but it didn't work.

Beth hugged Emma in the doorway and smoothed her hair. "Oh, baby. I'm so sorry."

"It's okay, Mom. It's not your fault."

"Your dad is an ass."

Gio couldn't agree more.

"I know," Emma said.

Beth let her daughter go and walked into the house. She hugged him. "Hi, Mama B."

She smiled. "I like that title."

"Can I get you some coffee?" Gio asked.

"I would love that."

Gio went to work to fill her request as she and Emma sat at the kitchen island.

"You don't have a suitcase with you . . . does that mean you're not moving out?" Emma asked her.

Beth's nervous laugh suggested she'd packed one.

"Your father left this morning to return to Napa. I have no idea where Richard went."

"He's with Ryan. Nursing a hangover, I'm sure."

Beth looked relieved. "That's good. Your brothers could use some bonding time."

Gio placed coffee in front of Beth and set the cream and sugar to the side. *"Amore?"*

Emma smiled. "Please."

Gio poured her a cup.

"I'm sorry. I'm sorry we didn't tell you kids earlier. I'm sorry for not standing up to him before now."

"Mom . . . it's okay."

"It's not, honey. When all of you left last night your father and I fought for hours. Before he left, we made some decisions. I know you don't believe this, but he does love you."

Emma huffed.

"His love language is providing," her mom said.

"Controlling," Emma corrected.

"Maybe. Your father is signing everything on this property over to you."

Emma paused. "I won't take more from him."

Gio placed a hand on her shoulder. "We'd rather do it ourselves."

"Then don't take it from him. Take it from me." Beth fixed Gio with a stare. "Both of you."

"Your money is his money," Emma said.

"Yes! It is. Believe me, I reminded Robert last night of that very fact. Just because I don't go into the office doesn't mean half of our worth isn't mine. Your father didn't want my assistance in the office any more than he wanted yours. That was his choice. I was more than willing to help. Then when you kids came around, I had my hands full and didn't offer again. Marriage is a partnership and your father agreed to that. I will see that the deed is solely in your name, and a fund is set aside to get you started on the right foot. That's what your father told me he was doing, and that is what is going to happen. No argument."

Gio could see Emma wanted to argue. "That's a lot of money, Beth."

Beth fixed him with a stare. "Giovanni, I take you as a family man. Am I right?"

"Yes, ma'am."

"Would give all he had if he needed to for that family."

"Without question," Gio replied.

"Am I not allowed to do the same?"

She had a point.

Gio glanced at Emma. "How do you argue with that?"

Emma relented. "Okay, Mom. For you . . . not for him."

"Good." Beth sipped her coffee. "When will you know about your liver?"

"Monday afternoon."

Beth looked like she wanted to cry. "Can I go with you for your test?"

Emma seemed surprised. "Sure."

"I can't lose you." Beth choked with her words.

Emma moved into her mother's arms and held her. "I'm not dying, Mom."

"But if your liver is—"

"Then we'll deal with it."

Gio watched mother and daughter and had to turn around to stop from choking up. His biggest fear was losing Emma and here her mother voiced that out loud.

He grabbed a cold water bottle from the refrigerator and placed it on his neck.

The temperature helped him get control of his emotions.

"I have a really personal question to ask you. Please don't be offended."

"Go ahead, honey."

Emma sat down, hesitated . . . and then asked, "Did you have an affair?"

Gio's back stiffened as he listened for Beth's answer.

Beth almost smiled. "That would have been so much easier. But no. Your father has trampled many of my nerves, but I've always been faithful."

"If you picked similar profiles for Richard, Ryan, and I . . ." Emma picked up the end of her hair. "Where did this come from?"

Beth's nervous laugh had Gio listening closer.

"Truth is, by the third time we went through this process, your father wasn't with me. We'd picked from a few profiles, but on the day of the treatment, the person we chose hadn't wanted to . . ."

Gio pictured a college-aged kid walking into a bathroom with a cup to pick up a few hundred dollars for beer money.

". . . so I made a decision. I saw Irish ancestry and thought . . . well, I liked Jamie from *Outlander*."

Emma started laughing, slowly at first and then so hard her body shook.

Beth joined her until they were both nearly in tears. She brushed aside Emma's hair. "Look at you. My beautiful girl. I wouldn't change it for the world."

Gio looked at Beth with an entirely new level of respect.

The intercom to the gate buzzed again.

"Are you expecting company?" Beth asked.

"Giovanni's family is coming over."

Gio answered the gate, heard Luca's voice.

Beth jumped to her feet. "I'm sorry. I should have called first."

"Mama B. You never need to call."

"I'll leave you to your guests." She moved to grab her purse.

"Mom. Stay, please."

"I'm a mess."

Gio touched her shoulder. "Your daughter has been through a lot these past couple of weeks. No one will judge you on the beautiful mess you think you are."

Beth sighed and glanced at Emma. "My God, where did you find him?"

Emma laughed. "Italy."

The front door burst open, and Franny ran in. "Zio Gio!"

"Francesca! You don't barge into someone else's home!" Brooke yelled from outside.

Gio scooped up his niece and hugged her hard. "My family is loud. Loveable, but loud."

CHAPTER THIRTY-SEVEN

The D'Angelos swooped into their home with hugs, kisses, and bags and bags of food.

Gio's mom took over her kitchen like she'd been there before.

Emma watched in fascination as Luca took Beth under his culinary wing and helped her make ravioli . . . from scratch.

"I didn't know you could cook," Emma teased her mom.

"I can't."

"If my daughter can make this . . . so can you," Luca told Beth.

Franny ran up to Emma's side and tapped her arm. "Can we go swimming?"

"Of course," she said.

Mari made a sweeping motion with her hands. "Please. There are too many people in the kitchen."

Gio picked Franny up and tossed her over his shoulder. "Who needs a swimsuit when I can toss you in like this."

Franny giggled as he carried her out the back door.

It wasn't long before Emma, Chloe, Brooke, and Franny were in swimsuits and took up residence at the pool.

"How are you really doing?" Chloe asked.

"I've been a mess," Emma admitted. "If it wasn't for your brother, I'd probably be rocking in a corner right about now."

Emma glanced over to where Gio and Dante were putting together patio furniture that Gio's family insisted on buying as a housewarming gift.

"We've all been worried," Brooke told her.

"Mama, look." Franny held on to the side of the pool, goggles covering her eyes, and waited for their attention. Once she had it, she sucked in a deep breath, put her face in the water, and swam to the opposite side of the pool.

She came up gasping with a smile.

"Much better," Brooke praised.

Franny went back to practicing her swimming skills while the three older women sat on the steps of the pool, chatting.

"I'm sorry for your worry," Emma brought the discussion back.

"Such a waste of an emotion. It isn't like our worry can take away yours." Brooke laid a hand over her very pregnant belly.

"Distraction . . . food. Food and distraction. That's about all we can offer," Chloe said.

"Pasta fixes everything." Emma laughed.

Franny splashed up to them, her smile covering her face. "Why aren't you swimming?"

Chloe pushed forward, submerging herself in the water. "Wanna race?"

Emma couldn't help but welcome the D'Angelo distraction.

When it was time to sit down to eat, Emma noticed that all the wineglasses on the table were filled with sparkling water. "You can drink wine. No reason everyone has to suffer," Emma told Mari.

"We'll celebrate when the doctor delivers good news," she said with a tap to Emma's cheek. "Now eat. You're getting too skinny."

"Maybe she'll listen to you, Mari. Lord knows she doesn't listen to me," Beth said.

"That's not true," Emma defended herself.

"It's a little true," Gio said.

"Hey!"

But they were all laughing.

Once dinner was over and the cleanup was complete, Franny was falling asleep on the sofa.

"We should get her home," Luca said to Brooke.

"You're driving back to San Diego tonight?" Beth asked.

"We are," Brooke said. "Dante and Chloe brought an air mattress."

"And I can sleep on the couch." Mari patted a hand on the cushion she sat on.

"Mari, that's ridiculous. Really. I live just up the road and have beds for everyone."

Emma thanked her mother for jumping in. "I'm sorry we don't have the spare rooms ready here yet."

"You've had other things to worry about," Luca told her.

Dante motioned behind them. "I've already set Chloe and I up, Beth."

Emma's mother looked at the others. "Please come over. I honestly could use the distraction."

Mari shrugged. "Then we come over."

Emma's heart filled with every sip of the D'Angelo cup.

"We want to be here tomorrow to support you . . . good news or bad," Chloe told Emma.

As the house emptied out, with the exception of Chloe and Dante, who closed themselves in a spare room that held one dresser and a plant, Emma curled up next to Giovanni in bed.

Her head buzzed after the sheer enormity of the day. And that was when all the worries of tomorrow came crashing down. "I'm scared," she whispered into Giovanni's chest.

"I know," he told her, his hand stroking her arm.

"I love your family."

"They love you, too."

∼

By the time Emma, Gio, and Beth left for her appointment Monday morning, the D'Angelos were back in the kitchen cooking for a village.

The FibroScan was in fact less invasive than the MRI. For the first time since all of this had started, Emma didn't have to be stuck with a needle.

Gio and her mother both sat in the waiting room while the exam was performed.

Less than thirty minutes later, they were walking out of the office.

"How was it?" Gio asked.

"Not bad. I didn't pass out," she told him with a smile.

Halfway home, Emma said, "I'm glad that's done."

"One less thing on the *then what* list," Gio said.

"The 'then what' list? What's that?" Beth asked from the back seat.

"Which doctor to see, what test to take, what treatment needs to be scheduled. It's what Gio and I call our 'to do' list."

"Are you trying to get control of my daughter's jumping from one thing to the next?" Beth asked Gio.

"Yes, ma'am."

Beth laughed. "Good luck with that."

Gio turned to Emma and smiled. "She knows you too well."

Emma started to relax right as her phone rang.

Dr. Sandy's name popped up.

"Oh shit." Emma wasn't expecting that quick of a reply.

Gio turned the radio down in the car.

Emma answered with the phone to her ear. "Hello, Dr. Sandy."

"Hey, how are you doing?"

"I'm on my way home from the scan. Do you have my results already?"

Gio kept glancing at her.

Her mother was leaning between the seats.

"No. I wanted to make sure you got there okay and had it done."

Emma deflated, put her hand over the receiver. "No results yet," she told them. "Yes. It went fine."

"I know you're anxious about the results. I'm keeping my eye on the portal and will call you as soon as I see them. Dr. Chow might beat me to it, so don't be alarmed if his call comes first."

"Thank you, Sandy."

Emma disconnected the call. "I can see how this day is going to go."

Her mom patted her shoulder from the back seat.

"Ryan called when you were in the testing. He wanted to join us at the house," Beth told her.

"Of course," Emma said.

"He called Nicole and she's on her way, too."

"Fine."

"Richard texted and asked to know as soon as we do."

"And Dad?" Emma had to ask.

"He called this morning and asked if you were seeing the best doctors."

Emma rolled her eyes.

"He wouldn't ask that if he didn't care, *cara*," Giovanni said.

She wanted to believe that . . . sadly, she didn't.

Back at the house, the entire family stopped chattering the second they walked through the door.

"We don't know yet," Gio informed them.

A collective sigh spread in the room, and the talking continued.

There was food, and talking . . . and people coming and going throughout the house.

And Emma watched the clock.

Even though everyone was there for the same reason . . . no one talked about it.

Except Giovanni.

Emma sat half listening to a story Dante was sharing about his time with Chloe in Bali, and while she kept a smile, and laughed when everyone else did, she couldn't tell you what Dante had said once he finished.

"You're going to be fine," Gio whispered in her ear.

"What if—"

He placed his fingertips to her lips. "We'll deal with it."

The hours ticked by.

Nicole was getting a tutorial on making ravioli.

Ryan was teaching Franny how to play poker.

Everyone seemed to be in some state of animation. All while Emma kept a fake smile on her face.

Sometime after three in the afternoon, Emma's phone finally rang.

She pulled it out of her pocket.

Gio locked eyes with her.

Dr. Sandy.

No matter the news, Emma didn't want to take it in front of everyone.

Emma grabbed Gio's hand and ran to the hall toward their bedroom.

A hush fell over those who noticed their quick exit.

Once they were behind their bedroom door, Emma answered the call and put the phone to her ear. "Dr. Sandy?"

"Hi, Emma. I have your scan."

"I'm listening." Emma felt dizzy and sat on the bed.

"You don't have cirrhosis."

Emma took the deepest breath she'd ever taken in her life and leaned forward as relief filled every cell in her body.

Dr. Sandy continued. "The scan measures for scarring of your liver. You do have some, but it's minimal. Not the kind of scarring we see in patients who have cirrhosis. So, when you see the numbers on the test results, don't worry."

"Cara?" Gio knelt down and looked up at her.

"I'm okay," she whispered as a smile swept over her face.

"I expect your liver enzymes to return to normal as soon as we get some of the iron out of there. This is good news, Emma."

Emma sobbed. "Thank you, Sandy."

"I already talked to Dr. Chow and he said he'd talk to you tomorrow to go over any details and questions you have."

"Okay . . . thank you so much."

"You're welcome. I'll see you in a few months." Dr. Sandy ended the call.

Emma stared at her phone while Gio buried his head in her lap and held her.

"I don't have cirrhosis. I'm not going to die." Saying the words out loud made them real.

Gio squeezed her harder. When he looked up, he was crying.

Smiling, but crying.

He picked himself off his knees, sat beside her on the bed, and held her. Emma's grip on his shoulders felt as if she were hanging on for dear life. "No more what-iffing."

"I can't lose you," Gio told her.

"Doesn't look like that's going to happen."

He kissed her softly . . . briefly, then went back to holding on. "I love you so much."

Emma used the edges of his shirt to wipe her eyes dry and let one last shaky breath free of her lungs. "We should tell the others," she told him.

"They're probably listening at the door." Gio pulled her hair behind her ears and placed his palm on the side of her face. "We're going to be okay."

"We are. I couldn't have done this without you."

"You don't have to do anything without me."

She blinked a couple of times. "I'm starting to figure that out."

Gio stood and helped her to her feet. "C'mon. Let's share the good news."

They walked into the living room with their arms around each other.

"Oh no!" Beth saw them first.

Emma shook her head, pointed to her face. "Happy tears."

Mari made the sign of the cross over her chest and Nicole, Chloe, and Brooke moved in to hug her.

"It's time to celebrate!" Gio announced.

Nicole was first to the wine fridge, removing bottles.

CHAPTER THIRTY-EIGHT

Three weeks to the day from when Emma had her last scan, Mari called to tell them that Brooke was in labor. At two in the morning.

For the first time in close to two months, Emma sat beside Gio in a hospital waiting room for someone other than her.

Franny was curled up in a chair, fast asleep.

The rest of the D'Angelos filled the room.

"Hospital coffee is the worst," Dante complained sometime around five in the morning.

"As soon as the sun comes up, I'm calling Salena to bring provisions," Chloe told her husband.

"Calling Salena before ten in the morning is a waste of your time," Gio said.

"I take it she's not a morning person," Emma said.

Dante, Chloe, and Gio all said no at the same time.

Emma had met the lifelong friend on one of their trips to San Diego. She was as beautiful in person as she was in the pictures Emma had seen.

"How are your treatments going, Emma?" Mari asked.

"I've only had four so far, but good."

"No more passing out?" Chloe asked.

"No."

"Thank God," Gio added.

The door to the waiting room opened and Luca popped his head in. "Not yet," he said immediately when the entire family leaned forward.

"How is she doing?" Mari asked.

"A champ. They just gave her the epidural and she's feeling much better." Luca lifted his hand in the air, Emma could see his red fingers. "I thought I was going to lose a limb for a while there."

Chloe winced. "I'm going straight for the drugs when I have babies."

"And when is that?" Mari asked.

"We practice all the time, Mrs. D'Angelo," Dante said with a wink.

Mari waved his comment away while the rest of them laughed.

Luca nodded toward his sleeping daughter. "Has she been okay?"

"Not a peep," Emma told him.

He rubbed his hands together and reached for the door. "I'll keep you informed."

Hours later Salena arrived with coffee and pastries.

Franny had finally stirred and was bouncing off the walls in a combination of boredom and excitement.

Every time the door opened, they jumped.

Gio had just gotten off the phone with someone at the restaurant with a request for lunch to be brought to the hospital for all of them when Luca opened the door one last time.

The expression on his face was a little shell-shocked, and a whole lot of happy. "It's a boy!"

Mari was the first to jump to her feet and rush in for a hug.

"I have a baby brother?" Franny asked.

"Leonardo Paolo D'Angelo," Luca told them with a nod.

Mari grasped her chest. "After your father."

"Of course, Mama."

Questions about how Brooke was doing were quickly followed with more congratulations.

Gio held Emma's hand as they laid eyes on the newest D'Angelo through a glass window in the nursery.

"He's beautiful," Emma cooed.

Gio leaned his lips to her ears so only she could hear. "Don't you want one of those?" he teased.

She bit her lip and for the first time since they met, she didn't reply with a steadfast "No."

~

For the first few weeks of Leonardo's life, Gio and Emma drove back and forth to Little Italy.

Gio used the opportunity to pack more of his things until only a bare minimum was left behind.

And when the time came for him to make a trip, one he knew Emma couldn't join him on because of her appointment with the vampire, Gio turned off his GPS tracking, which Emma could follow, to put their future in action.

"We haven't been apart since I moved in." Gio stood holding Emma at the front door.

"You'll survive," she teased.

"I'll see you in two days."

Emma kissed him and pushed him toward the door. "Get out of here. Nicole is coming over for pizza, ice cream, and talking about boys."

Gio hesitated. "Wait . . . I like this idea."

Emma pushed. "Go."

An hour and a half of traffic later, and he arrived in San Diego and parked. From there, Dante drove Gio to the San Diego airport.

"You sure about this?"

"I have to try," Gio told his friend.

"Good luck."

A few hours later he landed in Sacramento, where Richard picked him up and drove them to Napa.

"I'm not sure how this is going to go over," Richard said.

"I have to try."

At the R&R Wineries offices, Gio slid into a suit jacket and snapped up the buttons on his shirt and skipped the tie. He wanted to be presentable, but not a kiss-ass.

Richard walked him through the building and stopped at an office door. He looked at the secretary and said, "Hold all his calls."

She glanced between Gio and Richard. "Okay."

Richard knocked once and didn't wait for a reply.

He opened the door and Robert looked up from the desk. "What in the—"

Gio smiled and Richard shook his hand. "Good luck."

Robert stared at the closed door, both hands poised on his desk. "What are you doing here?"

Gio lifted his chin. "You're a smart man, Mr. Rutledge. Your daughter's boyfriend shows up uninvited, likely has only one reason to do so. I would have asked for an invitation but felt that would have been a waste of both of our time."

"This is a waste of your time, too."

Gio expected as much. "I'm going to ask your daughter to marry me, and I would like your blessing."

Robert sat back, folded his hands over his stomach. "Emma doesn't care about my opinion."

Gio moved farther into the room. "You'd think so, but you're wrong. I've seen Emma bleed, sweat, and cry as she's worked desperately hard to get your approval. When we first met, she was passionate in the fight to make you proud. Only in the last month . . . six weeks . . . I've seen that spark start to die. Not *her* spark, but the one she uses to keep your relationship with her going. What kind of man would I be if I didn't at least try and keep her love for you alive?"

"My daughter hates me." Robert looked away.

Gio shook his head. "No. She wants to. But she doesn't. You see, the opposite of love is not hate, Mr. Rutledge, it's complacency. It's nothing. Hate requires passion. Complacency requires nothing." And since

Emma still asked Beth about her father, Gio knew that complacency hadn't cemented in . . . not yet.

Robert looked beyond Gio, his lips a thin line.

Just when Gio thought he was getting somewhere, Robert said, "Honestly, D'Angelo. I don't think you're good enough for her."

The man's comment shouldn't have surprised him. "I'm going to marry her anyway."

Robert nodded a couple of times. "Good. She needs a strong man. Kyle was weak."

"Yet he still works here."

"A weak husband. But a good employee."

"Emma doesn't need my strength. Not in the way you speak of power." Gio started to turn toward the door to leave and stopped. "I can't help but wonder, who will walk her down the aisle? Who will stand in as the grandfather for our children?" Gio turned to face Robert, placed a hand on his chest. "My father is gone." He shook his head. "You're the only one left."

Silence filled the vast room.

When it seemed all that needed to be said was out, Gio reached for the door.

Three steps out of the office and Robert called Gio's name.

He turned.

"I've been told recently, mainly by my wife, that if I didn't work on my relationships with my children, I was going to die a bitter and lonely old man."

Gio adored Beth.

"I was never a fan of *A Christmas Carol*. Never thought of myself as Ebenezer Scrooge since I supported everyone around me. But throwing money around isn't enough . . . is it?"

A smile started to find Gio's face. He kept quiet.

"You have my blessing."

One step, and Gio planted his palm in Robert's. "Thank you."

~

The grapes on the vines were growing their way to perfection.

Emma wore a summer dress, soaking up the final rays of sunshine that would begin cooling off right about the time of harvest.

The winery part of Casa de Emma was complete, and everyone gathered for a massive party to celebrate. Their foreman, Raul, and his family . . . every one of the D'Angelo clan, Nicole, and Emma's mother, brothers, and sister-in-law were there. As a surprise, a last-minute car pulled in and Rob, Pierre, and Chris climbed out.

Emma squealed in delight and ran to them.

"We weren't going to miss this." Rob hugged her hard.

"There's going to be a long time before there's wine."

Chris looked around. "I see buckets full of wine."

Gio walked over, shook hands. "I'm glad you could make it."

"You did this," Emma accused.

"Guilty."

Brooke had hired a photographer and, with her expertise in the world of marketing, was directing the man to take pictures of everyone. Casa de Emma already had a website and a complete marketing plan for their first bottle.

Gio clapped his hands together and lifted his voice. "Let's get this started."

A celebratory bottle of champagne, wrapped in cloth to avoid injury, was waiting for Emma to smash against the side of the building.

But first . . . a speech.

Under dozens of lights strung over the space between the buildings sat small tables beautifully decorated with simple flowers and candlelight. Tucked into the vineyard, a long table was set under a newly built cover with two-year-old lemon trees planted at each post. More lights illuminated the space and long benches worked as seating on both sides.

It was still evolving, but Emma and Gio's vision for what Casa de Emma would become was taking shape.

Hired help walked around serving champagne.

"Bubbles first, red last," Nicole announced.

"I see nothing has changed," Chris called over to her, laughing.

The crowd gathered close.

Gio stood beside Emma, a hand on the small of her back.

"Emma and I want to thank all of you for coming. We know it's really not for us, but for the food and wine."

"Stop it!" Beth teased.

"It's been a crazy summer with a lot of changes, and I think I can speak for both of us when I say we might not have made this happen in time for our first harvest without you."

Emma nodded. "Raul and *all* your friends. We know how much work you've put in." She placed a hand on her heart.

"You humble me, Miss Emma."

"Every one of you have either helped practically or emotionally and it's that combination that made this happen," Emma said.

"Mama B . . . you know this wouldn't have happened without you." Gio winked.

"Are you going to smash that bottle against the building so we can drink, or what?" Nicole asked.

Laughter erupted.

"We just love you all so much and want to thank you."

"We love you, too," Franny yelled.

Emma glanced at Gio. "I guess we should do this."

"No . . . just you."

Emma shook her head. "If there is one person above everyone else here that I couldn't have done this without, it's you. We're in this together."

"Okay, *cara*."

Emma grasped the bottle by the neck and Gio placed his hand over hers.

"Don't cut yourself," Ryan yelled.

"And give the vampires a day off? They need the work," Emma teased.

Gio whispered in her ear. "Ready?"

"On three?"

He nodded.

"One . . . two . . . three!" They pulled back together and hit the corner of the building hard.

The bottle broke within the cloth and champagne dripped everywhere.

Emma and Gio both jumped back, laughing.

Those watching clapped.

Gio moved around her to a table where napkins were waiting for them to use to clean up the mess. He handed her one and then put the broken bottle into a bucket and turned. He stared at his hand.

Emma's smile fell. "Did you hurt yourself?"

"No . . . I found something."

"What is it?"

Gio didn't answer, instead he bent down to one knee and lifted up something he was holding between his fingertips.

For a split second, Emma had no idea what he was showing her.

But when every person standing there stopped shuffling and talking, and only the sound of a photographer could be heard above her breathing, Emma clued in.

"Emma, *amore*. From the moment you handed me that silly department store bag instead of a suitcase to put on our tour bus . . . and I heard the sass come out of your mouth . . . I knew I was in for a ride."

Emma started to shake, and tears started to flow.

"I was lost from your first kiss. And even when you got in my face and told me that this wasn't the beginning of forever . . . I knew you were wrong. I want to spend every moment of my forever with you at my side. I love you, Emma. With every fiber of my being. Will you please do me the honor of becoming my wife?"

She was crying too hard to speak. "I thought you'd never ask."

"Is that a yes?"

"Yes! Yes!"

Whistles and cheers went up all around them.

Emma placed a sticky hand on Gio's face as he stood and met his kiss halfway.

Her knees wobbled.

Gio caught her so she didn't fall.

"I love you," she whispered.

"I'm going to make you the happiest woman in the world."

"You've already done that."

He placed what looked like a two-carat solitaire on her finger. The exact setting she and Nicole had talked about on their girls' night.

"Did everyone know this was happening tonight?" Emma asked.

Gio nodded. "Pretty much."

Franny walked over to a tripod easel that had a massive piece of paper on it with a sign saying, "Casa de Emma Welcomes You." She moved the sign, and under it, written in giant letters, were the words "Then What?" Under that was an unchecked box that said, "Make Emma Say Yes."

Franny picked up the marker and made a big check inside the box.

Mari took the pen from Franny and wrote on the paper . . . *Babies.*

"And so it begins," Dante said.

Gio glanced up and stilled.

Emma tried to turn.

He stopped her. "Months ago, I went to Napa to ask your father for his blessing."

His statement shocked her. "You did?"

"I gave it."

Emma froze and turned around.

Her father, who she hadn't seen since the awful night that the truth came out, stood there.

"But first I told him he wasn't good enough for you." Robert looked around at the building and the people. "Then I realized I was the one that wasn't good enough."

"Dad?"

"I've been a complete shit. I just hope it's not too late to be a part of your life."

Emma offered a puppy-dog look Gio's way, her eyes filled with tears, then back to her father. "It's not too late."

Robert opened his arms, ever so slightly, and she slid into them.

When she stepped away, most of the women, and a few of the men, were wiping moisture from their eyes.

"You're ruining my mascara, Emma!" Nicole broke the crying and turned it to laughing.

Emma and Gio walked through their family and friends and accepted their congratulations.

She caught Ryan standing at their father's side, shaking his hand.

A strange sight if she were being honest.

It wasn't long before her dad made his way back to her. "Can I have a private moment?" he asked.

Emma smiled up at Gio and nodded to her father before walking away from the crowd and into the winery.

A few feet in, the sound from outside started to fade.

"I owe you an apology," he said on an exhale.

Instead of taking away his discomfort, Emma stayed silent and waited as they walked.

Robert caught her eyes. "You're not going to make this easy on me."

She paused, tilted her head.

"And you shouldn't." A deep breath later, "I'm sorry, Emma. I've been so wrapped up in what I wanted for your life, I didn't care to see what you wanted."

"I tried telling you."

"I didn't listen. I didn't want to hear it."

"You wanted me married and pregnant and far away from the executive room."

Robert studied his shoes. "I did."

It was nice to hear what she'd always known. "Why?"

"My mother didn't work. Your mother didn't work. I put you in the same category. When you called me out for being a misogynistic bastard, I had to take a closer look."

"I never called you a bastard." She'd thought about it repeatedly, however.

He smiled. "That would be your mother. And she'd be right. I have very few women working at R&R and none in management. I'm surprised no one has called me out on it . . . except you."

Emma smiled. "I'm pretty strong-willed. It's how I was raised."

"I should have done things differently."

They made eye contact. "You won't hear me correct you."

He smirked, nodded a couple of times, and glanced at the doorway. "I had to be a bystander when you were conceived. But that doesn't make you less of a daughter. I thought I was doing my part by making sure you and your brothers were financially taken care of, but I know that isn't enough."

"I needed my father, not a bank." Emotion started to fill the back of her throat. "I wanted you to believe in me."

"I see that now," he said. "I don't want to be a bystander in the lives of my grandchildren. I won't promise to make sweeping changes in my personality, I'm much too old to change everything . . . but I do promise to try and be a better father."

The door to possibility with her father opened enough for her to step inside. "I'd like that."

Her dad looked her in the eye and, for the second time that day, pulled her into his arms.

"I love you, Em."

"I love you, too, Dad."

He cleared his throat as he pulled away and offered a smile. "I'm proud of you. What you've done here," he said, looking around the empty vats just waiting for wine.

"I couldn't have done it without Giovanni."

Robert shrugged. "You could have. After all, you're a Rutledge."

"I'm about to be a D'Angelo."

"But you'll always be my daughter." He placed her hand in the crook of his arm and started back outside. "I heard you're already looking for more vines."

"Gio's been planning his own winery long before I thought of this place. We want to bottle the D'Angelo label right here at Casa de Emma."

"If you need any h—"

"We'll scrimp and save and do it on our own," she said, cutting him off.

Robert hesitated, looked at her, and seemed to change his mind on what he was about to say. "Fine. But I'm paying for the wedding."

Emma smiled as the sunshine from outside touched her face.

EPILOGUE

Gio stood back from all the chaos and held Emma in his arms.

Both of their families laughed and drank, teased and played. It was everything he'd ever envisioned for his life.

"I don't want a long engagement," he whispered in Emma's ear.

"I don't want a huge wedding. These people right here . . . maybe a few more, but that's it."

"We can do that." He kissed the side of her head.

"After harvest?"

"Sold."

"I can't believe you asked my father if you could marry me."

"Oh, I didn't ask, *bella*. I told him I was going to and wanted his blessing."

Emma chuckled. "Did he really tell you you weren't good enough?"

Gio nodded. "Asshole."

"I think he's going to try and redeem himself."

"Good. You deserve better."

She leaned into him and sighed. "I want one of those."

"One of what?"

Emma pointed to their family. "Leonardo."

Could this day get any better? Gio let her go and started to walk away.

"Where are you going?"

"To throw away your birth control pills." She'd taken the IUD out weeks ago and depended on a pill to do the job.

Emma grabbed his hand and pulled him back. "Stop. Let's get married first. Besides, the doctor said we should wait a little longer."

Gio brought her back into his arms. "And here I didn't think you were listening to my questions."

"I'm always listening."

"We're going to have the best life."

Gio kissed her for so long he thought for sure someone was going to turn on the sprinklers. "I'm the luckiest man in the world."

"We should probably get back to the party."

They walked to the table, took the ribbing of those who had watched them.

"We're going to make beautiful babies," Gio announced.

"Can you marry her first?" Robert asked.

"Leave their options open, Robert. I'm not getting any younger," Mari scolded.

The laughter at the table cut off when a stranger walked around from the front of the house, rolling a suitcase.

"I'm sorry to interrupt."

"Can we help you?" Gio asked the man.

"Is there an Emma Rutledge that lives here?"

Emma started laughing beside Gio. So much so that she started to double over. "That's . . ." Her laughter grew.

Next thing Gio knew, Nicole started laughing as well.

And as laughter does, everyone at the table started to chuckle even if none of them knew why.

Gio laughed with her. "*Amore . . .* what's so funny?"

She pointed. "My suitcase."

Rob, Pierre, and Chris chimed in the loudest. "Holy shit."

"It's a little late," Rob said.

The stranger looked at them as if they were crazy. "The airline sent me to a condo complex. They gave me this address."

Gio walked over to the guy, reached in his pocket, and handed him a tip. "It's okay. Her lost luggage gave me the chance to help her buy panties before our first kiss."

The stranger waved. "Thanks."

Emma looked at the tags on the bag. "It must have flown to Italy and back three times."

"Zio Gio?"

"Yes, darling?"

"Girls don't need boys to help them buy panties. We can do that all by ourselves."

Gio sucked in his smile with the seriousness of his niece's face.

"C'mon, Franny. Let's go get some cake." Mari grabbed her hand and started toward the house. "Stop talking about panties in front of your niece." His mother pushed a finger into his chest.

"Better start practicing what you say in front of children now," Emma suggested.

Gio gave her bottom a playful swat. "We need to make those babies fast."

"Wedding first!" Robert reminded them.

Gio and Emma locked eyes.

"Mrs. Rutledge?" Luca caught Beth's attention.

"Yes?"

"How soon can you plan a wedding?"

ACKNOWLEDGMENTS

When life hands you lemons . . . make *limoncello*. Or in my case . . . write a book.

This is the place I have the opportunity to thank my support system.

Thank you, Holly Ingraham, Maria Gomez, and every editor that had their hands inside the pages of this book to make it shine. The continued support of Montlake and Amazon Publishing is a blessing.

To my agent and friend, Jane Dystel, for making the calls not only about my work, but my health . . . I appreciate you more than you know.

To my friends Kari and Brandy, who dropped everything that one time for that one thing, to be by my side . . . I love you, ladies. And Kari . . . watch out for those loofahs at The Villages!

Now to Dr. Carrie. I never knew concierge medicine was a thing. But when I had one too many lab results come back crazy, and one too many specialists added to my list . . . I found you. And lady, your kind and compassionate care when I was spinning out of control kept me grounded in ways I can't explain. You of all people know that I have nicknames for all of my doctors. Liver-ologist, blood-ologist . . . coochie-ologist, but for you, the only nickname I have is *friend*. I know deep down that I would have survived the last few years without you, but it would have taken a Prozac salt lick and aerial spraying of Ativan to do it. Thank you for everything you do.

Catherine

ABOUT THE AUTHOR

Photo © 2022 Ellen Steinberg

New York Times, *Wall Street Journal*, and *USA Today* bestselling author Catherine Bybee has written thirty-eight books that have collectively sold more than ten million copies and have been translated into more than twenty languages. Raised in Washington State, Bybee moved to Southern California in the hope of becoming a movie star. After growing bored with waiting tables, she returned to school and became a registered nurse, spending most of her career in urban emergency rooms. She now writes full time and has penned the Not Quite series, the Weekday Brides series, the Most Likely To series, and the First Wives series.